Ann Taylor, Jane Taylor

Tales, Essays and Poems

Ann Taylor, Jane Taylor

Tales, Essays and Poems

ISBN/EAN: 9783337090043

Printed in Europe, USA, Canada, Australia, Japan

Cover: Foto ©Andreas Hilbeck / pixelio.de

More available books at **www.hansebooks.com**

ESSAYS AND POEMS

BY

JANE AND A

With a

By GRACE

BOST

ROBERTS BROTHERS

1884

John Wilson and Son, Cambridge.

CONTENTS.

———•◦•———

Poems.

Nursery Rhymes.

PAGE

MEMOIR.

THE Taylors of Ongar were a truly remarkable family.
Among the great number of writers of this name —
and Allibone gives more than three hundred in his Dictionary of Authors — there are none more beloved, more
worthy of mention, than this family, so called to distinguish them from all the others. From the time of the
eloquent Jeremy Taylor, and his scurrilous contemporary,
the "Water Poet," noted for his pasquils and ballads on
the Royalist side, and the vast numbers of these effusions,
every department of literature has had the name on its
list.

"The most eloquent of divines! had I said of men," of
whom Coleridge said, "Cicero would forgive this statement and Demosthenes nod assent," worthily heads the
long list of Taylors.

Among the contemporaries of Ann and Jane were so
many noted names that some distinctive appellation was
really needed for them.

There was Taylor, the "Platonist;" John Taylor, of
Norwich, the friend of Mrs. Barbauld, noted for his great
learning as a Hebraist: Tom Taylor, the dramatist, is a
very popular name; and William Taylor, of Norwich, one
of Mrs. Barbauld's scholars, takes rank as England's first
student of the literature of Germany. It was he who first
introduced modern German poetry to English readers by
his translations.

The eminent names of the Hebrew scholar and Platonist, the dramatist and poet, are still known to lovers of literature, but they have not overshadowed the modest, retiring, yet gifted Taylors of Ongar.

Theirs was not the fame of scholar, ballad-maker, or divine; they were simple untrained poets, wild-wood birds with a sweet, natural note peculiar to themselves. A spirit of pure devotion, unworldly simplicity, and deep religious aspiration, was their charm. A very tender chord is touched in many hearts when recollections come of the twilight hour, and the immortal lines, "Twinkle, twinkle, little star," repeated by the dear mother voice, as one by one the stars shone in the darkening sky in the evening shades.

Some mention should be made of the ancestry of these women. They were born in the "lower middle class," which it has been the fashion of late years for the critic and poet to decry. The apostle of "sweetness and light" has spoken often of the "Philistinism" of England, and the author of the operatic air, beginning, "Bow down, ye lower middle classes," has the same class in mind. The Taylor family, though gifted and of note, belong to this very much abused set. Matthew Arnold would have doubtless made them an exception to his sweeping denunciations had their merits been placed before him.

While their poems had immense popularity, they were also kindly welcomed by the critics. The "Quarterly Review" said of them, "The writers of these rhymes have far better claims to the title of poet than many who arrogate to themselves that high appellation."

Isaac Taylor, the grandfather of Ann and Jane, was eminent in his day as an engraver. The son of a brassfounder at Worcester, he early showed a talent for engraving. On the death of his father, who had fallen into

poverty in his latter days, Isaac walked to London. Finding employment in the cutlery works of Josiah Jeffreys, he
prospered so well that he married the daughter of Jeffreys.
Jeffreys meantime had retired from business, and settled
in Essex in a country home.

"Isaac Taylor had engraved crests and other devices at
Worcester, and so distinguished himself in that department
in Josiah Jeffreys's works, that it led to his adopting art engraving, then recently introduced, as a profession, to which he
added presently the business of an art publisher. His house
became in this way the resort of several personages of note in
art and literature. Goldsmith, the illustrations to whose works
are often signed 'Isaac Taylor,' was frequently there, and
upon one occasion, when consulted upon the title of a book
with an apology for troubling him upon so trifling a matter,
replied, 'The title, sir! why, the title is everything.' Barto-
lozzi, Fuseli, and Smirke, were among his friends, and he was
one of the original founders of the Royal Incorporated Society
of Artists of Great Britain, from which sprang the Royal Acad-
emy. The celebrated Woollett was for many years secretary
to the Society, and Isaac Taylor eventually succeeded him in
that office. Thomas Bewick was his valued pupil, who in his
turn speaks of him in his autobiography, as 'my warm friend
and patron Isaac Taylor.' And again says, 'He was in his
day accounted the best engraver of embellishments for books,
most of which he designed himself. The frontispiece to the
first edition of Cunningham's poems was one of his early
productions, and at that time my friend Pollard and myself
thought it was the best thing ever done.' The most important
work executed by this Isaac Taylor was a large plate, the
'Flemish Collation,' after Ostade."

Howard, the philanthropist, was a friend of his, and
took so much interest in one of his daughters that she
named a son for him.

Of the three sons of this Isaac Taylor, Charles, Isaac,

and Josiah, the second was the father of Ann and Jane. Charles was distinguished for his learning and peculiar erudition, and some very dry editing. Isaac, the brother of Ann and Jane, the third of his name, was the author of a large number of philosophical works of a popular character, which have excited considerable criticism and notice.

He began to write early in life, and his sister Ann records the first appearance of the author of the " Natural History of Enthusiasm " as " Imus," with the poetical solution of a charade on the word " consumption," at the age of thirteen. The publishers of the " Minor's Pocket Book," in which it appeared, were so pleased with the answer that they awarded him a special prize for it, as Ann under the name of " Maria " was judged the first in rank for the answer she sent to the same charade. A year or two later, she adds that he was in very ill health, and for hours would stand leaning his head against the mantelpiece where his mother was at work in the parlor. Years after she asked him, in talking over early life and its events, why he stood so, and if he remembered what he was thinking of at the time. " Yes, Ann," he replied, " I was, in fact, meditating on the evils of society, and wondering whether I could do anything to mitigate them." A consideration well fulfilled in his case by his works on " Enthusiasm," " Fanaticism," " Spiritual Despotism," and " Ancient Christianity," which, with many other less noted treatises, were his life work.

Sir James Stephen said his " History of Enthusiasm," published anonymously in 1829, " gave him his literary peerage." This was followed by the " Fanaticism," in 1833, and " Spiritual Despotism," in 1835. He was somewhat of a recluse, and his home at Stanford Rivers was well calculated for the life of quiet meditation and research which gave him leisure to send forth his popular and powerful books. With some exceptions, the critics of his day place him high as a writer and thinker. Somewhat lacking in originality, his manner was so popular and pleasing that in the mind of the great reading public he will hold an enduring place as a philosophical writer. The "Edinburgh Review" of 1840 contains the critique of Stephen on the "Natural History of Enthusiasm," long unacknowledged by its author, in which he says, "His books exhibit a character, both moral and intellectual, from the study of which the reader can hardly fail to rise a wiser and a better man." In 1862 he received the pleasant compliment of a civil service pension of £100 from the government for " his eminent services to literature, especially in the departments of history and philosophy, during a period of more than forty years."

Another brother, Jeffreys, was also an author of more than twenty works of a miscellaneous character, — some for children, — and religious in their style.

We have somewhat anticipated in noticing the career of Isaac Taylor and his brother, and must retrace our steps, and mention in this place the father and mother of this remarkable family of workers, thinkers, and writers.

Isaac Taylor, the father, was a man of mark, full of vital piety, and earnest in all he undertook. Early in life he embraced his father's calling and became an engraver; glad, as he said in his old age, to "engrave a dog-collar " with the same hand that executed the noted print of Stothard's great picture of the Meeting of Henry VIII. and Anne Boleyn. He began life in a very humble manner, as this remark will show, marrying very young on a very limited and precarious income. He was the author of a number of books, — we know of more than twenty, — some on travel, juvenile, and on religious subjects ;

curiously enough none related to his own profession, in which he was an expert, and which for years was the great object of his daily thought and interest. His character and life are so well traced by Ann in her reminiscences of early days that the reader cannot fail to be interested in their development.

He left London for Lavenham in Suffolk in 1786, and after practising his calling with great success for some years, his zeal for the welfare of the Independents, which led him often to supply the place of their minister, and preach during his absence, gave him note as a teacher and healer of souls. This deep feeling of religious devotion made him accept a "call" from a dissenting society at Colchester, where he ministered most acceptably for some years, — a change of life greatly to his worldly disadvantage. He left Colchester for Ongar, a village in the vicinity, and continued his pastoral care of that parish till his death in December, 1829.

Ann, in describing her father to her children, says : —

"My father was an unusually single-hearted man and Christian. His life till nearly thirty was spent in London, but he caught not a taint from its atmosphere. So long as he remained at home his father, a man of sense and ability, and a well-known artist of the time, was not, it seemed, under the influence of Christian principle, though a strictly moral man; and he exhibited towards his family an austere reserve which was little calculated to awaken the domestic affections to genial life.

"His mother, possessing no small share of practical good sense, and real concern for the interests of her children, was yet so more than occupied in the labors of rearing them, and withal of a temper so heedless of the graces of life, that it seemed scarcely possible for kind and tender dispositions to expand under her influence; but my father not only revered, but as his nature could not help, loved her also.

"At thirteen he commenced a life which became one of diffusive piety. At sixteen he joined the church under the Rev. Mr. Webb of Fetter Lane, and from those early years till he went down to the grave, at seventy-one, his character was one beautiful progress through the benignant graces of Christianity.

"His love of knowledge was early, strong, and universal. Nothing was uninteresting to him that he had opportunity to acquire, and when acquired his delight was to communicate. Apt to teach he certainly was, and ingenious as apt; all his methods were self-devised, and the life of few men devoted to teaching as a profession, would have accomplished more than he attained by husbanding the half hours of his own. Early hours, and elastic industry were the 'natural magic' by which his multifarious objects were pursued, and labors performed.

"Whatever I possess of knowledge came from his treasury, and far more than is now mine, for many engagements, and a memory never good, and perhaps in childhood too little cultivated, have deprived me of much. Too little cultivated, I say, because my dear mother having suffered from injudicious exactions upon memory when a child, erred perhaps in training her children in the other extreme. As far as I recollect, we were never required to learn anything by heart!

"It was my father's habit, whenever a question arose in conversation on points of science or history which we could not accurately determine, to refer at the moment to some authority, — the lexicon, the gazetteer, the encyclopædia, or anything from which the facts could be gained; so that much was in this way imbibed by his children without labor of any kind, and at the expense only of some little impatience at a digression with which they would at the time have been willing to dispense. 'Line upon line,' was, however, in this way gradually traced and deepened. Method, arrangement, regularity in everything, were the characteristics of his mind; as were a tranquil hoping for, and believing in the best, those of his heart.

"As a youth, he had accustomed himself to rise early, but

the habit declined through disturbed nights during the infancy of his children. After a few years, it was renewed and never abandoned, and, if I am not mistaken, it was by the following incident that he was induced to return to six o'clock as the commencement of his day. He had received a call from some poor minister, with a request that he would purchase from him a small hymn-book, beautifully bound in morocco; the price was half a guinea, a larger sum than he could prudently afford, but his open heart could not refuse the aid that was asked for in this form, and the little volume proved, in the end, of incalculable value to him, for, sensible of his indiscretion, he resolved to cover the loss by making a longer day for labor. This, though constitutionally disposed to sleep, he resolutely accomplished, starting from his bed at a quarter before six every morning, till within a short period of his death. It was not managed without difficulty. At first, an alarm clock at the head of his bed was sufficient, but becoming accustomed to the monotony, he placed a pair of tongs across the weight of the alarm, so disposed, that when it began to move, the sudden fall of the tongs should surely move him also.

"My father's habits of devotion formed a valuable part of his example. Rising thus early, the time from six to seven o'clock was always spent in his closet — really a closet, enclosed by double doors. But though thus secluded, and in a remote part of the house, we were, at times, near enough, in a room below, to be aware of the earnestness of his prayers, which were uttered aloud."

The aim of Isaac Taylor's early years had been devotion to the Ministry; but severe and continued ill health caused him to abandon then the hope resumed in later years, as we have seen. At twenty-two Mr. Taylor married, and the income on which he made this venture for himself and his young wife, "on which he calculated he could live" with comfort, was half a guinea certain for three days' work in each week, supplied to him by his elder brother, Charles, — then in business as a publisher, later known as the editor of "Calmet's Dictionary of the Bible," — and as much as he could earn the three remaining days on his own account. Thirty pounds of his own, with a hundred pounds of his wife's and the furniture given her by her mother, constituted the worldly possessions of the young pair.

Ann Taylor, the wife, was a woman of unusual strength of character and fortitude. She also courted literature ; somewhat late in life appearing as an authoress. Her books were on practical subjects, such as the duties of Children and Parents, advice to Servants ; and some tales of the homely scenes of English country life. With her daughter Jane she wrote " The Correspondence between a Mother and her Daughter at school." Her first book, " Advice to Mothers," was published in 1814. Her books, as well as all the Taylors' writings, were deeply tinged with the most intense religious views. The whole atmosphere of the home was one of domestic virtue and religious fervor, and this sentiment is impressed strongly on their books.

Ann says, after her reminiscences of her father, —

"My dear mother was a character more peculiar, and her disadvantages had been greater than those of my father. The sensibility of her frame, both mental and bodily, was extreme ; her affections were strong and lively, and her sufferings (irrespective of bodily pain) from the sorrows and bereavements of her seventy-two years, proportionably intense. My mother was the eldest of two children, and at six years old lost her father, who died of fever at twenty-nine. Of him I know little except that he was one of Mr. Whitfield's early converts, and thus happily prepared for early death. But he was probably alone in his religious preferences, for upon one occasion having taken his little girl to hear Mr. Whitfield, she suddenly stood

up in the pew and exclaimed, 'What have you brought me
here for, among a pack of Whitfieldites ? '

" His anxiety for my mother was more lively than discreet.
He thought it wise to exercise her infant patience by inflic-
tions which she recollected as producing paroxysms of anguish.
He once called her to see a new and favorite toy thrown on
the fire, hoping in this way to induce a salutary self-control ! "

The second marriage of Mrs. Taylor's mother made
her early years unhappy, and she was favored in the marriage she herself made, for it took her into a congenial
atmosphere of love and sympathy.   Ann, continuing her
narrative, says : —

"On their wedding day, April 18, 1781, my parents entered
their first home, in a house standing back from the street, and
exactly opposite Islington Church.   It was a first floor only,
but from the back room, the best one, there was a view over an
extent of country, including the Highgate Hills, and on the
day of their marriage, though so early in the year, a vine was
in full leaf over their windows.   There, on the 30th of January,
1782, on which day my youthful father reached his twenty-third
year, I was born ; and on the 23d of September the year following, their second daughter, Jane Taylor, known, perhaps, I
might say, on the four continents, and known only for good,
came into the world ; but at this time they had removed for the
convenience of business to Red Lion Street, Holborn, then a
sufficiently quiet place.

" Here their first son, and third child, was born and here,
scarcely allowing herself an hour of recreation either for body
or mind, practising the utmost economy, and with her children
filling every thought of her heart, my poor mother broke down
in health, and might have surrendered herself to be the mere
drudge of her family, had not a wise friend suggested to her
that it would be well if her husband found in her a *companion*,
as well as a housekeeper and nurse.   She took the hint immediately, and resolved to secure the higher happiness that had

nearly escaped her. For this purpose she commenced the practice of reading aloud at meals, the only time she could afford for mental improvement, and for nearly half-a-century it supplied her daily pleasure, while it sustained the native power of her mind."

A rapidly increasing family, expenses consequent, ill health and sufferings of the children shut up in the murky London atmosphere, decided Mr. Taylor to look for a country home for his little ones. Economy of course was a first consideration in seeking the new home, and for his business it must be near London. At last the little village of Lavenham in Suffolk, sixty-three miles from London, was found to have a vacant house suited to the very empty pocket of the young father.

Ann tells of the exodus, and her mother's grief at leaving early associations and friends, in her bright way. She says of the departure : —

"It was in June 1786, the fine old-fashioned weather of the eighteenth century, as my memory pictures it, that the little colony set forth — I well remember the freshness of that six o'clock on a summer's morning — in a hackney coach for the stage. My father had gone before to Lavenham to receive and arrange the furniture, and never was 'Queen's Decorator' more busy, more anxious (in some respects more capable), than he that everything should appear in tempting order, and in the best style of which it was susceptible. His materials, indeed, were few, but his taste and contrivance inexhaustible. The house, which a cottager described as 'the first grand house in Shilling Street,' was indeed so, compared with former residences.

"It was the property of, and had been inhabited by a clergyman. On the ground floor were three parlors, two kitchens, and a dairy, together with three other rooms never inhabited; and above them were six large bedrooms. An extensive garden, well planted, lay behind. A straight broad walk through the middle was fifty-two yards in length, with an open summer-house on rising ground at one end, and ha-ha fence separating it from a meadow, of which we had the use, at the other. There was also a large yard, with a pig-sty, uninhabited, till my sister Jane and I cleared it out for the purpose of dwelling in it ourselves. It was a substantial little building of brick, but, having no windows, and the door swinging from the top, it was somewhat incommodious, yet there, after lessons, we passed many a delighted hour.

"For this spacious domain (house and garden I mean, not the pig-sty), it will scarcely be credited that my father paid a rent of only six pounds a-year, but by such a circumstance the perfect out-of-the-wayness of the situation may be conceived. Neither coach road nor canal approached it, though I remember that the advantage the latter would be to the little town was often discussed. The postman's cart, a vehicle covered in for passengers, made its enlivening entrée every day from Sudbury, seven miles distant, about noon; and the London wagon nodded and grated in, I forget how often, or rather how seldom, — I believe about once a week.

"My dear mother had always the strongest objection to leaving her little girls to the care of servants, and seldom visited where we were not invited, — we were but two, not troublesome, perhaps something of favorites, so that completely social as these and similar parties were, we were often admitted to them at an age when now we should scarcely have emerged from the nursery. But nurseries at Lavenham, and at that time of day, I do not remember. The parlor and the best parlor were all that was known beside the kitchens, and thus parents and children formed happily but one circle."

This garden was a perfect joy to the sisters. Isaac Taylor remembered long after how the neighbors noticed the little girls, then five and six years old, early companions in song, pacing up and down the green walks and alleys of the garden, hand in hand, lisping a little couplet of their joint composition. "Nancy and Jenny," as the town folk called them, became great favorites. Ann says: "Jane was always the saucy, lively, entertaining little thing, — the amusement and the favorite of all that knew her. At the baker's shop she used to be placed on the kneading-board, in order to recite, preach, narrate, &c., to the great entertainment of his many visitors."

Mrs. Taylor was of a peculiar disposition; ill health, a large family, and the loss of little children, were very depressing to her. She had lost one child in London, her first boy, and before the year was out she lost another at Lavenham. All the affectionate assiduities of her good husband, and the charms of a country life, failed to make her feel at home; but after a while the natural scenes and pleasures of the new home touched and cheered her.

The first winter was a very sad time as her recent griefs were fresh, and the frequent absence of her husband on his professional work in London left her alone with the little girls and a servant. One incident of this sad winter was sufficiently startling for the strongest nerves. Mr. Taylor was in London at the time.

"It was a dark and stormy winter's night, the wind roared down the huge kitchen chimney, and screamed in the trees across the road. 'Ann and Jane' had gone early to bed, the last dear babe had recently found its resting-place in the churchyard, and my poor mother sat in her grief beside the parlor fire. Suddenly a dreadful crash was heard; the kitchen chimney was exactly over the room in which we slept, and her instant thought was that it had fallen, burying us in its ruins.

"She ran to the foot of the wide staircase and called. I was always a wakeful sleeper, but now there was no answer, and she felt no doubt of the terrible meaning of the silence. Her sister jumped out of the parlor window, and, my mother and servant following, fled up the dark street to Mr. Meeking's, the nearest friend in need. She fell on the high steps leading up to his shop-door, and his little dog, rushing out, tore off her cap before she could regain her feet. 'Oh! Mr. Meeking, Mr. Meeking, my children are both killed!' 'Let's hope not, madam, let's hope not,' and the worthy old man, with sons, staves, and lanterns, hastened back with her to the scene of disaster, first, of course, visiting our bed-room, where, holding a lantern at the foot of the bed, 'Nancy and Jenny' were seen sound asleep.

"That was enough; and when they had searched in vain through all the upper rooms of the large house, they began to smile at the alarm as one of imagination only, till entering the kitchen a mound of bricks upon the floor, that had fallen down the ample chimney, explained what had happened. The cracked grate long remained to attest the peril.

"But my father returned, — returned with sufficient employment in his art for months to come. Spring returned also, the winter had passed, the rain was over and gone, the time of the singing of birds was come, and my dear mother awoke to the beauties that surrounded her. Not that the style of country was particularly attractive. Suffolk, or at least that part of it, swells into shoulders of heavy corn land, with little wood, and these undulations shut out extensive prospects; a small river creeps dully through a succession of quiet meadows, and I think it must be partly owing to this tameness that a real taste for the country was not sensibly awakened in me till ten or twelve years later in my history.

"I can hardly otherwise account either for an impression of gloom which, though it was seen under the sunlight of childhood, still hangs over that Lavenham scenery. Enthusiasm must have been enthusiastic to be kindled among those flat meadows and cold slopes, with their drowsy river.

"And, whatever the surrounding country might be, there was at Lavenham a large and beautiful garden. We lived not in either of the big front parlors, but in a small pleasant room opening into it. There my father's high desk, at which, during his whole life, he stood, as the most healthy position, to engrave, occupied the corner between the fire and a large window; my mother sat on the opposite side, and we had our little table and chairs between them. One wing of the premises seen from this window was covered with a luxuriant tea tree, drooping in long branches, with its small purple flowers; on a bed just opposite was a great cinnamon rose bush, covered with bloom; a small grass plot lay immediately under the window, and beyond were labyrinths of flowering shrubs, with such a bush of honeysuckle as I scarcely remember to have seen anywhere. Then there were beds of raspberries, gooseberries, and currants, espalier'd walks, ample kitchen garden, walls and palings laden with fruit, grass and gravel walks, a honeysuckle arbor, and an open seated summer-house; flourishing standard fruit trees, and no end of flowers and rustic garden-seats.

"Here our habits and, to some degree, our tastes were formed, and here began our education. In that little back parlor we were taught the formal rudiments, and in the garden and elsewhere, constantly under the eye of our parents, we fell in with more than is always included in the catalogue of school learning at so much per quarter. Books were a staple commodity in the house. From my mother's habit of reading aloud at breakfast and at tea, we were always picking up something; to every conversation we were auditors, and, I think, quiet ones, for, having no nursery, the parlor would have been intolerable otherwise.

"There was a large room adjoining, having a glass door into it, and there, or in the garden, we were at liberty to romp. A closet in this room was allowed us as a baby-house, round the walls of which were arranged our toys; but I must acknowledge that here we were not the aborigines, an interminable race of black ants had taken previous possession, and we could only share and share alike with them.

"I do not know how far children so completely invent little histories for themselves as we did. We most frequently personated two poor women making a hard shift to live; or we were 'aunt and niece,' Jane the latter and I the former; or we acted a fiction entitled 'the twin sisters,' or another, the 'two Miss Parks.' And we had, too, a great taste for royalty, and were not a little intimate with various members of the royal family. Even the two poor women, 'Moll and Bet,' were so exemplary in their management and industry as to attract the notice of their Royal Highnesses the Princesses ('when George the Third was King'). When these two estimable cottagers were the subject of our personation, we occupied (weather permitting) either the summer-house or the ci-devant pig-sty. On the grassy ascent upon which the summer-house stood, terminating the long walk, the grass was mixed with a small plant, I fancy trefoil, but I have never been botanist enough to know; however, its name to us was Bob, why, I cannot imagine, unless from the supposed similarity of the three letters to its three small leaves. This we used to gather for winter food (so hard bestead were we), and the seeds of the mallow we called cheeses, and laid them up in store also. These were simple, healthy, inexpensive toys and pleasures, and, having such resources always at hand at home, and without excitements from abroad, we were never burdensome with the teasing enquiry, 'What shall we play at? What shall we do?' Yet we had always assistance at hand if needed. Both father and mother were accessible, and many a choice entertainment did we owe to their patient contrivances. My father, especially, was never weary of inventing, for our amusement or instruction. I have still a little glass case containing a cottage cut in cork, a few trees of moss, a piece of looking-glass for pond, a cork haystack, and so forth (a Suffolk idyll), which was one of these productions. Another was a small grotto fitted up with spars and minerals. But there was one of these home-made toys which I can hardly think of now without pleasure; it was a landscape painted on cardboard, cut out and placed at different distances, through the lanes of which, by means of a wire turning underneath, there slowly wound a loaded wagon and other carriages; it was contained in a box about seven inches by twelve, and two in depth, with a glass in front.

"Of course my dear mother, with health never strong, and

all the needlework of the household on her hands, could not undertake our entire instruction. Reading, the Needle, and the Catechism, we were taught by her, and as my father was constantly engraving at the high desk in the same room, it was easy for him to superintend the rest. We were never severely treated, though both my parents were systematic disciplinarians. But I record one instance of mistaken punishment only to show how possible it is, when a child is confused or alarmed, for parents to fall into that error. It must have been when I was very young, for it was owing to a supposed obstinacy in not spelling the word *thy*. I had been told it repeatedly, t-h-y, in the same lesson, still at the moment it every time unaccountably slipped from the memory. My mother could only attribute it to wilful perverseness, though I believe that was a disposition I could not be charged with. She felt, however, so fully persuaded that I knew, and would not say, that she proceeded to corporal punishment, very rarely administered, but not so entirely abandoned as is the fashion now."

Jane began as early as her eighth year to write more or less. A year or two earlier, it was noticed by her parents that she had furnished her memory with many historical anecdotes in the course of the instruction given her, and she used to recite these with such variations as the inspiration of the moment or a passing mood might suggest. As soon as she began to write at all, though the idea was never suggested to her by her parents, and no other persons had the confidence of the children who would have thought of such a thing, she cherished the fancy of writing a *book*. These childish scribblings all appear to have been prepared with a view to publication. Prefaces, title-pages, introductions and dedications, are among the MSS. preserved by the Taylor family, all the early spontaneous work of this untrained child.

The following preface appears to have been written in her tenth year : —

PREFACE.

To be a poetess I don't aspire.
From such a title humbly I retire;
But now and then a line I try to write;
Though bad they are, — not worthy human sight.

Sometimes into my hand I take a pen,
Without the hope of aught but mere chagrin .
I scribble, then leave off in sad despair,
And make a blot in spite of all my care.

I laugh and talk, and preach a sermon well;
Go about begging, and your fortune tell:
As to my poetry, indeed 't is all
As good and worse by far than none at all.

Have patience yet I pray, peruse my book;
Although you smile when on it you do look:
I know that in 't there 's many a shocking failure;
But that forgive — the author is Jane Taylor.

About a year later she addressed a poem to her father, beginning : —

PETITION.

Ah, dear papa ! did you but know
     The trouble of your Jane,
I 'm sure you would relieve me now,
     And ease me of my pain.

Although your garden is but small,
     And more indeed you crave,
There 's one small bit, not used at all,
     And this I wish to have.

The garden was evidently a sacred spot as in olden times, haunted by the Muses and Apollo: the little votaries of poetry found all the prose and poetry of their young lives in its sweet seclusion.

Ann, in continuing her recollections of their early years, says : —

" The precise hours allotted to our instruction I now forget, but they were regular, and regularly kept. I remember pleading once in vain for some temporary deviation. We breakfasted at eight, dined at half-past one, took tea at five ; then at eight we went to bed, and my father and mother supped at nine. On Sundays, however, we were indulged to sit up to supper, a treat indeed.

" Of our Sunday habits I am thankful to remember that, though never gloomy, they were after the olden fashion, — *strict.* It was a day unlike to other days — a feeling I should wish to preserve as a perpetual safeguard. I will not say how much I was profited by accompanying my father, at seven o'clock on a winter's morning, to the early prayer meeting, as I conclude, to be out of the way during early duties at home. The only vivid recollection now in my memory is of the astonishing noise made by the blower in raising the vestry fire. This, with the assiduities of Mrs. Snelling, the pew-opener, have survived the friction of much more than half-a-century. As Lavenham lies embedded in clay, and there was neither paving nor lighting, Water Street, which frequently well deserved its name, offered sometimes difficulties to Sunday chapel-goers, and not a few of the gentlemen wore pattens.

" Occasionally, when my mother was not well enough to go from home on the Sunday, I have been left to stay with her, and one of our quiet Sundays was signalized by an incident that shook my nerves. She had fallen asleep in the little back parlor, leaving me sole guardian of the premises. Suddenly I heard a tremendous noise somewhere in the kitchen, a knocking and a battering so long and loud, that nothing less than determined burglars could account for. My mother was so poorly that I dared not wake her, and even then so deaf that she did not hear the noise. With inexpressible terror I listened and watched to see the ruffians either enter the room or emerge from the back door into the garden, and, only eight or nine years old as I might be, armed myself with the poker for the worst. If I had not happened to catch sight of the culprit at the precise moment of escape, the mystery might have remained to this day unaccounted for. But I did; an immense dog issued suddenly with prodigious speed from the back door with the remains of a large, deep, stone milk-jar about his neck! Doubtless a small quantity of milk had been left at the bottom, the poor fellow had unwittingly thrust in his nose, the neck was narrow, the milk beyond his tongue tip; he thrust and thrust, till he found himself in dreadful custody. Then began the sound that had chilled my blood as he banged his portable prison about the kitchen floor, till the bottom giving way, he made use of recovered daylight, though still with a good portion of the pot about his neck, and decamped through the garden, wearing, to my astonished eyes, something like a close cottage bonnet. Whither his terror carried him I never heard, though if he scampered through the town in such a guise I think it would have made some stir.

"And another Sunday afternoon had its terror. From my earliest childhood I had a nervous apprehension of the sudden death of those about me, so that any inequality in the breathing, if asleep, or anything unusual in appearance, excited my alarm. This time, my father being slightly unwell, I was left at home alone with him. For our mutual edification he read aloud Wilcox's Sermons, not the liveliest volume in the world, and after a time I perceived something very singular in his pronunciation and tone, a confusion of syllables, a lengthening and a pause! I thought he was going to die! He did not die, but soon safely recovered; yet it was years afterwards that, recalling the symptoms of this appalling seizure, the true character of it occurred to me, my good father had been — almost asleep!

"I had always a conscience, whether or not enlightened, yet always a conscience, and especially with regard to the Sabbath. One Sunday I was myself alone at home, from some trifling ailment, and employed the morning in reading a little book by the Rev. George Burder, containing the

'History of Master Goodchild,' and various other strictly Sunday readings. Towards the end is the fable of the kite and the string, but this stopped me — a *fable* might not belong to Sunday reading ? — and I left the book open at the place till my father returned from Meeting, to know whether I might proceed. He silenced my apprehensions, while approving the hesitation."

It is interesting to note the first stirrings of poetry in the young mind. Ann says, —

" The time at which I began to string my thoughts (if thoughts) into measure I cannot correctly ascertain. It could not be after I was ten years old, and I think when only seven or eight, and arising from a feeling of anxiety respecting my mother's safety during illness. Not wishing (I conclude) to betray myself by asking for paper at home, I purchased a sheet of foolscap from my friend, Mr. Meeking, and *filled* it with verses in metre imitated from Dr. Watts, at that time the only poet on my shelves. What became of this effusion I do not know, but I should be glad to exchange for it, if I could, any of my later ones, —

> ' Not for its worth, we all agree,
> But merely for its oddity,'

as Swift says of learning in ladies.

" The earliest stanza that dwells in my memory, whether belonging to this production or not I cannot tell, is the following : —

> ' Dark and dismal was the weather,
> Winter into horror grew ;
> Rain and snow came down together,
> Everything was lost to view.'

" Certain it is, anyway, that from about this date it became my perpetual amusement to scribble, and some large literary projects occupied my reveries. A poetic rendering of the fine moral history of Master Headstrong ; a poem intended as antecedent to the Iliad ; a new version of the Psalms ; and an argumentative reply to Winchester on Future Punishment, were among these early projects, and more or less executed."

She adds : —

"I have certainly suffered by allowing the small disposable time of my youth to expend itself in writing rather than in reading. My mind was in this way stinted by scanty food. Of that I am fully sensible, and leave it as a warning to whomsoever it may concern. If I had not breathed a tolerably healthy atmosphere it would have been lean indeed. But there was always something to be imbibed; either from my mother's reading at meals, or that in which we afterwards all took turn in the workroom ; from my father's untiring aptness to teach, his regular habit of settling all questions by reference to authorities, and the books that were always passing through the family. Wherever my father moved there soon arose a book society, if there had not been one before. One word, however, about the reading aloud at meals. I believe my mother fostered thereby a habit of despatching hers too quickly, by which her digestion was permanently injured ; and, again, it hindered our acquiring readiness in conversation. To listen, not to talk, became so much a habit with us, as rather to impair fluency of expression — at least in speech."

One can easily imagine the young Taylors must have seemed marvels of genius to village people, where the gentry were so illiterate as Mrs. Gilbert says. The townsfolk she thinks less ignorant. At a party among the upper circles of Lavenham, " in honor of a bride who had belonged to this higher grade, the lady addressed my father across the room with, ' Mr. Taylor, who wrote Shakespeare ? ' The husband, feigning an amused laugh, could only say, ' Just hear my wife ! ' It was a question none of the humbler folk there needed to ask."

Mrs. Gilbert claims for her father the honor of being the originator of the Sunday school. She says he collected one at Lavenham as early as 1790. Robert Raikes of Gloucester has always had the credit of founding the first school, but Mrs. Gilbert's claim, which seems only just, proves that there is nothing new under the sun.

Sometimes the busy household at Lavenham had a little diversion. Ann says : —

"Quiet, and destitute of amusement as Lavenham was, we yet had our holiday seasons and pleasures, all in keeping with life in the country. In very fine weather, the tea, or even dinner, in the garden, for which there was a choice of spots whether in sunshine or in shade, was an occasion to the children. But the great thing was a whole day's ramble, on what would now be called a picnic excursion, — father, mother, children, and servants ; my father with his pencil, my mother with a book, the servant with provisions. And wherever there was a cottage, a stump, or a tree, worth sketching, there we gathered round him (those of us who did not prefer to hunt for violets), and my mother read till the sketch was finished. Well I remember my father's signal for attracting our notice to any slip of the 'picturesque' that might catch his eye : 'Lookye, lookye there ?'

"But of all our rural holidays the most exciting was an annual visit to Melford fair. Melford was, perhaps is, a very pretty town of a single street, terminating at the upper end in a large, open, and extremely pleasant green, with respectable houses on one side, a fine old church at the top, and fringed on the other by the park of Sir Harry Parker. On this green was spread the fair, not, as my recollection serves, rude and riotous, but attracting an assemblage of respectable country people from several miles round. Yet the fair made but a part of the pleasure, for on the return walk of about four miles was there not tea at Mr. and Mrs. Blackadder's, a worthy couple, the perfect personification of farmer and wife far up in Suffolk, say a hundred years ago, for they were still quite of the olden times. Their little homestead was the very centre of old-fashioned hospitality, and tea from the best china in the best parlor was no small delight. *Best* parlor, however, I should not call it, for the 'House, or houseplace' as it is called in Lincolnshire, on the other side of the entrance, could not aspire to anything like so genteel a name. There the 'min' were admitted to regale themselves, — master and men together after their daily labor, unless there was 'company.'"

The excitement of an annual fair was also to be had at Lavenham. The little Taylors were able by peeping from a dark, mysterious attic chamber, — a horror to them in the daytime, — to gain a glimpse of the fire-works let off by the boys at Mr. Blower's young gentlemen's school, on Guy Fawkes day. They knew their father would order them to bed; so they braved the dangers of the dim chamber haunted by their fancies, rather than let him see them. Then too Guy Fawkes appeared in all his glory, making an immense excitement for their young minds.

As we shall see by the description given of the household ways of the Taylors by Ann, it was a very strictly ordered, busy and methodical world into which these little maidens, singing hand in hand, came. This work-a-day world was early seen by them in its sternest aspect. Ann really reproaches herself at length for building castles in the air, to the extent of imagining how some poor people of the village would feel if she helped them to a home. She vividly relates the whole affair, and the singular pleasure she took in breaking to them the secret. Then after dressing them all in clean, new clothes, of which she had even chosen the colors, she took them in procession, " two and two to their new habitation."

What a strange, strange contrast between the inner workings of such a poetic fancy, and the outside life which encompassed and influenced it, so that the little creature actually thought her pretty dreams wrong, and calls the habit "ruinous, and an evil"! Jane, too, unconsciously felt her wings beat against the bars. The bright dreams of childhood must have been sadly depressed in such a mental and moral atmosphere. The hardest part of it is that the father and mother were so kind, affectionate, and well-meaning. The story of the hen who raised a brood of young ducks, comes to mind as one reads of the regrets and pain felt, as these bright young creatures tried to repress their natural gifts of poetry, and to banish the airy dreams which visited them. Later in life, under the increase of a very marked religious sentiment, never foreign to her but exaggerated by circumstances, Jane confessed and lamented the tendency. "I know," she said, "that I have sometimes lived so much in a castle as almost to forget that I lived in a house."

In June, 1789, Mrs. Taylor took her two little girls to London. She had been in the country three years, and had a great desire to visit her friends in town. This fancy was increased by the expected visit of George III. to St. Paul's, to return thanks for his recovery from the first attack of insanity. Ann says it was "a scene of excitement little calculated to continue a sane condition, but there was probably some unacknowledged political reason for amusing the public by the fearful venture. Among the thousands who on that occasion flocked to the metropolis were my mother and her two little girls. I was then, June, 1789, somewhat more than seven, and Jane not quite six years old. We were to travel by the Bury coach, which passed through Sudbury, seven miles distant, as early as seven in the morning on its road to London. Between one and two, therefore, that summer morning we left our beds in order to start by 'Billy East,' by which must be understood the postman's cart. Loaded, and covered in as we were, behind our single Rosinante, I soon began to feel very sick; and being asked how I was, replied, 'I am inclined for what I have no inclination to.'"

She recalled very little of this early London visit; but here and there a trace lingered in her memory. She says, —

"We had friends in Fleet Street, on the left-hand side, looking up to St. Paul's, and there we were to take our stations. A better position could scarcely have been selected from which to witness the cavalcade. We went to the house at five in the morning of the 25th of June, the room, a first floor, being fitted up with seats rising from the windows a considerable height behind, but we as little folks were happily placed in front. There we waited, oh, so long! There was amusement, however, in watching the throngs below less fortunate than ourselves, and the ladies in the room, many in full dress with their hair curled and powdered, and head-dresses adorned with white ribbons carrying in gold letters the words, 'God save the king.' At length, towards noon, the splendid pageant arrived, and fortunately for us a carriage with several of the princesses was detained a considerable time under our windows. They were dressed in white, and some sort of golden ornament lay in the lap of one of them. Poor things! I have thought since, for the lot of English princesses has not always been enviable. So the cavalcade passes into the mists of memory, which refuses to produce more of that long forgotten day.

"The evening of the following day London was splendidly illuminated. We children saw a little of it in Holborn, but my poor mother was induced reluctantly to accompany a party to the India House, which was reported particularly brilliant, and from that night dated much of her after life of suffering. Whether from fear of fire, or some local accident, the plugs in that neighborhood were up and the streets under water, while, to make matters worse, in the midst of the overwhelming crowd both my mother's shoes were trodden off. Many others it seems were equally unfortunate, for in the course of the night she met a woman with a barrowful of lost shoes, amongst

which she had the strange luck to pick out first one, and then
the other of her own! The cold thus taken, however, became
so threatening that my father was summoned to town, and
though she recovered the immediate effects, her health was
never sound afterwards."

Prosperity began to brighten the home of Mr. Taylor.
Some admirable work on an edition of Shakspeare, illustrated by him for his brother, caused Mr. Boydell to offer
him work for his great edition of Shakspeare. For his
plate of the death of Rizzio, by Opie, Mr. Taylor received
250 guineas. He exhibited it at the Society of Arts, and
it obtained the gold medal and a premium of ten guineas,
as the best engraving of the year.

The life of an engraver is full of anxious hours : who
but an engraver knows the meaning of a " touched proof ? "
says Ann. A few alterations made in as many moments
by the artist mean days or weeks of work for the engraver.
The parlor at Lavenham was quite a show place for the
townspeople when Stothard's " Henry VIII. meeting Ann
Boleyn," containing sixteen figures larger than life, filled
the side of the great room. Others came in rapid succession, and apprentices were taken in order to lighten the
details of the work. A printing press was bought for
" proving," and a young woman hired to work it.

Mr. Taylor seemed to be favored by fortune, and his
prospects of success appeared assured, when a most painful
rheumatic fever resulting from exposure confined him,
helpless and suffering, in his bed. For three months the
poor man was in his bed, and little hope was given of his
recovery. After five months he was able to appear
among his family ; "but there were large bills to pay, —
besides physicians' fees, £30 to the surgeon, the cost of a
bushel of phials left as perquisites on our hands," — innumerable derangements to rectify, anxious work to resume,

and strength wasted all but to the grave to recover ; but,
nothing dismayed, he took his place among various and
pressing duties, with thankfulness, faith, and hope.

A new house for his little flock was necessitated by the
impossibility of longer hiring the first ; and by buying an
old house, and repairing and contriving and building, Mr.
Taylor contrived a home and plenty of room for his workshops.   Ann says of this great event in a child's life : —

"At the mid-summer of 1793 our new house was deemed
habitable, and thither, as to a new life, we were delighted to
remove. By his unfailing contrivance, the house was made to
suit us exactly, and the garden, beautiful and pleasant, to our
heart's desire. The best parlor (a 'drawing-room' was not
then known in Lavenham), till a little of the pecuniary pressure was worked down, was left unfurnished at the disposal of
'Ann and Jane' to whip their tops in, but the common parlor
was as pretty and comfortable as it could be, with a door and a
large bay window into the garden, and a sliding panel for convenient communication with the kitchen. China closets and
store closets were large and commodious. The garden, too,
was an especially nice one. Happily there were several well-
grown trees already on the ground, and a trellis arbor covered
with honeysuckle, stood on a rising ground underneath a picturesque old pear tree. A poultry yard, containing sometimes
seventy fowls of different sorts, was on the premises behind,
and an excavated and paved pond for ducks.

"We had, in our new house, a large room, running the entire
length of one part of the building; this was appropriated to
business. My father's high desk was placed at the upper end ;
a row of windows facing the yard, was occupied by the apprentices, and another, overlooking the garden, was filled by the
children pursuing their education."

Pupils were taken, and apprentices also added to the
busy family circle ; yet the large household never boasted

but one maid of all work. Punctual, orderly habits were inculcated, and methodical and regular supervision in workshop, kitchen, and house, kept all running pleasantly and smoothly. Mrs. Taylor was evidently a notable housewife. The mother of eleven living children, herself an authoress, she yet found time to instruct her daughters in all the feminine occupations suitable to their station.

Ann made a visit with her father and mother in Islington, about this time, renewing friendships and making some new friends; among whom the Conders became lifelong intimates. Josiah Conder, the editor and author, was one of the children of this family, and, with his sisters, soon became very much attached to the Taylors.

During the exciting times in England, which accompanied the fearful scenes enacted in France during the Reign of Terror, and the succeeding horrors of the Revolution, dissenters were the objects of popular dislike. Priestley was mobbed, his house destroyed, and many others suffered. Even the quiet town of Lavenham, and the inoffensive Taylors, shared the trials of the time. They were only saved, once, by the coolness and courage of the clergyman of the parish, who urged the mob to leave Mr. Taylor's house, which they were about to destroy, by the plea of his sister's ill-health. The Church of England's authority probably saved them from a very distressing calamity.

Mr. Taylor had long been a deacon of the Independent meeting of Lavenham, and in the absence of the minister, often held services in his own house. His early aspirations had been directed to the ministry, only ill health had barred the way. Mr. Hickman was called to another charge, and he urged his society to ask Mr. Taylor to assume the pastorate. Some jealousy was felt at the elevation of one from among them, though many wished his acceptance. Of course, he did not accept a divided charge. This condition of affairs being made known, neighboring clergymen called on him to relieve them, and presently an Independent society at Colchester called him, and he accepted their invitation.

Colchester was a gay garrison town, containing fourteen parishes and twelve churches, some in a rather dismantled condition, with dilapidations dating from the rough work of the civil war, and especially from the siege of the town by Fairfax. Many parts of the town wall were then perfect, and the fine ruins of St. Botolph's Priory and St. John's Gate, with the Castle which had braved the storms of a thousand years in one or another form, and the broken ivied tower of St. Martin's Church, made a very picturesque view, and gave historic interest to a place full of association for artist and antiquary.

Dissent was not fashionable, intelligent, or popular in Colchester. The " Round Meeting," which held a thousand people when full, — and it was generally well filled, — was presided over by a dull old man whose perfunctory services interested no one. There were a few wealthy and substantial families connected with the dissenting chapel to which Mr. Taylor was called, but as a rule no young people of education, position, or intelligence were to be found among the ranks of Nonconformists in the town. The dissenters of the place were too often without thought or interest in their church, and habit only made them attendant at chapel or meeting. There was little life either in the Established Churches, and religious feeling was at a low ebb.

Mr. Taylor, who was a man full of life and spirit, threw so much animation and vigor into his preaching and lecturing, that thronged houses soon gathered to enjoy his services. He still occupied his days with engraving, and his evenings were passed in village preaching when not engaged in his own parish.

Ann was fourteen at the time of this removal to Colchester, and Jane a year younger. So childlike were they, that their earliest care was to fit up anew their doll's house; but Colchester life, and the rapid development which new scenes and faces brought to their expanding minds, drove the dolls into oblivion. Ann was much liked, and received many attentions, as well as Jane. The friendships and intimacies made at Colchester were very gratifying. Several excellent offers were declined by them, and their presence was most welcome at social gatherings. Ann had never cared for Lavenham outside the charmed circle of home, but Colchester she loved for itself.

Years after, she said of it to her children : —

" It is a nice old town, and the country has just that cheerful pleasantness about it which is inviting to the evening walk or the social ramble. The town, clean, open, and agreeable, is situated on a healthful gravelly hill, descending towards the north and east, commanding from many points a view of the Colne, the meadows through which it winds, and the horizon fringed with wood,—'the High Woods,' which formed the most delightful portion of our longer evening excursions. Large barracks adjoined the town on its southern side, and an air of business and activity was given to the place as a great military station, while the High Street was quite a gay promenade. The music of the evening bugle is still a pleasant note in my ears, as well as that of the eight o'clock curfew bell from the tower of Old St. Nicholas."

She often spoke of the beauties of the town as seen from the meadows, which lay to the north of it, and made a delightful walk.

A sudden change in the state of the foreign market for

engraving, closed by the continental wars, produced great distress in the profession. Many young men were driven from the practice of the art to other occupations, and tried veterans like Mr. Taylor found a lucrative and absorbing employment sunk into a precarious and uncertain business, in which they could not support a family.

The move made by Mr. Taylor to Colchester was indeed fortunate. What seemed a renunciation of some worldly advantages, in becoming a minister and devoting more precious time to that good work, instead of his art in which he was earning large sums, was for a time a great blessing. The moderate stipend of a dissenting clergyman, eked out by taking pupils in engraving and the help of his daughters, was barely sufficient to keep his large family in comfort. Wants were limited to necessities, but even necessities were many in so large a circle of little ones.

Ann records her engraving life as dating from July, 1797, when she was in her sixteenth year. Jane began the study at the same time. In order that they might not lose their taste for domestic employments, it was wisely decided that they should work only on alternate weeks, resuming each her household duties; the one employed in the work being known that week as "Supra," the housewife as "Infra," — an improvement on the name "Betty," which had been bestowed before on the sister keeping house. Washing and fine ironing, sweeping, dusting, and cooking, all were expected of "Infra." And sewing was in some way interpolated, for they made their own clothes as soon as it was considered possible.

A large workroom joining the main house was the scene of Ann and Jane's daily life for many years. Pupils filled other tables, and there also their brothers, Isaac and Martin, began a life of toil. Ann says : —

" Happy days, — mornings, evenings, — Happy years ! — have I spent in that shabby old room ! From the windows we could just see over the garden, and beyond the roofs, Mile End church and parsonage in the pretty distance, reminding us of the evening walk by which the day's business was so often closed.

" Our many callers in after years never thought of finding us 'in the parlor,' like other young ladies, but regularly turned into a back yard from the street, ascended the short flight of brick stairs, and placed themselves each on some wooden stool beside Jane and myself, watching what they were sometimes pleased to call our 'elegant art.' I must say we were never ashamed of it, and why need we have been ? We had, I might almost say, the honor of stepping first on a line now regarded as nearly the one thing to be accomplished, the respectable, remunerative, appropriate employment of young women."

Jane did not much enjoy the drudgery of this life. Her more lively nature and literary aspirations made her dislike the monotony of the work.

An article on " Female Industry," in the " Edinburgh Review " for 1859, in alluding to employments suitable for women, named the Taylors, saying, " The young women were incessantly at work, so as to be abundantly weary of it, as Jane's letters plainly show." Ann resented this statement, and said : —

" The life in that 'shabby old room' was a happy one ; and if Jane did at times dislike the monotony, it never reached habitual weariness. For myself, what I have said, I have said, and that most truly. Nay, the time has been, when I have risen in the morning with exhilaration to put on the brown-holland bib and apron, with sleeves to match, in preparation for two or three days of 'biting,'—this not very charming employment frequently falling to my lot.

" Well, then, as to ' biting.' A plate of polished copper (not steel at that time), of the size intended for the print, having been thickly covered with a sort of waxy ground, the subject to be engraved is etched upon it with a steel point, as you might say *drawn* with a strong needle, much as you might with a pencil or pen, but cutting through the ground to the surface of the copper. The lines, however, are of no depth, and of course all alike, and to increase and vary both depth and width, the work must be ' bit.' To effect this a wall of wax is raised round the plate, with a spout, moulded at one corner, by which to pour off the liquid, and a dilute preparation of aquafortis (nitric acid) is poured on, which eats away the copper in the exposed lines. It is now a delicate matter to watch the operation, ascertaining when the needful depth of the lightest portion is attained ; at the moment, the acid is poured off, water plentifully applied, and then dried out of the lines. A thin coat of varnish is now painted over the parts that are sufficiently deepened, technically speaking they are ' stopped out,' and the process of biting is recommenced. But all this is subject to accidents ; and one trying misfortune is, when the ground, from some defect in its composition, or from being laid on under too great a heat, ' blows up,' as it is called, and the acid penetrates to the copper where it is not wanted, causing innumerable specks which must be immediately stopped out, and requiring a grievous amount of labor afterwards with the ' graver ' to repair. An engraving after Ostade, the interior of a Dutch kitchen, was etched by me, and covered almost entirely with work, but in biting, the ground blew up largely, and it was my business for three months afterwards to sit at the patient repair of it, speck by speck. I should not wonder if during this time I did feel ' abundantly weary.' So much for weariness, and for ' biting,' a part of the process for which it will be seen there was good reason to be armed with bib, apron, and sleeves."

Jemima Taylor, the youngest of this great family, on reading this passage by Ann about the " biting " and other dull processes described with so much enthusiasm, gave an insight into the good woman's character when she exclaimed, " Ah ! Ann was always such a dog trot."

Ann and Jane were considered by a large number of young friends very clever girls, and of the two Ann was supposed to take the lead. Jane herself had this impression, when she addressed these lines to her sister : —

> " My Ann, you had taken the lyre ;
>   And I, from the pattern you set,
>   Attempted the art to acquire ;
>   And often we play a duet.
> But those who in grateful return,
>   Have said they were pleased with the lay,
>   The discord could always discern ;
>   And yet I continued to play." — JANE TAYLOR.

Curiously enough the public considered Jane as the leader, and publishers, taking advantage of this, Ann said, would often announce, "by ' Jane Taylor,' when ' Ann Taylor ' was the guilty person." " Dear Jane never needed to steal," she adds, " while I could not afford to lose."

Ann's first published production was an election song, for home reading only. It happened to be seen, and was evidently valuable enough for one side to print for party purposes. She was somewhat dazzled by her appearance in print, and gives the date as 1797.

Sometime before a friend accused her of literary vanity, and she felt the remark so keenly that she made " a magnanimous conflagration " of all her MSS., and " resolved to go humbly " all her days. For a time her favorite amusement was laid aside ; but it could not be borne, and she resumed her pen. The necessity of giving expression to the emotions constantly roused by various objects of daily life, was too strong ; she continued her poetical effusions.

ˈIn 1798 the girls entered with great enjoyment into the
formation of a little literary society proposed by their
father. The title " Umbelliferous Society " was intended
to indicate the buds, blossoms, and flowers so gathered
on one stem ; and it was suggested by Mr. Taylor. This
society, which was intended to stimulate the fancy, and
encourage the study of literature, lasted about two years.
Of the mode of life at this time, when full of business, and
also trying to save every moment for self-improvement,
Ann wrote : —

" We always breakfasted at eight o'clock, were allowed an
hour's interval for dinner, half-an-hour for tea, and closed the
daily routine in ' that dear old workroom ' (as more than one
of our friends called it) at eight in the evening. It was chiefly,
therefore, or according to the letter of the law, *only* by rising
early and supping as late as half-past nine, that we could effect
anything. But I must confess to having had pencil and paper
generally so near at hand, that a flying thought could be caught
by a feather, even when engraving or biting was going on ; or,
in cases of extremity, when it was to be feared that all would
escape me before eight o'clock came. I have made a sudden
exit, and in honest haste and unintelligible scribble, pinioned
the fancy or the lines to the first slip of waste paper I could
find, there to abide till happy evening. Instead of engraving,
I was going to say etching, but this would be scarcely correct,
for while etching it was generally desirable to keep the ' point '
unchanged in the fingers from meal to meal. Only a very
beautiful point indeed would be so exquisitely true, that no
inequality of stroke would result from changing it. To render
the point perfect by grinding all the angles, was often not a
little difficult, and would cost much time; as a hone for this
purpose, a fragment of Roman brick, picked up among the
ruins in the town, proved the finest and hardest substance we
could meet with. And if I have said ' bitings,' it must be understood to mean, at times when the water was off, and the plate
safely dry."

About this time the indefatigable Mr. Taylor was urged by some friends to invite the public to his lectures on astronomy, illustrated by diagrams, which were rough and picturesque, but very effective. He continued these lectures to full rooms, for some time. He prepared successive courses on astronomy, anatomy, geography, geometry, mechanics, and general history.

The removal of some friends to Bergholt, — "Constable's Country," as it has been called, since his hand made its rural scenes familiar, — caused an intimacy between the families Of the early introduction there is an amusing anecdote, told by Ann with great good-nature : " We had been invited to walk over to Bergholt to see his paintings, together with a portrait recently taken of him by his friend Mr. Reinagle ; and availing ourselves of this, one morning, we found his mother, Mrs. Constable, a shrewd-looking, sensible woman, at home. There we were, five girls, all ' come to see Mr. John Constable's paintings,' and as we were about to be shown up into his studio, she turned and said, dryly, ' Well, young ladies, would you like to go up all together to my son, or one at a time ?' I was simpleton enough to pause for a moment, in doubt, but we happily decided upon going *en masse.*"

Small events often lead to important results. Ann had bought an annual known as the " Minor's Pocket Book," in 1798 ; and this chanced to rouse her fancy, as we shall see by her own words : —

" On reading the solutions of enigmas, and other poetic contributions to which prizes were adjudged, it struck me that, without great presumption, I might aim at as much literary distinction as these prizes conferred. With lively interest, therefore, I possessed myself of the prescribed conditions, unravelled enigma, charade, and rebus, and forwarded the results under the signature of ' Juvenilia,' as directed, to 55 Gracechurch

Street. I little thought that it was bread I thus cast on the waters, or rather that it would return as bread after many days. I had, indeed, to wait long, and as the interesting season approached for the new pocket books to make their appearance in the window of old Mr. Gibbs the bookseller, frequent and anxious were my glances in passing by. At last they arrived, and on turning them over on his counter with as much indifference as could be assumed, I ascertained that the first prize — six pocket books — had been awarded to ' Juvenilia. ' "

The year 1799 may be fairly considered as the period when Ann was launched on the sea of literature. For some twelve or fourteen years she with Jane was a regular contributor, and latterly she had the editorial charge for Darton and Harvey, who also became publishers of some of their works.

Finding that plates were used in the " Pocket Book," the Taylors applied for work on the illustrations, and were frequently employed in that department. Their literary work was at this early period subordinate, and only done for their own relaxation. Ann made a visit in London when eighteen years old, and found much to interest and stimulate her artistic and literary taste. She met a young lady, Anna Forbes, who became the dearest friend of a lifetime. She met Josiah Conder, who became, in a few years, the editor of the " Wreath."

Constant work in an overheated room left its mark on the Taylors. They paid the penalty of close application, and want of active exercise in the open air, in after years. Ann happily was exempt ; but none of the others were strong or well. When Mr. Taylor finally allowed them a run at dinner time, as their mother so strongly urged it, the mischief was done. Isaac long felt the effects of the close confinement, and Jane was prematurely cut off in her prime.

In 1800 the pressure of business was so great that Mr. Taylor withdrew both Ann and Jane from the housework on alternate weeks, and they spent all their long working days in the preparation of the portraits engaged by him for " The Theological Magazine," with the exception of a day once in a fortnight for their own needlework. Jane thoroughly enjoyed all feminine accomplishments, and the use of her pen, but there is abundant evidence that she was very averse to engraving. Isaac Taylor has recorded that Jane's "taste for the arts was such as to make her excel in the lighter branches ; and many of her drawings, still in possession of her family, display a true feeling of the beautiful in nature, and a peculiar niceness and elegance of execution ; but the business of engraving was not altogether suited to her talent, or taste, and it was relinquished without regret, when other paths of exertion opened before her. In a letter of an early date, she says, — ' The more I see of myself, and of the performances of others, the more I am convinced that nature never intended me for an artist : . . . no one can tell how my feelings are excruciated, when I am referred to, or my opinion asked, as an *artist.* — I look at the girls in the milliners' shops, with envy ; because their business and their genius are on a level. I think it is what I shall come to at last.' "

There was hope for Jane ; and the envy with which she jokingly said she looked at the milliners' girls, soon was forgotten, when her talent was discovered. She then found her vocation ; and though she for a time continued the daily occupation of engraving, the interest and inspiration of her new life cheered her daily round of uncongenial labor.

Jane's first appearance in public was with the printing of "The Beggar Boy," in the " Minor's Pocket Book."

The pathos, simplicity, and animation of this poem attracted attention ; and the following note from the publishers will show that they saw the value of the sisters'
work.

LONDON, 1st 6 mo. 1803.

" ISAAC TAYLOR.

"RESPECTED FRIEND, — We have received some pieces of
poetry from some branches of thy family for the Minor's
Pocket Book, and we beg that the enclosed trifles may be
divided among such as are most likely to be pleased with them.
My principal reason for writing now, is to request that when
any of their harps be tuned, and their muse in good humor,
if they could give me some specimens of easy Poetry for
young children, I would endeavor to make a suitable return
in cash, or in books.   If something in the way of moral
songs (though not songs), or short tales turned into verse,
or, — but I need not dictate.   What would be most likely to
please little minds must be well known to every one of those
who have written such pieces as we have already seen from
thy family.   Such pieces as are short, for little children would
be preferred.

" For self and partner, very respectfully,

" DARTON AND HARVEY."

One can fancy the eager and delighted girls round their
father's desk as he read this kind note.   His remark, " I
do not want my girls to be authors," was seconded by
their mother, whose watchful care and narrow views made
her dread any new departure from the old established
customs of her day.   Female authorship was long de-
cried by all ranks and many intelligent people.   Like
many another fetich, it has been laid by patience and
tried skill.

The Taylors were both conscientious and poor.   The
desire to be useful went hand in hand with a very laudable wish to add to the common store.   Death had

several times visited the family; times were hard, and
mouths were many, in this large family. Mrs. Taylor
herself, as we have seen, appeared later in the field as an
author.

The field of poetry for children was almost an un-
trodden one when Ann and Jane took up their pens. Dr.
Watts was the first in his work for the young. It was
true that Dr. Aikin, Mrs. Barbauld, and others, had begun the good work of judicious, practical, and elevating
writing for the children, but the greater part of these
writers' work was done in prose. The beautiful "Prose
Hymns," of Mrs. Barbauld, fill a very important place for
the use of little children ; but hymns and verses appeal
most powerfully to the young mind. There is something
in every child's nature, responsive and alive to poetry.
Poetry is the happiest way of communicating great truths
in a simple way to the young.

The "Original Poems," published as the result of Darton and Harvey's note, appeared in 1804, and a second
edition was called for within the year.

The following extract from the preface will show the
ideas of the Authors : —

" If a hearty affection for that interesting little race, the race
of children, is any recommendation, the writers of the following
pages are well recommended ; and if to have studied in some
degree their capacities, habits, and wants, with a wish to adapt
these simple verses to their real comprehensions and probable
improvement, — if this has any further claim to the indulgence
of the public, it is the last and only one they attempt to make.
The deficiency of the compositions as poetry, is by no means a
secret to their authors; but it was thought desirable to abridge
every poetic freedom and figure, and even every long-syllabled
word, which might give, perhaps, a false idea to their little
readers, or at least make a chasm in the chain of conception.

Images, which to us are so familiar that we forget their imagery, are terrible stumbling-blocks to children, who have none but literal ideas."

A few pieces by another hand were added to the "Original Poems," but after the second volume appeared the authors always stood alone in their work. They received £10 for the Poems, and the "Rhymes for the Nursery" brought them £20. Not large sums, but to their simple ideas full of encouragement for the future. Thousands were sold, and translations were made into many languages.

Work was constantly given them; and among their principal prose works, which are not so well known as their poetry, were some translations and adaptations from the French, "City Scenes," "Rural Scenes," "Bible Stories," "Limed Twigs," and many others. Among other "jobs" given them was the revision and improvement of a queer book, "The World turned Topsy-turvey." The publisher, Sir Richard Philips, gave them twenty-four guineas for adding some poems and working over the old ones.

Ann attempted an imitation of Roscoe's "Butterfly's Ball," in her "Wedding among the Flowers;" and in a happy fortnight, by availing herself of the extra hour of daylight in the spring of 1808, when Jane was in London, she completed her poem; for which Darton and Harvey sent her what she thought the "Munificent gift" of twelve guineas.

"The Hymns for Infant Minds," printed in 1807, went through forty-five editions before 1860. Mrs. Gilbert herself corrected the thirty-fifth in 1844. During the twenty-four years since 1860, the sale has continued, and the works of the sisters are in no way superseded by more modern productions.

The preparation of hymns for children's use was a peculiarly difficult task. Jane wrote, in a letter of this date, " I think I have some idea of what a child's hymn ought to be ; and when I commenced the task, it was with the presumptuous determination that none of them should fall short of the standard I had formed in my mind. In order to this, my method was to shut my eyes, and imagine the presence of some pretty little mortal ; and then endeavor to catch, as it were, the very language it would use on the subject before me. If, in any instances, I have succeeded, to this little imaginary being I should attribute my success. And I have failed so frequently, because so frequently I was compelled to say, — ' Now you may go, my dear, I shall finish the hymn myself.'"

The Authors, in their preface to this volume, say very truly, " The Divine Songs of Dr. Watts, so beautiful, and so justly admired, almost discourage, by their excellence, a similar attempt; and lead the way, where it appears temerity to follow."

The want of hymns of this kind has always been felt by parents, and the immense sale of this book would seem to imply that the Authors' success was all they could have hoped or wished. Some years after, Ann's husband, Mr. Gilbert, proposed a similar volume for the use of Sunday Schools ; and the sisters prepared it. Ann records, shortly after her marriage, the singing of some of these " Hymns for Infant Minds," saying, —

"*May* 18, 1815.— You would have enjoyed a scene we witnessed last Monday. The Sunday schools of Sheffield, containing six thousand children and thirteen hundred teachers, assembled in an open space in the outskirts of the town, where they formed into a hollow square, sang the " Old Hundredth," and then marched in procession through the principal streets to a very large chapel, where a sermon was preached to them. Our hymns were sung, and the first, which was the first in the 'Infant minds,'[1] had a beautiful effect from so many little English voices. Large hustings were erected round the pulpit, where the principal ladies and gentlemen of the town were placed, and in front a gentleman beat time with one of our books. Montgomery told the committee in choosing the hymns that the middle one — 'Among the deepest shades of night' — was the finest hymn of the sort in the English language. The last in the volume concluded. Mr. Gilbert enjoys such incidents."

The intense excitement produced by the rumors of a French Invasion made a great panic at Colchester, and as a measure of safety, the younger children were sent in charge of Jane and Isaac to Lavenham, where the unoccupied house still owned by Mr. Taylor nicely accommodated them. Mrs. Taylor, in writing to Jane, "describes to her children the rigors of the fast-day — no cloth laid; half a round of toast at breakfast, and no dinner! She dwells, too, upon 'the wonderful sermon' of her husband, of which she had chosen the text — David's words to Goliath of Gath. 'Goliath, he said, had three significations, Revolution, Captivity, and Passing over. People came round him afterwards begging to have it printed.' There was plain speaking in those plain days; for he failed not to set forth, 'in most affectionate terms,' to the volunteers present in their uniforms, that many might probably 'wallow in their blood.'"

Ann, being in London visiting, could speak only from hearsay of all this, but she shared in the general commotion.

In the year 1807, as before said, appeared the "Rhymes

---

[1] "I thank the goodness and the grace."

for the Nursery," and "Hymns for Infant Minds." During this year Ann says, in writing of a visit to London, —

" Through the kindness of various friends, I gratified my intense, but humble yearnings to see ' Poetry ' in the shape of man or woman.' On this occasion I was introduced to both Dr. Aikin and Mrs. Barbauld. A call I was privileged to make at Newington upon the latter, I cannot forget, nor the strange feeling of unearthly expectancy with which, in a small parlor, I waited her appearance. At length the door opened, — for she did not float in on a cloud or a zephyr, — and a small, plain, lively, elderly lady made her appearance ; but it was Mrs. Barbauld, and that was enough ! During the same visit I was introduced to a literary nucleus of a different but interesting description, consisting of Daniel Parken, then editor of the ' Eclectic Review ; ' Theophilus Williams, who succeeded him ; and Ignatius Montgomery, a relative of the Poet. Of James Montgomery himself, Kirke White, and others, we, from time to time, heard a good deal from our now intimate friend Josiah Conder, whose correspondence, through the ' monthly parcel,' was made intensely interesting to us by the literary intelligence it conveyed."

Josiah Conder was a frequent visitor at the Taylors', and he urged on the sisters the publication of some of their more ambitious efforts at poetry.

In 1809 they collected several pieces and jointly printed them, though rather reluctantly, by his advice. He was editor as well as publisher. Ann's share of " The Associate Minstrels " was quite large, being eleven poems. The book was first called the " Wreath ; " but the editor probably changed the title, for Jane wished the volume to retain its original name, saying, " Since I have had time to think soberly about the ' Wreath,' — for this must always be its title, — I have felt far less anxious about it." She had not at this time displayed the vigor her writings later showed, and the poems, which were none of them prepared for publication, are pleasing, simple, expressive of feeling occasioned by various circumstances. They show her natural tenderness of heart, and the playful fancy always natural to her, but not the spirit later developed in her work.

The book, which was dedicated to Montgomery the poet, included poems from Ann and Jane, and the elder Mr. Conder, the lady afterwards Mrs. Josiah Conder, and a friend of the Taylors, Mr. Jacob Strutt. It went to a second edition soon, and received the kindly notice and commendation of Sir Walter Scott, Maria Edgeworth, Southey, James Montgomery, Hayley, and others. Scott and Miss Edgeworth greatly liked the poems for children.

Sir Walter Scott, writing to Josiah Conder, says, " My young people are busy with the ' Rhymes for the Nursery,' and it is perhaps the highest proof of their being admirably adapted for their benevolent purpose, that the little students have most of them by heart already."

Miss Edgeworth, in thanking Ann· for something sent her, says : " In a book called ' Original Poems for Children,' there is a pretty little poem, ' The Chatterbox,' which one of my little sisters, on hearing your letter, recollected. It is signed Ann T——. Perhaps, madam, it may be written by you ; and it will give you pleasure to hear that it is a favorite with four good talkers of nine, six, five, and four years old."

When Southey received from Josiah Conder the " Associate Minstrels," after some general remarks on the state of poetry at that day in England, and the work under his notice, adds : " The ' Original Poems ' of your friends and associates have long been in my children's library, and equally favorites with them and with me. There is a cast of feeling in them which made me suppose the authors to be Quakers, a society with which I am almost, yet not wholly in communion. Whoever these ladies are, they have well and wisely employed their talents, and I am glad to have this opportunity of conveying my thanks to them through you, for the good which they are doing, and will long continue to do."

Montgomery writes of it : — " Ann is to my mind the Queen of the Assembly. She is a poet of a high order, the first, unquestionably, among those who write for children, and not the last, by hundreds, of those who write for men. The ' Maniac's Song ' has not only the melancholy of madness, but the inspiration of poetry."

In 1811 the sisters published the third edition of " The Hymns for Infant Minds," for themselves, with the entire profit. They realized £150 from the first edition, but all their little savings were lost by the failure of their publisher, and this decided them to publish for themselves, which produced very substantial returns.

In 1810 Mr. Taylor resigned his pastoral charge in Colchester, and the following year received a call to Ongar, a pretty village near Epping Forest.

Fourteen years of workroom life for Ann and Jane was at an end. It was decided that they should forever abandon this work, so distasteful to Jane. Great changes were in store for them, and the projected school to take the place of engraving was talked of, but soon dropped. Ann gives a distant friend a picture of Castle House, Ongar, her home till her marriage in 1813.

" And now, how I wish I could show, instead of describe it to you! but, alas! Ongar and Barnstaple! Well, then, I must e'en tell you of the pleasant places in which our lines are fallen. The house was built upon the site of the ancient castle, in the

reign of Queen Elizabeth, who once honored it with a visit.
The hall-door, studded with clump-headed nails an inch in
diameter, measures 6 feet, by 4 feet 7. The front is covered
with a vine ; before it is a flower garden ; on the right, as
pretty a village church among the trees as you ever saw ; and
close on the left the castle trees rising upon a high mount, with
a moat of deep water encircling it. From every window in
front we command a rich and beautiful valley, and behind see
the town just peeping through a line of elms on a terrace beside
an outer moat. Immediately adjacent is a farm-yard, and we
have not only the usual live stock of such a scene, but a fine
pair of swans, three cygnets, moorfowl, and solan geese upon
the moat ; rabbits running wild upon the mount ; a rookery,
wood doves, and, we are told, nightingales in the castle trees.
Now, you may fancy, perhaps, that with all this appropriate
scenery the house must be haunted, or, at least hauntible ; that
there are nooks and vaults, and niches at every turn ; and that
sitting, as I now do, a broad moon shining in at my window,
and the village clock striking eleven, the next thing must be a
tall gliding figure patting down the stairs which wind from my
room door, within the northern turret. But I assure you we
are the picture of cheerfulness and comfort. The rooms are
light and pleasant, not in the least ghostly, and fitted up with
every modern convenience. We have a hall, two parlors,
kitchen, store-room, &c., on the ground floor ; three chambers
above ; and a good workroom, study, two bed-chambers, and a
light closet on the attic floor. We had to *saw* the ivy from the
back parlor window before we could see it, but some still remains to fringe the mullions ; we have beautiful walks in every
direction ; and we have placed our garden seat at the end of a
retired field, surrounded by the moats and the terrace elms
immediately behind the house."

After some very pleasant visits to friends in London, the girls went home, in February of 1812, looking
forward to a new era in their lives. This period was
of short duration for Ann, who passed but a few months

there. Before leaving Colchester, Hannah More's popular tale of " Cœlebs in Search of a Wife " was the
subject of a long letter from Ann to Josiah Conder. He
was intimate with Daniel Parken, the talented editor
of the " Eclectic Review," and probably showed him
this letter; for Mr. Parken presently asked if Ann would
undertake an article, and he so far diverged from the
customary range of the " Review " as to propose a
tale of the day by Mrs. West, " Self Control." This
" Review " numbered several able writers on its list,
among them, Robert Hall, John Foster, and Olinthus
Gregory. In its pages the merits of Washington Irving
were first recognized in England, by an article contributed by Isaac Taylor, Jr. Ann says of this, her first
Review article : " With anxiety, excitement, and delight,
I undertook it. After writing every morning till about
weary, I used to take the MS. to a clump of trees a
little in the valley as seen from my window, and sitting
beneath them, read it aloud, for until able to judge from
the ear I could never form an opinion of what I had written. It appeared in the ' Eclectic ' for June, and, being
favorably received, I was forthwith continually employed.
The next review was of Miss Edgeworth's Tales, I forget
which series, sent up in August of the same year."

Their quiet life was little broken by company; but " a
visit about this time from Josiah Conder and James
Montgomery gave great pleasure to us. Few and far
between had been our glimpses into literary society, and
in Montgomery, from first admiring his poetry in the
' Athenæum,' we had felt the most lively interest, — yes,
and notwithstanding the remark of a young lady belonging to our higher circle in Colchester, who, hearing from
me that he was printer at Sheffield, exclaimed, ' La ! how
terrible.' It was scarcely worth while to remember it

for half a century, but how can we get rid of anything
that chooses to stay? On the afternoon of their visit, our
walk with the two poets across the meadows, and up the
winding lane to Stondon Church, was indeed delightful;
and yet the only shred of conversation that clings to my
memory was the simple remark of Montgomery, when I
mistook distant thunder for artillery (that of Woolwich
sometimes shook our windows). 'Yes, the artillery of
Heaven.'"

In 1812 Isaac Taylor, Jr.'s, health began to fail. His
occupation in London was abandoned, and it was considered absolutely necessary that he should seek a different climate. Ilfracombe, in Devonshire, was chosen for
its soft climate; and the family decided that Ann and Jane
should go with him. So, armed with their writing, and
he equipped with his materials for miniature-painting and
engraving, the little party set out. It was sad and anxious
time. The journey of three hundred miles was made by
stage, from the celebrated "Castle and Falcon," Inn in
Aldersgate Street, London, in three days and nights.

Jane wrote of the place of their six months' stay, after a
few weeks' study, —

" Ilfracombe is situated in a deep valley, surrounded on one
side by barren hills, and on the other by stupendous rocks,
which skirt the sea. Our lodgings very pleasantly overlook
the harbor, which affords us constant entertainment. The sea
is close behind the house; and is so near a neighbor that, during the last high tides, the waves rose in immense sheets of
foam, and fell over a high wall opposite our chamber windows:
it also flowed into the house in front, and kept us close pris-
oners. Our walks in every direction are so interesting that,
while the weather permitted, we spent a great part of the day
abroad. Our rambles among the rocks I enjoy most; though
at first they excited sensations of awe and terror, rather than

of pleasure. But now we climb without fear amid a wilderness of rocks, where nothing else can be seen, and nothing heard but the roar of the distant sea : here the only path is over the huge fragments which lie scattered in all directions, and which it requires some courage as well as dexterity to scale. Besides these, we have several cheerful walks, commanding the sea, bounded to the north by a beautiful line of the Welsh mountains. Their aspects are very various; at times appearing only like faint clouds in the horizon; but when the weather is clear, and the sun shines upon them, they exhibit an exquisite variety of light and shade, and delicate coloring, finished, by distance, like the finest miniature. From some of the highest hills we have distinctly perceived the buildings on the nearer part of the coast ; — to the west the wide ocean is before us,

'Now sparkling with sunbeams, now dimpled with oars,
    Now dark with the fresh-blowing gale.'

The rocky cliffs of Lundy island add beauty and interest to the scene."

This new field of study, and the enlarged circle of friends made by the sisters, was very desirable in many ways. Jane was naturally of a retiring disposition. She wrote a few years before this : " How many mortifications should we escape, if we were always more solicitous to deserve the love of a few valued friends, than to excite general admiration ! A proud indifference to the opinion of the world is no amiable feeling. But to be independent of its smiles, by valuing chiefly the sweets of inward tranquillity, is indeed a most desirable state of mind, — only to be attained by cultivating the best principles, and by seeking approbation from the *highest* source."

She never fully threw off the extreme diffidence with which she started on her literary career. She continued to address herself to young people and children, because she felt herself safe in that humble and less ambitious sphere.

Jane spent much of her time at Ilfracombe in rambling about and gathering impressions for future work. Ann and Isaac were fully occupied. Ann wrote for the "Eclectic" several excellent reviews, — among them that pungent one on Hannah More's "Christian Morals." She was much stimulated in her new field of work by finding that an article by Dr. Gregory was laid aside for her review of Miss Edgeworth's book. But the chief event of the winter at Ilfracombe, was the arrival of a visitor on a peculiar errand. A minister, for a short time resident in Essex, but now associated with Dr. Williams as classical tutor in Rotherham Theological College, had been so impressed with Ann Taylor's writings, and had heard from those acquainted with her so much eulogium upon her personal merits, that he took the singular step, without having seen her, of writing to inquire, whether "any peremptory reasons existed which might lead him to conclude that a journey, undertaken with the purpose of soliciting her heart and hand, could not possibly be successful."

The Rev. Joseph Gilbert first visited Ongar, and took the wise step of enlisting the sympathy of Ann's only confidant and best friend, her mother, who wrote : " But as to the *man*, it would be vain and fruitless for me to say — 'like or dislike him.' Your own observations, your own eyes, your own heart, must be your directors. But I may say, *I like him*, and that he grows upon me most rapidly. I soon discovered a vivacity, a gracefulness, and even a fascination in his manner, which I thought might in due time render him acceptable. Poor fellow! There was no place inside, and he had to travel on the roof this bitter weather, and was so absorbed in love and learning, that he had left behind his warm travelling cap, and, but for your father, would have gone away again without his overalls ! "

At this time Mr. Gilbert was assistant classical Professor at Rotherham College. He was a widower of thirty-three, without children. At the death, in a few months, of the Principal of Rotherham, he was asked to take the entire charge of the college. After several visits on the way, the little family party returned to Ongar. Ann had received Mr. Gilbert's visit with courtesy, but given him no decided answer. She naturally was surprised, and it would seem not quite pleased, by his abrupt wooing.

After ten months they reached Ongar in July, 1813. Quite a correspondence had taken place between Mr. Gilbert and Ann, and at last he arrived in August at Ongar for a decisive answer to his offer.

Ann Taylor virtually closed her literary career when she replied *yes* to this suitor. It gave her forty years of a happy and useful life with one in all ways worthy of respect and love. Her heart and hands were soon too full for any but the practical duties of life. She lived that "duty, praise and prayer," she had so well written of in her verse. She was thirty-one when she took this important step. She had already received attentions and good offers, but this only touched that tender heart.

Jane was left alone by this event, and the last ten years of her life were passed without the constant companionship of her beloved Ann. She had written before this of preparations for work, to a friend, during the Colchester life: —

" My verses have certainly one advantage to boast, beyond any that ever before escaped from my pen; — that of being composed in my own study. Whether instigated by the sight of your retired literarium, or what, I cannot exactly tell; but certain it is, that one of my first engagements on my return home, was to fit up an unoccupied attic, hitherto devoted only to household lumber; this I removed by the most spirited

exertions, and supplied its place with all the apparatus necessary for a poet; which, you know, is not of a very extensive
nature, — a few book-shelves, a table for my writing-desk, one
chair for myself, and another for my muse, is a pretty accurate
inventory of my furniture.   But though my study cannot boast
the elegance of yours, it possesses one advantage which, as a
poet, you ought to allow surpasses them all: it commands a
view of the country, — the only room in the house, except one,
which is thus favored; and to me this is invaluable. You may
now expect me to do wonders. But even if others should derive
no advantages from this new arrangement, to me, I am sure,
they will be numerous. For years I have been longing for such
a luxury; and never before had wit enough to think of this convenient place : it will add so much to the comfort of my life,
that I can do nothing but congratulate myself upon the happy
thought; and I demand a large share of your poetical sympathy
on the occasion.   Although it is morning, and, I must tell you,
but little past six, I have half filled this sheet, which capability
I attribute, chiefly, to the sweet fields that are now smiling in
vernal beauty before me."

At Ongar, during her first years, she was hardly settled
enough to make a study.   Isaac's health obliged her to
again leave home for Ilfracombe and Marazion.

In October the brother and sister left Ongar, and from
there she addressed Ann as follows on the occasion of
her approaching marriage : —

"ILFRACOMBE, December 18, 1813.

"MY DEAR ANN, — I cannot suffer this interesting morning
to pass without something of a salutation from Ilfracombe ; and
I dare say this letter will arrive in good company; but I am sure
no one will address you who can feel on this occasion either so
glad, or so sorry as I do.   So far as you only are concerned, I
think I am entirely glad, and feel as perfectly satisfied and happy
as one can do about untried circumstances. But I cannot forget

that this morning which forms one indissoluble partnership, dissolves another, which we had almost considered so. From the early days of ' Moll and Bett,' down to these last times, we have been more inseparable companions than sisters usually are ; and our pursuits and interests have been the same. My thoughts of late have often wandered back to those distant years, and passed over the varied scenes which chequered our childhood and youth : — there is scarcely a recollection, in all that long period, in which we are not mutually concerned, and equally interested. If this separation had taken place ten years ago, we might, by this time, have been in some degree estranged from each other; but having passed so large and important a portion of life in such intimate union, I think we may confidently say it never will be so. For brothers and sisters to separate, is the common lot ; — for their affection and interest to remain unabated is not common ; but I am sure it is possible ; and I think the experience we have already had proves that we may expect its continuance. Farewell, my dear Ann ! and in this emphatical farewell I would comprehend all the wishes, the prayers, the love, the joy, and the sorrow, which it would be so difficult to express in more words. If there is a dash of bitterness in the grief with which I bid you farewell, it is only from the recollection that I have not been to you the sister I might have been. My feelings have been so strongly excited to-day, that I cannot bear more of it ; and must leave you to imagine what more I would say on this occasion.

" I cannot — no, I cannot realize the busy scene at the Castle House, nor fancy you in your bridal appearance. I intend to place myself before the view of the house, about the time I imagine you are walking down the gravel-walk, and stand there while you are at church, and till I think you are coming back again. How strange — how sad, that I cannot be with you ! What a world is this, that its brightest pleasures are, almost invariably, attended with the keenest heart-rendings."

Ann's wedding day was the 24th December, 1813. It was a bright winter's day ; and Ann wrote a friend she should "not soon forget the dearest group in all the world to me, left at the garden gate to watch the chaise out of sight. I had a last look as we ascended the hill. It was one of those bitter pains which we sometimes have to pay for pleasures of an earthly kind." Jane and Isaac were present only in spirit, as his health had driven them away, even in the weeks before the wedding. "It was then the fashion for ladies to travel in a riding-habit; a friend had undertaken to purchase the cloth for that required by the bride at a wholesale warehouse in London, and she was not a little gratified to learn, that when the proprietor heard for whom the purchase was intended, though he only knew Ann Taylor from her works, he begged her acceptance of the four guineas' worth of cloth as a token of respect."

The quiet and retirement of the second winter in Devonshire were passed by Jane in writing the tale published later, under the title, "Display." Her brother says : —

"She commenced it with a specific idea of the qualities she designed to exhibit, but with no definite plan for its execution. In pursuit of the same general object she followed, every day, the suggestion of the moment; and this was, perhaps, the only way in which she would ever have written. It was her custom, in a solitary ramble among the rocks, for half an hour after breakfast, to seek that pitch of excitement without which she never took up the pen. This fever of thought was usually exhausted in two or three hours of writing, after which she enjoyed a social walk, and seldom attempted a second effort in the day; for she had now adopted the salutary plan of writing in the morning only. To this plan she adhered ever after, with only occasional exceptions."

Mrs. Barbauld, writing to Miss Edgeworth in 1816, criticises it somewhat. Miss Edgeworth had spoken of it to her in a previous letter, saying, —

" We have just got a little book called 'Display,' a tale for young people, which we like much. It is written by the daughter of a physician, a Miss Jane Taylor, who keeps a school near Dublin. I am not acquainted with her. The *good* people in this book, are more to my taste, than those in Cœlebs, because they are not so meddling. I only wish they had not objected to young people going to balls. Before I could finish my sentence, in praise of all the good sense and excellent writing of this tale, a circle of young and old ladies were open-mouthed with the question, — But why object to balls ? "

To this pleasant recommendation from a sister author-ess, Mrs. Barbauld replied : —

" 'Display' we sent for on your recommendation, and are much pleased with a good deal of it, but we are entirely of your opinion with regard to balls, and indeed there is a great deal in her system that I should object to, particularly the doctrine, which I think a very pernicious one, that all, the innocent and good as well as the bad, must undergo a myste-rious change before they are in a safe state. Emily was very good for aught that I could see before her conversion. I trembled, as I drew near the close, lest Elizabeth should have a fine fortune left her by somebody, and was much pleased with the author's good sense in handing her to her post behind the counter. By the way, are you not mistaken in the Author ? We take it to be the production of *Jane Taylor* of *Ongar*, who has written several pieces, both verse and prose, for children."

" Display " went through many editions. Twelve were printed in London, before 1835 ; and it was reprinted elsewhere several times. The good sense and evident sincerity of the writer are everywhere noticeable ; and the plain unaffected· English, the perfect simplicity of the plot and incidents, all disarm criticism. Written with a

e

desire to inculcate religious and devotional sentiments, it is neither sectarian nor bigoted, like too many stories of similar style. One cannot help wishing that fate had allowed Jane a wider scope for her playful fancy and quick observation. " Display" belongs to a very serious class of stories, and is well calculated to awaken thought, and assist the young to a better knowledge of their wants and shortcomings.

For Mr. and Mrs. Gilbert, in Ann's own words,

> " Life's uncertain scope
> In pleasant haze before them lay,
> A land of Love and Hope."

Their first home was at Rotherham, in Yorkshire. It was from the first a very busy life for both, made very happy by mutual love and confidence. For a time Ann attempted to keep up her writing. She gave Mr. Gilbert assistance in his work. After his Greek instruction he devoted some time to literary work each day ; and in this his wife aided him. She had also engaged to review Miss Hamilton's " Popular Essays," and Miss Edgeworth's " Patronage."

Her letters to her mother are full of questions as to various housekeeping mysteries, showing her desire to make an acceptable housekeeper in her new home. She had to visit more or less, dining with the new friends in Yorkshire frequently. Sheffield, where her husband preached, was not distant, — six miles through pleasant field and wood walks. There she often visited and, while staying with James Montgomery, " witnessed the phenomenon of a poet smoking two pipes after supper."

She wrote of her new experiences, and the difficulty she found in keeping up her literary work, — " There is always ' some bed or some border to mend, or something to tie or to stick.' I endeavor to get to writing about eleven, and write during the morning, more or less, as I am able." She says in another letter, —

"I am persuaded that many here are expecting to find me a dawdle. Mr. G. says that people have been continually fishing for information on this head, 'Is Mrs. Gilbert always writing?' Mr. G. is very desirous that 'Mrs. Gilbert' should be as well known as 'Miss Taylor;' but he has invested me with other characters, and he does not feel, perhaps, that to be well known at the expense of these, would be disgrace, rather than fame. I hope, by prudence and activity, to be able in time to unite the different occupations and characters, so as not greatly to injure any; but if one must suffer, it should certainly be the literary."

Mrs. Taylor about this time made her first appearance as a writer; and soon after, with Jane, published the " Correspondence between a Mother and Daughter at School." Her little book on " Maternal Solicitude," was very popular, running through four editions immediately after its publication. In October, 1814, Ann's first child, a boy, was born; and to remonstrances about her unused pen, she would answer, " Never mind, the dear little child is worth volumes of fame." Her heart overflowed with tenderness and a welcome for all the little ones sent her. Her days and nights were full of thought and care for them. She had eight children born to her. Of this, the first born, there are many little anecdotes which run through the family letters. It was her one topic for a while.

She describes the old nurse as talking to the newly born baby: " I wish you could have heard her talk to him; it amused me many an hour in bed, for she speaks the broadest Yorkshire I have heard, except from a coal miner. ' Wale, wale, ma little lud, wha d'ye mack sic a

din, an croy soa? Oh, for shaam! I mun whip ye, happen ye wornt loyke that. Coom, coom, I mun hap ye oop,
an lig ye int' bed for a soop a bottle. Hoosh, hoosh,
thenna, an' dunna croye soa, ma little piggin, an' dunna
foight soa, an' tear ya screed.' "

Meantime Jane at Marazion was busy on " Display"
and "Essays on Rhyme." She was also meeting a new
set of friends, and enlarging her views of people and life.
She wrote of the place : " Marazion is pleasantly situated
on the margin of Mount's Bay, which forms a fine sweep :
on the western side lies Penzance, nearly opposite to us,
at the distance of three miles : — it is a fine ride by the
sea-side. This morning we have been there : it is a large
and very pleasant town ; and being so near, we can have
many of the conveniences it affords. The views here are
open and agreeable : St. Michael's Mount is a fine object,
distant about half a mile, and Penzance and the adjacent
villages very prettily skirt the Bay."

Here she met with very agreeable people and saw
much of members of the Established Church and the
Wesleyan Methodists. Her father's position as an Independent preacher had deprived the family of the free
social intercourse, so desirable for the young, and really
indispensable to the formation of a liberal mind and a
well-balanced literary judgment. Jane Taylor was much
hampered by the circumstances of her early life. The
humblest position could not have been more narrowing
than the isolation to which these children were doomed
by their father's pastorate.

The favorable reception accorded " Display," gave Jane
that confidence in herself so greatly needed. She had
always before persisted in attributing to Ann all the success of the works published jointly with her. This tale
was all her own, in plan, execution, and style. She had

long been urged to attempt a work of the kind, and this showed her ability for such writing. She wisely confined herself to a simple narrative, and her modest sketch is the groundwork of as unambitious and natural a story as one often finds.

The strictures of some critics on Jane's views were thus answered by her, in a letter to a friend : —

" As to the dancing, I certainly did not think I had erred on the strict side ; and I think I have observed the distinction you mention, of not objecting to dancing in *itself*. The children at Stokely, you may remember, were all dancing very merrily one evening. But, in fact, except with mere children, there is no such thing as 'select Christian dances.' — Go where you will, it is the world who dance ; and the serious who do not. . . . As to what Mr. Leddenhurst says about 'dancing through the world,' it is a remark I have heard made by those who are very far from being puritanical in their manners, or narrow in their views ; and I merely understand by it, that a person of a contemplative and serious turn of mind, impressed with the grand realities of religion, and intent upon remedying, as far as possible, the sin and misery of the world, will not be much disposed to go 'dancing through it.' "

Being urged by many to continue her writing for the general public, Jane, feeling her own judgment was best, resumed her work in the " Essays in Rhyme." She preferred the form, and really enjoyed versification. She also began, in 1816, her contributions, under the well-known signature of Q. Q., to the " Youth's Magazine : " among these sketches are many old favorites, and some justly celebrated. " Essays in Rhyme," were finished in 1816, and Jane never wrote anything with so much enthusiasm and interest as this book. She had received the just praise to which her other works entitled her, and her health was still fair ; she was then at the height of her maturity, and felt all the pleasure which capacity for work, and the appreciation of that power expressed by others, give to an earnest writer.

Her own consciousness of duty well done would have sustained her through arduous labor, or unremitting drudgery like that of the engraving shop, but for continuous literary occupation she needed the stimulus of others, the expression of the public that she was doing a good and necessary work.

Children were born to Ann in rapid succession, and she found little time for poetry ; now and then verses dropped from her facile pen ; some hymns for the Sunday-school were prepared by Jane and her, during the early years of her marriage. The changes of a dissenting minister's life took the Gilberts from Rotherham to Hull, in 1817.

" Eight happy and successful, though truly laborious years," says Ann, " were spent at Hull by Mr. Gilbert, as pastor of the Fish St. Chapel. What shall one say of her own share of that life ? During those years six children were added to the little ones she carried there, and the mother was always ready for her part of her husband's work, as well as her own household duties. Her correspondence was very large and full, as all the Taylors were scattered and distant from her. Visits to her father and mother were rare pleasures to her, and long anticipated by her affectionate heart.

Frequent and long visits from Jane also gladdened her heart. Jane had become very serious in her feelings, and with her own increasing ill health, and anxiety for her father, who had a long illness, her mind was more than ever drawn to the contemplation of the future. She was naturally cheerful in temperament, but suffering and weakness naturally somewhat affected her spirits. She wrote less and less, under the pressure of pain and weakness, and confined herself to short letters to friends. She continued to the last the interest she had always expressed for her friends, and her devotional duties, Sunday-school work, and active parish visiting. She calmly anticipated the change : and in January, the last time she visited the Meeting House to meet her Sunday-school class, she pointed out to a friend the spot where her grave was to be. She never attended the Meeting again, as all her symptoms were aggravated by the exposure of the wintry day; and she gradually sunk, passing away the 11th of April, her last articulate words being, "Well, I don't think I shall now see Ann again ; I feel I am dying fast," — and Ann on her way to Ongar arrived too late for the sad parting.

One who knew her well described Jane's appearance as follows: "In truth, the expression of her face was of that kind which is the most difficult to be seized by the pencil ; for it was the expression of the finest feelings, habitually veiled from observation. Her features were delicately formed, and regular, — her stature below the middle size ; every movement bespoke the activity of her mind ; and a peculiar archness and sprightliness of manner gave significance and grace to all she did."

The mind was as alert and active as the body ; wit and spirit enlivened her conversation, as well as her writings. Her pensive fancy was relieved by playful yet genuine feeling. She had a great dread of all literary affectations, and often restrained herself for fear of appearing to be a blue. Her seriousness of feeling developed more fully as the years of youth passed, and never a trifler, she gave her best efforts to her religious convictions.

Jane had so great a desire to escape the imputation of literary affectation that she often would omit gratifying herself in matters of fancy. She was eminently practical .

in her ideas. She restrained her wit, frequently, from the great earnestness which was the motive power ; the under current of feeling was too deep to allow a light touch. One traces this in many of her letters : "Some people," she says, "think it a great recommendation to be able to write *a clever letter;* but if there is any thing I dislike to receive, or that I am unambitious of writing, it is *a clever letter;* by which I mean a letter that exhibits, obviously, an endeavor to be smart and pointed ; or, worse still, fine and sentimental."

Carlyle expresses something of the same feeling where he says : " A resolution to be piquant is the besetting sin of innumerable persons of both sexes, and wofully mars any use there might otherwise be in their writing or speaking."

Ann, in writing her children after the funeral services of Jane, says : " She was in her life kind, tender, active, generous, and always anxious to be useful to others. She was willing to deny herself of everything, and was never so happy as when she was doing a kindness to her brothers and sisters. Above all, she feared God from her youth, and did not leave that great work till she came to die."

In 1825 Mr. Gilbert removed to Nottingham, called thither by a new charge. The only literary work we hear of there, was an address to the women of Nottingham by Ann on the subject of Infidelity. Sympathy with her husband's work kept her mind fully occupied, and every-day duties left little time for other work. She finally became much interested in seeing so much of " the then popular, vulgar infidelity, — the deism and atheism, of workshops and alehouses," as she herself expresses it, that she wrote a poem, later enlarged, but never published, " The Prisoner Infidel."

The year 1830 broke up the old Ongar home, always dear to Mrs. Gilbert's heart, by the death of both Mr. and Mrs. Taylor. Mrs. Gilbert had already been called to part with one of her own little flock, a bitter grief to the mother love. During a visit at Skegness she wrote the " Twelve letters on Recovery from Sickness." The MS. was published in the following year under the title of " The Convalescent." A serious illness of one of her daughters impressed her so deeply, that she answered what she felt the needs of one re-entering the world, after a long confinement in a sick room.

Mrs. Gilbert often employed her pen to celebrate local events, and commemorate important occasions, for home entertainment. The advent of the penny-post, and the introduction of steam travelling, received her enthusiastic praise ; she called the first " the glorious penny postage," and made great use of the cheaper system. She welcomed the rapid mode of travelling, dearly as she loved all old associations ; and though the old coach made a picture she enjoyed, as it passed along the road with the horn, and the scarlet coat of the mail-guard, which gave a bit of color and life she revelled in. Too many weary hours had been passed by her on the way to her friends in early years, for her not to rejoice in the new force which shortened distance and united families.

" The enthusiasm of humanity " was always natural to Ann. New books, new ideas were always welcomed by her. She continued to grow and learn all her days. In 1849, one new movement which was brought to her notice, the rights of women, as regarding the Elective Franchise, elicited a reply from her which contained her views on the political duties of women. I extract a few words from it. After objecting to women's burdening themselves more than they need with outdoor politics,. she says:

" Indoors she may do much, even politically, — that is, I should say, it is her duty to instil *principles* into her children, principles affecting all the great questions, — Freedom ; Slavery ; Justice ; Humanity ; War ; Monopoly ; Private Judgment ; Voluntaryism, with as many more as may be thought of ; and, supposing she do all this well, wisely, effectively, and see to it at the same time that dinners come *secundum artem*, that shirts have buttons (and buttons shirts), — that everything, in short, within the homestead is 'done decently and in order,' — she will have, to my thinking at least, enough to do ! "

In 1853 came the death of Mr. Gilbert. The devoted pastor, loving husband and father, was called, and his wife with her daughters made themselves sadly a new home. Several years were left her, and she tried to do her best to occupy them. She prepared a sketch of her husband's life and character, which was published, with "Recollections of his Discourses."

The breaking up of her home was very painful, and the severance of the one dear tie left a great blank. Mr. Gilbert was as tender and devoted in his family as he was in his ministry. Isaac Taylor writes of him, and his influence on the listeners who came to him. After remarking on his " eminent faculty for clear, continuous, and sustained abstract thought," he says, " but, as a preacher and writer, Mr. Gilbert earnestly desired to be *useful*. This desire manifestly was always paramount to the ambition to shine or to win popular applause. He scorned not to be intelligible to every one. He would leave nothing untried that might avail to bring him close home to the convictions of his hearers, — educated and uneducated. Far from him was the arrogance that might make him content to be wondered at as a philosopher by a gaping crowd. He loved his hearers, he earnestly desired to promote their highest welfare."

Something of the home life of Ann Gilbert as a minister's wife, may interest the reader. With a crowded nursery, poor servants much of the time, all the details of a minister's household to care for, one might fancy her living in the midst of disorder, for limited means do not make easy housekeeping; but such was not the case. One who lived in her household some years wrote these recollections of the home: —

" I can never forget the strong, clear, definite outlines of her character, nor the delicate beautiful touches that gave such an indescribable attraction to it. There was a firmness and straightforwardness in her gait that was essentially indicative of her moral strength; while a clear, distinct, sonorous utterance impressed one with the order, perspicuity, and justice of her ideas. She was a lover of peace and order, and though I lived with her for several years, I never saw her temper ruffled, or heard her say a harsh or unreasonable word. . . . The kitchen, the nursery, the library, the school-room, all felt the gentle restraint of her never-varying propriety.

" Mrs. Gilbert was habitually an early riser. When I knew her she rose at six, and was accustomed to do an hour's needle-work before the rest of the family were out of bed. She was indefatigable with her needle, and her love for keeping things in repair must often have been at the great sacrifice of her love of reading. Yet I have heard Mr. Gilbert good-humoredly remark, 'Though Ann seldom indulges herself in looking into a book, I don't know how it is, she is always up to everything that is going on in the literary world.'

" Her discipline with her children was gentle, yet very firm; and her remonstrances had always a tone of earnest, tender entreaty, that it was difficult to resist, so that force or punishment was seldom resorted 'to.

" Her manner was alike easy, affable, and kind to persons of every rank, and her sprightly repartees, interspersed through all her conversation, constantly took you by surprise, and elicited a laugh at the most unexpected moment, while she passed it by with scarce a smile. Her puns were inimitable, so natural, easy, and adroit, that you wondered they had not struck you before she uttered them.

"One of her greatest charms was her charity,— not speaking ill of any one, and always hearing, with regret, anything unfavorable against any person. She was a true friend, and a true woman, not lavish of endearments, but with a wealth of love in her heart, ever ready in the service of all with whom she had to do. Few women, with so elevated a poetic nature, have combined so much practical utilitarianism, and energetic self-abnegation; for a strong and healthy conscientiousness regulated every spring of her actions."

Of her own experiences as a minister's wife she wrote a poem, showing that she fully felt the daily and hourly needs of the people, and their demands on the sympathy and judgment of the pastor and his wife. She saw worth in that lower middle class, the rank and file of English life, where many have latterly detected only " Philistinism." She says —

> . . . . " 'the folks in trade,'
> Our pastor knew them, often gathered thence
> Lessons of self-denial, patience, sense ;
> The trust in Providence, the worth of prayer,
> The energy of manly bearing there ;
> Sore struggle 'twixt the dangers of the day,
> A ruined prospect, or a crooked way ! "

The last years of Ann Gilbert's life were passed in a peaceful and serene old age. Many pleasant little journeys filled the milder season of the year. Her children vied with each other in kind attentions, and loving friends were not wanting to cheer and soothe her declining days.

She survived her husband fourteen years, sinking gently
into rest, after some hours of insensibility, December 20,
1866. Her six surviving children were around her as she
passed calmly away.

The difference between the poetry of Ann and Jane was
quite marked. Ann loved the business of life, and the
social circle ; Jane, dreamy, shy and sensitive, sought
nature with its peace and pathos. Ann's " My Mother,"
perhaps the most quoted of her poems, will illustrate this.
Jane, who has written what her latest critic, Mrs. Oliphant,
calls " immortal " " Twinkle, twinkle, little star," loved
the contemplative side of life ; Ann, the dramatic and practical. Yet Ann has left lovely bits of natural description,
— notably the " Michaelmas Daisy ; " " A Pretty Thing,"
and the little nursery song which follows, is as perfect as
anything of its kind ; as good in its way is " My Mother,"
termed by one eminent writer " the finest lyric of the
kind in the English language."

> " Dance, little baby, dance up high,
>   Never mind, baby — mother is by ;
>   Crow and caper, caper and crow,
>   There, little baby, there you go ;
>   Up to the ceiling, down to the ground,
>   Backwards and forwards, round and round ;
>   Then dance, little baby, and mother shall sing,
>   With the merry gay coral, ding, ding-a-ding ! ding."

One will remember, in remarking on the perfect simplicity, the drollery, and the truth of the poems, Goldsmith's brilliant repartee to Dr. Johnson, who was amusing
himself about making animals talk in literature. " The
skill," said he, " consists in making the little fishes talk like
little fishes." Whereupon, observing Johnson shaking his
sides with laughter, he smartly added, " Why, Dr. Johnson,

this is not so easy as you seem to think, for if you were to make little fishes talk, they would talk like WHALES." And so would many other writers besides old Sam Johnson. Goldsmith hit the keynote of the whole subject of writing for children when he said this. There are few who understand writing for children. It requires a clear and eminently practical mind to divest itself of the worldly, in the way of addressing the undeveloped mind. Old Fuller long ago wrote truly, " Every boy can teach a man, whereas he must be a *man* who can teach a boy. It is easy to inform them who are able to understand, but it must be a masterpiece of integrity and discretion to descend to the capacity of children." A worthy saying, and to be well noted by writers for the young. To "descend " well is a great art. Miss Yonge, in her paper on children's literature, speaks of "the astonishing simplicity without puerility, the pathos and arch drollery, of the secular poems of the Taylors."

Dr. Arnold of Rugby said, in one of his sermons, " The knowledge and love of Christ can nowhere be more readily gained by young children, than from the hymns of these most admirable women."

Archbishop Whately, also, bears testimony to the value of the Taylor sisters' work, when he says, in " Essays on Christian Faith," " A well-known little book, entitled ' Hymns for Infant Minds,' contains, Nos. 14, 15, a better practical description of Christian humility, and its opposite, than I ever met with in so small a compass. Though very intelligible and touching to a mere child, a man of the most mature understanding, if not quite destitute of the virtue in question, may be the wiser and better for it." The poems here referred to are those entitled, " How to Find Out Pride," and " How to Cure Pride ; " and were written by Ann Taylor.

These poems exhibit a searching analysis of motive, common to both the sisters' work. After some close inquiries, the poem says : —

> " Put all these questions to your heart,
> And make it act an honest part ;
> And when they 've each been fairly tried,
> I think you 'll own that you have pride."

On Ann's last birthday, Jan. 30, 1866, at the age of eighty-four, she wrote in her diary, " Oh, what a length of mercy ! " She addressed her only remaining brother in that year, as follows ; showing that, always cheerful and trying to interest herself in those around her, her thoughts were busy, her mind was ready for the future life.

> " I breathed a sigh that spake of tears
> At thought of life's departing years !
> Well !   Speed they must, but oh, to stand
> Equipped for that near — distant land !
> My soul stands trembling but to think
> Of that unseen, that awful brink,
> And for herself, and all, she prays, —
> ' Lord search our thoughts, and try our ways,
> And see in that vain world within
> Or error's blight, or hidden sin.' "

DISPLAY.

CHAPTER I.

"I wish we were not going this evening," said Elizabeth; "they say Mrs. Fellows is so clever, and so satirical, that I shall be afraid of speaking a word."

"Dear now, I am glad we are going," replied Emily, "we have heard so much of Mrs. Fellows; and I had not thought about being afraid of her."

"I trust of all things they will not ask us to play. I would not play before Mrs. Fellows for all the world," added Elizabeth.

"I had rather not, certainly," said Emily; "and yet I do not think I should mind it so very much."

"How I envy you having so much courage," said Elizabeth; "I am such a silly, timid creature!"

It was true that the dispositions of these young people differed essentially: they belonged to opposite classes of character; which — to borrow terms used long ago in a different sense, in scholastic controversy — might be called *Nominalists* and *Realists*.

Emily was a *Realist*. Whatever she did, said, or *looked*, was in earnest: she possessed the grace of SIMPLICITY, — a simplicity which appeared alike in her virtues and her faults. It was neither from insensibility nor self-conceit that she thought of her introduction to this formidable lady with so much composure. Modest people are not the soonest frightened. "I wonder

I

what they will think of *me?*" is not the inquiry of humility, but of vanity.

Now this inquiry Elizabeth was making perpetually. To speak, to move, to weep, or to smile, were with her but so many manœuvres, which she was practising for *effect*, and to attract attention. The prospect, the picture, or the poem, which Emily admired with all her *heart*, Elizabeth admired with all her *eloquence*, — too intent upon exhibiting her taste or sensibility, to be truly the subject of either.

It was this disposition to *display*, that made her anxious about the expected visit. Emily was going that she might see Mrs. Fellows ; Elizabeth, that Mrs. Fellows might see *her*.

From the conference with her friend, Elizabeth went directly to her dressing-room. She would have given away half her ornaments to know whether Mrs. Fellows wore ornaments. "As she is a literary lady, I dare say she despises dress," thought Elizabeth, as she looked at her pearl bracelets ; and she clasped and unclasped them several times ; but at last put them on in a hurry, because there was no time left to deliberate.

Elizabeth and Emily went together to their friend's house. Emily happened to take off her glove in the hall. "You have no bracelets on !" said Elizabeth. This was a comparison she could not bear : Mrs. Fellows would think her a mere doll. "Wait one moment," said she ; but in snatching one of the bracelets from her arm it broke ; and the pearls wandered deliberately to every corner of the hall. "Oh, your beautiful pearls !" said Emily. But just as she and the footman were beginning the search, a rap, long and loud, announced the arrival of other company. It was Mrs. Fellows herself. "Oh, never mind, never mind," cried Elizabeth, shocked at the idea of being caught by a learned lady in the act of collecting beads ; "Thomas will look for them." And, drawing on her glove still more eagerly than she had taken it off, she hurried much discomposed to the drawing-room.

The first glance at Mrs. Fellows when she made her appearance, convinced Elizabeth that this literary lady was no despiser of dress ; and she now regretted the misfortune that had befallen her bracelet.

Mrs. Fellows was reputed a universal genius : besides excelling all the masters in all the usual accomplishments, she was a botanist, and a chemist, and an anatomist. She had written sonnets, and a novel, and a tragedy ; and appeared — at least among the *noblesse* of an obscure country town — a prodigy of learning and genius.

Nothing could be more ill founded than Elizabeth's expectation of attracting the attention of this gifted lady. Satisfied with being herself the object of attention, and engrossed by the display of her own accomplishments, she had little leisure or inclination to observe those of others. She was presently engaged in conversation with two or three gentlemen ; and the whole evening would have passed without Elizabeth's being able to ascertain whether she had once attracted her notice, if she had not happened to hear her say — after catching her eye for a moment — " about the height of that young lady."

How much anxiety and vexation do they escape, who mix in society with a simple, unambitious temper !

The business which brought Mrs. Fellows from town, was to dispose of an estate in this neighborhood to a relation.

" I understand we shall have a great acquisition in this new family," observed a lady.

" Very much so, I assure you," replied Mrs. Fellows ; " my cousin is a very sensible, excellent, clever, worthy man ; and educates his family in a vastly superior manner."

" Any of the young gentlemen grown up ? " inquired a matron.

" Oh, no ; the eldest I think is but ten years old."

" Only ten years old ! " said three young ladies in a breath.

" There is a tutor, and a governess, I suppose," resumed the lady.

" No tutor ; my cousin at present superintends their education entirely himself.   Mrs. Leddenhurst has a governess, I believe ; but really I can give you very little information about them," said she ; " I have scarcely seen anything of them of late ; indeed, my cousin and his wife have some peculiarities, which render them not altogether so entirely agreeable as one could wish."   And here she changed the conversation ; leaving the company in a state of suspense about these " peculiarities : " but it was not insupportable suspense, because the family was expected in six weeks ; " and then we shall know all about it," thought Mrs. P——, and Mrs. M——, and the three Miss C——'s, and old Mrs. G——, and young Mrs. G——, and Dr. W——.

At length it was requested that Mrs. Fellows would play.   The lively terms in which Elizabeth expressed her pleasure at this proposal were lost amid the general din of solicitation.

" What taste ! what execution ! " she exclaimed repeatedly, during the performance.

When it was over, Mrs. Fellows insisted that some of the company should take her place.

Elizabeth advanced a step or two within the line of observation.

" Miss Palmer, my dear," said the lady of the house, turning towards her : but in the meantime another lady had been prevailed upon.

" What an escape for you ! " whispered Emily.

" Yes, indeed," replied Elizabeth faintly, " what an escape ! "

When the party broke up, Elizabeth, as she wished her friend Emily good night, added in a whisper, " How much I am disappointed in Mrs. Fellows ! "

Elizabeth and Emily were friends, as it often happens, rather from accident than congeniality. They had been playfellows from their infancy ; and when they ceased to play, they had continued to associate.

Emily was affectionate, and she loved Elizabeth sincerely. Elizabeth felt as much regard for Emily as for any one she knew : but vanity chills the heart ; and in proportion as she became conscious of the slightness of her affection, she grew lavish in her professions of it. But notwithstanding the difference in their tastes and dispositions, there were some respects in which they suited each other. Elizabeth could by no means have tolerated a friend, who had been taller, or fairer, or considered more clever than herself. Perhaps she was not aware how much of her regard for Emily, and the pleasure she felt in her society, depended upon her own acknowledged superiority in these respects.

Elizabeth was now more than nineteen years old ; Emily nearly a year younger ; and most people thought " Elizabeth Palmer much handsomer than Emily Grey." They had always lived among people who allowed their full value to external advantages. Elizabeth's superiority to her friend was a circumstance entirely taken for granted between them ; and the deference naturally claimed by the one was peaceably yielded by the other.

As for Emily, a companion who would talk, and leave her to think and feel as she pleased, suited her better than one who had been disposed to interfere with her thoughts and feelings. Yet she occasionally sighed for something more like her own idea of friendship than she had ever found in associating with Elizabeth.

CHAPTER II.

ONE morning Elizabeth and several others called upon Emily. There was now an opportunity, they said, of going over the house and grounds at Stokely, as it was open to the workmen; and a great many people had been to see it.

It was a pleasant walk from the town: the house stood on a rising ground, and, embosomed in fine trees, was a picturesque object in all directions.

"What a pity that such a pretty place should be shut up!" had been said year after year by many a traveller. But now everything indicated that inhabitants were expected.

"Let us go over the house first," said several of the party, as they sprang nimbly up the steps to the hall door.

"You must take care of the paint, young ladies," said the workmen, as they flocked into the hall.

While they steered their way among work-tables and scaffolding, and over heaps of shavings and sawdust, and passed from one apartment to another, they expressed their opinions in various tones and terms of admiration. "What a charming room *this* is!" and "what a delightful room *this* will be!"

"What a sweet place this would be for a ball-room!" said one, bounding in upon a fine smooth floor, and humming a few notes of a country dance.

"If I were Mrs. Leddenhurst, I would have this for my dressing-room, or study, or something," said another, as they passed on.

"This is exactly such a kind of a room as I should like for myself," cried a third. "I wonder what *this* is to be? I wish there was somebody to tell one what the rooms are to be," said a fourth. "I wonder

whether I shall ever live in such a nice house as this ! "
exclaimed a little girl. " Silly child ! " said her sister,
who was old enough not to wonder *aloud*.

They next attempted a door which they could not
open. " That room is locked up, and I can't part with
the key upon no account," said a person who seemed
to be a superintendent.

" Dear, I wonder what there can be so particularly
curious within," said Elizabeth, looking through the
key-hole.

" Nothing particularly curious within ; they are my
books, ladies, which I shall be very happy to show you
when they are in better order," said a gentleman who
at that instant appeared on the staircase, and passed
on. This was said with a graceful bow, and a very
good-natured smile. They were all silent in a moment ; and stood coloring, and looking silly at each
other. For when a party of·young ladies are rambling
at large over an empty house, it is highly probable that
some silly and impertinent things will be said ; and
each was now trying to recollect what *she* happened to
be saying when the stranger appeared. Elizabeth remembered *her* speech very distinctly.

" It must be Mr. Leddenhurst himself, I suppose,"
said she, in a low voice.

" Oh, you may depend upon that, for you know he
said *my* books," replied one of her companions.

" I thought he was to go away with Mrs. Fellows ; I
had no idea he was here now," continued Elizabeth, in
a vexed whisper.

" Don't you wish you had not been looking through
the key-hole ? " said another of her friends.

" Oh, I don't believe he saw that ; I am certain he
could not possibly see that," said Elizabeth, sharply.

" Well," said Emily, " I believe we have been all
over the house now." So the party returned quietly
home.

The trees of Stokely were bright with the tints of autumn, before it was in complete readiness for its new inhabitants.

One fine evening in October, a travelling carriage, covered with dust, was seen driving through the town; and it was observed to take the road leading to Stokely Park. The travellers were fatigued with their journey; for they had come from a great distance.

"Where are we come to now?" said a little girl, in a sleepy voice, who was roused by their stopping at a turnpike.

"Just coming into Broadisham," said her father; "and now, children, in a few minutes we shall get a sight of Stokely."

"Of Stokely! and is this Broadisham?" They were all alive in an instant, and looked out eagerly from one side of the way to the other. "Ladies' Boot and Shoe Warehouse; Hodson, Dyer, and Hodson; Eve's Fancy Dress and Millinery Rooms; Ladies' School; Phœnix Fire-office; Pryke, Haberdasher," read little Lucy, as they drove through the town.

"What a handsome bridge we are coming to now!" said Richard. "And there is Stokely," said Mr. Leddenhurst; "those dark trees just in the sunset."

The children now expected to stop every moment; but the road had many a tiresome sweep to make still. At length it became shaded by a row of graceful elms; and a fir-grove with park-paling bespoke their near approach. And now the gate flew open, and they drove straight up the avenue.

"What a different looking place it is to what I expected!" said Richard.

"Yes," said Lucy, "but a great deal prettier."

While the father listened to their eager observations, Mrs. Leddenhurst and her friend beside her sat in silence. It was not the extent of the estate, nor the beauty of the scenery, but life and its vicissitudes, that occupied her thoughts as she drove up to her new residence.

In a short time Mr. and Mrs. Leddenhurst had been visited by most of their neighbors.

Being people of good sense and discernment, they were not particularly gratified by these specimens of their new society. Nevertheless, their guests were received with much courtesy and kindness; for their good sense was graced with good-breeding, and their discernment was softened by benevolence.

It was generally agreed that Mr. and Mrs. Leddenhurst were very agreeable people; and no one had detected the peculiarities which had been hinted at. They were well dressed and well bred; they wondered what Mrs. Fellows could mean. Emily was the first to unravel the mystery.

On the morning that she and her father called, Miss Weston — of whom nobody could determine whether she was a friend or the governess — was inquiring if there were any one in the town who took in needlework. Emily said there was a young woman who used to work very neatly, but she remembered hearing of her being ill, and did not know whether she could undertake it at present. "But I will inquire about it immediately," said she. Miss Weston said she intended to be in the town the next morning; and that if she pleased they would go together.

Emily was glad of this proposal; for there was something in Miss Weston — the expression of her countenance, and the sweetness of her manner — that attracted her attention. There was other company in the room, and they did not sit near enough to converse together; but she could not help looking at her continually; and their eyes met so often that at last Emily felt quite ashamed.

Miss Weston called the next day at the time appointed. They had to go a little way out of the town;

and during their walk she engaged in such agreeable conversation that Emily could not help wishing she might have Miss Weston for a friend.

When they arrived at Eleanor Jones's, her mother opened the door. " Does your daughter take in plain work, Mrs. Jones? " said Emily.

" Yes, Miss; that 's to say, she used to do," said the widow Jones; " but my poor child is so ill, ladies ! "

" Mother," said a feeble voice from within, " ask the ladies to please to walk in."

" Yes, let us go in," said Miss Weston.

They found Eleanor Jones sitting by the fire in a tall arm-chair. She looked extremely weak and ill, but her cheeks were flushed at the entrance of strangers. She spoke with difficulty.

" If it is not much in a hurry, ladies, I think I could undertake a little job, " said she, coughing.

" I am afraid it would fatigue you too much," said Miss Weston; " you appear very unwell. Has your daughter had advice, Mrs. Jones? "

" The doctor as 'tends the parish, ma'am, he sent her some drops in the spring; but he has n't been up here o' some time now — only the young gentleman; and he says the cough 's of no consequence; but dear me ! she coughs sadly o'nights."

" Can she take any nourishing things? " said Miss Weston.

" Oh, she 's no liking at all to her meat, ma'am," said the mother; " she takes nothing scarce but fruit, and such like, and now the fruit is just over."

" Do you think you should like some grapes? " said Miss Weston.

" Yes, I should like some grapes very much, I think," said Eleanor Jones; " but my wants are very few now, and I know that all the doctors in the world could do me no good; my time here is very short."

" Oh, you will get better soon, I hope," said Emily; " you must not be so lowspirited."

" I am not lowspirited," she replied ; " I am very happy, and if it was not for my poor mother I should not have a wish or a want."

Emily looked rather puzzled at this, but Miss Weston seemed to understand her. There was a Bible open upon the table ; and Miss Weston, laying her hand upon it, said, " It is *this*, I hope, that makes you happy ; whether we are sick or well, there is no real happiness but what is to be found here."

At this the invalid looked up with great animation, saying, " O ma'am, I am glad to hear you say so ; I am rejoiced to think you know that. Yes, yes, the Bible made me happy when I was well ; and now that I am ill and dying, it makes me still happier."

Emily listened in silence to the conversation which now commenced ; and she was surprised and affected at what she heard. She had often read in the news-paper, and heard among her acquaintance, about "bear-ing a long affliction with Christian fortitude ;" and about "resignation to the will of Heaven ; " but she now heard sentiments expressed which were entirely new to her. She was surprised that Miss Weston and this poor girl, although entire strangers, and in very different circumstances, seemed so completely to un-derstand each other, and to think and feel so much alike upon the subjects about which they were convers-ing.

" You have talked long enough now," said Miss Weston at length, in a kind voice ; and she took leave, saying she would call again to see her in a few days.

" Miss Weston, I have a favor to ask you," said Emily, after they had walked a little way in silence.

" What is that ? "

" I scarcely know what I mean, exactly," said she, " but I did not understand several things poor Eleanor Jones said just now ; indeed, I am afraid my religion must be very different from hers; would you be so good as to explain to me — "

" My dear," said Miss Weston, " you could not have asked anything that would give half so much pleasure."

Her countenance, as she said this, beamed with benevolence; and there was something so kind and encouraging in the manner of her speaking that it brought the tears into Emily's eyes.

" If I were not such a stranger to you — " said she.

" We will be strangers no longer," interrupted Miss Weston; " let us be friends, and talk to each other without reserve; and there is no subject of so much importance, none that can afford such a rational and interesting topic for conversation."

"And yet," said Emily, " I have never been in the habit of conversing upon it, nor of thinking about it much; but I am certain your religion must be very different."

" You must not call it *my* religion," said Miss Weston, smiling; " there is, there can be, but one true religion, which is that the Bible teaches; and they who most clearly understand, and most consistently practise it, are the wisest and happiest people in the world."

" I read the Bible on Sundays," said Emily, " and I hope I have always done my duty."

" That is saying a great deal," observed Miss Weston.

" But I never knew the Almighty required anything besides," continued Emily.

" Certainly he requires nothing more than that we should do our duty," replied Miss Weston; " but that is a very comprehensive phrase; are you sure you entirely understand it? "

" Not quite sure," said Emily.

" You have read the Bible," continued Miss Weston, " and so have many people; who yet, from pride, prejudice, or indifference, never appear to have understood its meaning. Let me advise you now to read

the New Testament with great attention and seriousness; and, my dear, it must be with *humility:* it is
God's word, His own message to mankind; and it becomes us to receive it humbly as His creatures. Did
you ever make it a subject of earnest prayer, that God
would teach you to understand the Scriptures? Without this, there is the greatest danger of making some
important mistake about them; for it is in this way that
He directs us to study His word; and in which alone
He promises us instruction. And when you have read
it in this spirit," continued she, " you will be better
able to judge whether there is not something in the
Christian religion beyond the observance of outward
forms and duties; whether there be any tendency in
these alone to produce such effects at the near approach
of death as you have just witnessed; the same willingness to resign life, the same peaceful serenity at the
thought of death, and the same humble joy in the prospect of a heaven of holiness."

Emily listened with interest as her friend proceeded:
they parted at the turning of the road, having agreed
to renew the conversation in their future visits to Eleanor's cottage. She walked home musing on what had
passed; her mind was affected and elevated; a new
world seemed to have opened to her view, notwithstanding her very indistinct ideas as to its nature and
reality.

Mr. and Mrs. Leddenhurst, as well as their friend,
were intelligent Christians: they knew religion to be
the most important of all concerns, and they uniformly
acted as though they believed it. They felt the disadvantage of coming to reside in a neighborhood where
they had reason to fear its true nature was little understood by those with whom they would be expected to
associate; but the hope of being useful reconciled them
to the circumstance. There was a general consterna-
tion when it was discovered that the new family at

Stokely were, as *they* called them, "quite Methodists : "
all marvelled, many murmured, and some mocked.
There were a few poor and despised people in this
town who had generally borne that or similar names :
but then, as a lady observed, " It was all very well for
that sort of people ; but what could induce such a
family as the Leddenhursts to make themselves so remarkable, was to her a complete mystery : though, to
be sure," said she, " people of property may do anything."

Miss Weston was both " a friend and the governess."
A friendship had subsisted between her and Mrs.
Leddenhurst from their early youth, which time had
strengthened and matured ; but it was only of late that
she had become an inmate in her family. Though it
was perceptible to none but accurate observers of feelings and faces, Miss Weston was a sufferer. It is easy
to wear a pensive smile, but hers was a smile of cheerfulness ; and she was generally spoken of as being
" remarkably cheerful."

As to the cause of her sorrow, only a conjecture can
be formed ; because Mrs. Leddenhurst, who was the
only person in whom she had confided, never betrayed
her confidence. Among the numerous sources of human woe, the reader may fix upon that which to her
may appear most difficult to endure with fortitude and
resignation. One may conclude she had lost her friend ;
another her heart ; and a third, her fortune ; but perhaps, after all, it was something very different from any
of these.

Miss Weston's idea of *resignation* was not as one
may see it in the print shops, — a tall figure, weeping
over an urn in the middle of a wood ; it was, in her
opinion, an active, cheerful, and social principle. It
was not, indeed, without an effort, that she resisted her
inclination to seek relief in rumination and seclusion ;
but strength of mind, that is, strength of principle,

prevailed. Without waiting to confer with her inclinations, she wrote to her friend Mrs. Leddenhurst, offering to assist her in the education of her little girls.

"You know," said she, "how much I love children, and that of all children none are so dear to me as yours. I am quite in earnest in saying that I will come and be the governess for whom you are inquiring. Do not raise needless scruples; some employment, that will engage both my time and attention, is essential to me just now; and I think I should engage in the work of education with an interest that would enable my mind to recover its self-possession. Indeed, I am impatient to forsake this retirement, — sweet and soothing as it is. Let me come, dear Caroline, and exchange these dangerous indulgences for the more wholesome pleasures of social intercourse and useful occupation."

Mrs. Leddenhurst, who understood enough of the human heart, and of the character and feelings of her friend, to know that her resolution was as wise as it was courageous, gladly welcomed her to the bosom of her family; where she soon learned to "smile at grief," without sitting "on a monument."

CHAPTER III.

OF all the young people who had been introduced to the Leddenhursts, there was not one whose appearance pleased them so much as Emily's. They observed that in some important respects her education had been defective; but she seemed amiable, modest, and unaffected; and possessed of good sense and a strong desire of improvement, which greatly encouraged them in their wishes to serve her.

They perceived that Elizabeth was a less hopeful

subject than her companion; but this did not make them less willing to attempt her improvement; for they were not accustomed to shrink from a duty because it was unpleasant, nor to despair of one that was difficult. They were both invited to join the family circle at Stokely as often as they felt disposed. They were not backward to accept this invitation; and an early evening was fixed upon to pay their first friendly visit.

Elizabeth and Emily set off on this occasion with high expectations of gratification and enjoyment. Hitherto they had only seen them with other company; "but now," thought Emily, "we shall be alone, and be able to enjoy their conversation." "Now," thought Elizabeth, "we shall be alone, and they must take notice of *me*."

On their way, they met one of the servants from Stokely, with a basket of grapes.

"There goes a present for somebody: who can it be for, I wonder," said Elizabeth; " the Tomkinses, — or the Davisons, perhaps."

"No, no," said Emily; " I can easily guess who it is for, — poor Eleanor Jones, who is so ill. I know they send her fruit or jellies every day."

"Well, very likely," replied Elizabeth; " for I heard, — but really I can scarcely believe it, Mr. Leddenhurst looks such a pleasant, different kind of a man, — they say, however, that he and Mrs. Leddenhurst were there the other day, and had such a strange conversation! Oh, I cannot remember half the extraordinary things I heard they said to her."

"I know they have been to see her," said Emily, " and that she was very much pleased with their conversation; I do not think *she* thought it strange."

"Well, I sincerely hope we shall have no such gloomy, stupid doings to-night!" exclaimed Elizabeth.

"Elizabeth," said Emily, "I have heard and thought more about religion since I conversed with Miss Weston than I ever did before; and I really think nothing is so likely to prevent one from being gloomy and stupid. Besides, do not the Leddenhursts appear remarkably pleasant and cheerful?"

"Yes, in company; people, you know, must be agreeable in company: but I have heard those over-religious kind of.folks are miserably dull when they are alone."

"Well, we shall see," said Emily.

When they reached Stokely, and entered the room, they found Miss Weston playing a lively tune, to which the children were dancing by the light of the fire. They were cordially welcomed; and Emily felt very happy as the circle formed, and she took her seat by the side of Miss Weston. She looked round, and saw none but cheerful faces; it did not appear to be that kind of cheerfulness which is made at a moment's warning by the rap at the door; they looked as though they had been cheerful and happy all day long.

Elizabeth appeared this evening dressed with taste, but rather over-dressed for the occasion. And this did not pass unobserved; for in the simple action of walking from the door to her chair there was a *manner* that asked for observation; that is, it was *not* a simple action.

Mr. Leddenhurst was looking over a review. "Poetry! poetry in abundance for you, ladies," said he, "if you like it."

"Oh, indeed, I am passionately fond of poetry," said Elizabeth.

"Passionately fond, are you? Here is an article then, that, perhaps, you will do us the favor to read."

Elizabeth readily complied, for she was fond of reading aloud.

"We select the following passage," said the injudicious critic, "for the sake of three lines which we are persuaded no reader of sensibility will peruse without tears."

" No reader of sensibility ! " thought Elizabeth ; but how should she discover for certain which they were in that long quotation ? To cry at the wrong place, she justly calculated, would be a worse mistake than not crying at the right ; but, fortunately, as she approached the conclusion, the lines in question caught her eye, considerately printed in Italics. She read them with great pathos ; and, as she read, tears — two undeniable tears — rolled deliberately down her cheeks. Having succeeded in this nice hydraulic experiment, she looked at Emily, and observed with some satisfaction that there was no trace of tears on *her* cheeks ; but glancing round at the rest of the company, she felt rather disconcerted to see how perfectly composed everybody was looking. " Are they not extremely affecting ? " said she, appealing to Mrs. Leddenhurst.

" Really, I can scarcely tell," said Mrs. Leddenhurst ; " I always find, that nothing more effectually drives away my tears than having them bespoke. Pathetic touches, to produce their effect, should take the reader by surprise, I think."

" I question if those lines could have *surprised* me into tears," said Mr. Leddenhurst.

" Oh, not *you*, papa ! " said Richard, laughing ; " men should never cry, should they, if they can help it ? "

" Neither men nor women should cry, if they can help it," answered his father.

" I can remember seeing papa cry, though," whispered little Lucy, " when he was telling mamma how glad the shabby looking gentleman looked at the sight of the guinea ; I saw a tear in the corner of his eye, just for a moment."

Elizabeth was so much absorbed by the little vexation she had just experienced, and by endeavoring to ascertain the precise construction that had been put upon her sensibility, that the conversation had taken a different turn before she was aware, and she found Mr.

Leddenhurst in the middle of a long story. He had travelled; and was giving an account of a night he once spent in a Laplander's hut; which the children thought so very entertaining that they often begged their father to tell it to them over again; and they now came from the further end of the room, where they were quietly at play, saying, " Oh, papa is telling about the little Laplanders ! "

Elizabeth suddenly roused herself to the appearance of lively attention. They who feel interest have no need to feign it; but it rarely happened that Elizabeth was really interested by conversation to which she was only a listener. The vain and selfish deprive themselves of most genuine pleasures. There was nothing now for her but to wait till the recital was finished; to wait for *her* turn, with that sort of impatience which good-breeding itself can sometimes scarcely conceal, in those whose sole object in society is *to make an impression.* But Mr. and Mrs. Leddenhurst had seen the little artifices of vanity practised by greater proficients than Elizabeth. She was not the first person in whom they had observed a greedy impatience to squeeze into conversation every scrap of information that can be collected upon the point in hand. Little do they imagine, who angle for admiration by this and similar methods, how completely their end is defeated, at least with respect to acute observers. They who are intent upon being heard and seen, are not often observers; nor can they believe how easily they are detected by those who know how to hear and see. The involuntary admiration which is inspired by wit or beauty, and especially the respect for talents and acquirements, are, to say the least, neutralized, if but a suspicion be excited that they are used as articles of display.

Elizabeth would have been really agreeable, if she could but have forgotten to be charming. Her form was delicate ; her face handsome, — and it might have been interesting, if the constant effort to make it so had not given a restlessness to her features which was far from pleasing : her eye first shot its spark, and then looked about for the damage. In her sensibility, especially, there was an appearance of artificialness, which rendered it difficult to feel real sympathy with her.

"There is nothing I have ever wished for so much as to travel," said Elizabeth, when Mr. Leddenhurst had finished his narration ; "it must be so excessively interesting, I should think, especially with an intelligent companion."

"We who are obliged to stay at home," said Mrs. Leddenhurst, "may, however, enjoy, by our firesides, most of the information and a considerable share of the entertainment of going abroad ; we are now so abundantly supplied with the observations of travellers."

"Yes," replied Elizabeth ; "and there is no kind of reading I am so partial to as voyages and travels ; they are so uncommonly interesting."

"Very interesting indeed," said Mrs. Leddenhurst ; "though I cannot say there is *no* kind of reading that I am so partial to."

"Oh, certainly not ; I did not mean to say *no* kind of reading, but — but really I am surprised," continued she, "that Mr. Leddenhurst was never prevailed upon to publish his tour ; it would, I am sure, have been such an acquisition ! "

At this Mrs. Leddenhurst only smiled, and began talking to Emily, who had fallen into a revery in *her* turn ; but it was not about herself nor the company : her imagination had been carried by Mr. Leddenhurst's narrative to polar regions ; and was wandering over fields of ice, and arctic snows, where

"—— the shapeless bear,
With dangling ice, all horrid, stalks forlorn,"

when Mrs. Leddenhurst recalled her recollection.

The evening passed rapidly away; and to Emily it was passing very happily. But Elizabeth felt an uneasiness which she would have been at a loss to define; there was nothing to complain of, but she was not gratified. She had been brilliant, and arch, and playful; she had caressed Lucy, and admired Caroline, but without effect; and there was a certain expression in Mr. Leddenhurst's eye, when she happened to meet it, that did not quite please her. The vexation she really felt suggested a new experiment. Her animation gave place rather suddenly to an air of pensiveness: she was silent and thoughtful; and started when spoken to as though waked from an interesting revery. Notwithstanding this, conversation went on very briskly, and even became increasingly lively. As she appeared disinclined to converse, she was suffered to be silent. At length Mr. Leddenhurst observed it, and said, " My dear, cannot we think of anything that will entertain Miss Palmer?"

" Here is a new botanical work, with colored plates: perhaps you will like to look at it," said Mrs. Leddenhurst; and the book and the candles were placed before poor Elizabeth, mortified beyond measure to be treated like a child, dull for want of amusement. Her assumed pensiveness now degenerated into real ill humor, which was but ill disguised during the remainder of the evening.

The fresh air sometimes produces a surprising effect in restoring people to their senses; and Elizabeth, when she had taken leave, and walked a few minutes in the wind, began to repent of her behavior. However, they had bade her good night, and repeated their invitation so kindly, that she hoped it had not been particularly observed: and when Emily, who had been too much occupied to remark her friend's disappointment, observed what a pleasant evening they had passed, Elizabeth assented, saying, " A delightful evening, indeed!"

Happy are they who do not go into company to *perform;* who can think an evening pleasantly spent, that has been unproductive of compliment, and afforded no particular opportunity of displaying the favorite quality, or talent, or acquirement.

There are some unfortunate persons who seem to make little other use of conversation than as a means of petty, personal aggrandizement; and who, in consequence of this wretched propensity, little as they suspect it, subject themselves to the contempt or pity of those whose opinions are most valuable.

There is a class of *speechmakers*, who contrive by ingenious allusions, and hints casually dropped, to let you know what they feared you might not otherwise find out. They are letting off fireworks; and when it seems all over, and there are only a few pitiful sparks dropping about — off goes another! But it never succeeds. For, whether it be "my uncle's carriage," or "my friend the colonel," or "the general," or "when I was on the Continent," or " only a *jeu d'esprit* of mine, a very foolish thing," or "Latin? Oh, scarcely a word, I assure you," or "a cousin of mine knows him intimately," or "when I write to Lady so and so," or all these one after another, — such hints afford a kind of information which is not intended to be conveyed. They prove, not only that her uncle keeps his carriage, that she knows a colonel and a general, that she has been on the Continent, that she writes poetry (and foolish things), that she learns Latin, that her cousin knows a learned man, that she corresponds with Lady so and so, but they show that she is anxious you should *know* it; that *she* considers such things as distinctions; and that they are to her new or rare; for people seldom boast of that which they have always been accustomed to. And, what is worst of all, it must create a suspicion that she has nothing more left to boast of. For she who gives out that she reads

Latin, is not likely to conceal her knowledge of Hebrew or Greek; and she who intimates that she writes to Lady A., would assuredly let you know it if she had any connection with Ladies B., C., or D.

But the symptoms of vanity are almost infinitely various; there is no genus comprehending a greater variety of species. The silly girl, vain of her dress and complexion, is really one of the least offensive and most pardonable of all; for in proportion to the value of the thing boasted of is the meanness of the boast. Hence a pedant is more contemptible than a coxcomb.

But whatever particular character it assumes, that mind is in miserable bondage whose happiness is dependent on the opinion, especially on the applause of others. It is a bondage which seems always the concomitant of a general moral imbecility, whether that imbecility be cause or effect.

CHAPTER IV.

EMILY's introduction to her new friends at this period of her life was a more important circumstance than she was aware of, highly as she felt disposed to value their friendship. Notwithstanding her many good qualities, she was not free from faults. She was sensible, modest, and ingenuous, but she was — *eighteen.*

She lost her mother early; and her father, although desirous to do everything in his power for the welfare of his only child, was not aware of the best means to promote it. He was a man of business, and it did not occur to him that anything more was requisite than to send her for several years to an established school, from whence he expected her to return completely educated. He did not consider that it is often not until the time when, young persons leave school, that the real ardor for self-improvement is excited, which it is of so great importance to direct and cultivate.

Girls of entirely common minds take leave of their books, and often of the accomplishments which they have acquired at such a vast expense of money and time, at the conclusion of the last half year, — delighted to exchange them for the pleasures from which they had been reluctantly restrained during the tedious periods from Christmas to Midsummer, and from Midsummer to Christmas. Revelling for a few giddy years in vanity and idleness, they by and by settle in life ; and, as the vigor and interest of youthfulness subside, sink into those ordinary beings who, with thousands of their kind, eat, drink, and sleep, dress, visit, and die ; while young people in whom the spark of intelligence has been enkindled are exposed to different dangers. Pride, pedantry, romance, and many other evils, according to the accidents of disposition and education, are the frequent consequences of partial and uncorrected cultivation.

Emily's simplicity was her grand preservative from many of these perils ; and she possessed a native delicacy of taste, which defended her from others. With the choice of all the volumes in the circulating library of a country town, her reading had been tolerably select. When she left school, her father informed her that " he did not approve of young girls reading novels ; " but he had little hope that the prohibition would be regarded, because he firmly believed that " young girls *would* read novels." But in this instance, Emily had less temptation to disobedience than many : from whatever was common, low, or profane, she always shrunk with dislike. Good taste had in some measure supplied the place of good principle ; and of all the gifts of nature, that instinctive fineness of feeling is most estimable, of which education itself can but produce an imitation.

Emily read and felt poetry, and lived in its atmosphere; but as none of the beings around her did the same, she shut herself up in her own world of enjoyment; neither desiring to interfere with the pursuits and pleasures of other people, nor wishing them to participate in hers. She loved her father tenderly, and was obedient and attentive to him; but he was so wholly incapable of entering into her feelings concerning those things which she thought most interesting that she never attempted to address him in a language which she knew would have been quite unintelligible; while he, satisfied with her cheerful looks and dutiful conduct, dreamed not of the ideal world his daughter inhabited. He studied to make her happy by supplying her with all the comforts and pleasures his circumstances would allow; but it was not for these things that Emily felt most obliged to her father. Having never known the want of a constant supply of those daily comforts which are as really necessary to the intellectual as to the unrefined, she had not learned to value them. It was the liberty she enjoyed to pursue her own pleasures, the luxury of being alone, the inestimable privilege of not being obliged to talk, &c. that inspired her with gratitude, and made her think him the best and kindest of fathers. And indeed this gratitude was not misplaced; for that sort of kindness which allows the object of it, as far as possible, to pursue its own plan of happiness, is that alone which makes the difference between *gratitude* and *thanks*. It is but a selfish kind of generosity to load persons with favors they do not value, and thwart them in the very point on which their pleasure depends.

There was one standing trial of Emily's good nature; this was, that her father expected her to read the newspaper to him every day after dinner. The sight of the newspaper was disagreeable to her; and politics were worse than uninteresting. However, she thought of

Milton's daughters, and made the daily sacrifice with a good grace ; and by degrees attained so great a proficiency in the art of reading and carrying on her own train of thought at the same time, that it became less burdensome. The kind "Thank ye, dear," with which her father always repaid her when she finished her task, reproached her more than anything, if she had performed it with reluctance.

The company of "uninteresting people," as Emily secretly styled the whole circle of her acquaintance, would have been grievously burdensome but for this habit of abstraction, which enabled her to take some apparent share in conversation, and to enjoy her own delicious musings at the same time. It could not, however, escape the observation of her friends, that her own contemplations seemed more agreeable to her than their company ; and she had sometimes been called proud ; but it was not by those who knew her, — those who had opportunities of witnessing her invariable sweetness and good-nature, and the obliging alacrity with which, when once roused from a revery, she would do anything, for anybody ; though it sometimes happened that her services were required before her attention was excited.

Notwithstanding this indifference towards most of those she had hitherto known, Emily had very sublime notions about friendship ; and from her first conversation with Miss Weston, she believed she had found that concerning which, as yet, she had only speculated. Her heart soon glowed and expanded with affection and respect towards the whole family at Stokely. Although the acquaintance was so recent, she felt more at home there than in the circle of her old associates ; for she was with beings who understood her, to whom she could express her feelings without the dread of being stared at for eccentricity. Not that her new friends by any means coincided in all Emily's feelings

and opinions; but they were not misinterpreted, nor
ridiculed; and when corrected, it was with a tenderness and reasonableness that made her quite sure she
had been in the wrong.

But it was not likely that a girl of Emily's age and
disposition should love such friends as the Leddenhursts — especially as they were new friends — with
entire sobriety and moderation. In comparison with
them, everybody appeared uninteresting and insignificant; and everything belonging to Stokely appeared to
her to possess some peculiar excellence, incommuni-
cable to any other place or thing. The children seemed
more lively and engaging than all other children; the
flowers more fragrant; the trees more picturesque.

When she walked out with her father, she always
pleaded to go that road, or at least some walk where
the house was in view; and it was a sort of pleasure if
they happened to meet even a greyhound belonging to
Stokely. For on such an occasion — perhaps after she
had been wondering that her father should seem so
much interested in what he was talking about — she
would exclaim with sudden animation, "There's Leo-
pard! pretty fellow! See, papa, is not he a graceful
creature?"— and be disappointed that her father appeared so little interested by the interview. But when
once affection, however well placed, exceeds the
bounds of reason, it becomes a source of at least as
much torment as delight. They who live on imaginary
pleasures must expect a balance of *real* pain. Emily
did not expect, and she thought she did not even wish,
for an *equal* return of affection from these friends; but
she was too anxious about it: and although they gave
the most substantial proofs of their regard for her, she
tormented herself when any little expression of it was accidentally withheld. It is not until persons enter upon
the realities of life, that they learn to distinguish between what is essential and what is trifling, in friendship

as well as other things; and Emily had this and many
other lessons to learn, which are never effectually taught
but by experience. She possessed, however, a certain
nobleness of temper, which prevented her from feeling
jealous of Elizabeth. If ever she detected in herself
a tendency to that meanness, she instantly discarded it,
and thought, " Is not she my *friend ?* "

As Emily became better acquainted with them, she
saw and heard many things at Stokely that surprised,
and even disappointed her. Mr. Leddenhurst, for instance, appeared really interested about politics, or
rather public affairs; and Mrs. Leddenhurst engaged in
her domestic concerns, not so much as matters of dry
duty as Emily had generally considered them.

She observed, too, that they entered into conversation with their guests, with a degree of interest that
exceeded, she thought, the requirements of politeness;
instead of practising that dexterous conciseness of reply
which brings a tiresome subject to the quickest possible
termination.

But what surprised her most of all, and occasioned
her the most pain, was a confession one day from Miss
Weston, that she was by no means devoted to poetry.
She felt no higher delight in it than every cultivated
mind must derive from the productions of the best
poets; and she assured Emily, that she had more satisfaction in reading works addressed to the understanding than in the finest productions of imagination.

Observing that her young friend looked disappointed,
she added : " But, Emily, you must not suppose that
I despise or undervalue the taste in others, because I
do not possess it myself. I not only tolerate, but I
admire it, where it is correct, and does not stand in
the place of better things."

" But yet," said Emily, " I wish you felt exactly as I
do about it."

Now Emily possessed more genuine poetical taste

than many who talk a great deal about poetry. It was not the fashionable admiration of the poem or poet of the day; nor the pedantic taste of the classic, or the critic; nor the indiscriminating rapture of youthful enthusiasm; but she had an eye to see, a heart to feel, and taste to select, the truly poetical, not only in books — but in nature, in life, in sentiment.

She did not often yield to the temptation of *scribbling;* when she did, it was to express and gratify some feeling of the moment; not to show about among her acquaintance, nor to send to a magazine or a newspaper. She was quite convinced that her own compositions were juvenile at best, and far inferior to the productions of poets that she did not greatly admire. This was one instance in which her good taste proved of essential service to her. It saved her from the unhappy mistake of those, who perceive no difference between writing *verses* and writing *poetry;* and who accordingly go on writing verses, as many as you please — or more : which is an art as easy of attainment as that of doing cobble-stitch, or making patchwork, or painting sprigs on a thread-paper.

They were just entering on a disquisition upon poetical taste, when a morning call interrupted the conversation. It was Miss Oliver, — one of the standing inhabitants of the town.

She belonged to a class of ladies, of whom it may be said, that they are good for nothing but to be married. Let no intellectual *Cœlebs* object to the expression; it is not intended to recommend her to *him.*

At eighteen she was tolerably pretty; and about as lively as mere youth will make those who have no native spring of vivacity. Her education, like her mind, was common. If she had married, she might have performed the ordinary offices of domestic life as well as they are ordinarily performed. Though she had not cared much for her husband, she would probably have loved her children ; and the maternal duties and affections of themselves impart a degree of interest to any character. But she did not marry, although trained to consider marriage as the grand object at which she was to aim.

Year after year passed away ; during which, her attendance at the Christmas rout, the Easter ball, the summer races, was tiresomely punctual. At length it became necessary, by extra attention to dress, and studious vivacity, to show that she was still young ; but even that time was gone by, and she now only labored to prove that she was not *old*. Disappointment, and the discontent occasioned by the want of an object in life, had drawn lines in her face which time might still have spared. It sunk down into dismal vacuity after every effort at sprightliness ; for, without mind enough to be pensive, she was habitually dull.

Her circumstances did not allow her the relief of frequenting places of fashionable resort ; she contrived to exist with no other air, and no better water, than were to be obtained in her native parish. The few families in the neighborhood with whom, in her youthful days, she used to spend her Christmas or her Whitsuntide were dead, or dispersed, or the acquaintance was broken off : so that the routs and card-parties of this little town were the only relief to her monotony ; where she went to meet the same faces, and to say and hear the same *nothings* as ever.

It was no wonder, therefore, that the veriest trifle — a new stitch, or a new pattern — became to her an affair of importance ; that the gossip of the neighborhood seemed essential to her existence ; and that, without malignity, scandal should become an entertainment, and mischief a recreation.

Having conversed for a short time with Mrs. Leddenhurst, in a strain of commonness that forbade the supposition of an original thought having ever by any

accident strayed into her brain, she took leave. As
Mr. Leddenhurst shut the door after her, Emily was
greatly surprised to hear him say, " Every human being
is interesting." Thinking her, and most other human
beings, uninteresting, she could not understand this at
all. But to Mr. Leddenhurst, who was an observer of
human nature, and studied it as the most important
and interesting of sciences, every specimen was valuable, for every specimen presents *some* shade of variety.
But there was a still higher interest, which the meanest
of his fellow-creatures did not fail to excite. Christian benevolence was with him an active principle ;
and the earnest desire of doing good led him to seek
and cultivate the society of those whom the pride of
intellect, or the selfish indulgences of taste, would have
taught him only to shun.

" What an alteration," said he, " an interest in religion would make in such a countenance as that
lady's ! "

Nor was it uncharitable of him to apprehend that
she was one of the many who pay no decided regard
to it. There is a vulgar cant belonging to people of
the world, which as effectually betrays their frater-
nity, as any peculiar phraseology called religious cant
can do.

" I never remember," continued Mr. Leddenhurst,
" observing such an expression of listless vacuity in the
face of the meanest Christian. Habitual thoughts of
God, and of eternity, will impress some trace of mind
upon the countenance. What a new world of hope
and happiness might be opened to such a character !
Caroline, let us cultivate her acquaintance."

CHAPTER V.

ELIZABETH and Emily accepted, with apparently equal eagerness, the offer of their friends at Stokely, to assist them in their course of study and self-improvement. They had free access to Mr. Leddenhurst's ample library, and the advantage of his advice to direct their choice of books. The course of reading recommended to Emily was calculated to inspire her with a taste for solid acquirements and general information; and to correct, without impairing, the liveliness of her fancy and the originality of her mind.

They found it more difficult to ascertain what plan of study was most congenial to Elizabeth's taste, or most likely to improve it. The pleasure she took in reading, or in any kind of study, for its own sake, was but small. It was less, perhaps, than she was herself aware of; because she was not accustomed to analyze her motives; and she might possibly mistake the avidity with which she often sat down to read a book in the morning, which she intended to talk about in the evening, for the pure love of knowledge, or the gratification of genuine taste.

How many books Elizabeth would have read, and how many things she would have learned, if she had been *Robinson Crusoe,* she never inquired.

A very superficial kind of knowledge had been hitherto sufficient to answer all the purposes to which she applied it; but now that she was associating with persons who possessed, and evidently valued, more substantial acquisitions, she began to apply herself to them with avidity: for Elizabeth could accommodate herself to the different manners, tastes, and opinions of different people — which she possessed some sagacity in discovering — in a way truly astonishing to simple beholders.

There was now nothing so dry, so difficult, or so wholly foreign to her real taste, which she would not have set herself about if it had been recommended at Stokely, or if Emily had been going to apply to it.

What a pity that so much labor should be lost ! — lost, not only with respect to the particular end aimed at, but as to any sterling advantage to her own mind ; and her new friends were pained to perceive that, with all her laborious efforts to obtain it, she missed the only method of gaining solid approbation. They did not, indeed, wish to discourage her in the pains she was willing to take ; but above all they would have been pleased to see her aiming to extirpate the radical evil ; and becoming simple, honest, unobtrusive, and in *earnest.*

Elizabeth's studies were interrupted one morning, by revolving a scheme, which was suggested to her by something she heard Mrs. Leddenhurst say the evening before, about establishing a Sunday school for the poor children of Broadisham ; and as soon as she had breakfasted, she stepped into the disorderly cottage of a neighboring cobbler, who had seven or eight dirty children that were always either playing or fighting in the street, and, to the great surprise of the whole family, she offered to teach them all to read.

At first they did not seem to understand her ; and when they did, they appeared less struck with her generosity than she had expected. The father went on with his work, with a proud sullen countenance. The mother grinned stupidly ; and said, " I don't know as they 'll choose to larn. Bill, boy, oo'll ye like to larn to read ? Sal, do ye hear ? oo'll you choose to larn to. read, child ? "

Bill said " No ; " Sal said " Yes ; " while Elizabeth, indignant at their rudeness and ingratitude, would have left them to their ignorance ; but recollecting her object, she condescended to expostulate, representing the

3

importance of the acquisition ; and " You know," said she, " you cannot get them taught for less than two-pence a week anywhere in the town ; and I tell you I will teach them all for nothing."

Finding, however, that she made no impression on the parents, she turned to the children, saying, " Well, if you 'll come and let me teach you to read, I will give you all a halfpenny apiece every Sunday morning."

These words, " a halfpenny apiece," were the only ones the children seemed to understand.

" I 'll come, if you like," said one of them ; " And so 'll I," " And so 'll I," said some of the others. So, in consequence of her liberal promise, she had four or five dirty scholars the next Sunday morning.

But while the children were thinking of their half-penny, and Elizabeth of her reputation, A B C was a dull subject to both parties.

" B, I tell you, you stupid little creature ! " said she, again and again ; but at last her scholars were dis-missed, with scarce any other notion about A, B, and C than that there was some connection between them and a halfpenny.

The very next day, as Elizabeth was walking with Miss Weston and Emily, they met a party of young ladies, who asked Elizabeth what made her " so un-commonly late at church yesterday morning? "

" Why, I was detained rather longer than I intended by my little scholars," said she.

" Scholars ! " said Emily.

" What scholars have you ? " said Miss Weston.

. " Only a few poor children, that I teach to read on Sundays," answered Elizabeth, carelessly.

" Indeed ! I am pleased to hear that : I did not know there was any one here who — indeed I am *very* much pleased to hear it," said Miss Weston ; and as she spoke, she looked at Elizabeth with such an expression of approbation as she was not accustomed to receive.

For Miss Weston's was a charity that not only "hoped all things," but "*believed* all things" in a wider sense than would have been possible, had she possessed a little more intuitive perception of character. But it was not

"Her nature's plague to spy into abuses."

Herself perfectly upright and sincere, any species of dissimulation appeared to her almost impossible; and the actual discovery of artifice, at which the malignant would be gratified and the sarcastic amused, filled her only with grief and pity.

That evening Elizabeth was invited to Stokely, to assist in forming a plan for a Sunday-school.

"We have certainly injured poor Elizabeth," said Miss Weston, when she mentioned the circumstance to Mr. and Mrs. Leddenhurst. "Not that I should think so much of her having raised a little school of her own when no one else had thought of it, but she has never told us, never boasted of it, even when we were speaking on the subject; Emily herself did not know of it."

"I am surprised at that," said Mrs. Leddenhurst.

As soon as Elizabeth arrived they began consulting about the school.

"We have no wish, Elizabeth," said Mrs. Leddenhurst, "to interfere with your arrangements; as you were the first to begin, we shall be quite contented to follow you. What plan, my dear, have you pursued with your scholars hitherto?"

"Oh," said Elizabeth, coloring, "I have no very particular plan; I hear them read, you know, — and so forth: but I am sure you and Miss Weston understand these things much better than I do."

Mrs. Leddenhurst then described some of the arrangements and methods of teaching which had proved

successful in schools she had formerly been engaged
in: and as they entirely met Elizabeth's approbation,
it was determined to proceed without delay.

A convenient room was provided in the middle of
the town; and Elizabeth and Emily, with a few other
young people, undertook to attend regularly, twice
every Sunday. The poor families around were not
all so insensible of the privilege as Elizabeth's cobbler;
for a school of fifty children was presently raised, and
the numbers increased continually. More teachers
were soon wanted; but of all the ladies who were applied to, few were found willing to lend a helping hand.
Many were too indolent; and others were afraid of
having anything to do with what they thought a
Methodistical concern. There were some who appeared very eager in it at first; but as soon as the
novelty was over, they became irregular in their attendance, and dropped off, one by one: for to submit
to the self-denial and exertion requisite to a regular
and persevering attendance at a Sunday school, requires,
in general, some stronger motive than mere caprice;
although many motives beside the *right* one may be
strong enough.

In this exigence, they gladly accepted the assistance
of two or three young women of a lower class, who
came forward to offer their services. They appeared
quite competent to the undertaking, having been formerly engaged in a small Sunday school, which fell off
for want of the means to support it.

One of these, well known by the name of "Betsy
Pryke," was a person of some repute among her friends
and acquaintance.

She was a sharp, neat, compact, conceited-looking
person, who kept a little haberdasher's shop in the
market-place. By the aid of some quickness, a good
memory, and what was called a great taste for reading,
she had accumulated a curious mass of heterogeneous

lore, with which she was accustomed to astonish, if not to edify, her simple neighbors. She was particularly fond of hard names and words of many syllables; and her conversation was frequently interspersed with quotations from Young, Hervey, and Mrs. Rowe.

Her customers, in addition to their purchase, were generally favored with a little learning, gratis, while she was weighing the pins or measuring the tape; and even before those whom she could not venture to entertain with familiar discourse, some fine. word, or knowing remark, was dexterously dropped, to let them know what she was; and her behavior to this class of her customers was marked by that mixture of pertness and servility which is commonly produced by self-conceit in dependent circumstances.

To these qualifications, Miss Pryke added a flaming profession of religion. She was one of the very few inhabitants of this town who appeared to pay any serious regard to it; and among those pious, simple people, who possessed little of the wisdom or knowledge of this world, she passed for a pattern of zeal and sanctity. Miss Pryke's creed was all *creed:* she was fond of holding argumentations upon a few points on which she considered herself to have attained more light than the generality of plain Christians. She appeared to take little interest in the practical parts of Christianity, about which there is no controversy; and upon those who made anything more than a distant or casual reference to these subjects, she readily bestowed her enlightened pity. They were "persons in the dark;" and if they were ministers, they were "blind leaders of the blind," and knew nothing of the *gospel.* She valued comfort much above consistency, and was more observant of her *frames* than of her temper.

She could quote Scripture with great facility; but was fonder of hearing it *allegorized* than explained. She had by rote the whole string of those phrases,

and particular modes of expression, which pass current
among some good people, and which, although frequently used with the utmost sincerity, are very far
from being evidences of it.

Susannah Davy was a person of a very different
description : she was an humble, serious, and superior
young woman. Her father was an ale-house keeper, a
profane, violent man ; he scoffed at religion, and had
treated his daughter with great severity since she became acquainted with its value. But she submitted to
his harsh treatment with patience and meekness, and
conducted herself in his riotous house with such strict
propriety that she was respected by the lowest who
frequented it.

Whenever she could be spared from the business
below, she took refuge from the disorderly company in
the kitchen, in her quiet chamber ; where, with her
Bible and a very few good books, she passed many a
tranquil and happy hour.

She had a pleasing, intelligent face ; and while her
manners were perfectly unassuming, there was a dignified
reserve in her deportment. Her dress was neat and
plain. She had that nice sense of propriety which
secured her from the vulgarity of dressing beyond her
station.

She showed that she respected *herself* by her uniformly respectful behavior towards her superiors ; and
the circumstance of the ladies she was now introduced
to being her fellow-Christians did not dispose her to
forget what was due to them. She had read that
superiors are "not to be despised because they are
brethren;" and she felt no inclination to practise that
unbecoming familiarity which in some instances has
proved a hindrance to profitable Christian intercourse
between the brother of high and of low degree.

The fault, however, is not always on one side ; there
is a *manner* in which some good and very charitable

people behave towards their inferiors in rank, which must be grating to those who retain any independence of mind.

It was not thus with the Leddenhursts; they always remembered and respected the *natural* rights of the poor, — those rights which belong to them in common with the rich, and which, in so many essential respects, place all the ranks of mankind upon an equality. They considered their services as voluntary, their dwellings as sacred, and above all, their minds as free as their own.

There were few families more beloved, and more justly, by their poor neighbors, than the Leddenhursts·; and few, perhaps, whose intercourse with their needy tenantry was so entirely free from the debasing spirit of *feudalism*, — that spirit which has so long survived the system. They were the friends of the poor, without calling themselves, or wishing to be called, such names as patrons, benefactors, and the like. Their offices of charity were never performed with that superlative condescendingness of tone and manner, which, though it may be thought excessively amiable, is but a creditable way of being proud; and which does, in fact, neither become nor belong to one being, in its transactions with another of the same species. Nor were their religious instructions and advice given with an air of persons invested with the authority of Church and State. They always used to *reason*, as well as to exhort; and to reason *first*. They well knew that authority can no more bind opinion than chains can bind sunbeams.

They took particular care to instil proper notions on this subject into the minds of their children; that when they were going about on little errands of kindness to their cottages, they might not fancy themselves such con-descending little cherubs as some foolish people might call them. They were told that a child *cannot* condescend to a grown person : and the little Leddenhursts were remarked for their modest, respectful behavior to servants, and to the poor. Nor were they ever encouraged in anything that might make their charities look *picturesque :* for their parents were aware that, with every possible precaution, it is difficult enough to prevent a frightful mixture of motives in the performance of any good work.

But all this time Susannah Davy is waiting to speak to Mrs. Leddenhurst. Her appearance very much prepossessed them in her favor ; and they accepted the offer of her services with still more readiness than that of her sagacious friend. They both, however, seemed well qualified for the employment ; and Elizabeth and Emily, to whom such engagements were entirely new, appeared at first, in comparison with them, to some disadvantage as teachers of a Sunday school.

Indeed, they both experienced some disappointment in this concern. In *itself* it was wholly uninteresting to Elizabeth : for what is there in a row of poor children, to interest a vain, selfish mind? And she found it more unproductive in other respects than she had expected. Although she would lose a great deal by withdrawing her attendance, there was but little to be gained by continuing it. She was but one of a number, undistinguished among the other teachers, who were too busy with their own classes to observe Elizabeth's attention to hers.

Emily's disappointment was of a different kind. She had surveyed the form of children allotted to her — which consisted of the usual proportion of the stupid, the brisk, the idle, the diligent, and the froward — with sanguine expectations of what instruction would do for them ; not calculating on the dull comprehensions, feeble powers, or perverse dispositions of the little beings she had to deal with. She soon discovered that the pleasant reward of immediate or cer-

tain success was not that which could be depended
upon ; and Miss Weston told her that the only way not
to feel discouraged, was to be contented with the satisfaction of *endeavoring* to do good to our fellow-creatures. She knew better than Emily what consequences
to expect from such exertions ; and was contented to
perceive, that the children were tolerably regular in
their attendance ; that they made a, real, though slow
progress in their learning ; and that they gradually
became more decent and orderly in their appearance
and behavior.

It struck Miss Weston that the new teacher, Miss
Pryke, regarded her friends Elizabeth and Emily with
an evil eye. Some hints she occasionally dropped
confirmed this suspicion ; but she had not given her an
opportunity to explain herself fully, having rather
avoided entering into conversation with Miss Pryke.
Her manner of talking, especially upon religious subjects, was not agreeable to Miss Weston. She had
much greater pleasure in conversing with Susannah
Davy. The poor in this world are often "rich in
faith ; " and many a lesson of patience, trust, and
cheerful suffering, may be learned from their " simple
annals." When this pious, humble girl told of the
peace and happiness she enjoyed during her hours of
retirement, even in the midst of hardships and insults,
Miss Weston felt that if her own sorrows were more
refined, her consolations were not more elevated.

The truth was, that Miss Pryke was not very well
pleased to find Elizabeth and Emily in office at the
school. She knew that they had always been numbered among the gay young people of the town ; and
she augured no good from admitting people of the
world to engage in such a service. Miss Pryke's
notions concerning this phrase, "people of the world,"
were neither liberal nor correct. It is a phrase which
cannot be particularly attached to wealth or station ; nor

is there any condition of life, any creed, or party, from which it must necessarily be excluded. They who love God supremely, and serve Him faithfully, are *not* of the world; they who prefer anything before Him, *are* of the world, though they may "call him Lord," and "prophesy in his name." And it is of little consequence whether the worldly mind be seeking its gratification from a display of dress and beauty in the glitter of a ball-room, or from a display of its *gifts* among a few poor brethren at a prayer meeting : each is loving "the praise of men more than the praise of God."

But this was not the view of the subject that Miss Pryke was accustomed to take. With the exception of herself and a few of her friends, she considered all the inhabitants of Broadisham, especially those of the higher class, emphatically, "*the world.*" And however true this appeared to be with respect to the majority, her charity would never stretch so far as to allow, no, nor to hope, that there might be *some* among them, who, humbled at heart, and essentially relying on their unhonored Saviour, might grope their way to heaven, through all the rubbish of ignorance, error, and pharisaic prejudice, which worldly connections, and unfaithful instructions, must throw in their way. But "God seeth not as man seeth."

One day, when Mrs. Leddenhurst and Miss Weston remained after the school was dismissed, to make some arrangements in the room, Miss Pryke seized the opportunity she had been wishing for. Mrs. Leddenhurst remarked that the children were making as much progress as could be expected.

"Yes, certainly, ma'am," said Miss Pryke, "as it respects their temporal instruction ; but for my part," added she, sighing, "I could have wished to see the work prospering in our hands in a different way to what it does. It would be a great encouragement to my mind, I must say, to see some of these dear children enlightened."

"We are not to expect miracles," answered Mrs. Leddenhurst; "there are very few of them who can read their Bibles at present."

"Oh," replied Miss Pryke, "we must have faith, and nothing will be impossible; but if I may speak my sentiments, Mrs. Leddenhurst," said she, now resolving to cast off the fear of man, "I do not wonder that our labors are not blessed; and I don't believe they ever will be while we have so many people of the world amongst us. What can be expected from such poor, dear, deluded, young creatures! and what an example to set before these dear children, Mrs. Leddenhurst!"

Here Susannah Davy ventured to remark, that "perhaps their attendance at the school might be made useful to the young ladies; she had heard of such instances, and thought it would be a great pity to discourage them."

To this Mrs. Leddenhurst assented; and observed, that "so far from disapproving of their assistance, she lamented that no other ladies had joined them: she knew not by what authority they should be justified in forbidding any, who were willing to unite in a good work;" and silenced, but not satisfied, Miss Pryke by adding that "there was nothing in the character or conduct of these ladies that, in her opinion, disqualified them for the task they were at present required to perform."

The conversation ended here; for Miss Pryke was not the kind of person with whom they chose to enter into a further debate. She could not, however, be more truly concerned for the religious welfare of the children than they were. The grand object of all their exertions, and of which they never lost sight, was to train them for heaven; and they steadily pursued those methods, which, in their opinions, were most likely to promote this end. They did not attempt to feed them with "strong meat," but with "milk," because they were "babes;" and communicated the simple ideas they could comprehend, in plain language, and short sentences, such as they might easily attend to and remember. They knew that most children will not listen to a long discourse, however excellent; but that their attention may be excited by a short, striking, personal address.

Such slow and simple methods did not satisfy Miss Pryke's zeal for the conversion of her pupils. Not considering the *usual* course of divine proceeding in spiritual, as well as in natural things, she expected to sow and reap at the same time. But instances of Sunday-school children's appearing seriously impressed are rare, and, generally speaking, doubtful; though there have been hopeful exceptions. At any rate, teachers may be satisfied with imparting that knowledge, and forming those habits, which are so frequently followed in after life by the divine blessing.

CHAPTER VI.

In the meantime Emily's friends witnessed with great pleasure the hopeful, though gradual change that appeared to be taking place in her mind. These friends could make allowances for the prejudices of education, the influence of early habits, and the various disadvantages which must attend the dawnings of religion in those who have not been taught to fear God from their youth.

They were pleased to observe in her a delicacy of conscience which made her extremely guarded in conversing on the subject, lest she should be led to express more than she felt. Without sincerity she saw that religion is but a name, and without earnestness, a shadow.

As soon as she began reading the Bible with attention and prayer, she perceived that she had never before read it to purpose. She was surprised that she had often passed over the same passages which now struck her so forcibly, with such total inattention to their obvious meaning. She began to feel that " one thing is needful ; " that the grand business of life, and that to which all others must be secondary, is to prepare for the life to come. Of the necessity and nature of this preparation she became increasingly conscious the more she thought of God, and of the nature of heavenly happiness. She was convinced that " His presence could not be fulness of joy " to any but those who are, like Him, holy and spiritual. When she compared the state of mind which the Scriptures call " meetness for heaven " with the vanity and earthliness of her present taste and pleasures, and with the distaste she felt to those that are wholly spiritual, she began to understand what is meant by being " born again," and to feel the necessity of it ; although her ideas of the way in which this change must be produced were still indistinct and uncertain.

She had bowed at the name of Jesus, and spoken of Him, and heard Him spoken of as " our Saviour," and " our blessed Saviour ; " but with notions the most vague, and feelings the most indifferent. But when she began to regard Him as a Saviour from sin and misery, as the Friend of *sinners,* a living and present Friend, and to hope that He might be hers, His being and His character appeared an astonishing reality, and it seemed to her as though she had never heard of Him before.

At first Emily set about becoming a Christian with the same expectation of success as she would have applied herself to a language or a science. She saw that she had it all to learn, and she thought there was nothing to be done but to learn it. She soon, however, began to experience some of the difficulties which will be encountered by all who are in earnest. She was sincerely asking, "What must I do to inherit eternal life?" But, like him who once "went away sorrowful," Emily found herself unwilling to make that entire surrender of the heart to God which he requires, and without which religion is but an irksome bondage, a fruitless effort to compromise between God and the world. She complained of a secret reluctance and disinclination to serious thought and engagements, and of a disproportionate interest in her own pursuits and pleasures. She sometimes expressed a fear to Miss Weston, that her solicitude about religion arose more from a dread of the consequences of neglecting it, than from a desire towards it for its own sake.

To these complaints her friend listened with sympathy, and administered such encouragements as were calculated, not to make her easy and satisfied with her present attainments, but to stimulate her to perseverance and diligence. She explained to her that these or similar obstacles ever oppose the entrance of real religion to the human heart; that all are naturally indisposed to embrace it; but that those who feel and lament this indisposition have every encouragement to expect assistance.

."Strength," said she, "is promised to those, and those only, who are sensible of weakness; who, acknowledging with deep humility and poverty of spirit their mental impotence, are willing to receive help of God."

"That change of heart which consists in new dispositions and affections, new pursuits and pleasures, new apprehensions of things unseen, and without which heaven could not be happiness, is," she said, "the immediate operation of the Spirit of God. It is that for which of ourselves we are absolutely insufficient. We must not, however," continued Miss Weston, "expect this assistance, unless we earnestly and constantly seek it. '*Ask*, and ye shall receive;' this is the invariable condition. And, Emily, we must watch as well as pray; and diligently use every means that God has appointed for the promotion of religion in the soul; never relaxing from that strict system of mental discipline in which Christian self-denial chiefly consists. It is to those who *do* the will of God that the promise is offered."

While Miss Weston was thus continually performing the noblest offices of human friendship, Emily's love for her became increasingly ardent; for she assumed no authority nor superiority in advising her: her manner was so humble and affectionate, and displayed at once such a delicate consideration of her feelings, and anxious solicitude for her happiness, that Emily's heart melted with grateful affection.

It has been said that there was nothing so dry, so difficult, nor so wholly foreign to her real inclinations, that Elizabeth would not have set herself about, if it has been recommended — or rather, likely to recommend *her* at Stokely. It was therefore less surprising — as religion was the one thing most attended to and valued there — that Elizabeth must now also become religious, or at least appear to be so.

Without premeditated and consummate hypocrisy, yet without sincerity, and wholly without earnestness, she professed to view the subject in a new light, and requested instruction upon it. She readily, and without gainsaying, acquiesced in new opinions: to many she might have appeared a more hopeful learner than Emily. But surely there can be no bondage so irksome, no drudgery so base, as counterfeiting, or from any mistake falling short of, that character which, when genuine, brings with it freedom and independence, pleasantness and peace.

Although they found it a difficult task to converse on the subject with Elizabeth, no pains were spared to give her right views, and to excite in her mind a real concern about it. She assented readily to everything that was said ; believed whatever was stated ; felt all that was described — and more ; but they could not feel satisfied with her professions.

Indeed, the manner in which the Christian character was described and exemplified at Stokely rendered it so difficult of imitation, — there was so little credit to be gained by mere outward appearances or particular expressions, while so much stress was laid upon sincerity, humility, and spirituality of mind, that Elizabeth soon began to feel the support of her new professions almost intolerably irksome, and almost hopelessly difficult : perhaps she might have abandoned the attempt altogether, if she had not accidentally discovered a style of religious profession far easier of attainment.

Miss Pryke was confirmed in her suspicions of the unsoundness of the new family by what had lately passed, and she attended the next Sunday, determined to make redoubled efforts at enlightening the school. The instructions she addressed to the children were indeed principally aimed at the teachers ; and Elizabeth's form being next to Miss Pryke's, she could not avoid hearing a great deal of it. She listened to her harangue, partly from curiosity, and partly from a desire of becoming familiar with a language which she wished to adopt. Perceiving from the whole strain of it that it would be comparatively easy to be very religious after Miss Pryke's manner, she determined to gain the notice and good opinion of this enlightened teacher. So, as soon as the school was dismissed, Elizabeth made up to Miss Pryke, and shaking her by the hand, with a particular kind of smile, said, " I am sure I have reason to thank you for what I have heard this morning."

Miss Pryke started at this very unexpected address : however, it put her prejudices to flight in an instant. Notwithstanding her jealousy of the gay or genteel, she was doubly gratified at having proselyted one of this class. Her answer was studiously seasoned with spiritual flattery ; but that and the succeeding conversation are not recorded, because it would be painful, and equally offensive to right feeling and good taste, to repeat a discourse in which expressions might occur, which to use professedly in earnest, but without sincerity and reverence, is the worst kind of profaneness.

The conversation was renewed in the afternoon, and on the following Sunday : and Elizabeth was invited to join a private meeting which was held once a week in Miss Pryke's parlor. She felt rather ashamed of accepting this invitation, and scarcely knew why she wished it ; however, as it was winter, she stole in one evening.

Her entrance seemed for a time to distract the devotions of the little assembly, the appearance of a gay lady was so very unusual among them. There was some bustle in dumb show, to make way for, and accommodate her ; and she was beckoned and jostled, and pointed, and pushed to the vacant arm-chair by the fire-side. But Elizabeth with gracious bows declined this distinction, and seated herself — for she was fond of contrast — on one of the forms, between a very old woman and a spare squalid-looking man, whose head was tied up with a blue handkerchief. Elizabeth's lace veil floated on his shabby shoulder, and her rich India shawl spread over the old woman's red cloak, who shook it off respectfully ; while the good man squeezed himself up to his narrowest compass, and drove at his next neighbor to make more room.

When the service was over, Miss Pryke made up to Elizabeth and shook hands with her ; and so did two or three others, saying a word or two expressive of

4

their pleasure at seeing her there : and there were some
present whose hearts glowed with true Christian benevolence when they did so.

CHAPTER VII.

By this time Emily, without having studied for it,
had gained the love and esteem of the whole family at
Stokely.　Elizabeth saw that she had ; and notwithstanding their impartial attentions — for none but the
children *appeared* the fondest of Emily — Elizabeth
perceived that she was not loved, esteemed, and, what
to her was still worse, not admired so much.　It was a
long time before she could believe this ; but when she
did, when she felt quite sure of it, her mortification
began to produce a degree of indifference to their
opinion, and distaste to their company ; and she wondered why she had taken so much pains to please
them.

From this time her visits to Stokely became gradually less frequent ; and as she felt Emily to be no longer
a foil, but a rival, her company also became irksome
to her ; and although her professions when they met
were the same as ever, Emily was hurt to perceive
that Elizabeth shunned her society.

Her connection with Miss Pryke tended much to
promote this coolness ; for it gave Elizabeth another
object and other engagements, — and such as were not
very compatible with her intercourse with the Leddenhursts.　She continued to attend the weekly meeting
at Miss Pryke's, — for vanity is seldom dainty, — and
the notice she attracted, and the distinction she obtained even *there*, were agreeable to her.　Her manners,
her accomplishments, her dress, excited little attention

among persons of her own rank, who could display much the same; but in all these respects she stood unrivalled in Miss Pryke's parlor, and they obtained for her that consideration which she loved.

Well had it been for Elizabeth if she had made as good use of these meetings as many, as most of those did, who frequented them. But unfortunately, she only imitated what was not worth imitating. She soon acquired a facility in using the phrases current among these poor people, and even caught something of their particular looks and gestures. These peculiarities, which, while they too easily pass among some as signs of grace, among others, are with as little discrimination concluded to be the symptoms of a canting hypocrisy; but which are, in fact, often, most often, the genuine and natural expressions of earnest sincerity, uncontrolled by the delicacy which teaches the educated to conceal their feelings.

But, truly, the least agreeable excrescences which are produced by earnestness in religion, are more reasonable, and ought to be less offensive, than that finished air of indifference which too often characterizes politer worshippers.

When a poor Christian turns the key upon her comfortless dwelling, and sets off with her lantern and her Bible, to spend an hour in thinking and hearing of a place where there will be no more want, it is not surprising if she be more deeply interested and affected than those, who leave a comfortable drawing-room, an intelligent circle, or some interesting pursuit, and whose " joy unspeakable " it costs them, perhaps, little effort to conceal.

But it is best to avoid *all* extremes; and those good people who are prone to make *such* " outward and visible signs of their inward and spiritual graces," would do well to observe the conduct which Jesus Christ seems plainly to recommend on this subject, — that decent composure of countenance and manner, which, while we are exposed to the eyes of others, answers the purpose of "entering into the closet, and shutting to the door." "Be ye not as the hypocrites, of a sad countenance; for they disfigure their faces that they may appear unto men to fast: but anoint thy head, and wash thy face," &c. When the repenting publican "smote upon his breast," he was not with the throng of worshippers in the Temple, but standing "afar off."

Elizabeth, however, found herself in high esteem among this little company, especially with Miss Pryke, by whom she was studiously flattered and extolled. She had little opposition to encounter at home, on account of her new profession; for her parents disliked trouble too much to persecute! and Mrs. Palmer contented herself with exclaiming sometimes, when her daughter was setting off for the market-place, "Bless me, Elizabeth, how can you make such a fool of yourself!"

Elizabeth's father and mother were people of the world in the most complete sense; they were "lovers of pleasure, and not lovers of God."

Mrs. Palmer was clever; and had a vast deal of taste in laying out gardens, and fitting up rooms, and setting out dinners. Her grand object in life was, to enjoy herself; and her selfishness was refined, and perfect in its kind. She was a good wife, a kind mother, an obliging neighbor, as far as ever she could be consistently with this object, but no further. She had an easy, pleasing address; and her politeness was so unremittingly attentive that it looked almost like friendship. Whatever did not demand any real sacrifice of her own pleasure or convenience, was done, and done in the most obliging manner possible; but really to deny herself for the sake of another, was a species of virtue which she left to be practised by such good sort

of people as chose it. To her it appeared foolishness;
especially as she could decline her services with such
masterly adroitness, with such a gentle, sympathizing
address, that the cold selfishness of her heart often
escaped detection.

Her feelings were naturally violent; but she had
such an extreme dislike of being uncomfortable, that
she rarely suffered them to be very troublesome to her.
When the news arrived that her only and darling son
had died abroad of the yellow fever, many people
thought she would not long survive the intelligence.
Her sorrow at first was ungovernable; she said she
should never have another happy hour. But it is
easier to be distracted for a week than to be sorrowful
for life; and Mrs. Palmer discovered surprisingly soon,
that she was still in possession of all those good things
on which her daily pleasure depended. She had no
son, it was true; but she had her pleasant house, and
handsome furniture; luxurious fare, and a healthy ap-
petite, a fine person and expensive ornaments. She
could still walk, and ride, and visit, and see company;
and build her grotto, and attend her green-house, and
arrange her cabinet; so that she recovered her cheerfulness rapidly. There was nothing in her mind with
which sorrow could *amalgamate*, it was an unwelcome
and unintelligible foreigner.

By her son's dying at a distance she was spared
what were, to her, the most shocking circumstances
attending such an event.

Death, that one thing which the sceptic *must* believe, and to which the worldly *must* submit, was
that which she most disliked to think about; and she
studiously avoided whatever was likely to remind her of
it. She shrunk from the survey of its gloomy apparatus; and was really glad that all that part of the affair
was transacted so far off as Jamaica. The opening of
the family vault was a circumstance she particularly

dreaded ; that was a place she did not like to think of ;
and still less to recollect that she must herself one day
lie down in that dark chamber. Whenever the unwelcome thought was forced upon her, she instantly
recurred to the soundness of her constitution, and the
vigorous means she used to preserve it. Besides
which, she avoided perils by water and perils by land ;
was the first to foresee evil and hide herself; and to
flee from contagion and every form of danger, — thus,
by a common but strange kind of deception, feeling
as though to delay death were to escape it.

She thought it prudent, however, to make some
provision for the distant day ; and was, accordingly,
constant at church, and charitable to the poor : by
which means she concluded all . would be safe, whenever she should be under the absolute necessity of
going to heaven.

Mr. Palmer was a gentleman of ordinary capacity ;
but he could hunt, and shoot, and joke, and swear ;
and contrived to do very well without thinking : for
with these accomplishments, a good table, and well
stocked cellar, he wanted neither for friends nor reputation.

It suited the taste both of Mr. and Mrs. Palmer to
live expensively. Whether it suited their income as
well, they did not often inquire ; for they avoided
everything that was disagreeable, and to them it was
disagreeable to think about debts and prudence.

A short time after Elizabeth had begun to estrange
herself from Stokely, Mrs. Leddenhurst received a
parcel of books from her, which they had lent her ;
with a note thanking her for the loan of them, but
declining the offer of others that had been proposed ;
adding, that " studies of this nature were too apt to
encroach upon pursuits of higher importance."

" This is very true indeed," said Mrs. Leddenhurst,
when she had read the note ; " and I wish Elizabeth

may now find herself more disposed to engage in pursuits of higher importance. But I am afraid she is making a mistake ; at least I should question whether she will really employ the time she would have spent in reading these books to more advantage. I have known some good people," continued she, "who would scruple taking up a volume of elegant literature, or of philosophy or science, alleging that they had not the time to spare from better reading, whose consciences would yet allow them to spend months in working a cap or a handkerchief; and who were in the habit of employing themselves in such domestic affairs as, in their circumstances, could be as well done by their servants."

" Elizabeth has learned this from some of her new friends," said Mr. Leddenhurst. " It is no uncommon thing for persons of low education and contracted views to entertain this kind of jealousy against general information, — indeed, most things which their own circumstances will not permit them to enjoy. Whatever they have not knowledge to understand, or taste to appreciate, they are apt to consider as inconsistent with real piety. Many very good people are subject to this prejudice, and are apt to consider as dangerous symptoms of conformity to the world, pursuits and refinements which a little more knowledge, and a little more liberality, would convince them are, in their way and in their place, aids and ornaments to Christianity."

" The opposite extreme is, however, so much the most general and the most abused," said Miss Weston, " and this is so much the safest of the two, that one had need be cautious in censuring it. Where one person abstains from general reading for conscience', or rather for prejudice' sake, how many are there who read bad books without any regard to conscience, and who are prejudiced against good ones ! "

The Leddenhursts were sorry that Elizabeth had

withdrawn herself so much from their society ; especially as they did not feel perfectly satisfied with the present style of her professions. They did not, however, venture to form so decided a judgment concerning her as was declared of Emily by some of the good people at Miss Pryke's.

Emily had no ambition to gain their favor ; indeed she paid too little regard to public opinion ; and her dread and abhorrence of *unfelt* professions led her to avoid those very appearances and expressions which might have induced them to form a more favorable judgment of her piety. They shook their heads at her youthful sprightliness ; while Elizabeth was pronounced " a gracious and growing character."

CHAPTER VIII.

ONE spring evening, Elizabeth had taken her accustomed seat by the side of Miss Pryke's counter. While they were talking, she sometimes put aside the shawls and ribbons that blinded the window with the end of her parasol, to see what was passing without. But there was nothing to be seen except some children at play in the middle of the square, and Mr. Preston standing in his usual position at his shop-door, and old Mr. and Mrs. Parsonson returning from their evening walk, and the setting sun shining on the old market-cross, just as it did a hundred years ago.

It was seldom that anything happened to disturb the tranquillity of this remote place, — except that a show, or a conjurer, or a company of strolling players, sometimes stopped to amuse the inhabitants for a night or two, in their way to the county town. But suddenly their conversation was interrupted by the

sound of distant music. Elizabeth started from her
seat, exclaiming :

"Hark, Miss Pryke ! what can that be ? The bass-
drum, I declare ! "

For now it came nearer and louder ; and presently
a full band, in gay green and white, playing a lively
march, followed by the regiment, and all the boys and
girls of Broadisham, crowded into the market-place.

"How partial I am to military music ! " said Elizabeth, as she stood nodding to the tune ; while rank
after rank passed the shop door.

This was a lively evening for Broadisham ; it was all
bustle and animation. Maids and mistresses, masters
and men, appeared at their doors and windows.
Trains of soldiers, stooping their tall caps, were seen
entering the lowly doors of the Angel, the King's
Arms, and the Red Lion ; while a party of officers
assembled before the gate of the new Hotel.

————

The teachers of the Sunday school had been employed for some time past in making a set of frocks
and tippets for the children ; and as soon as it was
completed, an evening was appointed for them to meet
in the school-room to receive them. This evening
being arrived, and the parties assembled, they were
about to proceed to business, when Emily proposed
waiting a little while for Elizabeth, who was not come ;
but at last they were obliged to go on without her.

It was a pleasant task to take off the patched, worn,
and torn, and fit on these new comfortable dresses.
The whole school soon appeared in a neat livery ; and
while the children in stiff attitudes kept surveying
themselves and each other, and looking almost as
much ashamed as they were pleased, the ladies, not
less pleased, stood beholding the happy crowd. Em-

ily enjoyed it exceedingly, as with great animation she stood rolling up the old tattered garments, and admiring the new.

It was nearly dark before the children were dismissed; and just as the ladies were coming down stairs, they observed a light dressy figure making her way rather impatiently through the crowd of children that was issuing from the school-room door. Till the moment she passed, when the light from a chemist's shop shone full upon her, they did not discover that it was Elizabeth. Emily spoke to her, but she was looking another way, and appeared not to observe any of the party, who stood gazing at her as she passed swiftly on.

"She is going to this officers' ball," said Mrs. Leddenhurst; "there is her mother, I see, just before."

"I am surprised at that!" said Emily.

"And I am concerned," said Miss Weston.

"I am concerned, but not much surprised," said Mrs. Leddenhurst.

"But I have heard her say so much against those amusements lately," added Emily.

"I should have been more surprised if she had said less," said Mrs. Leddenhurst; "but we will not condemn her; perhaps she is going against her inclinations. I only fear that if she once begin to break through the restraints she has lately imposed upon herself, she will return to these things with increased avidity."

As they passed the assembly-room they saw the chandeliers were lit up; the dancing had commenced; and they could distinctly hear the sound of the inspiring viol. Emily had trod many a measure there, and she could scarcely forbear stepping to the well-known air. She was really fond of dancing; but the company, the dissipation, were never very agreeable to her. She had declined attending this ball without regret. Mr. and Mrs. Leddenhurst had explained to her their reasons for abstaining from these diversions in a way that convinced her of their propriety. Without shaking their heads, and speaking of dancing as containing in itself some mysterious evil which could not be explained, they simply stated the difficulty, if not impossibility, of preserving that temper of mind in such assemblies which a Christian should always maintain; that they were universally allowed to indispose the mind to serious reflection and serious engagements, and to expose young and old to many temptations.

The offence it would inevitably give to many pious people, whose *prejudices* even we are expressly enjoined to consult, was mentioned as another reason, and a sufficient one, for abstaining, independent of all other considerations.

"And if resigning such paltry pleasures as these," said Mr. Leddenhurst, "be considered too great a sacrifice to be made for Christ's sake, what are we to understand by forsaking *all* to follow him? But even," said he, "if I could attend these places without any injury to my own mind, or any offence to the minds of others, I really should not feel disposed to go dancing through a world so full of sin and misery as this is."

Emily, however, needed not many arguments on this subject. When she began to *feel* religion, and to think of eternity, she did not want to dance, nor to mix much with people whose thoughts are all about this world; yet she had never before been so uniformly cheerful as now. She returned to Stokely with her friends, and spent the remainder of the evening so pleasantly with them, that she quite forgot the assembly-room.

How it happened that Elizabeth was at the officers' ball, must now be explained.

One of these officers was an old acquaintance of her

father's ; and he, with all the others, was invited to dine at his house.

Elizabeth had not quite finished dressing herself for this occasion, when she was called down stairs to Miss Pryke, who waited to speak with her in the hall.

"I did not hear till just now," said she, glancing as she spoke at the various parts of Elizabeth's dress, "I did not hear till this minute, that all these people were coming to dinner here to-day ; and as I was convinced you would not wish to be in the way of it, I came to request the pleasure of your company to spend the day at *ours*, and I hope — "

"Thank you," said Elizabeth, "you 're extremely good, I 'm sure, and I should enjoy it exceedingly, for, you know, it is excessively distressing to me ; but, indeed, I 'm afraid I could not get off anyhow, for, you see, my mother would be so much displeased. So thank you, *good morning*," said she, withdrawing rather abruptly, and leaving Miss Pryke not quite satisfied with the manner in which her invitation had been declined.

There are ways of being irresistible without flirting : and Elizabeth did not find it requisite on the present occasion to throw off entirely the character she had assumed. When she made her appearance, there was a look of childish simplicity and timidity, with a becoming expression of being distressed at the presence of so many gentlemen. Hastening to take refuge among the ladies, she seated herself beside Miss Oliver, who was one of the party, with whom she began chatting in an under voice, with playful familiarity.

During dinner the subject of the proposed ball was introduced, and Lieutenant Robinson, a young officer who sat next Elizabeth, began talking about the pleasure of meeting her there. But Elizabeth acknowledged she was not partial to these amusements. "There was too much publicity in them," she said, "to suit her taste :

she was aware she exposed herself to the imputation of singularity, but, in fact, she preferred pleasures of a more private and domestic kind." While the lieutenant was expressing his grief, surprise, concern, and astonishment at this declaration, a lady who sat opposite exclaimed,

"Oh, we must not expect to see Miss Palmer at the assembly-room; she has quite forsaken our innocent amusements since she has been such a saint."

At the word *saint* all the company laughed; laughed rather more than Elizabeth liked, and dreading further exposure, she joined in the laugh, saying,

"Oh, pray indeed, you must not call me a saint! I only wish I was more of one than I am."

"But, Mrs. Palmer, ma'am," said the lieutenant, appealing to her mother, "Miss Palmer surely cannot be serious; let me beg of you to intercede with her, that we may have the honor of her company to-morrow evening."

"I shall certainly endeavor to prevail with Elizabeth," said her mother.

"There," said he, "Mrs. Palmer takes our part; you will not refuse her, I 'm convinced."

"If my mother wishes it, certainly not," replied Elizabeth, with a submissive smile.

Thus she had promised to go to the ball before she recollected her pre-engagement at the school-room; and she could not break her promise. Besides which, in the course of this evening Lieutenant Robinson had rendered himself so agreeable that all prior considerations rapidly gave way.

When she was alone in her room that night, she began to speculate upon the posture of affairs. She thought for a moment of the opinion that would be entertained of her by her friends in the market-place for going to the ball; and she thought for two moments of what would be thought of it at Stokely. But Eliza-

beth now found herself engaged in business of importance, to which trifles must·be sacrificed ; and the tide
that was plunging her back into a world from which her
heart had never been alienated was but feebly stemmed
by principle or conscience.

Elizabeth had probably been deceiving herself as
well as others. They who are little accustomed to
self-examination, who look more at actions than at
motives, may go a great way in false professions without deliberate hypocrisy. Perhaps she was herself surprised to find how easily her scruples were overcome,
and her professions laid aside. She felt less dread in
doing so, than shame at the idea of their being discovered. Her mind was not indeed at this time in a
state for making cool calculations.

Religion, friends, reputation, were hastily thrown
into one scale and Lieutenant Robinson's gold epaulette
into the other — and thus the point was decided.

CHAPTER IX.

For more than a fortnight after the night of the ball,
Elizabeth had not been seen by any of her old friends.
At length Emily was surprised by a call from her ; and
still more, by her proposing to accompany her that
evening on a visit to Stokely.

" It is so long since I have been," said she, " that
they must think me quite inattentive ; and if you would
like to go this evening, I shall be happy to attend
you."

Emily readily agreed to this unexpected proposal.
Indeed she was very glad of it; especially as she
remarked a certain thoughtfulness and pensiveness in
Elizabeth's manner, which made her hope she was
sorry for what had lately occurred.

During their walk Elizabeth was unusually silent and absent; and she continued so after their arrival, although she had received the same free and cordial welcome as usual. Many ineffectual efforts were made to enliven her; and at last Mrs. Leddenhurst — who had remarked that Elizabeth liked to be asked to play — proposed that she should sit down to the instrument.

"What shall I play?" said she, turning over the leaves of the music-book. "'The Soldier's Adieu,'— that's a sweet thing; shall I try it?"

"If you please," said Mrs. Leddenhurst.

Elizabeth played and began to sing; but stopped presently, as though unable to proceed.

"Why don't you sing?" said Emily. "Do sing!"

"I cannot sing very well this evening," said she, looking distressed; and added aside to Emily, "You *must not* ask me to sing those words."

After attempting a few more notes, she stopped again, and leaning back upon Emily begged for air and water.

The window was thrown open, and Mr. Leddenhurst led her to the sofa; where, after a few hysterical sighs, she found herself a little better.

"Emily, my love, lend me your arm," said she, rising; "I shall soon recover in the air; it's nothing but the heat of the room."

So Emily led her friend to an arbor in the garden; where, as soon as they were seated, Elizabeth leaned her head upon Emily's neck, and burst into tears.

"What is the matter?" said Emily. "Are you ill, dear Elizabeth; or has anything grieved you?"

She continued to weep and sigh, but made no answer.

"I am sure," resumed Emily, after a short silence, "I do not desire to know anything you wish to conceal; but if I can guess why you are so unhappy—"

" Oh, then, I have betrayed myself!" exclaimed Elizabeth, hiding her face.

" Betrayed yourself! what do you mean, Elizabeth? I only thought that perhaps you were sorry about going to the ball and giving up the Sunday school; and if — "

" Oh, my dear!" interrupted Elizabeth, " you do not know, you cannot guess, it is quite impossible that any one should ever discover the cause of my uneasiness. That must ever remain a secret in my own bosom."

" Then certainly I shall not inquire," said Emily. " Will you like to walk?"

" No, stay a moment; forgive my weakness, Emily, and let me talk to you about my sorrow, although I cannot reveal the source of it."

" As long as you please, but take care, or I shall find it out."

" Oh dear! oh dear! oh dear me," said Elizabeth.

" Dear me," said Emily.

" Do you think Mr. Leddenhurst observed the words of that song?" inquired Elizabeth.

" I can't tell, indeed," replied Emily.

" How silly it was of me to attempt to play it!"

" Why so?"

Elizabeth looked down, and sighed.

" How beautifully the sun is setting!" observed Emily, who found it difficult to maintain her part of the conversation.

At length Elizabeth broke another silence by saying, " Emily, I know I may confide in you; will you promise faithfully never to betray me, if I tell you all my heart?"

" Yes, you may depend upon me," said Emily.

" But how shall I confess my weakness?" resumed Elizabeth; " cannot you guess? — Oh, Emily, if you had ever loved you would know how to feel for me!"

"Dear! are you in love?" said Emily, simply.

"Hush! my dear creature!" cried Elizabeth; "but what," continued she, in a low voice, "what but this fatal attachment could have led me to act as I have done?"

"Do you know now," said Emily, after running over in her mind the list of all the beaux and bachelors she knew, "do you know I am entirely at a loss to think who you can be at all attached to."

"Oh, my dear, that fatal regiment!" cried Elizabeth.

"Already!" said Emily.

"You do not know him, or you would not be surprised."

"Is it that tall, brave-looking officer that I have seen walking with your father?"

"No, that's Captain Scot. He is not particularly tall; you'd not be so much struck at first sight: but indeed he has paid me such attentions! though I know he is only flirting with me," said Elizabeth, sighing.

"Then indeed, Elizabeth, I hope you will endeavor to overcome it," said Emily, "and as it is so very recent, I should think with a little effort —"

"A little effort! O Emily, you know nothing about it; never, never; it cannot be overcome!"

"How are you now, Elizabeth?" said Miss Weston, who appeared at that instant.

"Thank you, better," said Elizabeth, starting.

"She is a great deal better," said Emily, blushing.

"I feared you would stay too long in the evening air," said Miss Weston; and, supported by her two friends, Elizabeth returned to the company.

Elizabeth had long wished for an opportunity of being a heroine; for which nothing had been wanting but a hero; and this being so unexpectedly supplied, it was no wonder that, mistaking ambition of conquest, and partiality to scarlet cloth, for love, she should presently exhibit its interesting phenomena.

5

She had not, however, been guilty of any misrepresentation in saying that Lieutenant Robinson had " paid her *such* attentions ; " for this young man had fallen in love with Elizabeth ; and a short time after this arbor scene, and after about a month's acquaintance, — during which time he spent every morning at her work-table, and every evening in her company, — he made his proposals to her father, which meeting with the approbation of the whole family, he became her acknowledged lover.

Elizabeth would have been more gratified at making a conquest of a man of sense ; and she would have preferred altogether having a sensible man for her husband. However, she had made a conquest, and she was going to be *Mrs. Robinson.*

Sometimes, indeed, she felt a little dissatisfied during the morning *tête-à-tête* with the strain of her lover's conversation : for it was surprising what silly things he would say rather than not say anything : but then Elizabeth thought it was because he was in love ; and any such unfavorable impression generally wore off during evening parade, when the lieutenant was manœuvring at the head of his company ; and always while the band was playing she was *sure* she was in love with him.

After evening parade the band was ordered to play for an hour in the market-place, for the amusement of the ladies, who were assembled on these occasions, and promenaded up and down the square.

It was then that Elizabeth enjoyed the *éclat* of her conquest. While she appeared laughing and talking with her lover among her less fortunate acquaintance, who were walking about in unattended rows, her purpose was served as well, or better, by a blockhead than a genius.

Sometimes she would stop awhile to chat with them, and her nods and bows were dealt about lavishly, and with unwonted cordiality, to everybody.

"Who are all these?" said Lieutenant Robinson, one of these evenings, as a new party entered the square.

"Gracious me! all the Leddenhursts," said Elizabeth, who would rather have avoided the interview.

"And who is that pretty figure in the cottage bonnet?" said he, as they came nearer.

"It's only Emily Grey," answered Elizabeth.

"How d'ye do, how d'ye do, Emily, my love, how are you?" said she, addressing her friends as they advanced.

She now introduced Lieutenant Robinson, and would have passed on, but they all seemed disposed to stay and chat, and Mr. Leddenhurst entered into conversation with her lover.

Never had he appeared to so much disadvantage to Elizabeth as at this moment; now that she saw him, not for herself, but for them, — saw him, too, by the side of Mr. Leddenhurst.

Her hand had fallen from his arm as they approached, and she now began talking as fast as possible to Mrs. Leddenhurst, Miss Weston, and Emily, to divert their attention from the conversation that was passing between the gentlemen.

Emily, who had raised her expectations rather unreasonably high, of a being whom it was possible to love in three weeks, was nearly guilty of the rudeness of starting when she first beheld the mean figure, and fiercely vacant countenance, of her friend's admirer.

"Is it possible!" said she to herself, and she looked about to avoid meeting the eye of Elizabeth.

In the meantime the lieutenant continued running on in his usual style of sprightly dulness to Mr. Leddenhurst, who stood looking down upon him with an eye of keen but candid observation.

"What a monstrous curious old cross you've got here!" said he, staring up, and tapping it with his cane.

"Well, good night!" said Elizabeth; "it's cold standing in the wind;" and she walked off with her lover, feeling more uncomfortable than ladies *always* do when they walk off with their lovers.

When they reached home, Elizabeth threw herself on the sofa, saying,

"Don't talk to me; I am tired this evening, Mr. Robinson."

Thus repulsed, he walked backwards and forwards in the room for some time, half whistling; till, stopping on a sudden, he exclaimed,

"That Emily what d'ye call her is a confounded pretty girl!"

"Do you think so?" said Elizabeth, rousing up; "well, she does look rather pretty in her bonnet."

Here the lieutenant resumed his walk and his whistle; but the remark had a fortunate effect upon Elizabeth. The momentary jealousy made him appear surprisingly more agreeable, and worth securing: and while she sat watching him as he paced up and down in the dusk, she said to herself, "He *whistles* uncommonly well!"

Very soon after Lieutenant Robinson's proposals were accepted, the regiment, which was quartered at Broadisham, received orders to remove to a distant county. It was expected they would march in six weeks; and as both he and Mr. Palmer were anxious to conclude the affair as soon as possible, it was agreed that the marriage should take place accordingly.

Elizabeth, therefore, suddenly plunged in the agreeable confusion of preparation, had little leisure to study the character and qualifications of her intended husband. He was but *one* of a great variety of important concerns that now distracted her attention. Crapes and sarcenets, laces and jewels, trunks and riding-dresses, her silver teapot, her satin workbag, and her scarlet beau, were objects of alternate and equal interest.

Wholly intent upon the *éclat* of her bridal, she had as little inclination as opportunity to look forward to the months and years when she would be a wife, but no longer a bride.

CHAPTER X.

ABOUT this time, Eleanor Jones, the invalid mentioned early in this history, having lingered through a painful winter, died peacefully. Miss Weston and Emily had visited her frequently during her illness, and they were present at the last scene.

Death, as personified and decorated by poetry, Emily had frequently contemplated; but she was unacquainted with the realities of a dying bed.

The moment they entered her room, they perceived the altered expression of her countenance; and although Emily had never seen it before, she saw it was *death* in her face. She felt the shock, but would not turn away; "for if I cannot bear to see it, how shall I endure it?" thought she.

Soon after they entered she was seized with a convulsive spasm which lasted several minutes.

" Oh, see ! " said Emily, " cannot we help her? Is there nothing that would give her any relief? "

" Nothing, my dear," said Miss Weston, softly; " it will soon be over."

" Dear, dear creature ! " cried her distressed mother : " please God to release her ! for I cannot bear this ! "

When the spasm was over, her features became composed, and she looked round upon them with an expression of joyful serenity.

" These are only the struggles of nature," said Miss Weston; 'the sting of death is sin;' she does not feel that."

At this she smiled, and her lips moved, but they could not distinguish what was said. She then lay for some time quite tranquil. They watched her in silence, and at length perceived that she had ceased to breathe.

Miss Weston led the mother down stairs; while Emily remained fixed to the spot, gazing on the placid corpse. She looked round on the low, tattered chamber, and thought she should never again wish for the vanities of so short a life. "This is how they must all end," she thought; "and death would look just the same if this poor bed were a state canopy." It seemed but a moment, not worth caring for, before she herself must lie down by her side.

Her contemplations were soon interrupted by the entrance of Miss Weston.

"Come, Emily, my love," said she, "we can do nothing more here, but we may still comfort her poor mother."

"I should like to stay longer," said Emily; "I never saw death before; how strange, and awful, and beautiful it is!"

"You have stayed long enough now," said her friend, and she led her out of the chamber; and as soon as they saw that the mourning mother had said and wept her utmost, they took leave, with many assurances of continued friendship.

When they opened the cottage door, they found it was noonday, and bright sunshine. Emily had not shed a tear before, but they overflowed at the sight of the bright fields and clear blue sky. They walked on silently to the entrance of the town.

"Had not we better go the back way? You will not go through the town this morning, Miss Weston?" said Emily.

"Why not, my dear?"

"I always avoid it when I can," replied Emily, "and just now especially."

"Unfortunately I have an errand in the town," said Miss Weston, "at Mrs. Eve's."

"At Mrs. Eve's!" said Emily.

They went on; and Emily was obliged to endure the sight of the shops and people, looking as busy as usual.

Mrs. Eve's windows were set out with spring fashions; and when they went in, they found Elizabeth, with her mother, and other ladies, making purchases, and examining the new assortment.

"I was just wishing for you," said Elizabeth, "to give me your opinion of these sarcenets. Which should you prefer, Emily, this rose color, or the pale blue?"

"They are both extremely pretty," said Miss Weston, "but the blue, I think, is the most delicate."

"I advise you to go up and see the millinery," said Mrs. Palmer to Miss Weston and Emily; "and really you'll be delighted. Mrs. Eve has some uncommonly pretty things come down, I assure you."

"We have something quite new in flowers, ladies," said one of the young milliners, taking down a tempting drawer. "That's a sweet thing, ma'am!" said she, holding up a quivering spray before Emily; who, sickening at the sight, made her escape as soon as she could to the opposite counter, where Elizabeth still stood, wavering between the rose color and the blue.

"Yes, Elizabeth," she said, "they are very pretty; but we are just come from Eleanor Jones's, — and have seen her die."

"Die! good gracious, have you? She is gone at last, poor soul! is she?" said Elizabeth. "Dear me!" added she, perceiving that Emily expected her to say something more.

"I wish you had been with us," said Emily; "you cannot think what a striking scene it was. I think I shall not soon forget it."

" It must indeed be very affecting, I should think,"
said Elizabeth, still glancing at the rival tints.

" I will walk back with you now, if you would wish
to see her," continued Emily. "She is looking so
placid and tranquil. Would you like to go?"

" My dear, you must excuse me," said Elizabeth;
" my spirits are so weak, I never could endure to see a
corpse."

" Why, she is only looking as we ourselves shall very
soon."

" La! my dear Emily!" cried Elizabeth; "but
really I have not a moment to spare — you know how
I'm circumstanced. Besides," said she, looking up
and down the street, " I am expecting Frederick every
instant. He was to call here for us half an hour ago."

" Poor Elizabeth!" said Emily, as soon as they had
got out of Mrs. Eve's shop, " how completely she is
absorbed again in these things; and how trifling, how
disgusting they are! I hope I shall never again waste
a thought, or a moment, about them!"

" They are trifling certainly," said Miss Weston;
" but I think they are only disgusting when they are
made affairs of importance, and suffered to engage a
disproportionate share of time and attention. 'There
is a time for all things,' you know, — a *little* time,
even for attending to the trifles of life. It would not
pain me, I confess, to see Elizabeth just now busily
engaged in these affairs, if I were sure they were kept
in due subordination to better things: but there is the
danger."

" I wish she had been with us to-day," said Emily,
" that she might have felt, as I did, the transition from
that room to Mrs. Eve's exhibition."

" It is very desirable sometimes," said Miss Weston,
" to view the gayeties of life in such strong contrast;
and we should be careful constantly to maintain such
an impression of these *realities*, as to counteract their

undue influence. But it is not intended that we should walk through the world only by a sepulchral light; nor that we should be always turning aside from its pleasant fields, to wander among the tombs. Indeed, the mind may take a melancholy pleasure in being familiarized with such objects, without making real progress in religion. It is far better for our thoughts to be habitually fixed on the world beyond the grave : that is more likely to stimulate us to run the race that is set before us, with patience, with vigor, and with cheerfulness ; and to give us at last the victory over the grave."

The first time Emily called upon the widow Jones after her daughter's funeral, she found her in a great deal of trouble.

The expenses of a long illness had reduced her so low that she was unable to pay her rent, which had already run on several quarters. By Eleanor's death she had also lost her chief means of support; being herself too feeble to go out to work as she used to do. So that, with grievous lamentations, she told Emily she must turn out of her cottage, and end her days in the parish poor-house.

Emily, much concerned at this account, set off to consult with her friends at Stokely. At the outskirts of the park there was a little building covered with ivy, which had formerly been a pleasure-house, but was now disused, and falling into decay. It struck Emily, as she passed, that with a little repair it might be made a comfortable asylum for the poor widow. She went in full of this scheme ; and before she had exhausted half her arguments, obtained Mr. Leddenhurst's free consent. He promised to have it put in proper repair, and commissioned Emily to superintend the alterations, — as she expressed much anxiety lest the workmen should tear down the ivy, or lop the branches, which spread so prettily over the thatch.

Mrs. Leddenhurst engaged to supply it with furniture ; and it was to be ready by Midsummer-day, — the day on which Mrs. Jones had warning to quit her cottage. To increase the pleasure, Emily proposed that in the meantime it should be kept a profound secret from the widow. But Mrs. Leddenhurst suggested whether, for the sake of that momentary surprise, it would be right to keep her so long in uneasiness at the thought of going to the poor-house.

" I forgot that," said Emily ; but she looked so much disappointed, that Miss Weston proposed to hold out only an indefinite hope, which might allay her anxiety, without letting her know the actual good fortune that awaited her.

Emily now went to work with alacrity. There was much to be done which she undertook to execute herself, besides giving directions to the workmen ; and she had a great deal of trouble in persuading them implicitly to follow her orders. They had so little notion of the picturesque that if she had not kept a constant watch over them, the place would, in her opinion, have been completely spoiled.

There was a little plot in front, overgrown with nettles, which she had cleared and was converting into a flower garden. The children were very much pleased with being employed under Emily on this occasion. They were permitted to weed and dig, and to do whatever services she required. To adorn the entrance, she contrived to form a rustic porch, with a seat, of mossy logs and branches ; and she led over it a wild honeysuckle and a white jessamine, which had long grown there, and crept over the front of the building.

One day, while Emily was busily employed in twining the sprays of her favorite jessamine over this porch, she was surprised by her friend Elizabeth.

" My dear Emily," said she, " I 'm just come to bid you good-by — I am going to be married to-morrow."

"To-morrow!" said Emily; and her hand fell from the bough.

"Yes, indeed," replied Elizabeth; "I did not expect it would be quite so soon; but the regiment is ordered off immediately, and Frederick is anxious we should spend a few days at Cheltenham before we join it; and I assure you I am quite fagged with packing and preparing. But I would not go on any account without seeing you," said she, with a voice and look of apathy that went to Emily's heart. She sat down in her porch, and burst into tears.

· But Elizabeth was too busy, and too happy, to weep. Just come from the important bustle of preparation, the sight of Emily in her garden hat and gloves, so intent upon fitting up a house for an old woman, excited that kind of contemptuous pity, with which the simple pleasures of simple people are commonly regarded by such observers as Elizabeth.

After standing an awkward minute, wishing Emily had not cried, she added,

"Well, Emily, my dear, I must not stay."

"Stay one moment," said Emily; "I was thinking of the old days when we were children, and used to play together under the chestnut trees."

Elizabeth was touched by the sudden recollection, and, without an effort, a tear came into her eye. She sat down by her friend, and they embraced affectionately.

"Elizabeth, I hope you will be happy," said Emily; "I hope Mr. Robinson is —"

"Oh, he is indeed," interrupted Elizabeth; "I have no doubt I shall. He is the most pleasant, generous creature in the world. I wish you had seen more of him, Emily; but really, of late, you know, I have been so particularly occupied. But, indeed, I must be gone!" said she rising; and they parted with a hasty embrace.

Emily followed her to the gate, and watched her with tearful eyes to the winding of the road, as she went briskly on.

Elizabeth slept soundly in consequence of this day's fatigue; and awoke the next morning with only a confused idea of what was before her. But the red beams of the rising sun, shining full upon her white hat and feathers, brought the strange reality to her recollection. She started up, but the clock struck four — only four ! So she lay down again; fell into a wakeful doze, and dreamed it was only a dream.

At six o'clock, the maid who had nursed her from her infancy came to awaken her. She looked at her young mistress as she lay asleep, and, brushing a tear from her eyes, she said, " Come, Miss Elizabeth, dear, it's time to get up, ma'am ! "

At ten o'clock the chaise that was to take Elizabeth away stood at her father's door. Soon after, she appeared, covered with a splendid veil, and was handed in by the smiling lieutenant; when, bowing and waving her hand to the party assembled at the street-door, they drove off.

It was a beautiful morning; the bells rang merrily, and as it passed the end of Church Street they outnoised the rattling of the chaise.

Elizabeth, in passing through her native town, felt an increased glow of satisfaction, from observing her friends and neighbors going about the ordinary business of the day. Some were washing, and some were brewing. Parties of children, with their workbags, were sauntering to school; and there were the pale teachers, peeping over the tall window-blinds, to see the bride; and there sat Miss Oliver with her hair in papers; and the row of young women at Mrs. Eve's all together raised their heads from their work, at the sound of the chaise,

— while she, a gay and youthful bride, was leaving them all to their monotonous employments. She was married ; and she was going to Cheltenham.

CHAPTER XI.

" No, this way," cried Emily, as she was conducting the widow Jones to her new dwelling.

" Dear miss ! where are you a fetching of me ? 'T was never worth a while to turn such an old woman as me out of my house and home," said she in a crying tone, as she went hobbling after Emily.

" But I tell you," said Emily, " you should not be thinking of your old cottage now." Yet, in spite of all her remonstrances, the widow Jones went groaning and grumbling all the way to Stokely.

Richard, and Caroline, and Lucy, were anxiously waiting their arrival at the garden gate. Emily, as she approached, called eagerly to them to stand out of the way, that they might not intercept the view of the dwelling ; which, with the little white gate and rustic porch peeping under the trees, had certainly a very pretty effect.

" What do you think of that ? " said she, looking eagerly at the widow.

" Deary me ! " said she.

" Do you think it pretty ? Then this is where you are to live. So do not be fretting any more about your old cottage, for you are to live here," repeated Emily. " Is n't it a pretty little retired place for you, now ? "

" I thank you, and his honor, and the ladies, a thousand and a thousand times, " said she, casting a forlorn glance at the thick shade that environed her dwelling.

"What, don't you like it?" said Emily.

"Why, dear, I can't mislike it," said she, "here's a power of trees, to be sure! but 't will be more lightsome come winter."

"But that is the beauty of it," said Emily. "Come, then, and see if it is not comfortable inside."

Emily indeed had spared no pains to make it so. The kettle was now boiling on the fire, and the little deal table was set out ready for tea. The widow's favorite cat had been dexterously conveyed away that morning, and Caroline and Lucy had kept her in safe custody all day. With indefatigable care and coaxing, and after various obstinate attempts to escape, they at last succeeded in making her lie down to sleep upon the hearth.

"Well-a-day, there's our puss!" exclaimed the widow, now looking *really* pleased.

This was the only thing that did not look strange to her; and novelty, much as it charms the young, is itself a grievance to the old.

Emily now only waited to point out some of the principal beauties and conveniences of the new abode.

"See," said she, setting open the door, "I'll tell you what you should do these fine summer evenings. You must bring your knitting, and sit here to work in the porch; you'll look so pretty sitting to knit in the porch! And be sure," added she, "that you do not tear down the ivy that grows over your little window."

The widow Jones having promised to do, and not to do, all that she thought it reasonable to require, Emily only stood a moment at the door, surveying with a picturesque eye the group formed by the old woman, her cat, and the tea-table; and then took leave, saying, she would "now leave her to enjoy herself."

The evening before this, Emily had put the finishing stroke to her work; and when it was done, she thought it looked such a snug little seclusion, that she very

much longed to live there herself. It was a calm
summer evening, she was alone, and she sat down in
the porch to enjoy it, just at the time when the moonlight began to prevail over the twilight ; and Emily
began to feel very poetically.

A scrap of paper that was left there rendered the
temptation irresistible : but she had written only a few
lines, when Mr. Leddenhurst appeared at the garden
gate.

"What are you about now, Emily?" said he.

Emily put by her verses, colored, and said, "Nothing, sir ;" and then took him in to admire her contrivances. He did admire them, and she thought no
more about her verses till she got home again, and
found herself alone in her father's parlor. She then
read them over, merely to see if they were worth finishing ; and she took a fresh piece of paper, and was just
getting into the spirit of it again, when she heard her
father's knock at the door, and he, with several other
gentlemen, came bustling in, talking all together, and
very earnestly, about a parish dispute which was to be
decided the next day at the county assizes.

"I tell you, sir, they must lose their cause," said
one of them, — "Miss Grey, how d'ye do, ma'am?
And I'll give you my reasons, Mr. Grey — "

"Take off these things, child," said her father,
pushing away Emily's papers rather disrespectfully, and
laying a pile of law-books on the table.

Emily took them off, and made her escape as fast
as possible to her own room, thinking, as she went,
how foolish it was of her to write poetry. The verses
were put by in a folio with several similar effusions, of
which some were better, and some worse. They were
mostly in a strain that to the uninitiated might appear
inconsistent with Emily's lively and flourishing appearance. But nothing could be more unreasonable than
requiring young writers of poetry to "prove their

words;" unless it were, inflicting upon them some of
the extraordinary things they sometimes wish for themselves when they are rhyming.

The verses Emily began writing this evening in the
widow's porch were as follows: —

> Say, spirit, if thou wanderest nigh,
>   Of every sylvan dale;
> What forms, unseen by mortal eye,
>   Frequent this leafy vale.
>
> Perchance 't was once the flowery court
>   Of merry elfin king;
> Where fairy people loved to sport,
>   And tread the nightly ring.
>
> The sun, descending down the sky,
>   In floods of misty light,
> Surveys it with his golden eye,
>   And makes the valley bright.
>
> The moon, who rideth in her pride
>   At solemn midnight hour;
> And sheds her radiance far and wide,
>   On turret, dome and tower,
>
> Here sleeps upon the checkered glade;
>   Nor finds a softer rest
> On myrtle bower, or classic shade,
>   Or ocean's silver breast.
>
> And oft would I, alone, resort
>   To this seclusion dear;
> Unchecked to breathe the ardent thought,
>   Or shed th' unquestioned tear.
>
> O Nature! how thy charms beguile
>   Or soothe our cares to sleep!
> Thou seem'st to smile with those who smile,
>   And weep with those who weep!
>
> The vernal tint, the summer breeze,
>   E'en winter's aspect drear,
> Thy woods, and vales, and skies, and seas,
>   Like friendship soothe and cheer.

/ The soul in thy serene retreats
  Communion sweet may find;
But gay assemblies, crowded streets,
  Are desert to the mind.

The throng where giddy mortals press,
  Is solitude to me;
But Nature, in her wildest dress,
  Refined society.

CHAPTER XII.

ELIZABETH had scarcely been married two months when she received the news of her father's death. He was taken off suddenly by a fit of apoplexy; and his affairs were found in so embarrassed a state that a narrow jointure alone secured his widow, and her recent settlement his daughter, from absolute want.

In consequence of this change of fortune, Mrs. Palmer immediately retired to a distance from Broadisham : and about the same time, Elizabeth despatched the following letter to Mr. Leddenhurst.

CHESTER, September 23.

MY DEAR SIR, — It would be absolutely impossible for me to attempt to describe the variety of painful emotions I experience at this moment, in taking the liberty of addressing you. Nothing indeed but a conviction of your extreme goodness could have emboldened me to undertake so awkward a task.

The poignant affliction occasioned by the loss of my lamented parent needed no aggravation; but I am persuaded you cannot be a stranger to the very unpleasant embarrassments in which, in consequence of his untimely decease, his affairs are involved. The

6

result to us, as you may readily imagine, has been particularly unfortunate. The truth is, my dear sir, that Lieutenant Robinson, depending on those resources of which we have been so fatally disappointed, has contracted some trifling debts, which it is, in fact, out of his power immediately to discharge. He has, you know, considerable expectations, but these are of no present avail; and I am persuaded you would be greatly concerned were I to relate the excessively unpleasant circumstances to which we have been exposed for some time past. In consequence of which I have been induced to address you; and encouraged by a recollection of your former goodness, to request the loan of two hundred pounds, if perfectly convenient; and which there is not the smallest doubt but we shall in a very short time be able to return.

You may be surprised that Mr. Robinson does not apply to his relations. The fact is, that the uncle to whom he has repeatedly written on the subject, is a low man, in trade, of very sordid and contracted ideas; who absolutely refuses the smallest assistance, except on conditions with which it is absolutely impossible we should comply.

This determined me to trouble you with the present application; indeed there is no individual in the whole circle of my friends on whose generosity and friendship I could so firmly rely. And need I say, under what infinite obligations we shall consider ourselves, should you be induced to comply with the request?

Lieutenant Robinson begs to join me in kindest regards to yourself and Mrs. Leddenhurst; and believe me, my dear sir, with the greatest respect, your most obliged friend and servant,

ELIZABETH ROBINSON.

A tremendous secret was discovered to Elizabeth a very short time after her marriage, in a letter from this uncle. Lieutenant Robinson had been — a linen-draper.

He was a weak, hot-headed young man. A dislike to business, that is, to employment, and an opportunity he once had of trying on a military hat, inspired him with an ardent desire for the profession of arms. And at the expiration of his apprenticeship to his uncle, deaf to the remonstrances of his prudent friends, he commenced the life of a gentleman.

In order to escape the ridicule of his brother-officers, and to remove, if possible, the suspicions they evidently entertained of his origin, he thought it requisite to plunge into most of their extravagances. In consequence of which — notwithstanding occasional supplies from his uncle, and the convenient practice of leaving every town at which they were stationed in debt — he was kept in perpetual embarrassments.

His alliance with Miss Palmer, therefore, appeared a very eligible measure. He had been confidently assured that her father was a man of handsome property, and this opinion everything he saw at his house and table tended to confirm.

Elizabeth thought this discovery at once released her from all obligation to love, honor, or obey her husband. From that time she conducted herself towards him with coldness and haughtiness, which he bore with tolerable patience until the intelligence of her father's death, and the unexpected state of his affairs, gave him, as he said, "a just right to resent it."

Trained in habits of show and expense, and wholly unaccustomed to economical calculation, Elizabeth had soon made alarming demands upon her husband's limited resources; which, depending upon her promised but delayed portion, he had not thought it necessary to check.

The news of Mr. Palmer's insolvency made an

immediate alteration in this respect. Nor did Elizabeth fully comprehend the nature of her misfortune, until the first time that, for want both of money and credit, she was really obliged to deny herself something she wished for. With a strange feeling of impatient astonishment, she then discovered that she *must* do without what she had said "it was absolutely impossible to do without." A scene of mutual upbraiding between herself and her husband was the consequence of this first lesson in economy, or rather in poverty. But they reproached each other, not for their faults, but their misfortunes, — not for being imprudent, but for being poor.

Elizabeth, however, had no sooner despatched her letter to Stokely than she felt relieved of her difficulties. She had witnessed so many instances of Mr. Leddenhurst's generosity that she was confident of receiving the requested supply. And she had not yet learned to look beyond the narrow extent of two hundred pounds.

She was engaged to dine at the colonel's, and had just finished dressing for the occasion, when her husband brought her the expected letter.

"This is fortunate indeed," said she. "Then, Mr. Robinson, be so good, while I read it, to step over to Levi's, and desire them to send the gold clasps. You may say, you know, I shall call and settle the account to-morrow morning."

They who have ever unfolded a letter, expecting at every turn to behold the fine texture and expressive features of a bank-note, which was really wanted, and found it was only a letter, will know better what Elizabeth felt on this occasion, than others who never met with such a circumstance. Having first turned it about in all directions, she sat down and read as follows : —

STOKELY, September 28.

My dear Mrs. Robinson, — I should be sorry to forfeit the opinion you are so good as to entertain of my readiness to serve my friends by every means in my power; and shall be happy should I succeed in convincing you, that I am sincerely desirous of doing so in the present instance, — although it may not be in the way that appears most expedient to you.

I should have been greatly at a loss to know how most effectually to serve you, if I had not been favored with an interview with Lieutenant Robinson's uncle, of whose character I conceive you have formed a mistaken idea. He appears to me to be a man of integrity, good sense, and benevolence; and highly deserving the esteem and confidence of his relations.

He has undertaken a journey to Broadisham, with the view of explaining to your friends the plan he had suggested to his nephew, in hopes of obtaining their concurrence, and influence with you.

Having himself been unsuccessful in former applications to you and Lieutenant Robinson, he has requested me to address you on the subject; a task which I undertake the more cheerfully, since you have already indulged me with your confidence.

Mr. Sandford informs me that Lieutenant Robinson was not intended for the military profession, having been trained to business; but entered it very recently, contrary to the advice of his friends. His uncle hoped, however, that after having experienced some of the inconveniences to which he would be exposed from such a change of habits and circumstances, he would more readily listen to proposals for returning to his former pursuits; and had determined, for a time, to urge him no further on the subject. It was not till he heard of his having formed an alliance, and with so young a lady, ill qualified to brook the difficulties of her situation, that Mr. Sandford became solicitous to prevail with his nephew to abandon his new profession immediately.

With regard to those expectations you allude to, Mr. Sandford requests me, as a friend, my dear madam, to assure you that they must prove wholly fallacious, unless Mr. Robinson founds them on his own diligent exertions. Should he be willing to enter into the prudent views of his uncle, he may depend upon every support and encouragement it is in his power to afford ; otherwise he must still submit to those distressing embarrassments to which the expensive habits so commonly contracted in his profession, and the limited resources it affords, unite to expose him.

Justice to his other relations, Mr. Sandford directs me to say, must forbid his continuing to answer Mr. Robinson's repeated demands, even if there were a probability of its proving of any ultimate advantage to him ; but so far from this, he considers that it would only be a means of encouraging those expensive habits, and, in the end, of plunging him in deeper embarrassments.

And now, my dear Mrs. Robinson, permit me to assure you, that I am solely influenced by a tender concern for your real welfare, when I earnestly recommend you to use every endeavor to prevail upon Mr. Robinson to accede to his uncle's proposals. I am not surprised that, at first sight, they should appear to you such as it was absolutely impossible to comply with ; and I readily admit that nothing less than an heroic effort can enable you to submit with a good grace to such a change of circumstances. But in making that effort you would find a noble satisfaction ; and in descending cheerfully and gracefully to an humbler sphere, more true independence and dignity of mind would be exerted than would probably ever be displayed throughout the whole of a gay life.

Considering that it might not be agreeable to his nephew to engage in business in his own immediate neighborhood, Mr. Sandford has been making inquiries in different directions, and has lately met with a very eligible offer from a respectable tradesman retiring from business. The only objection that I know of to the situation is, that it is at the village of Hilsbury, not more than fifteen miles distant from Broadisham; but as it is much secluded, and remote from any of your connections, perhaps you would not consider that a sufficient reason for declining it. The present proprietor has realized a considerable property in the concern, — it being the only one in that line in a populous neighborhood; and I should conceive a retired situation of this nature would be more agreeable to you than the publicity of a large town.

Should Mr. Robinson be willing to undertake this concern, his uncle and I will cheerfully unite to advance the capital; and with regard to the remittance you mention, it will be forwarded to Chester by the same day's post that informs us of his having agreed to this proposal.

In case of your concurrence, Mr. Sandford proposes to enter immediately upon the business at Hilsbury, in his nephew's name; where he would see everything properly prepared for your reception, and await your arrival.

After all, my dear friend, I am aware that no terms can be employed in this affair that will not be harsh and offensive to you; nor will I attempt to represent what might be called the pleasant side of it: for perhaps you have not yet had sufficient experience of the inconveniences of an unsettled life, nor of the miseries of showy poverty, to estimate the value of a peaceful home and a moderate competence.

I would rather remind you that we are never so safe, nor so truly well off, as when following the obvious

directions of providence. Our affairs are all ordered
by Him who is acquainted not only with our outward
circumstances, but most intimate with our hearts ; and
who knows by what means they will be most effectually subdued, and made willing to accept of real happiness. And be assured, my dear friend, that by whatever circumstances we are taught the nature and value
of real religion, and led cordially to embrace it, then,
and not till then, we shall find happiness.

　　　　Believe me your very sincere friend,
　　　　　　　　　C. L. LEDDENHURST.

　When Lieutenant Robinson returned from his commission to the jeweller's, he found his lady in strong
hysterics in her room.

　" Mercy upon us ! what 's the matter ? " exclaimed
he, stopping in dismay at the door. - " Elizabeth !
Betsy ! why don't you speak, child ? What 's the
matter, I say ? " continued he, advancing towards her.

　But Elizabeth took no notice, except motioning with
her hand for him to stand further off. Presently a
servant came in, saying,

　" If you please, ma'am, here 's Mr. Levi, with the
gold clasps for you to choose ; and here 's the bill he bid
me to bring up to you."

　" I can't look at them now ; tell him to call another
time," said Elizabeth. " There, Mr. Robinson, read
that ! " said she, pointing to the letter, and again falling
back in her chair.

　When he had read it, he walked up and down
thoughtfully for some time ; at length, going towards
his wife, he said, timidly,

　" I 'll tell you what, my dear, it does not signify objecting and objecting, we must, I know we must— "

　" Must what ? " said Elizabeth.

　" Must do what Mr. Leddenhurst says, my dear."

　" Do exactly as you think proper, " cried Elizabeth ;

" I am not in the least surprised, Mr. Robinson, that *you* are so willing to acquiesce in it ; but I never will — do you suppose I ever would submit to be the wife of a tradesman ? "

" I 'll tell you what, Betsy ! " said her husband, flying into a passion, " I can't nor I won't submit to this any longer !   You did n't bring me a penny, nor a halfpenny, nor a sixpence ; and what business have *you*, I should be glad to know, to talk in this unbecoming manner to *me ?* "

" O heavens ! " cried Elizabeth, " what a barbarian ! Let me escape ! " and rising hastily, she flew down stairs, and throwing herself tragically into the chair, which had been long waiting for her at the door, ordered to be taken to Colonel Harrison's.

While she was going there, Elizabeth, notwithstanding her complicated misfortunes, was far from feeling really unhappy.   She remembered a great many heroines who had been in debt and had bad husbands. Young, lovely, distressed, she was flying for protection from his cruelty.   Besides, she had fully determined to open her whole heart to her *friend* Mrs. Harrison ; and she was quite certain, that by some means or other, she should be rescued from the threatened degradation.

Elizabeth made her *entrée* at the Colonel's with an air of interesting distress.   There was nobody then present but the lady of the house, and the major of the regiment, with whom she was particularly intimate.

" My dear creature, how shockingly ill you look ! " exclaimed Mrs. Harrison.

" Indeed I am not very well," said she ; and throwing herself upon the sofa, she burst into an agony of tears.

While Mrs. Harrison was repeating her inquiries and condolence, the graceful major seated himself beside her, saying, tenderly,

"My dear Mrs. Robinson, what has happened to distress you? Only tell me if there is any possible way in which I can serve you."

Elizabeth could only reply by smiling on him gratefully through her tears, for other company entered at that moment. But she whispered Mrs. Harrison, that she would tell her all as soon as they were alone.

After dinner the ladies walked in the garden; when Elizabeth contrived to take her friend aside for a few minutes. She found it, however, an awkward task, notwithstanding the vague and general terms she employed, to disclose those parts of her story which related to her husband's connections.

"But, my dear child, what an unlucky thing you should ever have liked him!" said Mrs. Harrison. "Upon my word, my dear, I feel quite distressed for you."

"Only tell me what steps I ought to take," said Elizabeth; "I rely entirely on your friendship."

"Indeed, my dear, I should be excessively happy to advise you, and serve you, I'm sure, in any way that lies in my power, in this unpleasant affair; but really it's an awkward thing to interfere between man and wife. Indeed, I am not so much surprised that Lieutenant Robinson should consider it altogether most prudent to take the advice of his relations."

"But what then will become of me?" cried Elizabeth, weeping passionately.

"Come, come, my dear Mrs. Robinson, let me beg of you not to discompose yourself thus," said Mrs. Harrison. "To be sure," continued she, sighing. "We know it is our duty at all times to submit to what the Almighty is pleased to appoint for us. But really, I must insist upon it, that you do not distress yourself in this manner; I can't endure to see you so unhappy. Here are all our friends!—for heaven's sake, my dear, dry your tears. Shall I send you a glass of anything?"

"Nothing, thank you," said Elizabeth, who felt, at this forlorn moment, the difference between a friend and an acquaintance. The others now joined them; and as her eye wandered from one smiling, selfish face to another — faces from which the unhappy had nothing to hope — she involuntarily thought of Emily, and Stokely. The major, however, was a friend nearer at hand; but she saw no more of him during the evening. When she returned at ten o'clock to her comfortless lodgings, she was surprised to find him in earnest conversation with her husband.

The major, who was very good-natured, had frequently accommodated Lieutenant Robinson with small sums of money; which by this time had amounted to a debt that he was anxious to have discharged. He had been rather pressing on this subject of late; so that the lieutenant came to the resolution of disclosing to him the whole state of his affairs, and asking his advice on the present emergency. No sooner did the major understand that by resigning his commission he would be able to pay his debts, than he warmly urged him to comply: and it was not so difficult a matter to persuade him as it would once have been. He began to be weary of his present mode of life, of which the novelty had already worn off; and of the misery of being always in debt, and always short of money. His objections to business were less insurmountable than those of his lady. It was not pride, but idleness; and he now considered what a difference there would be between master and man.

"But then there's my wife," said he to the major. "If you had but seen the piece of work we had this morning! Let me beg of you, my dear sir, to try what you can do with her; she will not listen to me, that's for certain."

This task the major undertook; and when Elizabeth entered, he addressed her with an air of friendly interest, saying —

" Mrs. Robinson, we have just been talking over this awkward business of yours ; and I do assure you very seriously, as I 've been telling Robinson, I do not see any other plan in the world that as a man of honor he could adopt. In fact, if I were in his place, I should not hesitate a single instant about the business. Indeed, for my own part, I should not feel any particular reluctance to — to — engaging in mercantile concerns ; upon my life I should n't. If he were a single man," continued the major, observing the gathering gloom in Elizabeth's countenance, " it would be wholly a different affair ; but when a man is responsible for the honor and happiness of a young and lovely woman — "

" Oh, do not talk of *my* happiness," cried Elizabeth, glancing expressively at her husband ; " that is sacrificed for ever ! "

" Heaven forbid ! " said the major, looking at his watch.

" So the major 's been advising of me to lose no time about the business ; and he thought I had better write to my uncle and Mr. Leddenhurst by return of post. And so you see, my dear, it 's all settled," said Lieutenant Robinson, anxious to make the whole confession before his friend was gone.

" And I am extremely glad that everything is so happily adjusted," said he, rising ; and unwilling to wait the issue either of fainting-fits or remonstrances, he took leave.

As the door closed upon the gay, agreeable major, Elizabeth felt herself abandoned to wretchedness. She had no inclination to go into hysterics, nor to remonstrate with her husband ; but sat silent and motionless, watching him, while he was sealing and directing the letters for Stokely. And now she felt *really* unhappy.

The loss of rank *is* a misfortune : and Elizabeth

felt its utmost poignancy. She had always indulged that senseless contempt for trade, and trades-people, which is prevalent among the vulgar of her class; and she had not had opportunities of knowing that many of the truly noble, the excellent of the earth — that many persons of superior understandings, even of real taste, and respectable information — are to be found standing behind a country counter.

Having, however, no means of redress, Elizabeth suffered the necessary arrangements for their departure to take place undisturbed. During the few weeks they still remained at Chester, she never allowed herself to take any distinct view of the future, — only indulging a kind of vague hope, that anything so insupportable as the condition which threatened her, she should never be actually permitted to endure. And since nothing was now to be hoped from friends, relations, or acquaintance, she began to think that chance, or fate, or Providence, or something, would certainly interfere to prevent it.

CHAPTER XIII.

NOTWITHSTANDING these hopes, the day actually arrived on which Elizabeth and her husband took leave of Chester, and set off for their new home.

For, in this interval, no distant relation had died and left them a fortune; not a single individual in all the city of Chester had offered to lend them a thousand pounds; no banker, brewer, nor merchant, wanted a partner; no fashionable dowager a companion. In short, neither luck nor accident prevented their driving safely into the village of Hilsbury on the very day they were expected.

ROBINSON, in gold letters, over the door of a smart country shop, pointed out to Elizabeth her future residence.

"Is there no private door?" said she to her new uncle, as he handed her from the chaise.

"We have no other door; please to follow me, ma'am, and I'll show you the way," said he, conducting her through the shop, into a light, pleasant parlor. It was in reality far pleasanter than the dark and shabby apartment which Elizabeth used to call her drawing-room, in their lodgings at Chester.

"Welcome to Hilsbury, ma'am!" said the uncle, courteously.

Elizabeth bowed; and returned laconic answers to his repeated good-natured attempts to draw her into conversation.

But Mr. Robinson, who felt more at ease, and more in his element than he had done for two years past, was in high good-humor, and very talkative.

"Bless my heart, uncle, what a nice snug little place you've got for us here!" said he, rubbing his hands, and looking round the room.

There were some neat flower-stands, set out with autumn flowers; and a very pretty painted work-table; and various little decorations; at which, however, Elizabeth was rather surprised than pleased, when she observed them.

Every part of the house wore the same appearance of neatness and comfort; and seemed adjusted by a correct taste, careful to prevent an awkward contrast between the shop and the dwelling. It was something more than neat, and yet less than elegant.

Elizabeth, as she was conducted over it, could not help wondering that the old man should have so good a notion of doing things. For he had been strictly forbidden to inform her to whose taste and activity the credit really belonged. She was indebted to Mr.

Sandford for the desire of having everything comfortable for her reception, and for the willingness to pay for
it, — but it was her friend Emily who had done the rest.

Emily, having heard Mr. Sandford expressing a wish
that things might be made as agreeable as possible to
the young lady, and lamenting his own ignorance of
these affairs, earnestly requested permission to attend
him to Hilsbury, to assist in making the requisite
preparations : which was agreed to, upon Miss Weston's offering to accompany her. And during the
time that Elizabeth was waiting at Chester, thinking
herself abandoned by all the world, her two friends
were busily employed in planning and executing those
little contrivances to make her comfortable which
would not occur to the genius of an upholsterer.

It was not till the morning of the very day on which
Elizabeth was expected, that all was in complete readiness. Mr. Leddenhurst's carriage stood at the door
to take them home. Miss Weston was quite ready to
go ; but Emily still lingered, to see if everything was
in exact order. She replaced the flowers ; then returned to adjust the folds of the window curtains ;
and stood at the parlor door, to see how it would
strike Elizabeth when she first entered. She next
returned to that which was intended to be Elizabeth's
room, — which was fortunate ; for the wind had blown
up one corner of the white napkin on the dressing-
table. Emily laid it smooth, set the looking-glass in
precisely the proper angle, once more patted the
volumes on the book-shelves quite even, and after a
moment's thought took down the handsome new Bible
which had been provided, and laid it on the dressing-
table. She then went down stairs, and having repeated
sundry injunctions to Mr. Sandford, sprang nimbly into
the carriage and drove off.

When Elizabeth arose the next morning, refreshed
from the fatigue of her journey, and opened her

pleasant window, which looked across the village street upon a fine hilly country, her spirits experienced a momentary revival – a transient glow of comfort, such as will occasionally beam out upon the deepest gloom. But it *was* transient. The sight of Mr. Edwards, the shopman, in the street below, taking down the shutters, recalled her to a sense of her unhappiness.

Comfort sounds a dull word to those who are accustomed to live upon enjoyment : to Elizabeth it had few charms. In surveying her new situation, she was rather provoked than pleased, to find there was anything to render her discontent less reasonable. She had neither philosophy enough to *be* pleased, nor good-nature enough to appear so. Indeed it is nothing less than Christian humility, that can make persons willing to be happy in any way that is not of their own choosing.

Old Mr. Sandford's was the only pleasant face that was brought down to breakfast this morning ; for poor Frederick Robinson found that the two idle years he had spent in his Majesty's service had not had the smallest tendency to lessen his dislike to useful employment. He sighed heavily, when, as soon as breakfast was over, his uncle with the promptness of an industrious man, hurried him away to the counting-house ; while Elizabeth, who scrupulously avoided engaging in anything that would seem like acquiescing in her fate, shut herself up in her room, and employed herself in unpacking her portmanteaus. When she had done so, in spite of her reluctance, she found it most expedient to put away the things in her new drawers. With a heavy heart she put by the gay dresses and ornaments, which were now useless to her ; but it was with a deeper pang that she laid aside her husband's discarded uniform. She gazed at the faded scarlet, and tarnished gold ; and felt, that that was all she had ever admired in Lieutenant Robinson.

The reserve and coldness with which Elizabeth

conducted herself towards Mr. Sandford could not overcome his good-nature. He was particularly fond of young people, and longed to express the kindness of a relation; but he was careful not to offend her by unwelcome familiarity. He saw that she was placed in a new and mortifying situation; and while he regarded her with true pity and benevolence, he treated her with such respectful tenderness as would have dispelled the gloom from many a brow.

Emily loved the old man; and he, while witnessing her cheerful, disinterested zeal in the service of her friend, and while receiving from her himself those respectful attentions which she involuntarily paid to age and worth in every station, often wished that his nephew might have made as good a choice.

Mr. Sandford had been so long absent from his own concerns, that he could only remain a few days longer, to introduce his nephew to the business. During this period he observed with some uneasiness the unpromising disposition they both discovered towards their new duties. Elizabeth sat in state all day at her work-table, leaving her domestic affairs to fate and a servant; while Mr. Robinson wished excessively to be allowed to lounge about in the same gentlemanlike idleness he had been lately used to. As to the business, his uncle and Edwards, he thought, were quite sufficient at present; but as soon as his uncle was gone, he declared that he intended to give his mind to it — "upon his word and honor he would."

Accustomed to revel at his ease at the luxurious mess, he felt it a particular hardship to have to rise in the midst of dinner to attend a customer.

"Frederick — the bell, Frederick!" his uncle used to say; but he would be so long preparing to go, that his good-natured uncle usually went himself, — Frederick contenting himself with pretending to rise, and saying, "Don't you go, sir!"

7

It was not, therefore, without anxiety that Mr. Sandford took leave of his niece and nephew.   Just before
he set off, he called the latter aside, and gave him
some good advice, particularly on the subjects of industry and frugality.

"You know, Frederick," said he, "how handsomely
Mr. Leddenhurst has come forward ; and as for me, I
have done more than I ought, in justice to your poor
sister and your cousins.   So that if you get into fresh
difficulties, you must look to others to help you out, for
I have done my utmost.   And, Frederick," added he,
in a milder tone, "while we are speaking, let me beg of
you to treat poor Mrs. Robinson with as much respect
and delicacy as possible.   You should consider that
you have brought her into a very different situation to
what she was brought up to, and it's natural she should
feel it — quite natural.   You should consider, too,
what a delicate young creature she is, and give her
every indulgence that's prudent ; and make allowances.   A little tenderness and consideration may do
a great deal in reconciling her to her circumstances."

To all this, and more, Mr. Robinson continued
saying, "Certainly, sir ; certainly, sir."   As soon as
his uncle was gone, for which all the time he had been
rather impatient, he ran up stairs to unpack a new
violin which he had brought from Chester, but which
he had not thought fit to produce during his uncle's
stay.   He always believed that he had a fine ear for
music ; and to scrape on this instrument, was one of
the accomplishments he had acquired during his life
of leisure.

The village of Hilsbury was remarkably secluded in
its situation and appearance.   It consisted of a single
street, hidden amid the solitude of fine, but barren
hills ; and, with the exception of Mr. Robinson's house,
was formed entirely of stone cottages.   The business
depended upon the custom of the neighboring farms,

and of the poor inhabitants of many little hamlets that were scattered among the hills.

In this solitude Elizabeth's days passed with dreary sameness. She used to sit by her fireside during the dark afternoons of this November, and, watching the sparks from the blacksmith's shed that was directly opposite the house, muse upon scenes of past happiness. This was her only solace ; except, indeed, that she experienced a secret satisfaction from the contrast between herself and her condition. When she surveyed her delicate form, her white hands, her beautiful hair, her dress, though unornamented, still elegant, she felt that she was still a heroine in distress. But it was a satisfaction too slight to be a real alleviation ; because there were so few to witness it, and those few so insignificant. And she now discovered — what it required some experience to believe — that it is a far pleasanter thing to be a heroine *not* in distress.

Elizabeth had been some time in her new abode, before she had once made her appearance in the shop. The first time she did so, it was to procure some articles she wanted herself. "Pray do you sell silk fringe?" she said, in the same tone and manner with which she had been accustomed to make her purchases.

While she was examining the box of fringes, and turning over card after card with her delicate fingers, some ladies from a seat at some miles' distance happened to stop at the door in a barouche. Elizabeth took no notice of them as they entered, but continued looking over the fringes, and withdrew as soon as she had found some that suited her. But just as she was quitting the shop, she had the satisfaction of hearing one of them say to Edwards, in a tone of surprise, " Is *that* Mrs. Robinson?" Elizabeth was seen reading, very intently, at the parlor window, when the barouche drove past.

There was a green in the outskirts of the village, where the neighboring young farmers used to assemble to play at cricket. Mr. Robinson was fond of this diversion; and he soon became one of the most constant attendants there.

One day, just as he had snapped to his fiddle-case, and was reaching down his hat to go to this green, Mr. Edwards walked into the counting-house.

"I just wish to say, Mr. Robinson," said he, "that I shall be obliged to you to look out for some other person to do your business, sir. It's what I never was used to, and what I can't undertake, to have everything laying upon one pair of hands; and unless you think proper to give me some assistance, Mr. Robinson, the sooner you suit yourself the better, sir."

Much as Mr. Robinson was disturbed at this speech he could not give up going to the cricket-ground; but he told Mr. Edwards he would take it into consideration, and assured him he should have some help before long. He felt, however, very much perplexed and discomfited on this occasion. There were few afflictions he dreaded so much as that of being obliged to exert himself.

As he walked down the street, wishing Edwards would not be so unaccountably lazy, and wondering what he should do, some fine nuts caught his eye, that were exposed for sale in a cottage window; he bought some — and was comforted. He was very fond of good things in general, and of these in particular; and while he sat on a seat upon the cricket-ground, cracking his nuts, he forgot his troubles; at least, they did not oppress him. There were few of the evils of life for which an apple, a nut, and especially a good dinner, would not afford him temporary relief. And if this real interest in the sweet and the savory were peculiar to persons of no higher intellectual pretensions than Mr. Frederick Robinson, it would not be at all unaccountable.

But when both the feast and the sport were over, and he was returning late in the afternoon through the village street, the lights in his shop window brought it again to his remembrance. At supper time he appeared full of thought. Elizabeth did not take suppers; she was reading the newspaper, at the further end of the room.

" I say, Elizabeth ! " said he, all on a sudden, as soon as he had finished supper.

Elizabeth looked up from the newspaper.

" There 's one thing that I have been going to speak of ever since we have been here ; and it 's what I hope you 'll not make any piece of work nor opposition about, because it 's absolutely, indispensably necessary. "

" What is that, pray ? " said Elizabeth.

" I must say, then, " continued he, " that this is the first business I ever was in, in my life, where the mistress — where the lady — did not use to go in sometimes when she was wanted. "

" What do you mean, Mr. Robinson ? " said Elizabeth.

" I mean what I say, " replied he, " I mean that it is a sin and a shame to see a woman sitting all day long in her parlor, doing of work and nonsense, when there 's a shop full of customers that want to be waited on. Why, there was Mrs. Jones, and Mrs. Johnson, and — "

" Gracious goodness ! " exclaimed Elizabeth, " this exceeds all — everything ! I really did not imagine — I confess I had not the smallest idea that any one — that you, even *you*, Mr. Robinson, would ever have thought of proposing such a thing ! "

" Bless my heart, Betsy ! what a riot for nothing ! I say, then, whatever you may think of it, something must be done. There 's Edwards this very day been

giving of me warning, because he has so much upon
his hands, and nobody to help him. As for me, you
know very well that I am confined from morning to
night to the counting-house, and can't stir; and I see
plainly the business is going to ruin. And my'uncle
will lay all the blame upon me; and all because of
your pride and nonsense."

"If there is so much business that one servant is not
sufficient, pray why cannot you keep another?" said
Elizabeth. "Oh!" added she, falling into a violent fit
of weeping, "when I left my dear, dear father's house,
how little I thought of all I was to suffer!"

Her husband was always frightened when she went
into hysterics, and he thought she was going into hysterics now; besides, he was really good-natured. So he
said, "Well, well, child, I tell you what — I'll see if I
can't get another man, or boy, or lad, or something.
So don't go and flurry yourself into those foolish fits
now, for mercy's sake!"

Mr. Robinson, however, dared not venture to take
this step, without writing to consult his uncle. And
Mr. Sandford, in reply, strongly dissuaded him from
any such expensive proceeding; but he added, that
in order to afford him some present relief, until he
became more accustomed to business, his sister Rebecca had offered, if he wished it, to come and stay a
month or two at Hilsbury, and render them all the
assistance in her power. "We can ill spare her," said
the good uncle, "but I am willing to do everything in
my power to encourage you : and in the meantime, as
it must be a few weeks before she can be with you, I
shall expect, Frederick, that you make every possible
exertion yourself, with regard to business."

This offer Mr. Robinson very joyfully accepted; and
Mr. Edwards was prevailed upon to stay, upon the
promise of an accomplished assistant in "my sister
Becky."

CHAPTER XIV.

BUT by this time Elizabeth's cheek had grown pale. She was unhappy without *éclat:* there was none to admire, none even to pity, none to wonder at her hard lot; and she was deprived of all that had the power to gratify or to excite her. Irritated, impatient, and comfortless — a stranger to the balm of resignation — she sunk into despondency; and the effect was soon visible in her altered appearance.

After several days of feverish indisposition, she became so ill as to be confined to her room. And there she found herself alone indeed. Her husband was very sorry to see her so ill; but nursing, he thought, was *women's* business. He left that to the maid; and she was an unfeeling, selfish woman, who brought up her mistress's ill-made messes with gloomy looks, and frequent murmurings.

It was towards the close of the third day Elizabeth had passed on her bed, that as she was lying feverish and comfortless — watching, in the dusk, the light of the blacksmith's shop flashing on the ceiling — she heard the door open gently; so gently, that she was sure it could not be her maid. And in an instant she saw Emily at her bedside, her countenance glowing with health and cheerfulness; and she said,

"Dear Elizabeth, I heard you were ill, and I am come to nurse you."

Elizabeth started up without speaking a word; and throwing her hot arms around Emily's neck, continued to weep a long time, with a plaintive, piteous weak cry, upon her bosom.

"Dear, dear Elizabeth!" said Emily.

It was so long since she had heard the accents of kindness, that the soothing tones of Emily's voice quite overwhelmed her.

" I did not think there was any one in the world that cared for me now," she said, at length.

" Oh, you have never been forgotten by your *friends*," said Emily. " I should have come to see you long before this, if I had been sure you would have liked it. But we will not talk much to-night, dear Elizabeth ; let me try now to make you a little comfortable," said she ; and taking off her hat and pelisse, she proceeded quietly to smooth the tumbled pillow, and restore the littered room to neatness and comfort.

She next went, to prepare a cooling beverage for the night, into the disorderly kitchen ; where the maid and the shopman were carousing over a blazing fire.

Elizabeth took readily, and with confidence, what Emily had made for her ; said it was " very pleasant ; " and soon after she sunk into a quiet sleep.

Emily sat up with her friend that night ; and when she had done all that was requisite for her, she went to the book-shelves for something to read. She first took down Elizabeth's morocco Bible ; and she sighed to see that it had the appearance of an unused book.

Emily, since they last parted, was improved in her appearance, but still more in her mind : it was now under the settled, habitual influence of religion.

Her faults, though not extirpated, were subdued ; and her once uncertain virtues shone out with the steady light of Christian graces. Her good-nature was now charity : her sensibility, benevolence ; her modesty, humility ; her sprightliness, cheerfulness.

She found that in many of her intellectual indulgences there was much selfishness, and little use ; and her frequent abstractions from the common affairs of life had in great measure given place to a cheerful performance of its quiet duties, and a ready attention to the wants and interests of others. She had lost much of her romance, but her taste was rectified : she had fewer ecstasies, but more happiness.

For several days after Emily's arrival, Elizabeth continued so ill that little conversation passed between them but what related to her present wants and sufferings. When she began to amend, the effects of her disorder, and the returning remembrance of her misfortunes, produced a state of irritable fretfulness, which Emily's invariable tenderness was unable to soothe ; and she repelled with peevishness, and almost with asperity, every effort to enliven her, or to engage her in conversation.

Emily's eyes filled with tears, whenever she contemplated the alteration that illness and unhappiness had made in her late blooming and brilliant countenance ; and she fervently wished and prayed, that her friend might be led to seek for that consolation, of which she still appeared to be wholly destitute.

Having once the Bible open in her hand, Emily ventured to say, " Would you like me to read aloud a little while ? " But Elizabeth looked at her reproachfully, and said, " No, no, I cannot bear it ; pray do not disturb me ! " Emily shut the book, and gazed at her with heartfelt pity.

One morning, as soon as she arose, Elizabeth's spirits revived on finding herself decidedly better ; for in spite of other trials, the first feelings of returning health will be feelings of happiness.

When Emily came in, she found her for the first time disposed to enter into conversation, and to tell her of her troubles : for when people begin suddenly to talk of their misfortunes, it is generally in consequence of some temporary alleviation of their pressure.

" Oh, Emily ! " said she, " I have been too ill to talk to you ; but you do not know how unhappy I am. You see, indeed, what a situation I am in. What a situation ! Oh ! my happiness is sacrificed — sacrificed for ever ! "

" Indeed I feel for you deeply, dear Elizabeth," said

Emily, after hearing her expatiate upon her grievances. "How glad I should be if I could comfort you!"

"There is no comfort for me, Emily. Can there be anything in my circumstances that could possibly afford me the smallest degree of pleasure?"

"Not *pleasure*, perhaps," replied Emily; "but is it not possible to be happy — to be contented, at least — without pleasure?"

"Oh, do not take up my words," said Elizabeth; "I really don't understand those nice distinctions. If you will not allow that I have cause to be miserable, it is because you never knew what it is to be unfortunate."

"I know you have much need of patience and of resignation," said Emily; "but, Elizabeth, I have myself seen instances of people being really happy, who have had, perhaps, as much as you have to endure."

"Yes, I know very well what you mean; but as to religion, it would never, I am confident, make any particular difference to me, if I were to give myself ever so much concern about it. Now you are exactly the kind of person to be very religious; and I am not at all surprised that you view it in that particular kind of way that some people do."

"Indeed you are mistaken," replied Emily; "so far from being naturally disposed to it, it is impossible you should feel more averse to religion — *real* religion — than I did, or more difficulty in it; and I should always have remained as ignorant and as indifferent as I used to be, if God had not made me willing, and given me the desire to seek Him. And He will give it *you* if you ask for it: and then — oh, *do* believe it, Elizabeth! — then you would be happy; happier a thousand times here, in this humble solitude, than all the splendors of the world could make you."

"But even if I were ever so — so devotional, and all that," said Elizabeth, "I am persuaded it would only continue so long as I am deprived of other things. I am certain I should never care particularly about religion, if I had anything else to take pleasure in."

"Yes, if you had once felt the happiness of loving and serving God, you would prefer it to all other pleasures," said Emily.

"It may make some people happy, and it does you, I dare say," replied Elizabeth; "but as for me, I really do not believe it ever would. Indeed I feel a dislike to the thought of the thing; and to confess the truth, I always did, even at the time that I was hearing and seeing so much of it."

"And so did I — and so does every one," replied Emily, "until a new heart and a right spirit is given; and this is what we must pray for. But oh! do not let us talk of religion as a thing we may choose or refuse like an accomplishment, according to our particular taste. We *must* be religious, — we *must* come to Jesus Christ for salvation, and love God and His service, and learn not to love the world, — or we must perish. And what should prevent you? God is not willing that any should perish."

"I do assure you," said Elizabeth, after a short pause, "that sometimes since I have been in this miserable place, I have wished I were religious; but I know that it is quite impossible I ever should be."

"Impossible! oh, no; it is impossible that such faint wishes should make you so; but with God everything is possible; and if you sincerely desire, and earnestly ask His help, you will receive it."

"You do not know my heart," said Elizabeth; "it is very different from yours."

"If God had not promised to change the heart, I must have despaired as well as you; but He will."

"What, *my* heart?" said Elizabeth.

During the latter part of this conversation, there was an appearance of sincerity and solicitude in Elizabeth that Emily had never observed in her on any former occasion. She did not, however, continue it much longer at that time, lest she should be wearied; but she was overjoyed to find that for the two or three following days Elizabeth appeared willing, and almost anxious, to renew it.

During this visit, Emily had many opportunities of observing the neglected and declining state of the business. She had even heard Mr. Robinson making some lazy complaints of the discouraging state of his affairs. In writing to her father she had mentioned this, and expressed an earnest wish that some situation could be devised for them that would be less irksome to Elizabeth, and more likely to secure their permanent comfort. Very soon after, she had the satisfaction of receiving a letter from Mr. Grey, offering — provided it met with Mr. Robinson's approbation — to use his interest in endeavoring to procure for him the situation, then vacant, of superior clerk in a concern with which he was remotely connected. The salary, he said, was handsome, and the place considered respectable. An immediate answer was required, and Emily lost no time in submitting it to Mr. Robinson's consideration.

Most people, and especially idle people, expect to be better by a change of circumstances, and he accepted the offer without hesitation.

Emily found Elizabeth employed in reading the Bible, when she entered her room to communicate the contents of this letter.

"I am sorry to interrupt you," said she, " but here is something " — offering her the letter — "that perhaps will give you a little pleasure."

"My dear girl!" cried Elizabeth, when she had hastily read it, "how shall I ever repay you and your dear, good father for this kindness? Why this is the very thing for Robinson. Let me see — what does it say? 'the place considered respectable;' that means genteel of course. Oh, Emily," said she, shutting the Bible, and rising briskly from her chair, " I feel quite well and happy ! "

" But recollect, it is still very uncertain," said Emily.

" Not *very* uncertain, my dear, surely ; your father here speaks confidently, almost, does not he ? — ' think it not unlikely my application may be successful.' "

" Not unlikely, but he is not at all sure, you see," said Emily. " I am almost sorry I told you now," added she, as she looked at Elizabeth's animated and eager countenance, in which the *world* had already regained its recently banished expression.

" Dear, it would have been cruel not to have told me," said Elizabeth.

" But if you *should* be disappointed," resumed Emily, " you would *now*, I hope, know how to submit, and where to seek consolation."

" Yes, indeed, I hope I should," replied Elizabeth.

" It is the only satisfaction," continued Emily, " to commit such concerns cheerfully to Providence, know-ing they will be overruled for our real good ; it must, I should think, prevent all distressing anxiety."

" Very true," answered Elizabeth. " Emily," said she, after a short silence, " I wonder what your father means by ' a handsome salary ' — have you any idea, my dear, what it would be ? "

" No, indeed, I never heard," said Emily, sighing : and she almost regretted that the application had been made.

Nothing was now talked of but the expected ap-pointment ; and Emily found, with deep concern, that it was in vain to attempt engaging Elizabeth in the conversations which had lately seemed to interest and affect her. She either answered with indifference, or, — what was still more painful to Emily, and discour-aged her most from attempting it, — she adopted her old artificial manner, in talking about religion.

After only a week's suspense, a letter arrived from Mr. Grey, to inform them that his application in behalf of Mr. Robinson had been unsuccessful.

Elizabeth was busy at her drawers examining some dresses, which till now had not seen the light since she came to Hilsbury, when Emily, with a heavy heart, entered with her father's letter. She put it into her hand, and withdrew in silence.

Mr. Robinson's disappointment was more vociferous, but less acute, than Elizabeth's. In her mind a relish for the world had been aroused too actively to subside again with the hopes that excited it. She was first stunned, then irritated, by the intelligence. She referred again and again to the unwelcome letter; but still the decisive words " unsuccessful application," left her nothing to hope.

She had not learned to acquiesce in adversity, and at first refused to believe that she must actually submit to it. If *this* plan had failed, *something*, she thought, might be done; and her mind ranged with impatient ingenuity from scheme to scheme, as each appeared more impracticable than the former, — till at last she was compelled to believe, that there was nothing before her but submitting to present circumstances. When after a long train of thought she arrived at this conclusion, she again burst into a passionate fit of impatient sorrow.

When Emily joined her, she did not attempt to offer ill-timed reflections; they passed the greatest part of the day in silence; and it was not till Elizabeth had recovered from the surprise of disappointment, that she began to recollect there was still *one* way of being happy that was not unattainable. How many are driven to religion as a last refuge, who would never have chosen it as the first good !

As they were sitting together in the evening, Elizabeth broke a long silence by saying, in a voice between penitence and peevishness,

" Is not this exactly what I told you — that I should never care about religion if I had .anything besides to take an interest in? I have scarcely given it a thought the last week, Emily, and now what is there but that to comfort me ? "

" Oh, Elizabeth ! then is not this a happy disappointment? Be thankful that you were not *abandoned* to prosperity."

" But now," said Elizabeth, " now that I have been again as unconcerned, and indifferent, and ungrateful as ever — how can I hope to be forgiven? "

" God's ways are not like ours," answered Emily ; " His invitations are made to the unconcerned and the ungrateful. But when we have refused to surrender our hearts to Him till they have made trial of every other object, it should make us more humble and more thankful, that He will at last accept such a worthless, ungenerous gift."

The tears were starting in Elizabeth's eyes while Emily was speaking ; and when a little more had passed, she thought it best to leave her alone, and silently withdrew.

Elizabeth had sometimes said her prayers, but she had never *prayed;* and she now for the first time felt a real desire to do so. As soon as Emily was gone, she sunk down by the bedside ; she wept, but was unable to utter a word, — overwhelmed with the strange, glowing feeling of *sincerity*, and with the new and mighty effort to express a deep, inward sentiment, to a Being invisible and hitherto wholly unknown. They who do not know that prayer is an effort requiring all the energies of body and mind, may question whether they ever have prayed.

After a while, she knew not how long, Elizabeth rose up from her knees, exhausted, but yet relieved.

When Emily returned to her, she was struck with an expression of meekness and *reality* in her countenance, that was not natural to it.

" Emily," said she, in a faltering voice, " I have been attempting to — pray ! but I cannot."

"Then I believe you *have* prayed, dear Elizabeth," said Emily. ' "It is only in *real* prayer that there is any difficulty. It was easy to *say* our prayers, as we used to do ; but now you feel the difference between that formal service and calling upon God in spirit and in truth."

To Elizabeth, however, although a desire and a hope had suddenly sprung up in her mind, that gave her a new and strange sense of satisfaction, the difficulties in her way appeared at first insurmountable. Nor was it surprising that to a person of her character, religion, as it now appeared to her — an inward, heartfelt, all-pervading principle — should seem an almost unattainable good.

A single glance at its reality convinced her, that those things must be sacrificed to it from which she had ever derived her choicest gratifications. It was not so much that any particular pursuits were to be relinquished, — this had been the least and lightest sacrifice, — but the inmost recesses of her heart must yield up their long secreted idolatries.

CHAPTER XV.

IF Elizabeth's religion had expended itself in words and emotions, it would have been, as before, of a very doubtful character. But she soon gave the best evidence of its reality, by her anxiety to bring her daily conduct under its universal influence. She had, however, at present much to subdue, and much to learn. She and Emily had many conversations on the subject of her future conduct.

" I believe," said Elizabeth, as they were talking of these things one evening, " that I could be happy now in a cottage, almost in any situation, especially with a companion I could love ; but the business — the trade — I cannot tell you, Emily, how unpleasant it is to me ; only I hope I am now willing — more willing at least, to submit to what is unpleasant."

" But in time," said Emily, " may not you become almost reconciled even to this? — especially if you *could* so far overcome your reluctance as to take an interest in it yourself; and you are so clever, and have so much taste, that — "

" Dear, do you think so ? " interrupted Elizabeth.

" That I am sure," continued Emily, " Mr. Robinson would soon find an alteration in his affairs, if you were once to attend to them."

" But then there 's Robinson ! Emily, you know I *cannot* love him."

" Cannot you ? " said Emily. " But yet," added she, after a long pause, " I have thought sometimes, you might treat him with a little more respect and — kindness ; and then perhaps — "

" I know it — yes, I know I ought ; and I *will* endeavor," said she. And here the conversation ended ; for the time was come which Elizabeth now regularly devoted to her evening retirement.

She had learned the pleasure and privilege of daily " entering into her chamber, and shutting to the door ; " and it was there she could best fortify herself for any self-denying resolution. But in doing so, she was a wonder to herself. That *she* should find happiness in such engagements, — that an hour spent in meditation and prayer should to *her* be the happiest of the day, —

" Strange were those tones, to *her* those tears were strange,
She wept, and wondered at the mighty change."

That night Mr. Robinson came in to supper with a

8

gloomy countenance. Everything was going wrong. Business dull, money scarce, Edwards saucy ; but what really oppressed him most of all was the weight of his own indolence.

When Elizabeth came down from her room, she had evidently been in tears, but she did not look gloomy, and going towards her husband, she said, ·

" Are you tired to-night ? "

" Rather, my dear — not very, though, thank you," said he, unfolding his arms, and brightening up at the unexpected attention.

While they were at supper, after two or three unsuccessful efforts to speak, Elizabeth at length said,

" Mr. Robinson, you spoke to me some time ago about assisting you in the shop. I refused then, but now I have determined to do it ; and I intend to begin as soon " — and her voice faltered — "as soon as I am well enough to stand in the cold."

" Dear me ! will you ? " said her husband in unfeigned astonishment.

But Elizabeth, overcome by the effort she had made, burst into tears, and could not reply.

, " But I would not have you to do it upon any account, if it frets you thus," added he.

" Oh, she is not fretting, " said Emily, " she likes it ; only " — and here she stopped, at a loss how to make Mr. Robinson comprehend why anybody should *cry* at what they *like*.

" I shall be of very little service at first," resumed Elizabeth, in a firmer voice ; " but I hope I shall learn in time ; and as your sister is coming, and you find Edwards so inattentive and troublesome, I think it would be best to part with him, and we will endeavor to manage the business among ourselves."

" Well, I assure you I shall be glad enough to get rid of that idle dog, — that is, if you really intend it, my dear," said he.

" Yes, I really intend it," said Elizabeth.

And she retired to rest this night, with a calm sense of self-approval that she had seldom known. It was the genuine pleasure with which most instances of self-denial are rewarded — the pure satisfaction of sacrificing inclination to principle.

The next day, while they were at dinner, the stage coach, which once a week passed through the village, drove by their window ; and Mr. Robinson started up, exclaiming,

" There's my sister Becky ! " — and immediately set off to receive her.

" I wonder what sort of a being she is," said Elizabeth.

" We shall soon see," said Emily.

In a few minutes Mr. Robinson returned, laden with packages ; and introduced his sister to the ladies.

Elizabeth held out her hand to one of far less delicate texture, and endeavored to receive her new relation with cordiality : but Miss Rebecca's first appearance was not prepossessing. She was a plain person, much marked with the small-pox, and appeared about forty years of age. Her dress was far from untidy ; but it showed that total deficiency of taste which is betrayed by some persons, who without much ambition to be *smart*, would yet fain appear a little like other people : besides, she was now in her travelling *déshabille*. But when she spoke, there was a softness in her voice, and a propriety in her mode of expressing herself, that instantly made a favorable impression.

For a person in Miss Rebecca's circumstances to conduct herself with exact propriety towards such a sister-in-law as Elizabeth, would not appear very easy ; but she seemed to understand this secret to perfection. There was a certain independence in her character, that made her feel at ease, and enabled her to retain her self-possession on every occasion. Although fully conscious of her own inferiority in those respects, she was not to be overawed by such things as wealth, beauty, or elegance in others. Her behavior was uniformly obliging, courteous, and respectful; but it was never servile — never for a moment — to the grandest carriage customer that ever entered her uncle's shop.

Elizabeth took some pains to check the feeling of contemptuous pity, which the first appearance of her new relation had excited.

But she soon found that this effort was quite unnecessary. A person of good nature, sound sense, and consistent piety — and who makes no absurd pretensions — is not so easily despised as people may imagine. Miss Rebecca answered this description; and Elizabeth had not spent many hours in her society, before she found that she absolutely commanded her respect.

As they became better acquainted, Elizabeth and Emily were surprised to perceive how far removed she was from vulgar ignorance. This discovery, however, was not made by her introducing the names of all the books, and quoting all the authors she could recollect, on the first day of her arrival, but by the general superiority and intelligence of her conversation.

She had been in the habit of reading as much as her engagements would permit, from the honest desire of improving her mind, not with the most remote intention of making it a subject of vulgar boast. In the course of her life she had waited upon many a well-dressed supercilious customer, to whom it would have been in her power to have imparted some useful information; but she never felt disposed to make an unbecoming advantage of her acquisitions. If her mind was superior to her station, it did not disqualify her for its duties, nor lead her to despise them; for her little stock of knowledge had been turned to the

best account; it had made her not vain, but wise —
not ridiculous, but respectable.

There was no one who ever had so much influence
over Frederick Robinson as his sister. While he was
at his uncle's he was continually embroiled in some
dispute with his cousins, or the apprentices, or the
servants. A consciousness of his own weakness made
him exceedingly tenacious of his rights and privileges,
and jealous of his dignity: so that he was always imagining the one invaded, and the other insulted. In
these disputes his sister Rebecca was the universal
peacemaker; every one was willing to appeal to her;
and even Frederick would submit to her decisions.

Since her arrival he had been unusually attentive to
business; and the scraping of the violin was rarely
heard till shop was shut in the evening. Indeed, in
three days after she came, everything wore a different
aspect. Without bustle or parade, her pervading management had restored order in the counting-house, the
shop, and the kitchen. Her attentive and obliging
manner to the customers was soon noised abroad;
and many who had been offended by the neglect of
the master, and impertinence of the man, began to
return.

Elizabeth was not more agreeably disappointed in
her sister-in-law, than Miss Rebecca was in her. She
listened with tears of joy, while Emily related the
change which had recently taken place in her friend's
mind; and Emily was rejoiced, when she became
acquainted with her character, to commit Elizabeth's
yet weak and fluctuating principles to her superinten-
dence. Young as she herself was in Christian knowledge, she was glad to be relieved from the burden of
such responsibility, and to consign it to one on whose
experience and judicious management she could so well
rely.

When she had done this, Emily took leave of Hilsbury ; her heart glowing with joy and gratitude, as she contemplated the unexpected issue of her visit.

Elizabeth, who had dreaded the familiarity of a vulgar relation, was the more touched by the true delicacy of Miss Rebecca's manner towards her. A fair form and delicate complexion — much as one might wish to believe it — are not the invariable indications of a delicate mind ; while it often happens that this jewel is concealed within a plain, ungraceful exterior.

When Elizabeth witnessed how much might be effected by activity and management, she was strengthened in her determination to remain no longer a useless incumbrance in her own household : and having made an ingenuous confession of her ignorance, she requested to be instructed in all the mysteries of domestic economy. Miss Rebecca undertook this task with perfect simplicity. She took great pains in instructing her, without suffering her to feel it a mortification to be taught.

Emily had not flattered her, in saying that Elizabeth was clever. Her talents had hitherto been exercised to one unproductive end ; but now she felt the pleasure of exerting them usefully and honorably ; and she made rapid progress, not only in the attainment of those things of which she might feel ashamed of being ignorant, but also in her knowledge of the business, her ignorance of which was no disgrace.

It required, however, an effort — and an effort of something better than philosophy — on the morning she went in to take her first lesson behind the counter. Still pale from the effects of her recent illness, she appeared, wrapped in a large shawl ; but as she entered the shop, a deep glow passed over her cheeks. Miss Rebecca did not feel less on this occasion than Elizabeth, but she contrived to be quite engaged at the time with a customer, and did not seem to notice her as she walked round and took her station by her side.

A country girl happened to come in at the same instant, who, addressing herself to Miss Rebecca, said,

"I want a yard and three-quarters of — your servant, miss," said she, perceiving Elizabeth, and dropping a courtesy.

"What did you want, pray?" said Elizabeth, graciously.

While she was showing the article inquired for, Elizabeth observed that her customer's attention was diverted from that to herself. She was glancing at her, and at her dress; and seemed admiring the white hands that were unrolling the ribbons, still more than the bright, glossy articles themselves. When Elizabeth had dismissed her first customer, she whispered with a smile to Miss Rebecca, "Really it's not half so disagreeable as I expected!"

Elizabeth's good principles were too recently implanted to have attained the force of habits; and she found a constant reference to them necessary upon every fresh occasion. The exercise of patience, self-denial, forbearance, humility, was new and difficult. Indeed, had other dispositions, or better education, rendered them of easier attainment, the strength and reality of her piety had been less apparent. It was in no instance more so than in her conduct towards her husband. She was solicitous not only to fulfil her ordinary duties towards him, but to win him to partake of that happiness which she herself enjoyed.

"If religion," she said, "were to do as much for him as it has for me, we might be most happy together." And it was especially with this view that she endeavored to subdue the constant propensity she felt to treat him with harshness or indifference.

"That tiresome violin!" said she, one evening, as they caught its distant sound from the counting-house.

"I must say, however," said his sister, "that he does not suffer it to be very troublesome to us; I do not remember ever seeing it brought into the parlor."

"No, I confess he has never done that," said Eliza-beth.

"Do you think," she resumed, after a long silence, "do you think he would be pleased if I were some-times to ask him to play to me?"

"That he would, I am certain," said his sister.

That her resolution might not have time to relax, she went out immediately, and opening the door of the counting-house, said, good-naturedly,

"Mr. Robinson, you keep it all to yourself; why don't you come and play to us sometimes?"

"Dear me! I am sure I had no idea you would like to hear me play; why it's what I should like of all things," said he, gathering up the music-books, and proceeding briskly to the parlor.

"What shall I play to you now?" said he, in high good-humor, "anything you like, only say."

His sister chose something she thought Elizabeth would prefer; and Elizabeth, pleased with herself, found her spirits enlivened even by her husband's bad fiddling; and the evening passed more cheerfully than usual.

Accustomed to be despised, and to be thwarted, he was always particularly gratified by any mark of atten-tion or compliance; and a little such kindness and consideration produced the happiest effects upon his temper. It was in this way — and it was the only one practicable — that his sister recommended Elizabeth to attempt to acquire an influence over him. He had always been proud of his wife, and would have loved her, after his manner, if she would have permitted it; and now that her conduct towards him was so much altered, he began to be "very fond of her indeed."

Miss Rebecca did not offer to leave Hilsbury till she had the satisfaction of seeing her brother's affairs in a very different state to that in which she had found them. The business was increasing; he himself appeared disposed to take some interest in it; and as for Elizabeth, she was become both willing and able to superintend and conduct their concerns.

But she had derived still more important advantages from her sister's society. Herself an experienced Christian, she had led Elizabeth on step by step, as she was able to bear it, till she saw her making real progress both in the knowledge and practice of religion.

Having thus spent three useful months with them, she was at length obliged to take leave. They parted with mutual affection and regret; and Elizabeth was left alone to manage her house, her business, her husband, and — herself.

CHAPTER XVI.

ONE morning in the spring, a carriage stopped at Mr. Robinson's door.

Emily was the first who sprang out of it; and she was followed by the whole party from Stokely.

Elizabeth colored high as she advanced from behind the counter to receive them. But their easy, affectionate salutation quickly relieved her embarrassment. She led the way to her little parlor. Mr. Leddenhurst, as he followed her, looked neither to the right hand nor the left, but steered his way through the piles of goods that stood in the shop, and stooped beneath the festoons of drapery that decorated the passage door, as though he saw them not.

As this narrative is so near its conclusion, it may be imagined that the Leddenhursts were come to announce to Elizabeth some sudden change of fortune; or, perhaps, to make her a present of one : — but no ;

they were only come for the pleasure of seeing her —
for the pleasure of seeing Elizabeth happy in obscurity.

They were affected by the striking alteration in her
whole appearance since they last met, simple in her
dress, almost artless in her manner, the once restless
and ambitious turn of her countenance succeeded by a
subdued and tranquil expression.   As Miss Weston sat
gazing on her, her eyes filled with tears, in spite of her
efforts to restrain them.

The good opinion Elizabeth had once so unsuccess-
fully practised to win, was now spontaneously yielded.
She had never in former times received such gratifying
expressions of their regard.   It was not, as she had
dreaded, the affability of condescension to her reduced
station, but the open, cordial aspect of friendship and
esteem.

Their visit was prolonged to several hours, and they
had much conversation with Elizabeth; who, when
the first feeling of constraint had worn off, spoke of
herself and her situation without reserve.   This afforded them an opportunity of observing more minutely
the real change that had taken place in her character.
Their expectations were not disappointed, because
they were not raised unreasonably high.   They did not
expect to find propensities and habits of twenty years'
growth completely extirpated in the course of a few
months, even under the influence of the most potent
of all principles.

In Elizabeth's present retirement, there was, indeed,
little temptation or opportunity to *display*, if that
word be understood in its commonest import; but
there is no retirement, except that of the grave, where
the infirmities of human nature may not find opportunity to exhibit themselves.

Pride is rather provoked than checked by degradation, and never was vanity cheated into humility by
being placed in the shade.   Elizabeth still found no

duty she had to perform was so difficult, no act of self-denial so painful, as to watch, detect, and subdue it; especially in the new and more subtle forms in which it now frequently assailed her. But it was no longer a studied and cherished indulgence. Philosophy might have enabled her to detect, and pride to conceal it: but it was religion that had taught her to lament it as a sin, and to resist it as an enemy.

They found her even more reconciled to her condition than they had hoped. Time had already worn off the edge of mortification. She was no longer surprised, or shocked, to find herself where, and what, she was. She took an interest in her employments; and was alive to the honest pleasure of successful management. Besides, she was *occupied:* and the busy cannot, if they would, be as discontented as the idle. Employment, that *second* grand secret of happiness, had contributed more than anything, except the *first*, to reconcile her to her circumstances. Above all, she had inward peace; and a hope, that was better to her than either the vain pleasures or real comforts of life. It was "a hope, full of immortality;" and enabled her "in whatever state she was, therewith to be content."

During their visit, Elizabeth took her friends over her neat, orderly house; and into her pretty, retired garden, which was now looking gay with spring flowers.

"You would be surprised," said she, "to see how many little pleasures I have now; — and that from things which I never took any real pleasure in before. Even my taste is improved by religion. I am not so selfish — so engrossed in" — but here she checked herself, and began to speak of something else. Talking of *herself*, she observed, was particularly hazardous; and she found it a good rule never to do so — not even to speak of her faults unless it was unavoidable.

While Mr. Leddenhurst and Mr. Robinson were

gone aside to transact some business, Elizabeth and her friends conversed still more unreservedly. " I assure you," said she, looking on the carpet, " I am happier in all respects than I ever expected to be. Mr. Robinson is really much more — much less — much improved. Dear Emily," she added, " I often, very often, think of that dreary, feverish night, when you came to nurse and comfort me : from that I date all my happiness ! "

" Let us rather both think," said Emily, " of that happy day that brought our friends to Stokely ; it is to *them* we both owe everything that is good."

" We can all now," said Miss Weston, " look back to the time when we were unacquainted with God, and with ourselves, — when religion was uninteresting to us ; and to whatever circumstances we may trace the wondrous change, let us acknowledge *Him* as the sole and gracious author of it."

" And now, sir," said Mr. Leddenhurst, when they returned to the ladies, " we hope to prevail upon you to part with Mrs. Robinson, before long, to pay us a visit at Stokely."

" To be sure I will," replied he, " with a great deal of pleasure, Mr. Leddenhurst ; she deserves a little recreation now, as well as any woman in the world ; and I 'll be bound to say, that there 's no place whatever where it would give Mrs. Robinson so much pleasure to pay a visit."

" It would, indeed, give me a great deal of pleasure," said Elizabeth ; " I have nowhere such kind friends. I should like, too, to visit Broadisham once again, — if it were only to think of all that has passed since I last drove out of it."

" Ah, that was on our wedding-day," said her husband.

" Then you will come, my dear," said Mrs. Leddenhurst.

" Yes, she has promised," said Emily.

Her friends now took an affectionate leave of Elizabeth. Before the carriage drove off, they all looked out at her as she stood by her husband's side at the shop-door. There was a tear in her eye, but she strove to conceal it ; and her countenance shone with content.

" This is a sight," said Mr. Leddenhurst, " worth coming more than fifteen miles to see : — the subjugation of a propensity that I had almost thought incurable ; and I believe that nothing but *religion* will cure the love of — DISPLAY."

A DAY'S PLEASURE.

ONE fine May morning a large party of young people, of which I was one, set off for the purpose of viewing a nobleman's seat at some miles' distance. This was an excursion to which we had for some time been looking forward with much pleasure. It had been long promised us, and the day fixed more than once; but the weather, or some other untoward circumstance, had hitherto disappointed us. But now every obstacle was removed, the party assembled, and when, after many presages of bad weather, with which some of the least sanguine and more experienced of our number had alarmed us the night before, — when, after all these forebodings, the carriages drew up, and we found ourselves safely seated and driving off, there was not an eye that did not sparkle with pleasure.

The morning was bright and promising. Who does not know — who, at least, does not *remember* — how unusually blue and bright the sky appears on a holiday morning? The fields were yet sparkling with dew-drops. Some early husbandmen, going forth to their work, saluted us as we passed. The lark sang merrily over our heads. There was not a cloud — no, not one, to be seen from east to west. Oh, it was a lovely morning! We were in open carriages; which was the more agreeable as the first part of our road, especially, lay through a most delightful country, richly cultivated, and now all covered with the verdure of spring. We were, as may be imagined, in the highest spirits, and laughed we knew not why. When the first glow of happiness, occasioned by setting off, had sub-sided, we began to expatiate on the expected pleasures of the day. The place of our destination was one of the finest seats for many miles round. We had heard it talked of very often ; but none of us young ones had yet seen it. Most of the beauties and curiosities had been described to us, and on these our imaginations fixed with delighted anticipation ; — the grotto ; the hot-houses, with their rare collection of foreign plants ; the picture-gallery ; and, above all, the curious old tapestry hangings, which decorated one of the apart-ments, and which were esteemed the greatest curiosity of the place. Then there was the fine Belvidere at the top of the hill, which commanded, we were told, a most extensive prospect. You might from thence see five counties : and on a very clear day you might just distinguish Gloucester Cathedral. "Well, we could not have a clearer day than this," said we : "so we shall see five counties, and Gloucester Cathedral ! " Thus we went chatting along.

But we had scarcely reached the third mile-stone, before our pleasure was greatly damped by the indis-position of one of our party. She had risen with the headache, but strove to conceal it. However, it be-came so much worse with the motion of the carriage that she was quite unable to proceed : so with great reluctance we were obliged to leave her at a friend's house, which stood by the roadside. This misfortune cast a gloom upon us during the greater part of the ride. She was one of the most lively and intelligent of our whole party ; there was not one but could have been better spared. However, as we drew near the end of our journey our spirits revived, and our regret for the loss of our companion gradually subsided.

But now a new cause of uneasiness arose.   A few
rather threatening clouds had for some time been gathering in the southwest, which the elder part of the
company regarded with an anxious eye.   We young
ones, however, were persuaded they would soon pass
off; and as they began to gather overhead, we declared
that we should prefer it being cloudy during the heat
of the day.   "Yes, it would be much pleasanter!"
Just as I said the word, I felt a large drop of rain upon
my cheek, which was quickly followed by many more;
and now the most sanguine of us took the alarm.   When
we were yet a mile from the place of our destination, a
soaking shower came on, to which, being without any
shelter, we were completely exposed.   Still, we tried
to laugh at our misfortunes, — till, upon approaching
the place, the rain fell with redoubled violence; and as
we galloped up the avenue, it ran streaming off in
spouts and torrents from our hats and parasols.   We
had, therefore, little inclination to look about us.   The
first thing, as soon as we arrived, was to beg the charity
of the servants; and we were completely occupied, for
a full hour, in drying our clothes, and refitting, before a
large fire in the housekeeper's parlor.   By the time
this was done, and we had partaken of some refresh-
ments, we began to make ourselves so merry with the
adventure that some of us thought we gained as much
in fun as we lost in sunshine.

It still rained; so giving up all thoughts of an excursion without, for the present, we proceeded to view the
apartments.   They were splendid indeed, and we were
delighted.   For my own part, the only thing that prevented my being quite as much so as I expected was, that
my exposure to the rain had brought on a slight toothache; it was not violent, but yet just enough to take off
the edge of my enjoyment.   I went about holding a
handkerchief to my face; and when any of my companions pointed me to anything remarkable, I could

only nod assent, and smile somewhat piteously. Upon inquiring for the tapestry hangings, we were informed that they were always taken down when the family was absent ; they had been removed only the day before.

The continuance of the rain, while it prevented our expected ramble about the grounds, yet afforded us an opportunity of examining more at leisure the curiosities within. With this consideration we consoled ourselves. When we had viewed every apartment, and fully satisfied our curiosity, we were joined in the picture-gallery by the old house-steward, a venerable man, who, as he told us, had served the family for upwards of fifty years. He presently began recounting to us some of the family history, and many amusing anecdotes, pointing with his staff to the portraits of those to whom they related. "This," said he, "is poor Lady Susan, who died when she was only seventeen. And there is old Sir James, taken when he was a child, playing with his favorite spaniel. He was the present Earl's great-grandfather." We were much amused with this antiquated man and his stories ; and agreed it compensated to us for not seeing the tapestry.

It was now growing late in the afternoon. We had given up all hope of reaching the Belvidere, and viewing the gardens ; and were still lingering about the picture-room, when suddenly a bright golden beam of sunshine broke into the apartment. It streamed down the long gallery, and lighted up the pale faces and faded draperies of the old brown portraits, from one end to the other. An exclamation of joy burst at the same instant from the whole party. We hastened to the windows ; already a broad line of bright sky appeared along the horizon ; the clouds were dispersing in all directions ; the rain had nearly ceased ; and the heavy clouds that were rolling off on the opposite side exhibited a brilliant rainbow. By the time we were equipped for our ramble, all was clear overhead ; it was a beautiful evening. The grass was wet to the foot, and the trees were yet dropping with rain; but all was fresh, green, and sparkling. Once again our spirits revived: it was not, indeed, the lively, bounding joy with which we set off in the morning, but a more serene and chastened feeling.

We now visited the grotto, the gardens, and hot-houses. It was but a hasty inspection, as the ground was so wet that we were fearful of lingering; we were anxious, too, to reach the Belvidere before sunset. At length, with wet shoes and weary steps, we climbed the hill. The exhalations which were now rising in conse-quence of the heavy rain, in a great degree obscured the prospect, but at the same time added to its bril-liancy; for, being illumined by the setting sun, the whole wide expanse of country which the height com-manded, was, as it were, one flood of golden mist. The five counties we had thought so much of, were not indeed so distinctly discernible as we had seen them on the map; however, our attendant pointed to each, and we believed that there they were. As for the Cathedral, we were obliged to take it for granted that it lay in the direction of the guide's walking stick. We waited a few minutes to see the sun set behind the distant hills; it was a splendid scene; and, as he assured us, was almost as fine a sight as the Cathedral.

We now descended the hill, very well satisfied; and, being by this time considerably fatigued, were not sorry to find ourselves reseated in the carriages, and on our way home. The evening continued fine, but chilly; and the latter part of the way it was very dark. At first we talked over our adventures; but some of the party soon dropped to sleep, and conversation flagged with the rest. We were weary, and our heads ached. I question if anything we had seen during the whole day afforded us more real pleasure than the sight of the cheerful lights in our own house, as we approached it. We were certainly pleased with our excursion, notwithstanding its misfortunes; and yet I believe, had it been proposed to us to set off on a similar expedition the next day, we should none of us have been disposed to comply. The friend we left ill by the way, we found quite restored. She had spent the day at home very happily; and when she heard of our misfortunes, was glad she had escaped them. We were all thankful to retire to rest that night. The next morning at breakfast, at grandpapa's request, I related the adventures of the day. His reflections upon our excursion — to introduce which is my only reason for troubling the reader with this recital — shall be the subject of a following paper.

REFLECTIONS ON A DAY'S PLEASURE.

GRANDPAPA, having listened with great attention to the foregoing recital, and to our various animadversions upon it, began as follows : —

"I am an old man, children; and my *day's pleasure* is so nearly over that I am well able to compare it with yours. Our short life is but like a long day; and when I recollect the alternations of hope and fear, of success and disappointment, of pleasure and of pain, that have checkered the greater part of it, — the storms that I have seen blow up, and blow over, — the serenity of its decline, and the hopes I entertain of arriving, before long, at a safe and comfortable home, — I must say that my *day* has so much resembled yours, that what you have related has seemed like a relation of my own history. And since there has been nothing remarkable to distinguish my life from that of other men; since I have, undoubtedly, had my full share of success, prosperity, and enjoyment, I think I may fairly regard it, not only as a counterpart to my own life in particular, but to life in general. Or, to come to the conclusion I intended, that you, dear children, may consider your excursion as a fair specimen of what you have to expect in the *day of life ;* — so that the experience of this one day, may serve as a sample of all the rest. ·

"Here you are, all in fine spirits, just setting out on your journey. It is yet early morning with you ; the sun is up, and the sky clear ; the road fine and flowery ; and yet, pleasures in prospect rather than those at present possessed, are the chief sources of your felicity. The first circumstance that occurred yesterday to damp your pleasure was the loss of one of your party. Now, this is a misfortune which may be certainly expected early in the journey of life. Of a company of young people beginning life together, and hoping to pursue their course hand in hand, how commonly does it happen that one and another are stopped in their career, leaving their companions to pursue the journey without them ! And as it was with you, so it generally happens, that those who are taken are the loveliest, the liveliest, — those whose society can be least spared, and who must be the most regretted. Such a breach spoils our pleasure for a time ; but time, as you found it, and the new scenes that present themselves at every turn, reconcile us to the loss ; till at length it is little felt, perhaps, rarely remembered.

"The place of your destination, and its various curiosities, which you were so eager to see, may represent those favorite schemes and projects which we are apt to lay out for ourselves in life, and to which our chief hopes and efforts are directed. All goes on fair for a time ; we are in the direct road to our wishes ; but just as we come within sight of them, the clouds begin to gather, and down comes the storm, when, perhaps, we are driving straight up to their accomplishment. They who have marked well the ways of Providence, must have observed, that our earthly aims and wishes are oftener thus damped and embittered to us, than entirely frustrated. We are suffered to attain the object, but something unforeseen occurs to check the satisfaction we had expected in it. Now it is that our spirits sink, and we are ready to think our day's pleasure quite spoiled. But, like yours, it frequently happens that some unexpected alleviation, some little unforeseen circumstance attending our calamities, renders them supportable. Our very surprise at finding things not so bad to bear as we had expected, often amounts to positive pleasure.

" Well, you saw the apartments, and were upon the whole very well pleased. And thus it is, that we are generally indulged with a moderate share of the common comforts and enjoyments of life. We do not, perhaps, see the *tapestry*. That is, some particular gratification on which our hearts were most set is withheld. Now, while walking through the apartments, is the busy part of life ; and, notwithstanding some disappointments, our satisfaction would be considerable, if it were not for a *something*, like your toothache, my dear, to take off its edge. Nothing could more aptly represent the continual uneasiness occasioned by the little daily crosses of life, too trifling to be seriously complained of. And this is not *my* testimony alone ; the accumulated experience of ages will attest that some such nameless sources of dissatisfaction ever attend upon all our pursuits and undertakings, and mingle even with our holiday pleasures.

" It was a fine morning ; but it rained all day. Ah ! this is like life. You may not think it, children ; but I *know* it. Yet this very circumstance, it seems, was productive of some advantage. Thus every wise and good man will look back on seasons of adversity, and acknowledge that it was good for him to have passed through them. When you had given up all hope of fine weather, you were suddenly surprised with a ray of sunshine. Thus are some of the heaviest storms of life suddenly dispersed; not in the time and manner that we had expected, but in such a way as we could not have calculated upon. You did, therefore, at last, view the grounds, and climb the hill; but it was late in the day, with wet shoes and in haste. Just as we are often not permitted to arrive at the summit of our desires until the decline of life, when it can be possessed but for a short time, and when our capacities for enjoyment are greatly weakened. You reached the Belvidere, and had an indistinct view of the five counties; but that circumstance, which you had so long anticipated, disappointed your expectations; and as for the cathedral, it was not to be seen at all. Thus when we are permitted to reach the height of our wishes, the result is sure to disappoint us. Our imaginations had painted it too gayly; and our chief satisfaction arises, not so much from the success of our scheme, as from some simple circumstance attending it, which, like the fine glowing sunset, was unthought of in our calculation.

"You were cheered by the sudden fineness of the evening, and the late accomplishment of your hopes; but, like the chastened tranquillity of age, your cheerfulness was of a very different character from the lightsome, joyous spirits of the morning.

" After all, though you had some entertainments upon the whole, yet, if you had the offer of going over the same events to-day, you would not feel disposed to accept it. Now, this is what I, and every one, I believe, of my age, must say of *our* day's pleasure. Could our youth be renewed like the eagle's, yet we should decline the offer, if it must be upon the con-

dition of living over again all the vicissitudes and anx-
ieties, all the sorrows and sins of the past. Wearied
even with pleasure, you were glad to set off on your
return home. The evening was chilly and dark; and
you were more disposed to sleep than to converse.
This, as you see in your poor old grandfather, is not
unlike the condition and infirmities of old age.

"Thus far our comparison is pretty exact; and well
will it be for us if it need not stop here. The sight of
home at last, gave you, perhaps, more true pleasure
than anything you had seen in the day. And there
are some who can say the same of the long home to
which they are hastening. All are, more or less,
weary of life and need rest: yet, how many shrink
from, and at last come short of it. You had a kind
father to receive you, and a comfortable home; and
the companion you dropped at the commencement of
your journey was ready to welcome your return. And
if it should be thus with us at the end of the day of
life, it will signify little, indeed, what accidents befall
us by the way. 'In our Father's house are many
mansions.' 'There is a rest remaining for the people
of God.' And there, many dear friends who are gone
before await our arrival. They regret not that they
were stopped short in their course, but, like your friend,
rejoice that they got safe home so early, and thus
escaped all the misfortunes of the road.

"Your day's pleasure is now over: and you all feel
that the little accidents which disconcerted you yesterday, are of no consequence at all *to-day*. You can
now smile at its misfortunes; and as for its pleasures,
they are *past*, and are now nothing to you. But
suppose you had found no home to return to; or an
uncomfortable one, exposed to the weather, and filled
with bad, quarrelsome company! Of how much
greater value is the smallest convenience and comfort
you enjoy here, because it is to last for years, than all

the pleasures of that one day, put together! Or suppose that from morning to night it had been one continued storm; suppose you had not been able to reach the place of your destination at all; that *many*, instead of one, of your company had been left behind; that your carriages had broken down, and every other misfortune had befallen you that can be imagined, — what then? Your day's pleasure would have been spoiled, it is true; but it was only a day, and now all is over. Now, this is just the state of the case with regard to time and eternity; only the comparison falls far short of the truth. They who, devoted to the pleasures of this life, take no care to ensure an entrance into that rest, act infinitely more unwisely than you would have done, if, for the sake of enjoying that one day's recreation, you had left your house to be overrun with robbers, or destroyed by fire; knowing that upon your return at night, you would have no shelter, no home, no father to receive you.

"But is it true that our youthful hopes are so fallacious; that there are so many drawbacks to our pleasure; and that there is so large a mixture of pain? What does this teach us? First, not to give life a wrong name. After all, it is not a day of *pleasure*, but a day of *business*. We came into life, not to please ourselves, but to do the will of Him that sent us; and especially, 'to work out our salvation with fear and trembling.' Again, we should learn hereby 'not to set our affections on things below.' It is to teach us *this* lesson, which we are slow to learn, that so many trials are allotted us. Our Heavenly Father does not willingly afflict and disappoint us. He does it in mercy, to wean us from the world to which we cling. We should also learn, by the disappointments attending our schemes, not to desire to order our own lot in life; since we cannot foresee how they will succeed, nor what will most promote our welfare. Let us leave it to Him, who sees the end from the beginning, and who will then cause 'all things to work together for our good.' Above all, let us learn to care less for the things of time, and more for those of eternity. Do not our years pass like 'a tale that is told'? Let us therefore fear, lest a promise being given us of entering into His rest, any of us should seem to come short of it."

Thus grandpapa concluded his discourse; which, thinking it might prove instructive to others as well as to ourselves, I have, as I promised, transcribed for the perusal of the reader.

LUCY'S WISHES.

LUCY had been standing one afternoon for nearly an hour at the parlor window, watching the carriages and passengers in the street. Idleness ever begets discontent : but instead of laying the blame upon herself, she felt disposed to complain of her condition. Almost every stranger that passed, she concluded was in happier circumstances than herself. She observed stages and carriages of various kinds, driving up to the great inn on the other side of the way. She watched the passengers as they alighted and set off again; wondered who they were, whence they came, whither they were going, and envied them because they were not staying at home. A travelling chaise, with ladies in pretty riding dresses, stopped to change horses. "Ah," thought she, "how happy they are ! going some delightful journey — hundreds of miles perhaps, and to see thousands of curiosities ; or to live at some elegant country seat : at any rate they are not staying at home like me. How long have I been confined to this dull town, and this one house!" She then cast a forlorn glance around the room, every object in which had been familiar to her from her infancy. Then looking over to her opposite neighbors, she saw a blazing fire, and the family seated round it. "How comfortable they are!" thought she; "so cheerful, so sociable: telling some interesting story, perhaps; not all alone in a dull room like me!"

When it grew too dark to see distinctly what was passing in the street, Lucy slowly moved from the window and seated herself by the fire; where, fixing her eyes upon the red cinders, she fell into a deep revery; and began to consider what situation she would choose for herself, if she might but change her condition. Her imagination still followed the travelling party she had seen stop at the inn; and she first thought she should like to be a companion to those ladies; to read to them, walk with them, and attend them wherever they went. "But how foolish!" thought she; "while I am wishing, why not wish myself one of the ladies themselves? Yes, yes, a rich heiress, very handsome, fortune at my own disposal; a thousand a year — no, five, — or suppose ten thousand a year. Should my father and mother be alive? Perhaps they would not allow me to travel and do as I pleased; so they should have been dead some years and I would have a very agreeable young person for a companion. But poor papa and mamma!" thought Lucy, "no no, they should not be dead then; but still I should have the fortune in my own hands, and do just what I pleased with it. And I would be an only child, and not have any brothers or sisters to tease me." She next proceeded to settle the number of her servants, the color of her carriages and liveries; in what counties she would have her country seats, and in what square her town house: till the number of her

wants, and the splendor of her establishments, increased so surprisingly, that she began to fear her
means would be insufficient, and she found it expedient
at once to increase her income from ten to twenty
thousand a year.

Just as Lucy had arrived at this conclusion, her
mother entered the room, and put a stop to her meditations. She was beginning to converse with her
daughter about the book they had been reading together in the morning; but Lucy, finding that subject
very dry in comparison with her late brilliant specu-
lations, soon interrupted it by relating as much as she
thought proper of what had been just passing in her
mind. Her mother, when she had finished, endeavored to prove that she would probably not be at all
happier for such a change of circumstances. Lucy
knew not what to say to her representations; yet she
did not feel convinced, and said, " Well, then, mamma,
if wishing were of any use, and if you were exactly in
my place, what would *you* wish for? What is the happiest situation in all the world that you can think of ?"

" If wishing were of any use, then," said her mother,
" I might, in the first place, wish to be about that age
when the dangers of infancy and the follies of childhood are past; but when the opportunities and advantages of youth are yet to come. I would not wish to
be grown up, because then the character is fixed; and
I should lose the unspeakable advantage of having it
yet in my power to form a good one. I might also
wish for a sound, vigorous constitution. With regard
to personal beauty, as there are some disadvantages
connected with it, and as many who do not possess it
make greater proficiency in the things most important
to happiness than those who do, I would not wish
about it; but make up my mind to be contented with
whatever external appearance I happened to have. I
should certainly wish to have kind parents; not such

as would indulge my follies and spoil my temper; but parents able and willing to train me up in the way I should go, to impart useful instruction, and correct my perverse dispositions. I would also wish for brothers and sisters, some of them nearly of my own age; as it would not only render my life more social and cheerful, but give me an opportunity. of cultivating amiable and generous feelings, instead of growing selfish and self-important, as is sometimes the case with an only child. I might further wish my parents to be in easy circumstances, such as would allow them to give me a good, useful education, to supply my common wants, and to afford me a few rational pleasures. But I would by no means wish to be very rich, nor in the highest ranks of society, because it is universally allowed by men of the greatest wisdom and experience, that persons in the middle ranks of life are the most advantageously circumstanced for the attainment of virtue and happiness. Nor would I by any means wish for a fortune in my own hands till I was well qualified to manage it; for there cannot be a greater misfortune than for a person to be left to his own guidance at the early age we are supposing. I would only wish, therefore, for a moderate allowance from my parents, such as would enable me to indulge a few reasonable wishes, and that I might have a mite of my own to give to the poor, and to contribute towards some of the institutions for doing good to my fellow-creatures. In addition to all this, I might, if it were worth while, wish to live in an agreeable neighborhood, where there were a few young people of my own age and rank, with whom I might occasionally associate. I might also desire to live in a pleasant convenient house, with a garden; perhaps I might wish my parents to allow me a little garden of my own, to cultivate at my leisure hours; and that my own room should be furnished with a suitable library, and other means of instruction and amusement; and I would have regular hours for business and recreation."

"O how delightful!" exclaimed Lucy; "I can fancy exactly what kind of a house and garden it is, and what kind of people they are. I think you are a very good wisher indeed. Now that is exactly what I should like."

"Indeed!" said her mother; "and who do you think is the fortunate young person I have been thinking of all the time, with whom you would so much like to change places?"

Lucy thought for a moment, and then exclaimed,

"O mamma! you have been playing me a trick. You have been thinking of me, I do believe! Yes, for I am just the age that you said; and I have kind parents to instruct me, and they are not very rich; and I have brothers and sisters of my own age to associate with, and a few young friends besides; and I have an allowance to do what I please with; and I am not very handsome; and I live in a convenient house, tolerably pleasant, with a garden, and have a garden and room of my own, and books and globes, — dear, how foolish I was not to find it out at first! Well, but how is it then that I am not as happy as I thought I should be with all those things? Why was I so dull and uncomfortable this afternoon, that I thought everybody better off than myself?"

"I'll tell you the reason, my dear," replied her mother; "we have still left something out. The situation I have described, and in which precisely you yourself are placed, is certainly, as far as outward things can go, one of the happiest in the world; and in such a world as this, a change for you would almost certainly be for the worse; but then we must remember that no situation, no possible combination of circumstances, can make us perfectly happy in this world, because it is a sinful world. When we fancy others better off than ourselves, it is only because we know our own circumstances, but do not know theirs. Those ladies whom you imagined to be so happy only because they were travelling, and wore pretty riding dresses, have, very probably, some outward trial, or some secret uneasiness, which makes them less so than you. But besides this, there are, as I said, some things which we have forgotten to include in our list of desirables; and they possess this great advantage above all the rest, that if we wish for them aright, wishing will not be vain. I would therefore, in addition to all we have mentioned, wish for an amiable, obliging disposition; a cheerful, open temper; a peaceable and contented spirit. I would wish also, for industry and activity, which are the best securities against languor and discontent; and without which, no circumstances can make us happy. Above all, I would desire a good conscience, and a heart right towards God. These are things, my dear Lucy, which, if we wish for, not feebly and lazily, but seriously and earnestly, may certainly be obtained. With these, in any circumstances, we shall be happy; and without them, we should not be contented, even with twenty thousand a year!"

EVERY MAN HIS OWN FORTUNE-TELLER.

THERE is a strong propensity in the human mind to look forward to distant years, and to penetrate the secrets of futurity. This desire, in the minds of the vulgar and ignorant, has given rise to the foolish and wicked practice of consulting pretended fortune-tellers. In these enlightened days, I have little fear that any of my readers should wish to have recourse to such absurd

and sinful means of information ; and yet as, it is very
likely they may sometimes feel curiosity respecting their
future destiny, they will I hope listen to the plan I have
to propose, — which, without incurring either guilt or
disgrace, will enable them, each for himself, to foretell
with considerable accuracy, what they may have to expect in future life.

To prevent disappointment, I here candidly confess
that I do not pretend to enable them to divine the
amount of their fortunes, what connection they may
form, in what parts they may reside, nor at what period
they will die. Nor do I regret this ; nor need they ;
since these are circumstances which it is better for us not
to know beforehand. But with regard to things of still
greater importance than these, such as the degree of
success and of happiness they may reasonably expect
in their undertakings and situations in the world, they
will find the proposed method may be depended on.

I shall, then, suppose myself to be consulted by a
number of young persons, wishing to be initiated in my
secret ; but they will not find me commencing my instructions with any mystical ceremony, nor pronouncing
any unintelligible charm. I do not even wish to examine the palms of their hands, although I may perhaps
take the liberty to notice the expression of their faces ;
all I require is, some insight into their present characters and past conduct.

Suppose one of them, for instance, should appear to
be a lad of an indolent, inactive disposition ; to whom
exertion, whether of body or mind, was always irksome
and burdensome, performed as a task, and by compul-
sion ; he is looking forward anxiously to the time when
coercion will cease, and when he shall be free from the
necessity of exertion. In this case, I do not hesitate
to shake my knowing head, and in the technical language of my profession to pronounce " bad luck to
him." I need not ask, nor can I guess, what may be

his line of business, nor what the extent of his capital ; but I can foretell, with great confidence, that he will be neither successful, respectable, nor happy. That when restraints are removed, and he is thrown upon himself, life will be burdensome to him ; and that it will, very probably, end in poverty and disgrace.

I shall suppose my next applicant to be a gay young lady, desirous of knowing how soon she shall be her own mistress, and how large her fortune will be ; as she is in want of a thousand things that she is not allowed to purchase. She is very fond of jewels and laces, and of all that is showy and expensive ; and wishes extremely to be able to gratify her desires. Here again, I could augur no good ; so many husbands and fathers have been ruined by expensive wives and daughters. For, as poor Richard says, " silks and satins put out the kitchen fire." What could I see in her destiny but bills and bailiffs, a husband in prison, children in want, and herself in indigence ?

Another approaches with his pockets stuffed with gingerbread, and his hands full of macaroons ; he professes himself to be so fond of good things that he spends the greater part of his pocket money at the pastry-cook's ; his parents allow him to partake of every dish that comes on the table, and to stuff as long as he pleases ; and he owns that he considers dinner-time the best part of the day. I need not feel this young gentleman's pulse in order to predict to him an impaired constitution, and an early decay of his mental powers. Complicated disease, and premature old age are the invariable rewards of indulgence. These habits will increase with his years ; a listless, burdensome life, and early death is his probable destiny.

The next applicant appears with a frowning brow, and a discontented, clouded aspect. His temper is sullen and obstinate, or fretful and irritable. He wishes to know if anything agreeable will ever befall him, for at present he has known only unhappiness. Alas, nothing but unhappiness can I predict to him. He may grow rich and prosper in the world, but he will ever " dwell in *Meshech* : " his family will dread, and his neighbors dislike him ; and his gold, if he has it, will never purchase that ease and content which is the reward of good-nature only.

Another inquirer I shall suppose to be an undutiful son, who has ever rewarded his parents' care and kindness with neglect, disrespect and disobedience. Now, on this case I can pronounce with a greater degree of certainty than on any of the preceding. Some faults never appear to meet their proper punishment in this world ; but it is a common remark, founded on long observation, that unkindness to parents, above all other crimes, reaps its reward even here. This youth then, if he becomes a parent, will be taught by refractory, rebellious children the anguish he has inflicted on his own parents. A rebellious son, an ungrateful daughter, must expect in due time to become an unhappy father, or despised mother.

Another informs me he has had a religious education, and that he is in a great degree aware of the importance of religion, and of the value of his soul ; moreover, he intends before long to give it the attention it demands ; but hitherto he has delayed to do so, from time to time, hoping it would be less difficult at some future period than it appears now ; so that, at present, he is as far from being truly religious, as he was when first he began to think upon the subject. Now it requires little sagacity to foresee the probable consequences of this temper. I solemnly warn him that the same indisposition that has hitherto prevailed, will, unless strongly counteracted, continue and increase ; while he is intending and purposing, his heart will grow harder and harder, until it will finally be said of him, " Cut it down, why cumbereth it the ground ? "

I fear I shall be regarded as a gloomy prognosticator ; but I dare not depart from the rules of my art, which are founded on universal experience, and on the established laws of cause and effect. However, lest I be thought too discouraging, I am happy to proclaim that these destinies are, by no means, at present, to be considered as unchangeable. On the contrary, if the indolent should be roused, by a dread of the consequences awaiting his disposition, to become active and industrious ; the extravagant, moderate and frugal ; the indulgent, self-denying and abstemious ; the ill-tempered, mild and amiable ; the undutiful, affectionate and tractable ; and if the procrastinator resolves at once that he will serve the Lord, then it is obvious that all my dark predictions will be immediately reversed.

For instance, let us suppose an inquirer of a different description to any of the foregoing. A modest, ingenuous youth now approaches, wishing to know what encouragement he may expect in his exertions. He confesses that he is not gifted with superior talents, and therefore does not hope to arrive at any distinguished eminence. It appears, however, that he early acquired habits of attention and industry ; that he has courage and perseverance to press forward in his undertakings in spite of difficulties, till he has conquered them ; that although his real wants are amply supplied, he has been trained in frugality and self-denial ; therefore his wishes are few and moderate, so that he has always his mite to spare for the poor and the destitute. He cannot boast of rich or powerful patrons, but his temper is sweet, and his manners obliging, by which he obtains the good-will of his neighbors. Moreover, he is a good son and a kind brother ; and having been taught that " the fear of the Lord is the beginning of wisdom," he has already found " His ways to be pleasantness, and his paths peace." Now, without presuming to guess whether this will be a rich man, I hesitate not to pronounce him a happy one. He may encounter difficulties, and pass through trials, but "his bread will be given him, and his water will be sure," especially "that bread which he casts upon the waters will return" to him, when it is wanted, though "after many days." It is, besides this, more than probable that he will eventually he successful even in his temporal affairs ; that he will be "blessed in his basket and his store ;" rear an affectionate family ; be beloved by his friends, and respected by all ; finally, he will die in peace, and at last " enter into the joy of his Lord."

It is not unusual for fortune-tellers to predict the day of death ; and although, as I said, I make no such pretensions, it may yet be expected that I should not be totally silent on the subject. And while they who presume to do so are miserable deceivers, I can with the most absolute certainty foretell what it is much more important to know, namely, that "it is appointed unto all men once to die ;" the day and hour is indeed unknown ; and yet each one may, for himself, look forward to a period not very distant, when he may be quite certain that he shall have reached his "long home." To know that we must die one day is a far more interesting fact than to know *what* day ; and this is a circumstance which, surely, we may all foretell for ourselves.

Is it not strange, that the grandest event of our existence — that part of our fortunes which it is of infinitely greater consequence we should foreknow than whether we are to be princes or beggars — we should so seldom inquire about, although it is more easily ascertained than any question respecting our temporal affairs? I mean, whether we are going to heaven or hell. Now, to know this, we have only to ask whether or not we are Christians. If conscience allows us humbly to hope that we are so, in the Scriptural sense of the word, then we are sure that the Lord is gone " to prepare a place for us" among the "many mansions in his Father's house." But if we know that we are not true Christians, nor earnestly striving to become such, then, the awful probability is, that we are doomed to the place "prepared for the devil and his angels."

Thus, having explained and exemplified my method, so as to render it clear to their comprehensions, I trust that every one of my readers will be able to predict all that is good for them to know concerning their future lives ; and I doubt not they will find it profitable to do so. Should any think it an unsatisfactory and uncertain plan, or flatter themselves, that although they may answer some of the above descriptions, yet, that they shall escape the appropriate punishment, I must tell them that it is for want of knowing the world and themselves, and for want of considering the natural and inevitable consequences of things.

A new year is now commencing. Let every one inquire how they have begun it. Is it with a resolution to make renewed efforts to overcome their bad habits, and to improve their manners and characters ; and have they actually begun to make such efforts? Then I prophesy a happy new year to them ; and that if they persevere in their resolutions, it will be the happiest they have ever known. But if, on the contrary, they are beginning it in the old way, not more attentive to business, nor watchful of their tempers and conduct, not more concerned for their intellectual and religious improvement than heretofore ; then, although they may very likely have had a merry Christmas, I cannot wish them a happy new year, because I know it would be in vain to do so. For the saying is as true as it is trite, that to be happy we must be good. The knowledge of this is, in fact, the grand secret of my art ; and it is by consulting this simple rule, that every man may be his own fortune-teller.

THE LIFE OF A LOOKING–GLASS.

To the Editor of the "Youth's Magazine":

Sir, — It being very much the custom, as I am informed, even for obscure individuals to furnish some account of themselves, for the edification of the public, I hope I shall not be deemed impertinent for calling your attention to a few particulars of my own history. I cannot indeed, boast of any very extraordinary incidents ; but having, during the course of a long life, had much leisure and opportunity for observation, and being naturally of a reflecting cast, I thought it might be in my power to offer some remarks that may not be wholly unprofitable to your readers.

My earliest recollection is that of a carver and gilder's workshop ; where I remained for many months, leaning with my face to the wall ; and having never known any livelier scene, I was very well contented with my quiet condition. The first object that I remember to have arrested my attention was what I now believe must have been a large spider, which, after a vast deal of scampering about, began, very deliberately, to weave a curious web all over my face. This afforded me great amusement ; and not then knowing when the livelier objects were destined to my gaze, I did not resent the indignity.

At length, when little dreaming of any change of fortune, I felt myself suddenly removed from my station ; and immediately afterwards underwent a curious operation, which at the time gave me considerable apprehensions for my safety. But these were succeeded by pleasure, upon finding myself arrayed in a broad, black frame, handsomely carved and gilt ; for

you will please to observe that the period of which I
am now speaking was upwards of fourscore years ago.
This process being finished, I was presently placed,
very carefully, in a large packing-case, and sent a long
journey, by wagon, to London. That I may not be
tedious, I will not here stay to relate the surprise and
terror I endured during this transportation ; nor the
serious apprehensions I entertained that my delicate
frame would never survive the jolts and jars it underwent in the course of it. Indeed, I have reason to
believe that I was in imminent danger many times ;
not to mention the extreme darkness and dreariness of
my situation. How sincerely did I then wish to be
replaced in my old quiet corner ; which appeared
cheerfulness itself, compared with my present forlorn
condition. So little are we capable of judging what
circumstances will eventually prove most conducive to
our happiness ! At last, after many, to me, unintelligible movements, I found to my great joy that my
prison was being unbarred. The cheerful light once
again shone upon me ; and a person, whom I afterwards found to be my new master's apprentice (and
with whom I soon became well acquainted) lifted me
carefully out. No sooner had he cleared away from
my face the straw and paper with which I had been
well nigh suffocated, than, as I observed, he gave me
a very significant look ; which, to confess the truth, I
took, at the time, for a compliment to myself; but I
have since learned to interpret such compliments more
truly. Striking, indeed, was the contrast between my
late mode of life and that to which I was now introduced. My new situation was in the shop window,
with my face to the street, — which was one of the
most public in London. Here my attention was at
first quite distracted by the constant succession of
objects that passed before me. But it was not long
before I began to remark the considerable degree of

attention I myself excited; and how much I was distinguished, in this respect, from my neighbors, the other articles, in the shop window. I observed that passengers, who appeared to be posting away upon urgent business, would often just turn and give me a friendly glance as they passed. But I was particularly gratified to observe, that while the old, the shabby, and the wretched, seldom took any notice of me, the young, the gay, and the handsome, generally paid me this compliment; and that these good-looking people always seemed the best pleased with me; which I attributed to their superior discernment. I well remember one young lady, who used to pass my master's shop regularly every morning in her way to school, and who never omitted to turn her head to look at me as she went by; so that, at last, we became well acquainted with each other. I must confess, that at this period of life, I was in great danger of becoming insufferably vain, from the attentions that were then paid me; and, perhaps, I am not the only individual to whom a sudden removal from retirement to a more public mode of life, has proved a hazardous and trying event to the character; nor the only one who has formed mistaken notions as to the attentions they receive in society.

My vanity, however, received a considerable check from one circumstance; nearly all the goods by which I was surrounded in the shop window, though many of them much more homely in their structure, and humble in their destinations, were disposed of sooner than myself. I had the mortification of seeing one after another bargained for and sent away, while I remained, month after month, without a purchaser. At last, however, a gentleman and lady from the country, who had been standing some time in the street, inspecting, and, as I perceived, conversing about me, walked into the shop; and after some altercation with my master, agreed to purchase me: upon which I was once more packed up, and sent off on a longer journey than before. I was far less disconcerted, this time, by my unpleasant circumstances, than during my first journey ; concluding they would terminate, as before, in a change for the better, — another proof of our incompetence to judge of the real tendency of passing events. I was very curious, you may suppose, upon arriving at my new quarters, to see what kind of life I was likely to lead. I remained, however, some time unmolested in my packing case, and very *flat* I felt there. Upon being, at last, unpacked, I found myself in the stone hall of a large, lone house in the country. My master and mistress, I soon learned, were new-married people, just setting up house-keeping ; and I was intended to decorate their best parlor ; to which I was presently conveyed ; and after some little discussion between them in fixing my longitude and latitude, I was hung up opposite the fire-place, in an angle of ten degrees from the wall, according to the fashion of those times. I felt, at first, very well pleased with my new situation, and looked with complacency upon the various objects before me, which, like myself, were then new and handsome. But perhaps I should have experienced some dismay, if I could have known that I was destined to spend fifty years in that spot without undergoing any change myself, or witnessing any in the things that surrounded me, except, indeed, that imperceptibly produced by time.

Yes, there I hung, year after year, almost in perpetual solitude. My master and mistress were sober, regular, old-fashioned people ; they saw no company except at fair time and Christmas day ; on which occasions only, they occupied the best parlor. My countenance used to brighten up, when I saw the annual fire kindled in that ample grate ; and when a cheerful circle of country cousins assembled round it. At those times, I always got a little notice from the

young folks ; but those festivities over, and I was con-
demned to another half year of complete loneliness.
How familiar to my recollection at this hour, is that
large, old-fashioned parlor ! I can remember, as well
as if I had seen them but yesterday, the noble flowers
on the crimson-damask chair-covers and window-
curtains ; and those curiously carved tables and chairs.
I could describe every one of the stories on the Dutch
tiles that surrounded the grate ; the rich china ornaments on the wide mantel-piece ; and the pattern of
the paper-hangings, which consisted alternately of a
parrot, a poppy, and a shepherdess — a parrot, a poppy, and a shepherdess. The room being so little used,
the window-shutters were rarely opened, but there
were three holes cut in each, in the shape of a heart,
through which, day after day, and year after year, I
used to watch the long, dim, dusty sunbeams, streaming across the dark parlor. I should mention, however,
that I seldom missed a short visit from my master and
mistress on a Sunday morning, when they came down
stairs, ready dressed for church. I can remember how
my mistress used to trot in upon her high-heeled
shoes, unfold a leaf of one of the shutters, then come
and stand straight before me ; then turn half round
to the right and left ; never failing to see if the corner
of her well-starched handkerchief was pinned exactly
in the middle. I think I can see her now, in her
favorite dove-colored lustring (which she wore every
Sunday in every summer for seven years at the least),
and her long full ruffles, and worked apron. Then
followed my good master ; who, though his visit was
somewhat shorter, never failed to come and settle his
Sunday wig before me.

Time rolled away : and my master and mistress,
with all that appertained to them, insensibly suffered
from its influence. When I first knew them, they
were a young, blooming couple as you would wish to

see : but I gradually perceived an alteration. My mistress began to stoop a little ; and my master got a cough, which troubled him, more or less, to the end of his days.   At first, and for many years, my mistress's foot upon the stairs was light and nimble, and she would come in as blithe and as brisk as a lark ; but at last, it was a slow, heavy step ; and even my master's began to totter.   And, in these respects, everything else kept pace with them.   The crimson damask that I remembered so fresh and bright, was now faded and worn ; the dark polished mahogany was, in some places, worm-eaten ; the parrot's gay plumage on the walls grew dull ; and I myself, though long unconscious of it, partook of the universal decay.   The dissipated taste I acquired, upon my first introduction to society, had long since subsided ; and the quiet sombre life I led, gave me a grave, meditative turn.   The change which I witnessed in all things around me, caused me to reflect much on their vanity ; and when, upon the occasions before mentioned, I used to see the gay, blooming faces of the young saluting me with so much complacency, I would fain have admonished them of the alteration they must soon undergo ; and have told them how certainly their bloom, also, must fade away as a flower.   But, alas ! you know, sir, looking-glasses can only *reflect*.

After I had remained in this condition, to the best of my knowledge, about five and forty years, I suddenly missed my poor old master.   He came to visit me no more ; and by the change in my mistress's apparel, I guessed what had happened.   Five years more passed away ; and then I saw no more of her.   In a short time after this, several rude strangers entered my room ; the long, rusty screw, which had held me up so many years, was drawn out ; and I, together with all the goods and chattels in the house, was put up at auction, in that very apartment which I had so long

peaceably occupied. I felt a good deal hurt at the
very contemptuous terms in which I was spoken of by
some of the bidders ; for, as I said, I was not aware
that I had become as old-fashioned as my poor old
master and mistress. At last I was knocked down for
a trifling sum, and sent away to a very different
destination.

Before going home to my new residence, I was
sent to a workman to be refitted in a new gilt frame ;
which, although it completely modernized my appearance, I must confess, at first, set very uneasily upon
me. And now, although it was not till my old age, I
for the first time became acquainted with my natural
use, capacity, and importance. My new station was
no other than the dressing-room of a young lady, just
come from school. Before I was well fixed in the
destined spot, she came to survey me, and with a look
of such complacency and good-will, as I had not seen
for many a day. I was now presently initiated in all
the mysteries of the toilet. Oh, what an endless
variety of laces, jewels, silks, and ribbons ; pins, combs,
cushions, and curling-irons ; washes, essences, pow-
ders, and patches, were daily spread before me ! If I
had been heretofore almost tired with the sight of my
good old mistress's everlasting lustring, I really felt
still more so with this profusion of ornament and preparation. I was indeed, favored with my fair mistress's
constant attentions. They were so unremitting as
perfectly to astonish me, after being so long accustomed to comparative neglect. Never did she enter
her room, on the most hasty errand, without just
vouchsafing me a kind glance ; and at leisure hours I
was indulged with much longer visits. Indeed, to
confess the truth, I was sometimes quite surprised at
their length ; but I don't mean to tell tales. During
the hour of dressing, when I was more professionally
engaged with her, there was, I could perceive, nothing

in the room, in the house, nay, I believe nothing in the world, of so much importance in her estimation as myself. But I have frequently remarked, with concern, the different aspect with which she would regard me at those times, and when she returned at night from the evening's engagements. However late it was, or however fatigued she might be, still I was sure of a greeting the moment she entered; but instead of the bright, blooming face I had seen a few hours before, it was generally pale and haggard, and not unfrequently bearing a strong expression of disappointment or chagrin.

My mistress would frequently bring a crowd of her young companions into her apartment: and it was amusing to see how they would each in turn come to pay their respects to me. What varied features and expressions in the course of a few minutes I had thus an opportunity of observing!— upon which I used to make my own quiet reflections.

In this manner I continued some years in the service of my mistress, without any material alteration taking place either in her or in me. But, at length, I began to perceive that her aspect towards me was considerably changed, especially when I compared it with my first recollections of her. She now appeared to regard me with somewhat less complacency; and would frequently survey me with a mingled expression of displeasure and suspicion, as though some change had taken place in *me*, though I am sure it was no fault of mine; indeed, I could never reflect upon myself for a moment. With regard to my conduct towards any of my owners, I have ever been a faithful servant; nor have I once, in the course of my whole life, given a false answer to any one I have had to do with. I am, by nature, equally averse to flattery and detraction; and this I may say for myself, that I am incapable of misrepresentation. It was with mingled sensations of contempt and compassion, that I witnessed the efforts my mistress now made in endeavoring to force me to yield the same satisfaction to her as I had done upon our first acquaintance. Perhaps, in my confidential situation, it would be scarcely honorable to disclose all I saw. Suffice it then to hint that to my candid temper it was painful to be obliged to connive at that borrowed bloom, which, after all, was a substitute for that of nature; time, too, greatly baffled even these expedients, and threatened to render them wholly ineffectual. Many a cross and reproachful look had I now to endure; which, however, I took patiently, being always remarkably smooth and even in my temper. Well remembering how sadly Time had spoiled the face of my poor old mistress, I dreaded the consequences if my present owner should experience, by and by, as rough treatment from him; and I believe she dreaded it too. But these apprehensions were needless. Time is not seldom arrested in the midst of his occupations; and it was so in this instance. I was one day greatly shocked by beholding my poor mistress stretched out in a remote part of the room, arrayed in very different ornaments to those I had been used to see her wear. She was so much altered that I scarcely knew her; but for this she could not now reproach me. I watched her thus for a few days, as she lay before me, as cold and motionless as myself. But she was soon conveyed away; and I, shortly afterwards, was engaged in the service of another mistress.

My new station was, in some respects, very similar to my last; that is, I was again placed in a young lady's apartment, where I did not doubt but I should be called to witness the same appearances and operations as before; but in this I was mistaken. The first circumstance that made me suspect my new mistress differed from my late one, was, that when she

first entered her chamber after my arrival, I observed
that she remained there for a considerable time, and
at last went out again without taking the least notice
of me. This surprised me exceedingly. The first
time I had a full view of her, was the next morning as
soon as she arose, when she came and spent a very
few minutes in my company, adjusting a neat morning
dress, and combing out some pretty, simple ringlets
upon her fair forehead. It was not such a fine formed
face as I remember my last mistress's was, when I
first entered her service; but having, by this time,
from the nature of my studies, acquired considerable
skill in physiognomy, I confess it pleased me much
better. And although I soon found I should meet with
much less attention here than I had lately been accustomed to, I was now too old, and knew too well how to
estimate those attentions, to feel at all mortified at the
neglect. The visits my new mistress paid me were very
regular. About thrice in the day she used to avail herself for a short time of my services; and while on these
occasions I never remember to have received a cross
or discontented look from her, so I never, on the
other hand, witnessed that expression of secret satisfaction, or anxious inquiry, which I had often heretofore had occasion to remark.

My mistress spent much time alone in her chamber;
but it was rarely indeed, that she took any notice of
me, except at those times when I was really wanted.
I have known her sit many a time, for two or three
hours, working or reading at the table over which I
hung, without once lifting up her head to look at me;
though I could see her all the time. I have observed
her light figure pass and repass twenty times before
me, without her once glancing at me as she went by.
Thus we lived together very good friends; neither of
us making any unreasonable demands upon the other.
Time, as usual, passed away; but I was particularly

struck in observing the different effect of his operations on the countenance of my present possessor, and that of my last. There was, of course, in a few years some visible alteration; but although the bloom of youth began to fade, there was nothing less of sweetness, cheerfulness, and contentment in her expression. She retained the same placid smile, the same unclouded brow, the same mildness in her eye (though it was somewhat less sparkling), as when it first beamed upon me ten years before.

I saw here but few fine things and little variety, — except such as the changing seasons, and a moderate attention to changing fashions occasioned, — but then, I was never annoyed, as I had been in my last place, with that heterogeneous mixture of fragments of littered finery with which the room and dressing-table used to be scattered in all directions, after the grand operation was over; and which lay full in my view for hours, till my mistress's return at night, or more often till the next morning. All here was neat and orderly; which to me was a very great accommodation; having acquired, in early life, from the orderly habits of my poor old mistress, such a love of neatness, that anything untidy was particularly offensive to me. I became, as you may easily imagine, much attached to my present employer, and wished for nothing better than to pass the remainder of my days in her service; but herein I was disappointed.

One morning early, she appeared before me, surrounded by several fair attendants, and devoted to me a little more time and attention than was usual with her. I shall never forget the expression of her countenance, as she stood arrayed all in white, and gave me one more pensive look, which I little thought, at the time, would be the last I should ever receive from her; but so it was. There was a great bustle in the house that morning (whatever was the reason), and I saw my fair mistress no more !

Ever since, I have continued in quiet possession of her deserted chamber ; which is only occasionally visited by other parts of the family. Sometimes my dear mistress's favorite cat will steal in, as though in quest of her ; leap up upon the table, purr, and sweep her long tail across my face ; then, catching a glimpse of me, jump down again, and run out as though she was frightened. I feel that I am now getting old, and almost beyond further service. I have an ugly crack occasioned by the careless stroke of a broom, all across my left corner ; my coat is very much worn in several places ; even my new frame is now tarnished and old-fashioned ; so that I cannot expect any new employment.

Having now, therefore, nothing to reflect on but the past scenes of my life, I have amused myself with giving you this account of them. I said I had made physiognomy my study, and that I had acquired some skill in this interesting science. The result of my observations will, at least, be deemed impartial, when I say, that I am generally least pleased with the character of those faces, which appear the most so with mine. And I have seen occasion so far to alter the opinions of my inexperienced youth, that, for those who pass the least time with me, and treat me with little consideration, I conceive the highest esteem ; and their aspect generally produces the most pleasing reflections.

HOW IT STRIKES A STRANGER.

IN a remote period of antiquity, when the supernatural and the marvellous obtained a readier credence than now, it was fabled that a stranger of extraordinary appearance was observed pacing the streets of one of the magnificent cities of the East, remarking with an eye of intelligent curiosity every surrounding object. Several individuals gathering around him, questioned him concerning his country and his business; but they presently perceived that he was unacquainted with their language, and he soon discovered himself to be equally ignorant of the most common usages of society. At the same time, the dignity and intelligence of his air and demeanor forbade the idea of his being either a barbarian or a lunatic. When at length he understood by their signs that they wished to be informed whence he came, he pointed with great significance to the sky; upon which the crowd, concluding him to be one of their deities, were proceeding to pay him divine honors. But he no sooner comprehended their design than he rejected it with horror; and bending his knees and raising his hands towards heaven in the attitude of prayer, gave them to understand that he also was a worshipper of the powers above.

After a time, it is said that the mysterious stranger accepted the hospitalities of one of the nobles of the city; under whose roof he applied himself with great diligence to the acquirement of the language, in which he made such surprising proficiency, that in a few days he was able to hold intelligent intercourse with those around him. The noble host now resolved to take an early opportunity of satisfying his curiosity respecting the country and quality of his guest; and upon his expressing this desire, the stranger assured him that he would answer his inquiries that evening after sunset. Accordingly, as night approached, he led him forth upon the balconies of the palace, which overlooked the wealthy and populous city.   Innumerable lights from its busy streets and splendid palaces were now reflected in the dark bosom of its noble river; where stately vessels laden with rich merchandise from all parts of the known world, lay anchored in the port.   This was a city in which the voice of the harp and of the viol, and the sound of the mill-stone were continually heard; and craftsmen of all kinds of craft were there; and the light of a candle was seen in every dwelling; and the voice of the bridegroom and the voice of the bride were heard there.   The stranger mused awhile upon the glittering scene, and listened to the confused murmur of mingling sounds.   Then suddenly raising his eyes to the starry firmament, he fixed them with an expressive gaze, on the beautiful evening star which was just sinking behind a dark grove that surrounded one of the principal temples of the city.   " Marvel not," said he to his host, " that I am wont to gaze with fond affection on yonder silvery star.   That was my home.   Yes, I was lately an inhabitant of that tranquil planet; from whence a vain curiosity has tempted me to wander. Often had I beheld with wondering admiration, this brilliant world of yours, ever one of the brightest gems of our firmament; and the ardent desire I had long felt to know something of its condition, was at length unexpectedly gratified.   I received permission and power from above to traverse the mighty void, and to direct my course to this distant sphere.   To that permission, however, one condition was annexed, to which my eagerness for the enterprise induced me hastily to consent; namely, that I must thenceforth remain an inhabitant of this strange earth, and undergo all the vicissitudes to which its natives are subject. Tell me therefore, I pray you, what is the lot of man ; and explain to me more fully than I yet understand all that I hear and see around me."

" 'Truly, sir," replied the astonished noble, " although I am altogether unacquainted with the manners and customs, products and privileges of your country, yet methinks I cannot but congratulate you on your arrival in our world ; especially since it has been your good fortune to alight on a part of it affording such various sources of enjoyment as this our opulent and luxurious city. And be assured it will be my pride and pleasure to introduce you to all that is most worthy the attention of such a distinguished foreigner."

Our adventurer, accordingly, was presently initiated in those arts of luxury and pleasure which were there well understood. He was introduced by his obliging host to their public games and festivals ; to their theatrical diversions, and convivial assemblies ; and in a short time he began to feel some relish for amusements, the meaning of which, at first, he could scarcely comprehend.

The next lesson which it became desirable to impart to him, was the necessity of acquiring wealth as the only means of obtaining pleasure, — a fact which was no sooner understood by the stranger than he gratefully accepted the offer of his friendly host to place him in a situation in which he might amass riches. To this object he began to apply himself with diligence ; and was becoming in some measure reconciled to the manners and customs of our planet, strangely as they differed from those of his own, when an incident occurred which gave an entirely new direction to his energies.

It was but a few weeks after his arrival on our earth, when, walking in the cool of the day with his friend in the outskirts of the city, his attention was arrested by the appearance of a spacious enclosure near which they passed. He inquired the use to which it was appropriated.

"It is," replied the nobleman, "a place of public interment."

"I do not understand you," said the stranger.

"It is the place," repeated his friend, "where we bury our dead."

"Excuse me, sir," replied his companion, with some embarrassment, "I must trouble you to explain yourself yet further."

The nobleman repeated the information in still plainer terms.

"I am still at a loss to comprehend you perfectly," said the stranger, turning deadly pale. "This must relate to something of which I was not only totally ignorant in my own world, but of which I have, as yet, had no intimation in yours. I pray you, therefore, to satisfy my curiosity ; for if I have any clue to your meaning, this, surely, is a matter of more mighty concernment than any to which you have hitherto directed me."

"My good friend," replied the nobleman, "you must be indeed a novice amongst us, if you have yet to learn that we must all, sooner or later, submit to take our place in these dismal abodes. Nor will I deny that it is one of the least desirable of the circumstances which appertain to our condition ; for which reason it is a matter rarely referred to in polished society, and this accounts for your being hitherto uninformed on the subject. But truly, sir, if the inhabitants of the place whence you came are not liable to any similar misfortune, I advise you to betake yourself back again with all speed ; for be assured there is no escape here ; nor could I guarantee your safety for a single hour."

"Alas," replied the adventurer, "I must submit to the conditions of my enterprise ; of which, till now, I little understood the import. But explain to me, I

beseech you, something more of the nature and consequences of this wondrous metamorphosis, and tell me at
what period it most commonly happens to man."

While he thus spoke, his voice faltered, and his
whole frame shook violently ; his countenance was pale
as death, and a cold dew stood in large drops upon his
forehead.

By this time his companion, finding the discourse
becoming more serious than was agreeable, declared
that he must refer him to the priests for further information ; this subject being very much out of his province.

"How!" exclaimed the stranger, "then I cannot
have understood you. Do the priests only die? — are
you not to die also?"

His friend, evading these questions, hastily conducted
his importunate companion to one of their magnificent
temples, where he gladly consigned him to the instructions of the priesthood.

The emotion which the stranger had betrayed when
he received the first idea of death, was yet slight in
comparison with that which he experienced as soon as
he gathered from the discourses of the priests, some
notion of immortality ; and of the alternative of happiness or misery in a future state. But this agony of
mind was exchanged for transport when he learned,
that by the performance of certain conditions before
death, the state of happiness might be secured. His
eagerness to learn the nature of these terms, excited
the surprise and even the contempt of his sacred teachers. They advised him to remain satisfied for the
present with the instructions he had received, and to
defer the remainder of the discussion till the morrow.

"How!" exclaimed the novice, "say you not that
death may come at any hour? — may it not then come
this hour? And what if it should come before I have
performed these conditions! Oh! withhold not this
excellent knowledge from me a single moment!"

The priests suppressing a smile at his simplicity, then proceeded to explain their theology to their attentive auditor. But who shall describe the ecstasy of his happiness when he was given to understand that the required conditions were, generally, of easy and pleasant performance ; and that the occasional difficulties or inconveniences which might attend them, would entirely cease with the short term of his earthly existence. " If then, I understand you rightly," said he to his instructors, " this event which you call death, and which seems in itself strangely terrible, is most desirable and blissful. What a favor is this which is granted to me, in being sent to inhabit a planet in which I can die ! " The priests again exchanged smiles with each other; but their ridicule was wholly lost upon the enraptured stranger.

When the first transports of his emotion had subsided, he began to reflect with sore uneasiness on the time he had already lost since his arrival.

" Alas, what have I been doing ! " exclaimed he. " This gold which I have been collecting, tell me, reverend priests, will it avail me anything when the thirty or forty years are expired which, you say, I may possibly sojourn in your planet ! "

" Nay," replied the priests, " but verily you will find it of excellent use so long as you remain in it."

" A very little of it shall suffice me," replied he ; " for consider, how soon this period will be past. What avails it what my condition may be for so short a season? I will betake myself from this hour to the grand concerns of which you have charitably informed me."

Accordingly, from that period, continues the legend, the stranger devoted himself to the performance of those conditions on which, he was told, his future welfare depended ; but in so doing, he had an opposition to encounter wholly unexpected, and for which he was even at a loss to account. By thus devoting his chief attention to his chief interests, he excited the surprise, the contempt, and even the enmity of most of the inhabitants of the city ; and they rarely mentioned him but with a term of reproach, which has been variously rendered in all the modern languages.

Nothing could equal the stranger's surprise at this circumstance ; as well as that of his fellow-citizens appearing, generally, so extremely indifferent as they did to their own interests. That they should have so little prudence and forethought as to provide only for their necessities and pleasures for that short part of their existence in which they were to remain in this planet he could consider only as the effect of disordered intellect ; so that he even returned their incivilities to himself with affectionate expostulation, accompanied by lively emotions of compassion and amazement.

If ever he was tempted for a moment to violate any of the conditions of his future happiness, he bewailed his own madness with agonizing emotions ; and to all the invitations he received from others to do anything inconsistent with his real interests, he had but one answer : " Oh," he would say, " I am to die ! — I am to die ! "

SOLILOQUIES OF THE OLD PHILOSOPHER AND THE YOUNG LADY.

" ALAS ! " exclaimed a silver-headed sage, " how narrow is the utmost extent of human knowledge ; how circumscribed the sphere of intellectual exertion ! I have spent my life in acquiring knowledge, but how little do I know ! The farther I attempt to penetrate the secrets of nature, the more I am bewildered and benighted. Beyond a certain limit all is but confusion or conjecture; so that the advantage of the learned over the ignorant consists greatly in having ascertained how little is to be known.

"It is true that I can measure the sun, and compute the distances of the planets; I can calculate their periodical movements; and even ascertain the laws by which they perform their sublime revolutions. But with regard to their construction, to the beings which inhabit them, — of their condition and circumstances, whether natural or moral, what do I know more than the clown?

"Delighting to examine the economy of nature in our own world, I have analyzed the elements; and have given names to their component parts. And yet, should I not be as much at a loss to explain the burning of fire, or to account for the liquid quality of water, as the vulgar who use and enjoy them without thought or examination?

"I remark that all bodies, unsupported, fall to the ground; and I am taught to account for this by the law of gravitation. But what have I gained here more than a term? Does it convey to my mind any idea of the nature of that mysterious and invisible chain, which draws all things to a common centre? I observe the effect, I give a name to the cause, but can I explain or comprehend it?

"Pursuing the track of the naturalist, I have learned to distinguish the animal, vegetable, and mineral kingdoms, and to divide these into their distinct tribes and families; but can I tell, after all this toil, whence a single blade of grass derives its vitality? Could the most minute researches enable me to discover the exquisite pencil that paints and fringes the flower of the field? Have I ever detected the secret that gives their brilliant dye to the ruby and the emerald, or the art that enamels the delicate shell?

"I observe the sagacity of animals; I call it instinct, and speculate upon its various degrees of approxima-

tion to the reason of man. But after all, I know as
little of the cogitations of the brute as he does of mine.
When I see a flight of birds overhead, performing their
evolutions, or steering their course to some distant
settlement, their signals and cries are as unintelligible
to me as are the learned languages to the unlettered
mechanic. I understand as little of their policy and
laws as they do of Blackstone's Commentaries.

" But leaving the material creation, my thoughts have
often ascended to loftier subjects, and indulged in
metaphysical speculation. And here, while I easily
perceive in myself the two distinct qualities of matter
and mind, I am baffled in every attempt to comprehend
their mutual dependence and mysterious connection.
When my hand moves in obedience to my will, have I
the most distant conception of the manner in which
the volition is either communicated or understood?
Thus in the exercise of one of the most simple and
ordinary actions, I am perplexed and confounded, if
I attempt to account for it.

" Again, how many years of my life were devoted to
the acquisition of those languages by the means of
which I might explore the records of remote ages, and
become familiar with the learning and literature of other
times ! And what have I gathered from these but the
mortifying fact, that man has ever been struggling with
his own impotence, and vainly endeavoring to overleap
the bounds which limit his anxious inquiries.

" Alas, then, what have I gained by my laborious
researches but a humbling conviction of my weakness
and ignorance? Of how little has man, at his best estate,
to boast ! What folly in him to glory in his contracted
powers, or to value himself upon his imperfect acquisitions ! "

" Well ! " exclaimed a young lady, just returned
from school, " my education is at last finished. Indeed

it would be strange, if, after five years' hard application, anything were left incomplete. Happily that it is all over now ; and I have nothing to do but to exercise my various accomplishments.

" Let me see, as to French, I am mistress of that, and speak it, if possible, with more fluency than English. Italian I can read with ease, and pronounce very well, — as well at least, and better, than any of my friends ; and that is all one need wish for in Italian. Music I have learned till I am perfectly sick of it. But, now that we have a grand piano, it will be delightful to play when we have company. I must still continue to practise a little, — the only thing, I think, that I need now to improve myself in. And then there are my Italian songs, which everybody allows I sing with taste ; and as it is what so few people can pretend to, I am particularly glad that I can.

" My drawings are universally admired, — especially the shells and flowers ; which are beautiful, certainly. Besides this, I have a decided taste in all kinds of fancy ornaments.

" And then, my dancing and waltzing ; in which our master himself owned that he could take me no further — just the figure for it certainly ; it would be unpardonable if I did not excel.

" As to common things, geography, and history, and poetry, and philosophy, — thank my stars, I have got through them all ; so that I may consider myself not only perfectly accomplished, but also thoroughly well informed.

" Well, to be sure, how much I have fagged through ! The only wonder is that one head can contain it all ! "

THE PHILOSOPHER'S SCALES.

In days of yore, as Gothic fable tells,
When learning dimly gleamed from grated cells,
When wild Astrology's distorted eye
Shunned the fair field of true philosophy,
And wandering through the depths of mental night,
Sought dark predictions 'mid the worlds of light ;
When curious Alchemy, with puzzled brow,
Attempted things that Science laughs at now, —
Losing the useful purpose she consults,
In vain chimeras and unknown results, —
In those gray times there lived a reverend sage,
Whose wisdom shed its lustre on the age.
A monk he was, immured in cloistered walls,
Where now the ivied ruin crumbling falls.
'T was a profound seclusion that he chose ;
The noisy world disturbed not that repose.
The flow of murmuring waters, day by day,
And whistling winds, that forced their tardy way
Through reverend trees, of ages' growth, that made
Around the holy pile a deep monastic shade ;
The chanted psalm, or solitary prayer —
Such were the sounds that broke the silence there.

    *   *   *   *

'T was here, when his rites sacerdotal were o'er,
In the depths of his cell, with its stone-covered floor,
Resigning to thought his chimerical brain,
He formed the contrivance we now shall explain.
But whether by magic or alchemy's powers,
We know not, indeed 't is no business of ours.
Perhaps it was only by patience and care,
At last that he brought his invention to bear.

In youth 't was projected ; but years stole away,
And ere 't was complete he was wrinkled and gray ;
But success is secure unless energy fails ;
And at length he produced *The Philosopher's Scales.*

What were they, you ask.   You shall presently see
These scales were not made to weigh sugar and tea ;
Oh, no ; for such properties wondrous had they,
That   qualities,   feelings,   and   thoughts   they   could
      weigh ;
Together with articles small or immense,
From mountains or planets to atoms of sense.
Nought was there so bulky but there it could lay ;
And nought so ethereal but there it would stay ;
And nought so reluctant but in it must go ;
All which some examples more clearly will show.

The first thing he tried was the head of *Voltaire,*
Which retained all the wit that had ever been there.
As a weight, he threw in a torn scrap of a leaf,
Containing the prayer of the penitent thief ;
When the skull rose aloft with so sudden a spell,
As to bound like a ball on the roof of the cell.

Next time he put in *Alexander the Great,*
With   a   garment   that   *Dorcas*   had   made — for   a
      weight ;
And though clad in armor from sandals to crown,
The hero rose up, and the garment went down.

A long row of alms-houses, amply endowed,
By a well-esteemed pharisee, busy and proud,
Now loaded one scale, while the other was prest
By those   mites the   poor widow   dropped   into   the
      chest.
Up flew the endowment, not weighing an ounce,
And down, down, the farthing's worth came with a
      bounce.

Again he performed an experiment rare ;
A monk, with austerities bleeding and bare,
Climbed into his scale ; in the other was laid
The heart of our *Howard*, now partly decayed ;
When he found, with surprise, that the whole of his
    brother
Weighed less, by some pounds, than this bit of the
    other.

By further experiments (no matter how)
He found that ten chariots weighed less than one
    plough.
A sword, with gilt trappings, rose up in the scale,
Though balanced by only a ten-penny nail ;
A shield and a helmet, a buckler and spear,
Weighed less than a widow's uncrystallized tear.
A lord and a lady went up at full sail,
When a bee chanced to light on the opposite scale.
Ten doctors, ten lawyers, two courtiers, one earl,
Ten counsellor's wigs full of powder and curl,
All heaped in one balance, and swinging from thence,
Weighed less than some atoms of candor and
    sense ; —
A first-water diamond, with brilliants begirt,
Than one good potato, just washed from the dirt.
Yet not mountains of silver and gold would suffice,
One pearl to outweigh — 't was " the pearl of great
    price."

At last the whole world was bowled in at the grate,
With the soul of a beggar to serve for a weight ;
When the former sprang up with so strong a rebuff,
That it made a vast rent, and escaped at the roof ;
Whence, balanced in air, it ascended on high,
And sailed up aloft, a balloon in the sky ;
While the scale with the soul in so mightily fell,
That it jerked the philosopher out of his cell.

MORAL.

Dear reader, if e'er self-deception prevails,
We pray you to try *The Philosopher's Scales.*
But if they are lost in the ruins around,
Perhaps a good substitute thus may be found :
Let *judgment* and *conscience* in circles be cut, .
To which strings of *thought* may be carefully put ;
Let these be made even with caution extreme,
And *impartiality* use for a beam ;
Then bring those good actions which pride overrates,
And tear up your *motives* to serve for the weights.

"I CAN DO WITHOUT IT."

I.

THIS is one of the best mottos in the world, or one
of the worst, according to the meaning attached to it :
which will appear from the conduct of two young
people who were acquainted with each other ; each of
whom happened to take the above sentence into frequent use. Eliza disliked and ridiculed the manner
in which it was applied by Ruth ; and Ruth could not
but disapprove of the way in which it was used by
Eliza. The purpose to which Ruth appropriated the
words, and the way in which she came to adopt them
as her motto, shall be explained in the present paper.

Her parents were persons of superior education, but
their income was limited and narrow ; so that they were
compelled by their circumstances, as well as inclined
by their good sense, to study economy. Ruth entered
into the prudent and sensible views of her parents at
an early age ; and her general conduct gave them so

much satisfaction, that on the day she was fourteen, her mother informed her that from that time she should be intrusted with the purchase and entire management of her own dress, and that her annual allowance would be increased accordingly. The sum now allotted to her was such as her mother considered sufficient, with prudence and management, to meet all her real wants and reasonable wishes.

When Ruth received her first quarterage, the possession of a sum of money so much larger than she had ever been mistress of before, made her feel a little giddy. However, she deposited it safely in her desk, resolving not to touch it till it was really wanted. Economy, her mother told her, did not consist in grudging to supply our wants, but in restraining the desires for superfluities. Not many days after she had entered upon this new responsibility, Ruth accompanied her father and mother to a neighboring market town, where they frequently went to make purchases, as they lived in the country. She had often been with them on former occasions ; but it was with sensations entirely new that she now walked through the busy streets of this town, and passed its long rows of well-furnished shops. Heretofore she had surveyed the various tempting articles they exhibited merely as an amusing spectacle ; and with no more idea of possessing any of them than one has of purchasing the curiosities of a museum. But now circumstances were altered. Here were things, and pretty things too, that she might have if she pleased. And this thought, notwithstanding Ruth's prudent temper and good resolutions, presented itself to her mind temptingly.

The first thing that struck her as a real *desideratum* was a steel purse, of which she saw several glittering in a jeweller's window. There were also silver ones, but of these she did not allow herself to think. A new purse, now that she had so much more to do with money, appeared very suitable for a first purchase.

"Mamma," said she, touching her mother's elbow, "would you stop one minute? I think I should like one of those purses." Her mother, who was aware that this day's excursion would prove rather trying to her daughter's prudence, replied, "Yes, I will stop a minute; but we will wait here, that you may have time to consider, before you go in, whether you *want* a new purse." "To be sure," said Ruth, after a moment's thought, "I have my old silk one; but then, — ah well, I can do without it," she added; and without giving another look at the shop window, she hastened on. "Now," said her mother, "you have saved five or six shillings, by that moment's consideration."

At this time beaver hats, trimmed with satin, were much worn. There was a capital hatter's in the town; where two large bow windows, furnished with every variety of shade and shape, to suit all fancies, caught the eye of the fair passenger, — some loaded with nodding plumes, others with most becoming pink satin linings, and trimmings to match, and some with broad embossed bands, and dangling tassels.

"Mamma," said Ruth again, as they passed this shop, "would you stop one minute? Don't you think a beaver hat would be very warm and comfortable for me this winter? And besides how it would save my straw! This is a very pretty one, is it not? — just my size, I should think. Shall we go in and inquire the price?"

"If you wish it, we will," replied her mother. So they entered the shop, where a genteelly dressed lady was then in the act of purchasing one of the very same shape. Ruth seeing this, jogged her mother, that she might notice such a sanction to her own choice. They now inquired the price of the article in question. "That hat, ladies, is one guinea, only," said the shopkeeper.

Ruth darted an inquiring look at her mother, to know whether she thought it cheap or dear. "You recollect

your straw hat, I suppose, my dear," said her mother.
" Straws, ma'am," interrupted the shopkeeper, " are now
considered uncommonly common, — quite *out*, in fact.
We have a surprising demand for beavers at the present
time ; our manufacturer assures me he cannot get them
made up fast enough."

Ruth's respect for beavers and contempt of straws
were wonderfully heightened by this speech.

" Allow me, ma'am," continued he, " to recommend
the young lady to try it on." Ruth knowing this would
be a hazardous experiment, again looked at her mother.
She then reflected a moment (which it must be confessed is a difficult thing to do dispassionately in a
room full of hats and bonnets), and then whispered to
her mother, " I wish we had not come in, for after all
I could do without it." " I am very sorry we have
given you any trouble, sir," said her mother to the shopkeeper, " I believe we shall not purchase one this
morning." The shopkeeper bowed coldly ; and whether
he or Ruth felt most disappointed it would be hard to
determine.

Soon afterwards her mother had occasion to go to
the stationer's. This shop displayed a great variety of
articles of different sorts and value, from toys to tele-
scopes. After looking about for some time, Ruth said
to her mother, " I am very glad I did not buy a beaver
hat, how much better it would be to have something
that would *last!* See, are not these pretty? " added
she, pointing to some small plated inkstands, " they
are only fifteen shillings, I find." Her mother smiled.
" Ah, you are thinking of my writing-desk. Very
true I can certainly do without it," continued Ruth ;
and with this consideration she got safely out of the
shop.

Her mother had now finished her business in the
town ; but as they were returning to the inn, a pastry
cook's window reminded Ruth of a new want.

" Mamma," said she, " are not you hungry? I am, very ;
had not we better go in and have something?"

" I thought you brought some biscuits in your basket," said her mother. "True, so I did," said Ruth,
" so we can do without it."

When they reached the inn, the chaise not being
ready, Ruth's mother drew out her pencil, and wrote
something on the back of a bill ; which she then handed
to her daughter, saying, " See my dear, if I have cast this
up right."   Ruth took the paper, and read the following account.

	£	s.	d.
A steel purse.	0	5	6
Beaver hat	1	1	0
Plated inkstand	0	15	0
Sundry tarts	0	0	10
Total, saved by doing without it . .	£2	2	4

Ruth smiled, and said, " Yes, mamma, it is quite right ;
and if it had not been for you I should have been quite
wrong."   " Nay, Ruth," replied her mother, " I must
give you some credit this morning, for having yielded
so easily to my suggestion.   Prudence does not consist
in not being tempted, but in not yielding to temptation.
Yes, you have saved at least 2*l.* 2*s.* 4*d.* this morning
by the timely use of those few simple words ; and I
think they would form an excellent motto for you, now
that you are intrusted with the disposal of money."
" Yes," said Ruth, quite delighted, " I can do without
it : this shall be my motto ; I will write it on the lid of
my money box ; it is an excellent motto, mamma ! "

When Ruth returned home, she was pleased to think
not only that she had saved her money, but that not
one of the articles she had wished for was really wanted.
She now congratulated herself that, to the mere pleasure of novelty, which would have lasted but a few
hours, she had not sacrificed a sum which would, by

and by, purchase things that she would really want, and that she could *not* do without. Unnecessary expenses always rob either ourselves or others. We either deprive ourselves of something essential to our comfort afterwards, or defraud the poor and destitute of their just claims. *Economy* and *liberality* go hand in hand.

Ruth found, during many future years, that the motto thus early adopted, was of excellent use as a check upon her expenditure. Indeed, it led her to form habits of self-denial which were of essential importance to her during life. She was always dressed with a graceful simplicity, far more pleasing to persons of good sense and good taste than a more studied style ; and thus, by purchasing only such things as she could not with comfort and propriety do without, she had always a little overplus with which to relieve her poor neighbors, and for other useful purposes. " Ah," said she to her mother, as she was making up a flannel gown for an old " goody " who was " sadly bad of the rheumatize," " poor Betty Brown would have been obliged to do without this, if I had not sometimes recollected — *I can do without it.*"

There is no danger of economy degenerating into covetousness, when what is saved from our needless gratification is devoted to the real wants of others.

" If I had not remembered my motto," thought she, on another occasion, " when the man called yesterday with his box of lace, I should not have had three and six pence to spare for this Bible to-day. And oh, how much better I can do without a piece of lace to my frock, than my poor neighbor can do without a *Bible !*"

How many a superfluous article of dress, how many a trifle that wearies or disgusts almost as soon as possessed, how many a needless and injurious dainty to please the palate, would be dispensed with, and how many more of the destitute might be relieved, if persons would but recollect, and recollect in time, Ruth's excellent motto — " *I can do without it.*"   \

. II.

THIS, we remarked, was one of the best mottos in the world, or one of the worst. Its excellence has appeared in the use made of it by Ruth, the economist. We shall now, according to promise, proceed to show it in its opposite appropriation. This sentence, with some variations, though not professedly adopted as a motto, was frequently employed by Eliza, by way of excuse for the negligence to which the indolence of her disposition continually inclined her. She disliked, beyond everything, that patient care which is essential to success ; which is requisite in order to do anything properly ; and which experience proves to be the best, and, in the end, the shortest way in all the concerns of life.

This temper manifested itself in Eliza at an early age. Suppose, for example, she was writing an exercise with a bad pen that spirted, or blotted, or scratched like a pin ; rather than take the trouble of mending it, she would say to herself, " It will do without it," or " I can manage without ; " and thus her writing was rarely fit to be seen.

In like manner, if a slide broke in her frock, or if the string came out of her shoe, instead of replacing them immediately, she would exclaim, " How provoking ! there 's that tiresome slide gone ! " adding " ah, well, I can do without it," and then she would beg somebody to pin it for her, — a most untidy thing certainly ; or she would go half a day slip-shod for want of a shoe-string. It was just the same if a stitch came undone in any part of her dress, or if she had torn a small rent in her frock. Instead of recollecting that true saying —" a stitch in time saves nine," she would let it go, upon the strength of her favorite saying, till it became a long job to mend it ; so that her mother used often to declare that she had more trouble with Eliza's clothes in one month, than Ruth's mamma had with hers in a whole year ; and no wonder.

Eliza met with such frequent instances of the mischievous tendency of her favorite excuse that one would have thought she might have been induced to discard it. Scarcely a day passed but she, or those around her, suffered more or less from it. Not to mention such misfortunes as the frequent falls and bruises which occurred from loose shoe-strings, and the like.

One time she sustained a considerable loss for want of replacing a button to her pocket. She found it was come off one morning ; and saying, as usual, " I can do without it," she substituted a pin. Pins, though very useful things in their way, are certainly made most use of by lazy, untidy people. Things went thus for two or three days ; but at last, as she was returning from a long walk, upon feeling for her handkerchief, she discovered that the pocket with all its contents, had 'escaped. Eliza felt this loss considerably ; for besides her thimble, a silver knife, a pencil case, and a purse with seven and sixpence in it, her pocket that day unfortunately contained a beautiful coral necklace which had lately been presented to her. A very improper place for a necklace, it will be said. Very true ; but the case was this : Eliza, being fond of ornaments, came down that day, prepared for her walk, with this necklace slipped over her tippet. To this her mother very properly objected, as having a tawdry and ungenteel appearance, and desired her to take it off. Eliza complied reluctantly ; but instead of replacing it safely up stairs, she indolently slipped it into her pocket, and thus lost it, as related above.

Another time, one of her bonnet-strings coming unstitched, she fastened it on, as usual, with a pin, and going out with it in this state, it came undone when she was walking by the river side. The wind being high, it blew her bonnet off into the water, and there she saw it sailing irrecoverably down the river, like a swan. One day her mother gave her a small phial containing an acid for taking out ink spots, and other stains ; and desired her to write a label for it. " Dear !" said Eliza, when her mother was out of hearing, "it will do just as well without it ; " so she left it as it was. Soon after, her mother feeling unwell, desired Eliza to give her a few drops of sal volatile. She went carelessly to find the phial, and snatching up this in mistake, gave her mother a dose of the poisonous fluid. Being aware of her daughter's careless habits, she fortunately tasted a little, before taking the whole, and so discovered the mistake. Thus it was that indolent habits, sanctioned by a foolish saying, endangered even the life of her mother. Eliza felt these things ; but she considered them as accidents and misfortunes, not as the natural consequences of her faults, so that they made no useful impression upon her.

It too often happened that she varied her motto by the alternate use of all the personal pronouns. *He, she, they,* or *you,* can do without it, was as commonly heard as *it.* This was usually the case when any little service was required of her by those around ; in which case, the struggle between her inactive habits and a sense of duty was quickly decided by the use of this unfriendly sentence. Her father and mother, her brothers and sisters, as well as her neighbors, missed many a kind service by this means.

It must also be observed, that Eliza rarely applied

these words to *herself* in the way of restraint. When there was anything that *she* wished for, it was seldom indeed that she said, "I can do without it;" for, to exercise self-denial, requires an effort of mind much more painful to the indolent than any bodily exertion. Eliza accordingly treated herself with everything she liked that she could by any means get the money to purchase; at the same time laughing at the frugal habits of her friend Ruth; and often prophesying that she would die a miser.

The inactivity and carelessness of Eliza's disposition extended to everything in which she was called to engage, and lamentably retarded the progress of her education. Her father and mother were anxious to furnish her with every useful acquirement in their power, with a view to her future respectability, usefulness, and independence. But to Eliza the acquisition of knowledge, of whatever kind, was extremely irksome. Nothing is to be attained without trouble; and trouble was the thing she could not endure. Whatever was proposed to her as a desirable study, she used to think, if not to say, that she could do without it. Therefore, notwithstanding the cost and pains that were bestowed upon her, she grew up ill-informed and unfurnished. Even reading was a toil which she thought she could do as well without, unless a book happened to be merely entertaining.

It will not be imagined that a person so slothful in business should be "fervent in spirit," or active in "serving the Lord." The concerns of the soul, indeed, are the first to suffer from an indolent temper. If "the kingdom of heaven must suffer violence," and if even the violent can only "take it by force," how shall the feeble and languid efforts of indolence prevail? Alas, religion was one of the things that poor Eliza was contented to do without. In spite of a pious education, and occasional impressions, she too often excused her neglect of prayer, and other means of grace, by the secret application of her favorite sentence.

At length a time arrived, long anticipated by her parents, when their circumstances rendered it necessary that Eliza should do something for her own maintenance ; and now, notwithstanding all the pains that had been bestowed upon her education, the utmost that could be said of her, in an advertisement drawn up by her disappointed father, was to this effect :

" Wants a situation as governess to the younger children in a private family, or as under teacher in a school, a young person of respectable connections who is qualified to teach the rudiments of English grammar, to superintend plain work, or to make herself useful in any way that may be required."

How different an account would have been given of Eliza's qualifications, and in how different a sphere might she have moved, if she had not so often thought and said of this attainment, and of that pursuit, " I can do without it ! "

In these humbling circumstances, she amused herself with fruitless wishes for a fortune, in order that she might not be obliged to exert herself ; not considering that the same inactive temper which makes a poor person helpless and dependent, renders the rich discontented and miserable.

We cannot stay to detail the subsequent misfortunes of Eliza.   It is sufficient to say that a time arrived when she had some practical experience of the virtues of her motto, in a way little desired.   Instead of saying, as formerly, " I can do without it," she was compelled very often to say, " I *must* do without ; " and that, not in reference to the luxuries of life, but to some of its most essential wants.   How much better it is to say, " I *can* do without it," of a superfluity, than to say, " I *must* do without it," of a comfort !   Let those who would avoid all danger of the latter, early enter into the spirit of the former ; and let them learn nicely to distinguish between those things which, without any real privation may be done without, and those which cannot be neglected but by the sacrifice of respectability, usefulness, and happiness.

THE SORE TONGUE.

THERE was a little girl called Fanny, who had the misfortune one day to bite her tongue as she was eating her breakfast. It hurt her so much that she could scarcely help crying ; and even when the first smart was over, it continued so sore that whenever she spoke it pained her considerably. Finding this to be the case, she said very pitifully to her mother, " Mamma, you can't think how it hurts me when I speak ! " " Does it? " replied her mother ; " then I 'll tell you what I would advise you to do. Resolve all this day to say nothing but what is either *necessary* or *useful ;* this will give your tongue a fine holiday, and may answer more purposes than one."

Fanny, knowing that she had the character of being somewhat loquacious, could not help laughing at this, and said, " Well, I will try for once ; so, mum ! I am going to begin now, mamma."

MOTHER. Do so ; and whenever you are beginning to speak, be sure you ask yourself whether what you were going to say was likely to be of any use, or whether it was necessary.

FANNY. Yes, yes, I will ! but don't talk to me, mamma, for fear. So saying, she screwed up her lips, and taking her work, sat for about five minutes as still as a mouse. She then looked up, smiled, and nodded at her mother, as much as to say, " See how well I can hold my tongue," still screwing her lips very tight for fear she should speak. Soon however she began to feel a great inclination to say something ; and was glad to recollect that if she could but think of anything either useful or necessary, she might speak. Whereupon she endeavored to find something to say that would come " within the act." To aid her invention, she looked all round the room.

FANNY.   Mamma, don't you think the fire wants stirring ? (This question, she thought, savored of both qualifications.)

MOTHER.   Not at present, my dear.

Then followed another long silence ; for Fanny found it vastly more difficult than she had any previous idea of, to think of anything useful to talk about ; and she knew her mamma would laugh at her if she said what was obviously idle or silly, just now. She was beginning to repent having made such an agreement, when her three elder sisters entered the room. She now thought it quite reasonable, if not absolutely necessary, to tell them of her misfortune ; which she did at considerable length, and with many needless digressions (the usual custom with great talkers); upon which they all laughed, prophesying that her resolution would not last half an hour, and rallying her for telling such a long story with a sore tongue.

Soon after, some ladies called to pay their mother a morning visit. This gave Fanny's tongue such a long rest, that the moment they were gone it seemed irresistibly to resume its wonted functions.

FANNY.   What a while old Mrs. W. has had that brown satin pelisse ! Really, poor old lady, I am quite tired of seeing her in it !

MOTHER.   How is your tongue, Fanny?

FANNY.   Oh, better, mamma, thank you, almost well.

MOTHER. I am sorry for it: I was in hopes it would have been sore enough at least to prevent your making impertinent remarks upon anybody all this day.

FANNY. No, but really, mamma, is it not an old rubbishing thing?

MOTHER. I don't know, indeed. It is no business of mine; therefore I took no notice of it.

A silence ensued after this; but conversation revived when Caroline, who had stood for some time with her eyes fixed on their opposite neighbor's window, suddenly exclaimed, "I do believe the Jones's are going to have company again to-day! The servant has just been lighting the fire in the drawing-room; and there is Miss Jones now gone up to dress. I saw her draw down the blinds in her room this instant." "So she is," said Lucy, looking up: "I never knew such people in my life! they are always having company."

"I wonder who they are expecting to-day!" said Eliza, "dinner company, I suppose."

The proceedings of their neighbors, the Jones's, continued to furnish matter for various sagacious conjectures and remarks for a considerable time. At length Caroline exclaimed with the eagerness of discovery, "Look! look! there's the baker now at the door, with a whole tray full of tarts and things. Make haste, or he'll be gone in."

LUCY. So he is, I declare; it *is* a dinner-party then. Well, we shall see presently, I hope, who are coming.

CAROLINE. O no, they never dine till five when they have company.

ELIZA. And it will be dark then; how tiresome!

LUCY. If Miss Jones is not dressed already! She is this instant come into the drawing-room.

CAROLINE. Stand back, stand back! Don't let her

see us all staring.   Ah, there she is, — got on her pink
sarcenet body and sleeves to-day.   How pretty that
dress is, to be sure !

ELIZA.   And how nicely she has done her hair !
Look, Caroline — braided behind.

LUCY.   There, she is putting down the sash.   That
chimney smokes, I know, with this wind.

FANNY.   And there is that little figure, Martha
Jones, come down now.   Do look, — as broad as she
is long !   What a little fright that child is, to be sure !

MOTHER.   Pray, Fanny, was that remark *useful* or
necessary ?

FANNY.   Oh, but mamma, I assure you, my tongue
is quite well now.

MOTHER.   I am sorry for it, my dear.   Do you
know, I should think it well worth while to bite my
tongue every day, if there were no other means of
keeping it in order.

At this the girls laughed ; but their mother resuming her gravity, thus continued :

" My dear girls, I should before now have put a
stop to this idle gossiping, if I had not hoped to convince you of the folly of it.   It is no wonder, I confess,
that at your age you should learn to imitate a style of
remark which is but too prevalent in society.   Nothing,
indeed, is more contagious.   But let me also tell you,
that girls of your age, and of your advantages, are
capable of seeing the meanness of it, and ought to
despise it.   It is the chief end of education to raise
the minds of women above such trifling as this.   But if
a young person who has been taught to *think*, whose
taste has been cultivated, and who might therefore
possess internal resources, has as much idle curiosity
about the affairs of her neighbors, and is as fond of
retailing petty scandal concerning them, as an uneducated woman, it proves that her mind is incurably
mean and vulgar, and that cultivation is lost upon
her.

"This sort of gossipping, my dear girls, is the disgrace of our sex. The pursuits of women lying necessarily within a narrow sphere, they naturally sink, unless raised by refinement, or by strong principle, into that littleness of character, for which even their own husbands and fathers (if they are men of sense) are tempted to despise them. The minds of men, from their engagements in business, necessarily take a larger range ; and they are, in general, too much occupied with concerns comparatively important, to enter into the minute details which amuse women. But women of education have no such plea to urge. When your father and I direct you to this or that pursuit, it is not so much for the sake of your possessing that particular branch of knowledge ; but that by knowledge *in general* you may become intelligent and superior ; and that you may be furnished with resources which will save you from the miserable necessity of seeking amusement from intercourse with your neighbors, and an acquaintance with their affairs.

"Let us suppose, now, that this morning you had been all more industriously inclined ; and had been engaged in any of your employments with that ardor which some happy young people manifest in the acquisition of knowledge ; would you, in that case, have felt any desire to know the date of Mrs. W.'s pelisse ; or any curiosity in the proceedings of our neighbors the Jones's? No, you would then have thought it a most impertinent interruption, if any one had attempted to entertain you with such particulars. But when the mind is indolent and empty, then it can receive amusement from the most contemptible sources. Learn, then, to check this mean propensity. Despise such thoughts whenever you are tempted to indulge them. Recollect that this low curiosity is the combined result of idleness, ignorance, emptiness and ill-nature ; and fly to useful *occupation*, as the most successful antidote against the evil. Nor let it be forgotten that such impertinent remarks as these come directly under the description of those "*idle words*," of which an account must be given in the day of judgment. Yes, this vulgar trifling is as inconsistent with the spirit of Christian benevolence, and with the grand rule of 'doing to others as we would that they should do to us,' as it is with refinement of taste and dignity of character." "Who would have thought," said little , Fanny, "that my happening to bite my tongue this morning, would have led to all this?"

"It would be a fortunate bite for you, Fanny," said her mother, "and for your neighbors, if it should make you more careful in the use of it. If we were liable to such a misfortune whenever we use our tongues improperly, some persons would be in a constant agony. Now, if our consciences were but half as sensible as our nerves, they would answer the purpose much better. Foolish talking pains a good conscience, just as continual speaking hurts a sore tongue ; and if we did but regard one smart as much as the other, it would act as a constant check upon the unruly member."

THE DISCONTENTED PENDULUM.

An old clock that had stood for fifty years in a farmer's kitchen without giving its owner any cause of complaint, early one summer's morning, before the family was stirring, suddenly stopped.

Upon this, the dial-plate (if we may credit the fable) changed countenance with alarm ; the hands made an ineffectual effort to continue their course ; the wheels remained motionless with surprise ; the weights hung speechless ; each member felt disposed to lay the blame on the others. At length, the dial instituted a formal inquiry as to the cause of the stagnation ; when hands, wheels, weights, with one voice, protested their innocence. But now a faint tick was heard below, from the pendulum, who thus spoke :

" I confess myself to be the sole cause of the present stoppage ; and am willing, for the general satisfaction, to assign my reasons. The truth is, that I am tired of ticking." Upon hearing this, the old clock became so enraged that it was on the point of *striking*.

" Lazy wire ! " exclaimed the dial-plate, holding up its hands.

" Very good ! " replied the pendulum, " it is vastly easy for you, Mistress Dial, who have always, as everybody knows, set yourself up above me, — it is vastly easy for you, I say, to accuse other people of laziness ! You, who have had nothing to do all the days of your life but to stare people in the face, and to amuse yourself with watching all that goes on in the kitchen ! Think, I beseech you, how you would like to be shut up for life in this dark closet, and wag backwards and forwards, year after year, as I do."

" As to that," said the dial, " is there not a window in your house on purpose for you to look through ? "

" For all that," resumed the pendulum, " it is very dark here ; and although there is a window, I dare not stop, even for an instant, to look out. Besides, I am really weary of my way of life ; and if you please, I 'll tell you how I took this disgust at my employment. This morning I happened to be calculating how many times I should have to tick in the course only of the next twenty-four hours. Perhaps some of you above there, can give me the exact sum."

The minute hand, being quick at figures, instantly replied, " Eighty-six thousand, four hundred times."

" Exactly so," replied the pendulum. " Well, I appeal to you all, if the thought of this was not enough to fatigue one ! And when I began to multiply the strokes of one day by those of months and years, really it is no wonder if I felt discouraged at the prospect. So, after a great deal of reasoning and hesitation, thinks I to myself — I 'll stop."

The dial could scarcely keep its countenance during this harangue ; but, resuming its gravity, thus replied :

" Dear Mr. Pendulum, I am really astonished that such a useful, industrious person as yourself should have been overcome by this sudden suggestion. It is true you have done a great deal of work in your time. So we have all, and are likely to do ; and although this may fatigue us to *think* of, the question is, whether it will fatigue us to *do ;* would you now do me the favor to give about half a dozen strokes, to illustrate my argument ? "

The pendulum complied, and ticked six times at its usual pace : — " Now," resumed the dial, " may I be allowed to inquire, if that exertion was at all fatiguing or disagreeable to you ? "

" Not in the least," replied the pendulum ; " it is not of six strokes that I complain, nor of sixty, but of *millions*."

" Very good," replied the dial. " But recollect that although you may *think* of a million strokes in an instant, you are required to *execute* but one ; and that however often you may hereafter have to swing, a moment will always be given you to swing in."

" That consideration staggers me, I confess," said the pendulum.

" Then I hope," resumed the dial-plate, " we shall all immediately return to our duty ; for the maids will lie in bed till noon if we stand idling thus."

Upon this, the weights, who had never been accused of light conduct, used all their influence in urging him to proceed ; when, as with one consent, the wheels began to turn, the hands began to move, the pendulum began to wag, and, to its credit, ticked as loud as ever; while a beam of the rising sun that streamed through a hole in the kitchen shutter, shining full upon the dial-plate, it brightened up as if nothing had been the matter.

When the farmer came down to breakfast that morning, upon looking at the clock he declared that his watch had gained half an hour in the night.

MORAL.

It is said by a celebrated modern writer, " Take care of the *minutes* and the *hours* will take care of themselves." This is an admirable hint; and might be very seasonably recollected when we begin to be " weary in well doing," from the thought of having a great deal to do. The *present* is all we have to manage. The past is irrecoverable; the future is uncertain; nor is it fair to burden one moment with the weight of the next. Sufficient unto the *moment* is the trouble thereof. If we had to walk a hundred miles, we still need set but one step at a time, and this process continued would infallibly bring us to our journey's end. Fatigue generally begins, and is always increased by calculating in a minute the exertion of hours.

Thus, in looking forward to future life let us recollect that we have not to sustain all its toil, to endure all its sufferings, or to encounter all its crosses at once. One moment comes laden with its own little burden, then flies, and is succeeded by another no heavier than the last; if *one* could be sustained, so can another, and another.

Even in looking forward to a single day, the spirit may sometimes faint from an anticipation of the duties, the labors, the trials to temper and patience that may be expected. Now this is unjustly laying the burden of many thousand moments upon *one*. Let any one

13

resolve to do right *now*, leaving *then* to do as it can, and if he were to live to the age of Methuselah, he would never err. But the common error is to resolve to act right *to-morrow*, or *next time*, but *now*, just *this* once, we must go on the same as ever.

It seems easier to do right to-morrow than to-day, merely because we forget that when to-morrow comes, *then* will be *now*. Thus life passes, with many, in resolutions for the future which the present never fulfils.

It is not thus with those who, " by *patient continuance in well doing*, seek for glory, honor and immortality." Day by day, minute by minute, they execute the appointed task to which the requisite measure of time and strength is proportioned ; and thus, having worked while it was called day, they at length rest from their labors, and their " works follow them."

Let us then, " whatever our hands find to do, do it with all our might ; " recollecting that *now* is the proper and the accepted time.

BUSY IDLENESS.

Mrs. Dawson being obliged to leave home for six weeks, her daughters, Charlotte and Caroline, received permission to employ the time of her absence as they pleased. That is, she did not require of them the usual strict attention to particular hours, and particular studies, but allowed them to choose their own employments, — only recommending them to make a good use of the license, and apprising them, that, on her return, she should require an exact account of the manner in which the interval had been employed.

The carriage that conveyed their mother away was

scarcely out of hearing, when Charlotte, delighted with her freedom, hastened up stairs to the school-room, where she looked around on books, globes, maps, drawings, to select some new employment for the morning. Long before she had decided upon any, her sister had quietly seated herself at her accustomed station, thinking that she could do nothing better than finish the French exercise she had begun the day before. Charlotte, however, declined attending to French that day, and after much indecision, and saying, " I have a great mind to," three several times without finishing the sentence, she at last took down a volume of Cowper, and read in different parts for about half an hour. Then throwing it aside, she said she had a great mind to put the book shelves in order, — a business which she commenced with great spirit. But in the course of her laudable undertaking, she met with a manuscript in short-hand; whereupon she exclaimed to her sister, " Caroline, don't you remember that old Mr. Henderson once promised he would teach us short-hand? How much I should like to learn ! Only, mamma thought we had not time. But now, this would be such a good opportunity. I am sure I could learn it well in six weeks; and how convenient it would be ! One could take down sermons, or anything; and I could make Rachel learn, and then how *very* pleasant it would be to write to each other in short-hand ! Indeed, it would be convenient in a hundred ways." So saying, she ran up stairs, without any further delay, and putting on her hat and spencer, set off to old Mr. Henderson's.

Mr. Henderson happened to be at dinner. Nevertheless, Charlotte obtained admittance on the plea of urgent business; but she entered his apartment so much out of breath, and in such apparent agitation, that the old gentleman, rising hastily from table, and looking anxiously at her over his spectacles, inquired in

a tremulous tone, what was the matter. When, therefore, Charlotte explained her business, he appeared a
little disconcerted ; but having gently reproved her for
her undue eagerness, he composedly resumed his knife
and fork, though his hand shook much more than
usual during the remainder of his meal. However,
being very good-natured, as soon as he had dined he
cheerfully gave Charlotte her first lesson in short-hand,
promising to repeat it regularly every morning.

Charlotte returned home in high glee. She at this
juncture considered short-hand as one of the most
useful, and decidedly the most interesting of acquirements ; and she continued to exercise herself in it all
the rest of the day. She was exceedingly pleased at
being able already to write two or three words which
neither her sister nor even her father could decipher.
For three successive mornings Charlotte punctually
kept her appointment with Mr. Henderson ; but on the
fourth she sent a shabby excuse to her kind master ;
and, if the truth must be told, he from that time saw
no more of his scholar. Now the cause of this deser-
tion was two-fold : first, and principally, her zeal for
short-hand, which for the last eight-and-forty hours
had been sensibly declining in its temperature, was, on
the above morning, within half a degree of freezing
point ; and, second, a new and far more arduous and
important undertaking had by this time suggested itself
to her mind. Like many young persons of desultory
inclinations, Charlotte often amused herself with writing
verses ; and it now occurred to her that *an abridged
history of England in verse* was still a *desideratum* in
literature. She commenced this task with her usual
diligence ; but was somewhat discouraged in the outset
by the difficulty of finding a rhyme to *Saxon*, whom
she indulged the unpatriotic wish that the Danes had
laid a *tax on*. But, though she got over this obstacle
by a new construction of the line, she found these diffi-

culties occur so continually that she soon felt a more thorough disgust at this employment than at the preceding one. So the epic stopped short, some hundred years before the Norman conquest. Difficulty, which quickens the ardor of industry, always damps, and generally extinguishes, the false zeal of caprice and versatility.

Charlotte's next undertaking was, to be sure, a rapid descent from the last in the scale of dignity. She now thought, that, by working very hard during the remainder of the time, she should be able to accomplish a patch-work counterpane, large enough for her own little tent bed ; and the ease of this employment formed a most agreeable contrast in her mind with the extreme difficulty of the last. Accordingly, as if commissioned with a search-warrant, she ransacked all her mother's drawers, bags, and bundles in quest of new pieces ; and these spoils proving very insufficient, she set off to tax all her friends, and to tease all the linen-drapers in the town for their odds and ends ; urging that she wanted some *particularly.* As she was posting along the street on this business, she espied at a distance a person whom she had no wish to encounter; namely, old Mr. Henderson. To avoid the meeting she crossed over. But this manœuvre did not succeed ; for no sooner had they come opposite to each other, than, to her great confusion, he called out across the street, in his loud and tremulous voice, and shaking his stick at her, " How d' ye do, *Miss Shorthand ?* I thought how it would be ! Oh, fie ! Oh, fie ! "

Charlotte hurried on ; and her thoughts soon returned to the idea of the splendid radiating star which she designed for the centre-piece of her counterpane. While she was arranging the different patterns, and forming the alterations of light and shade, her interest continued nearly unabated ; but when she came to the *practical* part of sewing piece to piece with unvarying

sameness, it began, as usual, to flag. She sighed several times, and cast many disconsolate looks at the
endless hexagons and octagons, before she indulged
any distinct idea of relinquishing her task. At length,
however, it did forcibly occur to her that, after all,
she was not *obliged* to go on with it; and that, really,
patch-work was a thing that was better done by degrees, when one happens to want a job, than to be
finished all at once. So, with this thought (which
would have been a very good one if it had occurred
in proper time), she suddenly drew out her needle,
thrust all her pieces, arranged and unarranged, into a
drawer, and began to meditate a new project.

Fortunately, just at this juncture some young ladies
of their acquaintance called upon Charlotte and Caroline. They were attempting to establish a society
amongst their young friends for working for the poor,
and came to request their assistance. Caroline very
cheerfully entered into the design; but as for Charlotte, nothing could exceed the forwardness of her
zeal. She took it up so warmly that Caroline's appeared, in comparison, only lukewarm. It was proposed that each member of the society should have
an equal proportion of the work to do at her own
house; but when the articles came to be distributed,
Charlotte, in the heat of her benevolence, desired that
a double portion might be allotted to her. Some of
the younger ones admired her industrious intentions,
but the better judging advised her not to undertake
too much at once. However, she would not be satisfied till her request was complied with. When the
parcels of work arrived, Charlotte with exultation
seized the larger one, and without a minute's delay
commenced her charitable labors. The following
morning she rose at four o'clock, to resume the employment; and not a little self-complacency did she
feel, when, after nearly two hours' hard work, she still

heard Caroline breathing in a sound sleep. But, alas ! Charlotte soon found that *work* is *work*, of whatever nature, or for whatever purpose. She now inwardly regretted that she had asked for more than her share ; and the cowardly thought that after all she was not *obliged* to do it next occurred to her. For the present, therefore, she squeezed all the things, done and undone, into what she called her " Dorcas bag ; " and to banish unpleasant thoughts, she opened the first book that happened to lie within reach. It proved to be " an Introduction to Botany." Of this she had not read more than a page and a half before she determined to collect some specimens herself ; and having found a blank copy-book she hastened into the garden, where, gathering a few common flowers, she proceeded to dissect them, not, it is to be feared, with much scientific nicety. Perhaps as many as three pages of this copy-book were bespread with her specimens before she discovered that botany was a *dry study*.

It would be too tedious to enumerate all the subsequent ephemeral undertakings which filled up the remainder of the six weeks. At the expiration of that time Mrs. Dawson returned. On the next morning after her arrival she reminded her daughters of the account she expected of their employments during her absence ; and desired them to set out on two tables in the schoolroom everything they had done that could be exhibited, together with the books they had been reading. Charlotte would gladly have been excused her part of the exhibition ; but this was not permitted ; and she reluctantly followed her sister to make the preparation.

When the two tables were spread, their mother was summoned to attend. Caroline's, which was first examined, contained, first, her various exercises in the different branches of study, regularly executed, the same as usual. And there were papers placed in the books she was reading in school hours, to show how far she had proceeded in them. Besides these, she had read in her leisure time, in French, Florian's " Numa Pompilius ; " and in English, Mrs. More's " Practical Piety," and some part of Johnson's " Lives of the Poets." All the needle-work which had been left to do or not, at her option, was neatly finished ; and her parcel of linen for the poor was also completely and well done. The only instance in which Caroline had availed herself of her mother's license, was, that she had prolonged her drawing lessons a little every day, in order to present her mother with a pretty pair of screens, with flowers copied from nature. These were, last of all, placed on the table with an affectionate note, requesting her acceptance of them.

. Mrs. Dawson, having carefully examined this table, proceeded to the other, which was quite piled up with different articles. Here, amid the heap, were her three pages of short-hand ; several scraps of paper containing fragments of her poetical history ; the piece (not large enough for a doll's cradle) of her patchwork counterpane ; her botanical specimens ; together with the large unfinished pile out of the Dorcas bag, — many of the articles of which were begun, but not one quite finished. There was a baby's cap with no border, a frock body without sleeves, and the skirt only half hemmed at the bottom ; and slides, tapes, and button-holes, were all, without exception, omitted. After these, followed a great variety of thirds, halves, and quarters of undertakings, each perhaps good in itself, but quite useless in its unfinished state.

The examination being at length ended, Mrs. Dawson retired, without a single comment, to her dressing-room ; where, in about an hour afterwards, she summoned the girls to attend her. Here also were two tables laid out, with several articles on each. Their mother then leading Caroline to the first, told her that, as the reward of her industry and *perseverance*, the contents of the table were her own. Here, with joyful surprise, she beheld, first, a little gold watch, which Mrs. Dawson said she thought a suitable present for one who had made a good use of her time ; a small telescope next appeared ; and lastly, Paley's "Natural Theology," neatly bound. Charlotte was then desired to take possession of the contents of the other table, which were considerably more numerous. The first prize she drew out was a very beautiful French fan ; but upon opening it, it stretched out in an oblong shape, for want of the pin to confine the sticks at bottom. Then followed a new parasol ; but when unfurled there was no catch to confine it, so that it would not remain spread. A penknife handle without a blade, and the blade without the handle, next presented themselves to her astonished gaze. In great confusion she then unrolled a paper which discovered a telescope apparently like her sister's ; but on applying it to her eye, she found it did not contain a single lens, — so that it was no better than a roll of pasteboard. She was, however, greatly encouraged to discover that the last remaining article was a watch; for, as she heard it tick, she felt no doubt that this at least was complete, but upon examination she discovered that there was no hour-hand, the minute-hand alone pursuing its lonely and useless track.

Charlotte, whose conscience had very soon explained to her the moral of all this, now turned from the tantalizing table in confusion, and burst into an agony of tears. Caroline wept also, and Mrs. Dawson, after an interval of silence, thus addressed her daughters : —

"It is quite needless for me to explain my reasons for making you such presents, Charlotte. I assure you your papa and I have had a very painful employment the past hour in spoiling them all for you. If I had found on your table in the school-room any one thing that had been properly *finished*, you would have received one complete present to answer it; but this you know was not the case. I should be very glad if this disappointment should teach you what I have hitherto vainly endeavored to impress upon you, — that as all those things, pretty or useful as they are in themselves, are rendered totally useless for want of *completeness,* so exertion without *perseverance* is no better than *busy idleness.* That employment does not deserve the name of industry which requires the stimulus of novelty to keep it going. Those who will only work so long as they are *amused* will do no more good in the world, either to themselves or others, than those who refuse to work at all. If I had required you to pass the six weeks of my absence in bed or in counting your fingers, you would, I suppose, have thought it a sad waste of time; and yet I appeal to you whether (with the exception of an hour or two of needle-work) the whole mass of articles on your table could produce anything more useful. And thus, my dears, may life be squandered away, in a succession of busy nothings.

" I have now a proposal to make to you. These presents, which you are to take possession of as they are, I advise you to lay by carefully. Whenever you can show me anything that you have begun, and voluntarily *finished,* you may at the same time bring with you one of these things, beginning with those of least value, to which I will immediately add the part that is deficient. Thus, by degrees, you may have them all completed; and if by this means you should acquire the wise and virtuous habit of *perseverance,* it will be far more valuable to you than the richest present you could possibly receive."

TEMPER; OR THE TWO OLD LADIES.

In a huge old-fashioned red brick house, with a great many tall narrow windows in front, and a high flight of stone steps up to the door, lived two old ladies, commonly called Mrs. Abigail and Mrs. Dorothy. They had lived there for many and many a year. They never altered the fashion of their dress, and were very exact and regular in all their habits and customs. Every day of the week they were driven out at the same hour, in their old-fashioned coach, by their old-fashioned coachman; and at the same hour they returned home; so that when the coach passed through the town, either going or returning, everybody knew what was o'clock. They neither paid visits nor received company at their house; and the few servants they kept had lived with them so many years that none but the aged people of the place could remember the least alteration in the household.

The old ladies dressed exactly alike; and were nearly of the same age. Their customs, also, were quite similar; so that to observe them at a distance, it might be supposed there was scarcely any difference between them. And yet there was a difference. Mrs. Abigail was very rich, though nobody knew *how* rich; but not so Mrs. Dorothy, although she was her own sister. For having in her youth in some way displeased the old gentleman, her father, he left all his fortune to his eldest daughter; so that Mrs. Dorothy depended almost entirely upon the bounty — or rather upon the *justice* — of her sister. But this was not the greatest difference between them; for Mrs. Abigail was ill-natured, and Mrs. Dorothy was good-natured, — and it is this kind of thing that makes the greatest real difference between persons, in the mind of all those with whom they have to do. The consequence of this, in the present instance, was, that all the old servants loved Mrs. Dorothy better than they loved their mistress ; and waited upon her, not only with more affection, but with more respect. And as respect and affection are things which can neither be concealed where they are felt, nor successfully imitated where they are not, Mrs. Abigail saw as plainly how it was as if they had told her so in the most express terms. Now, this aggravated her temper beyond anything. She thought it so very strange, and hard, and ungrateful, that she to whom they were indebted for all they had, who paid them such handsome wages and made them such generous presents, should be in less esteem than her poor sister Dorothy, who had nothing of that sort in her power. No ; but " such as she had she gave them," — and that happened to be of more sterling value than their mistress's silver and gold. At first, Mrs. Abigail was so impatient under the grievance, that she turned away several faithful servants for no other real reason than this private one ; but finding that the new comers regularly fell into the same fault, she was soon glad to recall her old domestics.

Mrs. Abigail's temper did not soften as she grew older. She was vexed and tormented that she could not purchase, with all her money, that of which every human bosom feels the need ; and every year increased both the cause and the effect of her disquietude. There was not a tradesman, nor a tenant, nor a neighbor, but would touch his hat with more cordiality to Mrs. Dorothy than to Mrs. Abigail ; for nobody could help seeing the difference. It was even perceptible as they passed along in the old coach ; for, while Mrs. Abigail used always to sit back in an erect posture, looking neither to the right nor the left, the round, good-natured face of Mrs. Dorothy might always be seen, sometimes smiling at the children, and sometimes nodding to the neighbors as she passed their doors.

Mrs. Abigail used perpetually to complain of her wrongs and grievances to Mrs. Dorothy; who always heard her very patiently, and said what she could to soften and console her. She very rarely ventured to hint either at the reason or the remedy; for that irritated Mrs. Abigail beyond anything, and always brought forth the whole list of her benefactions to witness that the fault was not in *her*.

After a long succession of years, a circumstance occurred in the family which made a greater alteration in its aspect than if the China images on the best parlor mantel-piece had been transported to the sitting-parlor mantel-piece, — which would, however, have been considered a most memorable innovation. This was Mrs. Abigail's taking it into her head to adopt a little orphan girl, — a child scarcely five years of age, the daughter of a poor minister lately deceased.

Little Mary was a very pretty, artless, engaging child. Full of spirits, and unconscious of her misfortunes, she entered the great house without any adequate idea of its dignity, and felt herself quite at home the moment she found something to play with. At first, the old ladies could not exactly say whether they were most amused or most put out by the noisy frolics of their new inmate. Mrs. Abigail, at least, felt considerable uncertainty on the subject. But Mrs. Dorothy soon found that it added materially to her happiness. For although she certainly was *fidgeted* at the unwonted sight of doll's clothes strewed upon the carpet, and to see the covers to the crimson damask chair-bottoms unceremoniously pulled up and left in wrecks and wrinkles, and, above all, that the cat's back was sometimes stroked the wrong way, — yet the innocent smiles, the playful gambols, and engaging prattle of the child went to her heart and awoke sensations of delight and tenderness, which must needs languish, even in benevolent minds, when it is long since they were called

into exercise. So much were the good ladies sometimes amused that the wind might shift from southeast
to northwest without its being noted by either of them,
— a thing unprecedented heretofore. And often Mrs.
Abigail herself was so much diverted by her little
protégée that she had been observed not to gape more
than seven times during a whole afternoon.

But, notwithstanding all this, things did not go on
quite so smoothly as may be imagined. Mrs. Abigail's
grand object in adopting the little girl was, that she
might train up somebody to love her; and having
heard that you may teach a child anything, she thought
by taking one so young she should be sure to succeed
in her design. Accordingly, she resolved to instil it
into her youthful mind as her highest duty to love her
benefactress; and she did not fail by reiterated instructions, to give the child to understand, that, for everything she eat and wore and played with, she was
indebted to her alone. Now it was a little strange that,
after sixty years' experience, this good lady did not
know any better way of securing her object; and that
she should imagine that so very small a sacrifice as that
of giving out a little money from an ample store would
alone procure so invaluable a blessing as that of the
affection of a fellow-creature.

Children are excellent physiognomists, and little
Mary soon learned to whom to apply for any assistance
or sympathy in her play; and she never failed, when
she was tired or sleepy, to run and lay her head on
Mrs. Dorothy's lap. It happened not unfrequently
that she was very noisy in her mirth; so much so, that,
to use her own expression, "it absolutely went through
and through Mrs. Abigail's head," and even Mrs.
Dorothy's did not escape with impunity. Now on
these and similar occasions, when her patience was
quite exhausted (which generally happened pretty
early), Mrs. Abigail would begin to scold; but in spite

of this, and of Mrs. Dorothy's repeated admonitions of
" softly ! softly ! my little dear," the little dear would
continue romping about till she got such a thorough
trimming from Mrs. Abigail as made her cry sadly, and
wish that her own mamma would come again. When
the storm was over, the old lady often relented ; and
trotting to her china closet she would take a sweet
queen cake or macaroon (articles on which she placed
her chief dependence in the management of the child)
and hold it out to her with a beneficent smile, which
seemed to say, "Sure you *must* love me now."   On
one of these occasions, as soon as Mary had devoured
the bribe, Mrs. Abigail called her, saying, "Come
hither, my dear, come to me, and tell me now, don't
you love me?"   Retaining a lively remembrance of her
recent scolding, the child hesitated ; and on the question being repeated, she answered, " No."

"Then you are the most ungrateful little creature
that ever was," exclaimed the old lady ; " and you may
take that for your pains."   So saying, she gave her a
smart box on the ear.   Mary ran off roaring, and hid
her face in Mrs. Dorothy's lap.   Mrs. Dorothy knowing that would not do, raised her up, saying, —

"Oh, now you are a very naughty little Miss !
What, not love poor Mrs. Abigail, that gives you so
many pretty things, and such nice cakes !   Oh, fie ! I
am quite ashamed of you !   Sure, you love her, don't
you ? "

" I love *you*," said the child, " because you don't beat
me."

" Well, to be sure," exclaimed Mrs. Abigail, " there
is nothing but ingratitude in this world !   Nothing
else ; old and young, all alike.   Such a little creature
as that too, — who could have thought it ? "

Thus little Mary had her troubles, like other people,
in the midst of her apparent prosperity.   However, she
had a never-failing friend and solace in Mrs. Dorothy ;

and when they were alone she would often throw her little arms round her neck, and kiss her repeatedly, saying, —

" I do love you ; I do love you very much, Mrs. *Doroty.*" In return, Mrs. Dorothy used to kiss her fondly, and say, —

" And I love you, my darling ! my jewel ! my pretty one ! " never failing to add, " but you know you must love poor Mrs. Abigail too ; because she is so good to you, and gives you such nice things." At which little Mary used to slide off her lap, and run away to play.

One day Mrs. Abigail was taken very ill, and could not leave her bed ; and kind-hearted Mrs. Dorothy came down to breakfast with the tears in her eyes.

" What are you crying for ? " says little Mary.

" Because, my dear, poor Mrs. Abigail is very ill, and cannot come down stairs."

" Why then, you know, we shall have nobody to scold us all day ; so why do you cry for *that ?* " said little Mary.

In the spring little Mary was attacked with the measles, and had them very severely. Notwithstanding her ill-nature, Mrs. Abigail was really fond of the child ; and she attended her in her illness with much solicitude, took her on her lap, and rocked her to and fro. Once, when she was very restless, she spoke to her in soothing tones ; and when little Mary, in taking some barley water, spilt a little of it over her silk gown, and began to cry from the apprehension of being punished for it, Mrs. Abigail said, " Never mind, love, I 'll not be angry with you *now.*" Upon which little Mary raised her head, looked up in her face for a moment with surprise, and then said, " I love *you, now,* Mrs. Abigail."

Mrs. Abigail looked surprised in her turn. She pressed the child to her bosom with unwonted fondness ; the tears came in her eyes ; for those few words, uttered by a little child, gave her more real pleasure than anything that had happened to her for many a day. Being alone, she fell into a deep revery; but the thoughts of a person unaccustomed to reflection are too indistinct and crude for repetition. However, the sense and the substance of her meditation was something like this : —

"What ! will one kind word, one act of forbearance and good-nature, do more than all the favors I have bestowed? Oh, if I had considered this in early life, — if I had but seen that it is not money but kindness, not gifts, but good-nature, that purchases affection, — how differently would my life have passed. Ah, sister Dorothy ! Sister Dorothy ! I have had all the money, but you have had all the happiness ! "

THE MOTH.

A MILD September evening; twilight already stealing over the landscape shades yonder sloping cornfield, whence the merry reapers have this day borne away the last sheaf. A party of gleaners have since gathered up the precious fragments. Now all are gone. The harvest moon is up ; a low mist rising from the river floats in the valley. There is a gentle stirring amongst the leaves of the tall elm that shades our roof ; all besides is still. The gray and quiet scene invites reflection.

Wishing the reader to participate in our meditations, we were in the very act of committing to paper some sage considerations on the departure of another summer. But a very small and elegant moth, attracted by the candles, has this moment descended on the sheet,

14

within an inch of our pen, and with the light stroke of his wing has broken our thread of thought. Will the reader excuse it if it break his also?

The delicacy and perfection of its form, the exquisite lace-work of its airy wing, its swift and noiseless movements, a body nearly as ethereal and unincumbered as if it were a soul, its independence, its innocence, awaken admiration; and (contrasted with the inertness and languor with which our cumbrous frames are often oppressed) might excite envy too.

Who can guess what are its imaginings concerning the extensive plain on which it has just arrived? Is it a field of dazzling light, an enchanted region of pleasure and brightness? He flutters his wings as though his dreams of joy were at length realized. From the dun shades of the evening without, he has suddenly launched into a new world of magic splendor, illumined with radiant suns. How little does he think (of this at least we may be sure) that this shining plain is no other than a sheet of foolscap; that those glorious suns are inglorious candles! Such are the illusions of moths!

It would be very desirable, some young reader may think, if it were possible, to undeceive him; and supposing him capable of understanding it, to rectify all his mistakes, by addressing him in some such language as this: "You are only a *moth;* and you have no idea what insignificant things moths are! You know nothing at all; you can't imagine what an astonishing number of things there are that you have not even heard of. *We* think nothing of you; *we* are really of importance; but you are of no importance, — you are only an insect. You sometimes do us mischief by eating holes in our clothes, and very tiresome it is that such little creatures as you should be able to do *us* mischief. Having this opportunity, I must desire you not to do so any more, for what you eat is not at all

nice ; it is cloth, not food ; why should you eat *cloth ?*
I wish you would mention this to all your relations.
And as to the place that you now are upon, it is nothing
in the world but a sheet of paper that a person is writing on. But you don't know what writing means, I
dare say. Indeed, it is no use talking to you, you are
so extremely ignorant, moth."

With a few variations, how suitable would be such
an address to some things that are *not* moths ! And to
beings a little higher than ourselves in the scale of
reason, how similar to those of the moth must appear
the illusions of men ! How now the objects of
our ardent pursuit are as destitute of intrinsic excellence, as empty of happiness, as *we* know the glare of
the light to be in which an insect so joyously flutters
its wings ! It does not, indeed, require the intellect
of an angel to know this ; experience teaches it, at
last, even to dull scholars. Children can laugh at the
folly of an insect ; youths soon learn to ridicule the
toys and sports of children ; men smile at the vanities
of youth ; wise men at the pleasures of weak men —
and not seldom at their own ; while angels look down
with surprise and pity on all — smiling most at the
mistakes of the man, and least at those of the moth !

Fortunately enough for our moral, the little hero of
the piece has this moment expired in the flame of the
candle ; and that in spite of the most praiseworthy
exertions on our part to deter him from the rash adventure. In vain we whisked our quill in every dis-
suasive attitude (an employment, by the way, to which
we are but too much accustomed), he was resolved —
and could he have given utterance to his feelings, no
doubt he would have expressed his certain persuasion
— that it must be a desirable and a delightful thing
to sport in that elegant flame. Who can witness this
common catastrophe without observing the analogy,
and reading the oft-told moral? Even if it had not

scorched a single feather, if he could have lived there, still, we could assure him, he could not *find happiness in a candle.* He would have been a thousand times more comfortable, as well as more safe, hid in the dark folds of the curtain, or fixed within the protection of some broad shadow on the wall, or in any of the natural and customary haunts of his species. So is it with all unsanctioned pleasures. Even if they were not dangerous they would be disappointing. But we know they are both the one and the other.

How quickly was that most complete and delicate machine destroyed ! — an engine which not the united sagacity and ingenuity of man could restore ! No wonder that so fine and fragile a creature should be liable to swift destruction. But let not the strong glory in their strength, for behold " *we* are crushed *before* the moth."

THE MOTH'S SONG.

Ah ! what shall I do,
To express unto you
What I think, what I feel, what I know and pursue !

With my elegant face,
And my wing of lace,
How lightly the motes of the evening I chase !

Though I am but a moth,
And feed upon cloth,
To me it is pleasant and nourishing both.

And this region of light,
So broad and so bright,
It makes my heart dance with a strange delight !

If dismal to you,
'T is the best of the two,
For oh ! it is pleasant, this wide-shining view !

There are lights afar,
More bright than a star,
You say they are candles — I 'll see if they are.

I go, and I fly,
And so good-by ! —
Ah me ! what is it? — I die ! I die !

THE WONDERFUL BIRD.

Signor Pasqualini, just arrived from the Continent, announced to the inhabitants of a certain village his intention of amusing them, for one evening only, with a variety of entertaining exhibitions and performances, of unrivalled excellence and ingenuity ; amongst these, the manœuvres of "The Learned Bird," an accomplished German bullfinch, were particularly specified, and largely described in his advertisement. What this bird *could* do seemed not so much to be the question, as what it could *not* do ; so rare were its professed attainments. It could, for instance, go through the military exercise with a straw ; bow to the company at the word of command ; sing different tunes, when called for ; articulate some words ; draw a triangle with its beak ; and spell certain names by pointing to the letters with its claw.

Amongst the spectators of this entertainment were two lads, upon whom it made a strangely different impression. One of them, having read the advertisement in the

morning, had his imagination wrought upon all day by
the glowing descriptions of Signor Pasqualini's hand-bill.
It was not so much those attributes of the bird that
were particularly specified as the undefined intimations
of its sagacity over which his fancy hovered, and which inspired him with so much respect that it is a question if he
felt more veneration for the learning of the parish school-
master than for that of this gifted biped.   Full of these
expectations, when evening was come, Edward paid his
willing sixpence, and entered with trembling eagerness
from behind the curtain of green baize that formed the
entrance of the show.   As the company thickened, and
various preliminaries appeared to be going on behind the
scenes, his impatience increased to a degree that was
almost painful.   At length Signor Pasqualini made his
appearance and his bow, and after sundry performances,
not necessary here to specify, a cage with golden wires
was introduced, out of which solemnly stepped the wonderful bird, and immediately hopped upon a perch that
was raised for the purpose on the table. This bullfinch,
as to its outward appearance, looked much more like
other bullfinches than Edward expected.   Indeed, the
hard discipline and solitary life to which its profession
had subjected it had rendered its plumage less glossy
and brilliant, and its movements less natural and graceful, than those of most of its species.   Edward was a
little disappointed at this ; however, he concluded that
its mental endowments would abundantly compensate
for any external deficiencies.   The first thing required
of the hapless performer was to bow three times to the
company.   This Edward thought was not very gracefully done.   Indeed, the poor little bird, though for
some time accustomed to practise in private, had but
newly been introduced at public exhibitions, and it appeared to be half frightened and half ashamed at performing before so large a company.   Some of its tricks
were diverting enough ; but many mistakes and blun-

ders were detected. When, for instance, it was required to point to the letters that spell King George, it stumbled upon the last word first, and thus produced only the inglorious name of *George King.* And when asked where it was that Lord Wellington gained his great victory, whether the bird replied *Waterloo* or *water gruel* could only be guessed by the question. Edward could not help laughing at this ; yet on the whole he felt no small degree of disappointment, — so much so as to be weary of the performance some time before it was over.

Very different was the impression made by the exhibition on another spectator above alluded to. This lad had not happened even to see the advertisement ; moreover, he had never in all his life heard of such a thing as a learned bird. He only stepped in as he was passing, attracted by the lights, with no idea of what nature the amusement was to be. When therefore the little performer commenced its operations, this boy felt as much pleasure and entertainment as the thing was capable of affording. He laughed out several times, and protested it was " wonderful, really wonderful for such a little creature ! " He observed indeed some failures and mistakes, but for these he made the most charitable allowances ; because, as he said, " it was but a bird ; " and because *he had expected nothing*.

Such were the opposite effects produced by the same spectacle on these differently circumstanced observers : and yet, perhaps, both would agree, when they came to think about it afterwards, that it was a prettier sight to see the sparrows and robins hopping about in their natural haunts, in gardens and orchards, and pleasanter to hear their simple notes, than to stare at the performances of the most accomplished finch that ever exhibited.

MORAL.

But stay ; methinks before we part,
  A moral may be heard, —
A hint to many a sanguine heart
  From this accomplished bird ;
The truth impressed on every brow,
Where time has passed his noiseless plough.

Just thus from life, and what it yields,
  Hope steals the zest away :
We never tread the Elysian fields
  Through which we thought to stray ;
Of all the joys on which we seize,
The more we hope, the less they please.

Our pleasures rather seem to spring
  From things too low that lie
For fancy there to sweep her wing,
  Or hope to glance an eye ;
These humbler gifts, of all on earth,
Alone *surprise* us with their worth.

Reader, while eager hope arrays
  In flowers the youthful year,
Think too what storms and rainy days
  Will follow his career :
Expect these storms and clouds to lower, —
'T will brighten every sunny hour.

A CURIOUS INSTRUMENT.

A GENTLEMAN, just returned from a journey to London, was surrounded by his children, eager, after the first salutations were over, to hear the news ; and still more eager to see the contents of a small portmanteau, which were one by one carefully unfolded and displayed to view. After distributing amongst them a few small presents, the father took his seat again, saying that he must confess he had brought from town, for his own use, something far more curious and valuable than any of the little gifts they had received. It was, he said, too good to present to any of them; but he would, if they pleased, first give them a brief description of it, and then perhaps they might be allowed to inspect it. The children were accordingly all attention, while the father thus proceeded : —

"This small instrument displays the most perfect ingenuity of construction, and exquisite nicety and beauty of workmanship. From its extreme delicacy, it is so liable to injury that a sort of light curtain, adorned with a beautiful fringe, is always provided, and so placed as to fall in a moment on the approach of the slightest danger. Its external appearance is always more or less beautiful; yet in this respect there is a great diversity in the different sorts. But the internal contrivance is the same in all of them, and is so extremely curious, and its powers so truly astonishing, that no one who considers it can suppress his surprise and admiration. By a slight and momentary movement, which is easily effected by the person it belongs to, you can ascertain with considerable accuracy the size, color, shape, weight, and value of any article whatever. A person possessed of one is thus saved from the necessity of asking a thousand questions, and trying a variety of troublesome experiments, which would otherwise be necessary; and such a slow and laborious process would, after all, not succeed half so well as a single application of this admirable instrument."

GEORGE. If they are such very useful things, I wonder that everybody that can at all afford it does not have one.

FATHER. They are not so uncommon as you may suppose; I myself happen to know several individuals who are possessed of one or two of them.

CHARLES. How large is it, father, — could I hold it in my hand?

FATHER. You might; but I should be very sorry to trust mine with you.

GEORGE. You will be obliged to take very great care of it, then?

FATHER. Indeed I must! I intend every night to enclose it within the small screen I mentioned; and it must besides occasionally be washed in a certain colorless fluid kept for the purpose. But this is such a delicate operation, that persons, I find, are generally reluctant to perform it. But notwithstanding the tenderness of this instrument, you will be surprised to hear that it may be darted to a great distance without the least injury, and without any danger of losing it.

CHARLES. Indeed! And how high can you dart it?

FATHER. I should be afraid of telling you to what a distance it will reach, lest you should think I am jesting with you.

GEORGE. Higher than this house, I suppose?

FATHER. Much higher.

CHARLES. Then how do you get it again?

FATHER. It is easily cast down by a gentle movement, that does it no injury.

GEORGE. But who can do this?

FATHER. The person whose business it is to take care of it.

CHARLES. Well, I cannot understand you at all; but do tell us, father, what it is chiefly used for.

FATHER. Its uses are so various that I know not which to specify. It has been found very serviceable in deciphering old manuscripts; and, indeed, has its use in modern prints. It will assist us greatly in acquiring all kinds of knowledge; and without it some of the most sublime parts of creation would have been matters of mere conjecture. It must be confessed, however, that very much depends on a proper application of it; being possessed by many persons who appear to have no adequate sense of its value, but who employ it only for the most low and common purposes, without even thinking, apparently, of the noble uses for which it is designed, or of the exquisite gratifications it is capable of affording. It is, indeed, in order to excite in your minds some higher sense of its value than you might otherwise have entertained, that I am giving you this previous description.

GEORGE. Well then, tell us something more about it.

FATHER. It is of a very penetrating quality; and can often discover secrets which could be detected by no other means. It must be owned, however, that it is equally prone to reveal them.

CHARLES. What! can it speak, then?

FATHER. It is sometimes said to do so, especially when it happens to meet with one of its own species.

GEORGE. What color are they?

FATHER. They vary considerably in this respect.

GEORGE. What color is yours?

FATHER. I believe of a darkish color; but, to confess the truth, I never saw it in my life.

BOTH. Never saw it in your life!

FATHER. No, nor do I wish; but I have seen a representation of it, which is so exact that my curiosity is quite satisfied.

GEORGE. But why don't you look at the thing itself?

FATHER. I should be in great danger of losing it if I did.

CHARLES. Then you could buy another.

FATHER. Nay, I believe I could not prevail upon anybody to part with such a thing.

GEORGE. Then how did you get this one?

FATHER. I am so fortunate as to be possessed of more than one: but how I got them I really cannot recollect.

CHARLES. Not recollect! why, you said you brought them from London to-night!

FATHER. So I did; I should be sorry if I had left them behind me.

CHARLES. Tell, father, do tell us, the name of this curious instrument!

FATHER. It is called — an EYE.

THE TOAD'S JOURNAL.

IT is related by Mr. Belzoni, in the interesting narrative of his late discoveries in Egypt, that having succeeded in clearing a passage to the entrance of an ancient temple which had been for ages buried in the sand, the first object that presented itself, upon entering, was a toad of enormous size; and, if we may credit the assertions of some naturalists respecting the extraordinary longevity of these creatures when in a state of solitary confinement, we may believe that it was well stricken in years.

Whether the subjoined document was intrusted to our traveller by the venerable reptile as a present to the British Museum, or with the more mercantile view of getting it printed in London, in preference to Alexandria, on condition of receiving one per cent on the profits, after the sale of the five hundredth edition (provided the publisher should by that time be at all remunerated for his risk and trouble), we pretend not to say. Quite as much as can be vouched for is the manuscript's being faithfully rendered from the original hieroglyphic character.   The dates are omitted.

" Crawled   forth   from   some   rubbish,   and   winked
        with one eye ;
Half opened the other, but could not tell why ;
Stretched out my left leg, as it felt rather queer,
Then drew all together and slept for a year.
Awakened, felt chilly, — crept under a stone ;
Was vastly contented with living alone.
One toe became wedged in the stone like a peg ;
Could not get it away, — had the cramp in my leg ;
Began half to wish for a neighbor at hand
To loosen the stone, which was fast in the sand.
Pulled harder, — then dozed, as I found 't was no
        use ;
Awoke the next summer, and lo ! it was loose.
Crawled forth from the stone, when completely awake ;
Crept into a corner, and grinned at a snake.
Retreated, and found that I needed repose ;
Curled up my damp limbs and prepared for a doze.
Fell sounder to sleep than was usual before,
And did not awake for a century or more ;
But had a sweet dream, as I rather believe.
Methought it·was light, and a fine summer's eve ;
And I in some garden deliciously fed,
In the pleasant moist shade of a strawberry bed.
There fine speckled creatures claimed kindred with me,
And others that hopped, most enchanting to see.
Here long I regaled with emotion extreme ;
Awoke — disconcerted to find it a dream ;
Grew pensive ; discovered that life is a load ;
Began to be weary of being a toad.
Was fretful at first, and then shed a few tears."
Here ends the account of the first thousand years.

MORAL.

To find a moral where there 's none
Is hard indeed, yet must be done ;
Since only morals sound and sage
May grace this consecrated page.
Then give us leave to search a minute
Perhaps for one that is not in it.
How strange a waste of life appears
This wondrous reptile's length of years !
Age after age afforded him
To wink an eye, or move a limb,
To doze and dream, — and then to think
Of noting this with pen and ink ;
Or hieroglyphic shapes to draw,
More likely, with his hideous claw !
Sure, length of days might be bestowed
On something better than a toad !
Had his existence been eternal,
What better could have filled his journal?
True, we reply ; our ancient friend
Seems to have lived to little end.
This must be granted ; nay, the elf
Seems to suspect as much himself.
Refuse not then to find a teacher
In this extraordinary creature ;
And learn at least, whoe'er you be,
To moralize as well as he.
It seems that life is all a void,
On selfish thoughts alone employed ;
That length of days is not a good,
Unless their use be understood ;
While if good deeds one year engage,
That may be longer than an age.
But if a year in trifles go,
Perhaps you 'd spend a thousand so.

Time cannot stay to make us wise ;
We must improve it as it flies.
The work is ours, and they shall rue it
Who think that time will stop to do it.
    And then, again, he lets us know
That length of days is length of woe ;
His long experience taught him this, —
That life affords no solid bliss.
Or if of bliss on earth you scheme,
Soon you shall find it but a dream ;
The visions fade, the slumbers break,
And then you suffer wide awake.
What is it but a vale of tears,
Though we should live a thousand years?

ON VISITING COWPER'S GARDEN AND SUMMER-HOUSE AT OLNEY.

ARE these the trees?   Is this the place?
These roses, did they bloom for him?
Trod he these walks with thoughtful pace?
Passed he amid these borders trim?

Is this the bower?—an humble shed
Methinks it seems for such a guest !
Why rise not columns, dome bespread,
By art's elaborate fingers drest?

Art waits on wealth, there let her roam,
Her fabrics rear, her temples gild ;
But Genius, when he seeks a home,
Must send for Nature's self to build.

This quiet garden's humble bound,
This homely roof, this rustic fane,

With playful tendrils twining round,
And woodbines peeping at the pane ;

That tranquil tender sky of blue,
Where clouds of golden radiance skim,
Those ranging trees of varied hue, —
These were the sights that solaced him.

We stepped within.   At once on each
A feeling steals, so undefined,
In vain we seek to give it speech, —
'T is silent homage paid to Mind.

They tell us here he thought and wrote ;
On this low seat — reclining thus :
Ye garden breezes, as ye float,
Why bear ye no such thoughts to us ?

Perhaps the balmy air was fraught
With breath of heaven.   Or did he toil
In precious mines of sparkling thought
Concealed beneath the curious soil ?

Did zephyrs bear on golden wings
Rich treasures from the honeyed dew ?
Or are there here celestial springs
Of living waters, whence he drew ?

And here he suffered !   This recess,
Where even Nature failed to cheer,
Has witnessed oft his deep distress,
And precious drops have fallen here !

Here are no richly sculptured urns
The consecrated dust to cover ;
But Nature smiles and weeps, by turns,
In memory of her fondest lover.

THE TROUBLESOME FRIEND.

To the Editor of the " Youth's Magazine " :

SIR, — In the hope that some of your correspondents may offer a few remarks on the subject on which I am about to address you, I have been induced to lay before you certain grievances under which I have long privately groaned. And as it is possible that others besides myself may have similar things to complain of, you may, by the insertion of my letter, be rendering a public service while conferring a private obligation.

You must know that the house adjoining my father's is occupied by a family with whom we are on terms of intimacy. The eldest daughter especially, being a girl of my own age, I have always considered as a particular friend ; and notwithstanding the complaints I am about to lay before you, I really feel a sincere regard for her ; although I will not deny that the warm affection which I at first entertained is greatly damped by the continual vexations to which her conduct exposes me. In short, sir, she is one of those good sort of people whose misfortune it is to be very soon affronted.

Now it is needless to state how many occasions will perpetually occur, between such near neighbors, of taking offence where there is a disposition to do so ; and that, notwithstanding the most sincere and diligent efforts on one part to avoid them. Being myself one of a large family, my time is very much occupied by domestic affairs ; besides, my attention to those pursuits which are necessary to the completion of my education. Now it unfortunately happens that our neighbor, although in circumstances apparently similar to my own, has, or makes, a much larger portion of

leisure than I can command ; and hence arises one of
the principal sources of uneasiness between us.   She
is so much " hurt," as her phrase is, that I am not
ready and willing at all times of the day " to step in,"
or to have a gossip over the garden wall.   Now,
although no one can enjoy the pleasures of society
more than I do at proper seasons, yet I must say it is
no enjoyment to me to have the regular and agreeable
routine of my daily avocations liable to perpetual interruption.   It is, however, on this account that my
troublesome friend is perpetually reproaching me with
being " a bad neighbor," " unsociable," " proud ; "
and with being indifferent to her society.

I do assure you that I cannot pace up and down
our garden walk with a book in my hand, but at the
hazard of giving offence ; for if she should happen to
be within sight, and if I should not happen to raise
my head to nod to her, and say " Good morning," it
will take her a week to pardon the neglect.   Then, it
would surprise you to hear the plausible manner she has
of representing her grievances ; so that when her complaints have been repeated to me by some mutual
friend, I have really begun to fancy myself quite in the
wrong.   And yet upon the coolest reflection I cannot accuse myself of misconduct in this matter.

My friend is wont, with a very resigned, pathetic,
and reasonable sort of look and manner, to make such
complaints as the following : —

" I do feel a little hurt, I must confess, — so much
attention as I have shown to her, and so much regard
as, I can truly say, I feel for her.   Why, I have known
her pass our parlor window twenty times in a day,
when she knows I have been sitting there, without
once giving herself the trouble to turn her head to nod
to me !   Is not this a little strange, so intimate as we
are ? "

" Certainly, it is," says our mutual friend.

" Well, and then she makes an excuse of being so vastly busy. For my part, I 've no notion of being too busy to speak to a friend, — have you? "

" Certainly not."

" Well, one can never step in there but one seems to be interrupting them ; and it is quite a favor to get her to bring her work, and sit an hour with one in the morning. In short, I have done asking her. I don't deny that she is willing to come in and do one a kindness, when it is needed. But I like a friend to be a friend at all times ; and in my opinion there 's nothing so charming as a sociable disposition. For my own part, this is so much *my* temper that, as I often say, I feel these slights the more ; and certainly at times I cannot help feeling a little hurt."

In this style, as I have been repeatedly informed, she makes out a case against me. But as I never take any other notice of such charges than by doing all in my power to show her real friendship, we might go on tolerably, if it were not that sometimes, owing to some unforeseen occurrence or mistake, which it is impossible always to guard against, my friend takes more serious offence, — so much so, at times, that during many weeks she has refused to speak to me. I should be ashamed to call the attention of your readers to the detail of affairs so trifling, if it were not for the sake of illustrating my meaning. With this view, I will mention an instance or two of the kind.

The last time that she appeared so much offended, it was in consequence of my having omitted to send her a formal invitation to spend the evening with me. Wishing to see several of my young friends, I had previously consulted with her about the day ; and, having fully agreed together when it should be, I sat down to write the notes to my other friends, without its even occurring to me that she would expect any further notice. However, to my great surprise, she

did not join our party; and when I sent in to inquire
the reason, she returned me only a cold and formal
excuse. It was in vain that I endeavored to recollect
anything I had done or left undone that could have
vexed her; and it was not till weeks afterwards that
she condescended to explain the cause of her displeasure. Now really, if I had thought of writing her a
note of invitation, I should have been in equal danger
of giving offence; for then, it is probable, she would
have accused me of being too ceremonious with her.

I should be more ready to suspect that the blame
was on my part, if it were not that others of her acquaintance make the same complaints. We are both
of us teachers in our Sunday School; and there is no
situation, as you may be aware, in which a quarrelsome or peevish disposition is more likely to show
itself. You will not be surprised, therefore, when I
say that my poor neighbor is continually taking um-
brage with some of her fellow-teachers. When any
fresh arrangement takes place in the classes, she seldom fails to complain that all the most stupid children
are selected for her. Her attendance at the school is
not the most regular; yet no one can offer her the
kindest remonstrance on this subject, or suggest the
smallest improvement in her method of teaching, without the certainty of her being highly offended. If any
new plans are projected without consulting her, that is
sure to be considered as a personal affront; and·if, on
the other hand, she is consulted, we are equally sure
of her objecting to what is proposed. She is always
complaining that she has so little to do with the management of the school; and indeed she is so constantly
dissatisfied that her services are much less acceptable
than they would otherwise be; for there is, you know,
trouble and difficulty and fatigue enough in a Sunday
School, without having our embarrassments increased
by disagreements among the teachers.

Having been so long used to the peculiarity of my friend's temper, I was really scarcely aware of the degree of bondage and restraint which it imposed upon me, until lately when she was absent from home on a visit of some months. I cannot adequately describe to you how much I felt at liberty as soon as she was gone. I could now walk in the garden without looking fifty ways to see if she was within sight. I could go out or come in, read or write, or take a walk with any other friend, — and all with a degree of freedom and comfort unknown heretofore. And the glow of sincere pleasure with which I should otherwise have welcomed her return was (I do not deny it) damped exceedingly by the recollection of the trouble it would inevitably bring upon me.

Now, surely that must be a serious fault in a person's character which, in spite of many good qualities, renders her company burdensome and her absence a deliverance ; and if anything could be suggested that might successfully represent the weakness and unreasonableness of such a disposition, it would at once do a real service to all such troublesome friends, and inspire with the warmest gratitude all their troubled acquaintance.

I am, sir, your obedient servant,

PENELOPE.

A LETTER TO WHOMSOEVER IT MAY CONCERN.

DEAR READER, — Happening to glance my eye upon the title of a paper in the last number of the "Youth's Magazine," I was induced to put on my spectacles, and give it a reading. And although many of those who contribute to its pages are doubtless better prepared in most respects than myself to reply to it, yet on one account I feel peculiarly qualified to accept the challenge there given : it is that I myself, for a considerable portion of my life was one of the society of " troublesome friends."

I can assign more reasons than one for my having long withdrawn from that society ; but must frankly acknowledge that the primary cause was my having few friends left to be troublesome to. This circumstance at once afforded me leisure for reflection and roused me to it. For, observing that my society was shunned, first by one, and then by another of my associates, I began to employ many solitary hours in endeavoring to discover the cause ; and after various unsuccessful attempts to trace it to the misconduct of others, I was at last compelled to suspect that, after all, the fault might be in myself.

Without troubling you with the long course of experiment and observation by which I was led to this unpleasant conclusion, I shall content myself with stating it to be my settled conviction that an excessive sensibility to injury — a readiness to take offence on small occasions, a disposition to jealousy — proceeds from nothing so much as a tendency to overrate our own worth and consequence. Hence it is that we entertain unreasonable expectations of the attentions due to us from others ; and the inevitable disappointment which ensues mortifies our vanity and self-love, and produces that fretful, complaining, or resentful temper which gives so much trouble to our neighbors and tenfold more uneasiness to ourselves.

Persons whose misfortune it is to magnify their own consequence, instead of making a liberal allowance for similar infirmities in their neighbors, expect that everybody should regard them in the same disproportionate view ; and are first astonished, and then hurt, when they discover how far this is from being the case. She who is always thinking of herself imagines that others must be always thinking of her; at least she thinks it ought to be so; though of all persons, such a one is the least likely to excite a lively interest in those around her.

Another cause of the disposition in question I discovered to be, in my own case, the want of a sufficient interest in the useful employments of life, which left me at leisure to indulge that idle and gossiping turn of mind from whence mischief of one sort or another is sure to arise. When, as a resource from the painfulness of my reflections, I began to engage more heartily in my pursuits, it was astonishing how much less inclination I felt to watch the motions and arraign the conduct of my neighbors. Being fully occupied myself, I often quite forgot to notice whether they paid me proper attentions or not; and a thousand little things passed unnoticed at which I should most certainly have taken offence, had I been on the look out for it. I also acquired by this means a little more charity in judging of the conduct of my neighbors; for it could not but occur to my mind that whereas, while I was busily engaged in my own occupations, I had little leisure to think of *them*, so they, for a reason equally good, might sometimes lose a lively recollection *even of me*. That very common admonition, to *mind one's own business*, is really an excellent one; for while an energetic attention to one's own affairs effectually checks an impertinent and mischievous curiosity about the conduct of other people, it by no means prevents a benevolent concern for their welfare or activity in their service, when they may happen to require it. Thus I found that while I became less and less inclined to break off an interesting employment in order to watch whether one neighbor went by without calling, or whether another paid me some expected attention, I was yet much more willing than heretofore to give up some portion of my time to them when I could do them any good by that means.

There was another consideration which had great efficacy in curing me — if I am cured — of my troublesome propensities ; and that was the utter unavailingness of my resentments. When I was affronted, and determined to show it, I soon discovered that nobody cared much whether I was pleased or angry. People in general seemed perfectly contented to wait till my anger was over. A few more good-tempered ones, who endeavored to explain and to conciliate, I could see smiled secretly at my infirmity ; while the more ill-natured laughed at it without disguise. So that I found I was always the chief sufferer and the chief loser by my ill-humor. When from motives of pique I absented myself from any company, the circumstance, as I have had opportunities enough of discovering, excited no regret, but very often the reverse ; so that I began to be thoroughly tired of indulging resentments which punished no one but myself.

As it is common to pass from one extreme to another, so I am suspected by some of having now become too insensible to this sort of injury. Whether that be the case I will not determine ; but this I know, that if I err on this side it is the most peaceful and comfortable fault I ever fell into. In fact it is so difficult a thing to offend me now, that those — if there are any such — who would wish to do so, must I am sure give up the attempt in despair. I am far from being ignorant that I occasionally experience, like other people, little slights and neglects from the carelessness, selfishness, or ill-nature of my neighbors ; but as this rarely happens from those whom I love and esteem, I must confess that it gives the smallest possible disturbance to my tranquillity. If any one treats me with rudeness or neglect, I perceive that that person knows not how to behave ; and I feel the same sort of compassion and indulgence towards the party that one does on remarking any other species of awkwardness in ill-bred people.

As to my happiness, that is so greatly independent of others — so much regulated by my own conduct and internal tranquillity — that it cannot be moved by such things. It is, indeed, since I have learned the happy art of looking within for entertainment and satisfaction, and depended on my own resources, that I have become so much less troublesome to others than formerly. And it is well for me that this change has taken place ; for as I am now growing old, and have nothing to recommend me to the notice of any one, being neither rich, nor witty, nor entertaining, think, I beseech you, what an unhappy and forlorn creature I should be if my happiness still depended upon the flattering attentions of my neighbors. I assure you if that were the case, I should have little enough ! And while I am upon this subject I will take the liberty to say that it does appear to me that much of the dissatisfaction, fretfulness, and uneasiness visible in persons in the decline of life, especially in those who are solitary, is owing to their not having independence of mind enough to make them indifferent to the neglect which is too often the lot of age. The most obscure and despised individual who thus rises above her circumstances and finds content within, is far more respectable, and enjoys a much more permanent and sterling species of happiness, than the most admired coquette, or the most richly bedizened dowager, who depends for the maintenance of her happiness, like the meanest mendicants, on the crumbs of admiration and respect that are thrown to her by the surrounding crowd.

But I perceive that, like other old folks, I have wandered from my subject, and, forgetting that I am writing for the young, have been lecturing the old. However, I am well persuaded that the same dispositions that are necessary to respectability and happiness at one period of life are equally so at another ; and she or he who would have a cheerful, peaceful, and respectable old age, must learn in youth to build happiness on a true foundation.

To return to the subject on which I set out, I will just say that, while I am so remarkably backward in taking offence, I hope I am equally reluctant to give it ; and I should be sincerely sorry if any remarks I have at present made should have such an effect on any of my readers. If, however, I may have unintentionally *hurt* any one, I humbly hope that they will prove that my advice has not been quite lost upon them, by a generous act of forgiveness towards the unknown offender, and that in future, as often as occasion may require, the same indulgence may be extended towards others. For truly, when one comes impartially to consider the degrees of uneasiness that the temper of which we have been speaking occasions, I doubt if one should find a very great deal to choose between a troublesome friend and a troublesome enemy.

I am, my dear reader, your humble servant,

DOROTHY.

GOVERNMENT OF THE THOUGHTS.

THERE is a prevailing desire in the minds of many young people to be freed from the restraints of authority, — an impatience for that period to arrive when they shall be at liberty to direct their own actions. It is not, perhaps, very uncommon for them to imagine that they should be more willing even to do right, — that it would be easier, and far more agreeable, — if it were no longer a matter of constraint, but of choice.

To any who may have entertained such ideas, I would propose a method by which they may already ascertain their powers of self-government, and direct them to a sphere of action which, whatever their present circumstances may be, is subject to no external control; where parents, tutors, friends, have no dominion; where they are already emancipated from every outward restraint. Here, then, they may try their strength and prove their skill; and if they fail here, it is but reasonable to conclude that they would be, at least, equally unsuccessful if intrusted with the direction of their own conduct.

But in what way, it may be asked, are persons whose time, pursuits, actions — whose very recreations — are in a measure regulated by others, at liberty to command themselves? There are, indeed, several ways in which this question might be profitably answered; but we shall at present confine ourselves to one, and reply, *Thought is free.* Here is a boundless field, over which the youngest and most strictly guarded possesses unlimited dominion. Here the eye of the most watchful friend cannot penetrate. At the very moment that a child is gratifying a parent's feelings by some act of obedience, the thoughts may be so employed as would incur his severest displeasure. There is but One whose eye discerns " the thoughts and intents of the heart; " and a lively recollection of that eye being ever present, beholding and recording all that passes within, would indeed supersede every other consideration.

Here then let the proud spirit, impatient of control and confident of his strength to resist temptation and avoid danger, begin to exercise his self-command. And here let the modest and ingenuous, who cheerfully submit to wholesome restraint and parental guidance, give double diligence in guarding and regulating that to which parental authority cannot extend.

All self-government begins here. He who cannot

command his thoughts, must not hope to control his actions. The smallest attention to our own minds must convince us that the thoughts require restraint. If left to pursue their own course, they will assuredly take a wrong one. Three different descriptions of thought might be mentioned, closely indeed connected with each other, but which generally, perhaps, occur in the following order: *idle* thoughts, *vain* thoughts, and *wicked* thoughts.

Idle thoughts are those which ramble wantonly about the mind, ranging from one object to another, just as they will, without any effort being made to divert them into a useful channel. It might afford a profitable illustration of our meaning, if the train of thought passing through the mind of a young lady, for instance, while sitting for an hour alone at her work-table, could be taken down as it occurs. Perhaps she would herself be startled to peruse the motley record. Or, should she be disposed to plead in her excuse that it was rather silly than sinful, let her remember that " the thought of foolishness is sin." It is not said the thought of *wickedness*, but the thought of *foolishness*. And it is so, because it wastes time and talents which might be profitably employed, and for which we must render an account. It is not sufficient that the hands are occupied, — the mind may be idle whilst they are busy ; and how much mischief and misery may be traced to indolence of mind ! Thought is the chief prerogative of our being, the great means of ennobling and reforming it ; it makes the grand distinction be-tween the man and the brute. And yet, would it be paying too high a compliment to the capacities of the linnet or the lapdog (who we may suppose to be the aforesaid young lady's companions at her work-table), to presume that the train of ideas or sensations passing through their brains at the same time would be at least as well worthy of note as those of their mistress?

I would gladly amuse my readers with the alternate cogitations of the lapdog, the linnet, and the lady ; but being unwilling to hazard a conjecture with regard to the two former, I leave them to furnish those of the latter for themselves. If " Satan finds some mischief still for idle hands to do," it is no less true of idle thoughts. They are the first means he employs to ensnare us. Of them we are not much afraid ; and therefore are easily led on to the next step, which is short and easy indeed.

By *vain* thoughts, we may understand those wilful excursions of the imagination, those airy visions of future happiness (as improbable as they are indeed undesirable), which, it is to be feared, are by many not only admitted but encouraged. If any young persons should yield to this kind of mental indulgence, under the idea of its being a harmless amusement, it can only be for want of observation of their own minds, or for want of sufficient experience of its consequences. Its effects on the mind are much the same as those of intemperance on the body, — enfeebling its powers, rendering every present occupation insipid, every duty dry, and creating a distaste for all mental improvement ; at the same time that it cherishes the love of self, and blunts every benevolent and generous sentiment. Nor is it too much to say, that an habitual indulgence of these visionary pleasures is absolutely incompatible with religious improvement. The mind, whose favorite employment is forming plans and wishes for possessing the pleasures, honors, riches, vanities of this world, cannot be seeking, "*first*, the kingdom of God ; " cannot be " hungering and thirsting after righteousness ; " cannot have " fixed its affections on things above." Well, then, might David exclaim, " I hate *vain* thoughts, but thy law do I love." He knew that to love both was impossible, for he sets them in direct opposition to each other.

It is not necessary to describe, and we hope not needful to warn our readers against, the last mentioned kind. Indeed, if the two former be carefully guarded against, and dismissed from the mind as soon as they enter, there will be little danger that *wicked* thoughts should gain admission. But let none hope to escape even from these, if license be given to the others. The distance and difference between *vain* and *wicked* thoughts, is much less than may be imagined; it is but another step, a step soon and easily and often unconsciously taken. Who, then, will dispute that "the thought of foolishness is sin?" Who but has need to watch and pray that they enter not into this temptation!

If a habit of indulging vain and sinful thoughts be so injurious to the moral and intellectual powers, how healthful, how desirable is a well-regulated mind, which has acquired such a command over itself as to be able to call off the thoughts instantly from unprofitable wanderings, and fix them on useful and important subjects! Youth is the time for forming this habit. If neglected then, it will in after life be by painful laborious efforts only that the mind can be brought to profitable reflection and meditation; from which it will be ever liable to be diverted by every trifle that presents itself to the senses.

All mental superiority originates in habits of *thinking*. A child indeed, like a machine, may be made to perform certain functions by external means; but it is only when he begins to *think* that he rises to the dignity of a rational being. Are we at a loss for subjects of improving and interesting thought? Oh, look around; regard the heavens above and the earth beneath! The wonders and beauties of nature are of themselves inexhaustible sources of delightful contemplation. That must be a low, frivolous mind, in which a glance at the starry heavens excites no interest, no curiosity, no admiration, no reverence for the great Creator. Many of our employments (and this remark especially applies to female employments) are happily of such a nature as to leave the mind at liberty. Let no one imagine that she is not responsible for the manner in which that liberty is used. While the useful needle is performing its humble functions, what a noble privilege it is, that the mind may be engaged in the grandest pursuits that can occupy an intelligent being!

Why is it that so many who acknowledge generally the supreme importance of religion, yet from year to year neglect that great salvation? It is for want of thought. Idle and vain thoughts are the "weeds which spring up and choke" every good impression, and prevent all serious reflection. Oh, we should be ashamed to mention the trifles that, it is to be feared, occupy hours and years of eager, anxious thought, and cause such subjects as death, heaven, and eternity, to appear dull, insipid, and unimportant! Let our young readers inquire for themselves to what themes their thoughts most gladly and naturally recur. And happy, happy they who after such an investigation can sincerely exclaim, "Oh, how love I Thy law; it is my meditation all the day!"

Let none be discouraged from attempting to acquire the right regulation of their thoughts by the difficulties they may have to encounter. Habit will render that easy and delightful which at first appears dry and difficult. The mind will gradually become enlarged and ennobled; will feel disgusted at the trifles which used to satisfy it, and aspire to pursuits and pleasures of the highest order. To be prepared for the great change — meetened for a world of intellectual and spiritual enjoyment — will then appear to us the grand concern of life, the "one thing needful." Then shall we be able to say with the Psalmist, "I thought on my ways, and turned my feet unto Thy testimonies."

FASHIONS FOR OCTOBER.

" Be clothed with humility," and have " the ornament of a
meek and quiet spirit, which is in the sight of God of great
price."

THIS is the most graceful, becoming, and at the
same time novel costume that has ever solicited public patronage. The mantle is of the most exquisite
hue and delicate texture, tastefully decorated with the
above-mentioned costly brilliants, and will be found to
unite every advantage of utility and elegance. This
dress is suitable to all seasons, and is considered
equally becoming to the young and the old. It possesses extraordinary durability, is less liable to take a soil
than any other material, and retains its freshness and
novelty to the last. It falls over the person in the
most graceful folds, and is so adjusted as to veil every
blemish and set off the least favorable figure to the
best possible advantage. The color usually preferred
for this costume is invisible green ; which casts the
most delicate shade upon the whole form, and produces
an effect indescribably agreeable and prepossessing.
Nothing can be more tastefully imagined than the
ornament with which this mantle is finished ; and
although this jewel is pronounced by the best judges
to be of immense value, it may be obtained upon very
reasonable terms. It is so delicate in its hue, and so
chaste and simple in its workmanship, that it has been
mistaken by unskilful observers for an ordinary pebble ;
but connoisseurs instantly recognize it, and allow it to
be " more precious than rubies." Notwithstanding
the many recommendations it possesses, this dress has
never become common, although universally approved.
It was once worn as a royal robe, and has ever

since been held in high estimation and general use amongst the subjects of the great Prince who first introduced it.

The figurative language of the Bible will always allow of the most plain and practical interpretation. When our Lord, for instance, relates the parable of the merchantman seeking goodly pearls, who sold all that he had to obtain one of great price, we are not to regard it as an entertaining fable. Its meaning is plainly this, — that eternal life is of such incalculable value that it is infinitely worth while to part with everything which must be sacrificed to its attainment. The merchant sold his all to gain one pearl; for by this means he would abundantly enrich himself. He acted wisely, therefore; for " the children of this world are, in their generation, wiser than the children of light." In like manner, whatever we may resign of present pleasure or advantage with a view to our eternal welfare, will prove so unspeakably advantageous in the end that nothing but the grossest blindness and inattention to our own interests could make us unwilling to do so.

The language of the apostle Peter, quoted above, is no less plain and practical in its import. The apparel he recommends is no fancy dress which we are not really expected to wear. On the contrary, we may — we *must*, if we are Christians — be thus clothed with humility, and have this ornament of a meek and quiet spirit. Some of our young readers would probably hear with considerable interest that the most becoming dress and the most brilliant jewels ever worn were offered for their acceptance. Now, this is truly the case. Clothed with humility and adorned with a meek and quiet spirit, they would be more richly attired than in the most costly array. Who then will turn away disappointed from such a gift, and think some sparkling bauble more desirable? Oh, remember in whose sight this ornament is of " great price ! " It is well to pause and reflect closely upon such an assertion. Many such passages of Scripture are, it is to be feared, passed over with slight attention, so that their force and beauty are little ·perceived. Many, perhaps, who spend some precious hours every day in reflection upon their outward decorations have never stopped to meditate upon this striking declaration, — *in the sight of* GOD *of great price.* He who forms the most accurate and impartial estimate of the true and comparative value of all things, He who formed and gave their lustre to those shining gems we so greatly admire, is fully aware of whatever beauty and value they possess. Yet He says " *not* with gold, and pearls, and costly array," but " with the ornament of a meek and quiet spirit."

It is not our present intention to enter upon that part of the subject to which the words just quoted would afford so suitable a text ; nor to inquire how far the expression " not with gold and pearls " &c., may be supposed to imply a direct prohibition of a showy style of attire. That they condemn that excessive attention paid to appearance which so greatly prevails among professing Christians cannot, however, be doubted. But our present purpose is to recommend " that inward adorning of the mind," which is here described. Indeed, there is little fear that they who eminently shine with these internal graces will be prone to excess in external decoration. Humility, whose chief characteristic it is to be contented to pass without attracting observation, will surely seldom be found excessively arrayed in those ornaments which expressly invite it. There may be some, however, who, though not destitute of this Christian grace, yet conform too much to the customs of those around them, merely from the want of a due consideration of the subject.

"Be ye clothed with humility." There is grace in the very word; an attraction which they who feel not must be as destitute of true taste as of right principle. There is no age to which it does not belong; but to the young, how eminently becoming! Humility is the very foundation of Christianity. We must be abased, before we can be exalted; and our highest exaltation must, at last, consist in the depth of our humiliation. He who is the "High and lofty One that inhabiteth eternity," exhibited, during the whole period of his abode on earth, a perfect pattern of this virtue. He not only "was found in fashion as a man," but "took upon Him the form of a servant;" and let us remember that He set us this example in order "that we might follow His steps." When we are conscious of the swellings of pride, or the risings of vanity, let us think of the Lord Jesus Christ, — endeavor to realize His appearance, His manner, and to ascertain what conduct or feelings He would display or recommend on the present occasion. Above all, let us remember, — however we may imagine the secret workings of our vain hearts to be concealed from those around us (though even this is rarely the case), — that His eye beholds them all, and with what sentiments we are fully informed. "The Lord resisteth the proud;" "the proud He knoweth afar off."

Be ye *clothed* with humility: there is a peculiar beauty in this figure. It is to cover us completely, like a garment, and without it we must never appear. This simple attire need fear no injury. A person walking the streets in delicate and costly clothing is perpetually in danger of its being soiled and torn; while another in plain garments may go about without fear of inconvenience from the common accidents to which he is exposed. So a vain, showy mind is continually exposed to pain and mortification, from which one of a humble unassuming temper is per-

fectly secure.   The freedom, ease, and tranquillity he
enjoys can, indeed, scarcely be conceived of by those
of an opposite spirit.   And the garments of humility
are armor as well as clothing.   They form an invul-
nerable covering, which malice itself cannot penetrate.

> " He that is down need fear no fall ;
>   He that is low no pride.
> He that is humble ever shall
>   Have God to be his guide."

Bunyan's shepherd boy sang sweetly when he sang
thus.

And what is this ornament on which we ought to
set so high a value? A meek and quiet spirit.   Oh,
what a different world ours would be, if this heavenly
jewelry were to become fashionable ! But alas, how
rarely do we see it worn ! We hear much outcry of
wrong, insult, ingratitude ! The peace of every private circle is interrupted, more or less, by some petty
contention, — and here is a simple means which would
heal every breach, calm every storm, allay every irri-
tation.   There is a certain temper called *spirit* in
some young people, which is altogether opposed to
meekness and quietness.   The very terms, indeed,
would probably excite in them a smile of contempt.
But this would only prove them to be unacquainted
with the nature of true dignity and real manliness.
That the most perfect dignity of character and manner is consistent with these virtues was eminently
manifested in Him who was, beyond all others, " meek
and lowly in heart."   That *spirit* which is by some so
greatly admired, would upon investigation be found
to be made up of the most mean and pitiful qualities,
and to proceed from a contemptible species of vanity.
But can it be necessary to insist on the excellence of
those tempers which the Bible itself recommends?
Can that be mean, unmanly, or of small value, which
in the sight of GOD is of great price !

Every word of God is true. It is therefore true, however reluctantly we may be disposed to admit it, that even a child who subdues a rising fit of passion, or submits patiently to some little grievance that he felt disposed to resist, is " greater than he that taketh a city."

Do we need other inducements to cultivate this temper? Let us make the trial for one day; let us be peaceable, meek, forbearing, submissive ; determining not to be provoked by provocation ; and remark if that day will not be more productive of happiness to ourselves, as well as to all around us, than another in which rights have been maintained, privileges asserted, insults returned, and wrongs (ever so successfully) revenged. This, indeed, must be the case ; because holiness and happiness, our duty and our interest, are inseparably connected.

Let our young readers, then, while they wisely repress that inordinate attention to external decoration which so generally prevails, be ambitious to win and wear this choice array, these precious ornaments. Let them " learn of Him who was meek and lowly in heart, and they shall find " peace in their consciences, " and rest to their souls."

THE USE OF BIOGRAPHY.

That " what man has done man may do " is a most stimulating and encouraging truth. It is this consideration chiefly that renders the lives of individuals who have distinguished themselves in their day and generation so interesting to their fellow-creatures ; and it is a remark which should be borne in mind, whether we are studying the actions of *great good men* or of *clever bad men.* In the former case, we should inquire whether we are not possessed of the same qualities, powers, and opportunities — generally speaking — with which they were favored ; and in the latter, that we partake of the same depraved nature, and are liable to the same temptations that led them astray. It is not the history of other beings, — of those above or below us in the scale of intelligence ; it is neither of angels nor of brutes, but of men like ourselves that we read.

It is a common remark, that biography is one of the most useful studies to which we can apply ; but we must remember that its usefulness to us entirely depends upon our right application of it. It is idle, indeed, to take up a book of any kind, merely with a view to entertainment : we hope our readers are all of them, by this time, above so childish a practice ; but it is possible to read with a general desire to derive benefit, and yet without that close, personal application of it to ourselves which alone is likely to do us good. We would therefore recommend, especially to the reader of biography, to keep one grand object in view, and to make this close inquiry whenever such a volume is opened : In what respects is this applicable to me? How can I make it subservient to my own improvement? We shall endeavor to offer some suggestions that may assist the reader in this inquiry.

Suppose that a young person in the quiet and humble walks of life should meet with the annals of some great warrior or statesman. He would probably say, " This is nothing to me, except as mere amusement. I have no ambition, at least I have no talents or opportunities to distinguish myself in public life ; I am quite contented with my humble lot ; I seek not great things for myself." Herein, indeed, he would show his wisdom ; and yet it might not be true that such a history was nothing to him. Whatever is in itself excellent is worthy of our attention and more or less of our imitation, however widely our circumstances may differ. Great talents and splendid achievements are necessarily confined to a few; and as we may be virtuous and happy without them, this is not to be regretted. But it is the duty and interest of every individual to aim at excellence in his own sphere, however humble; and while it may be the farthest from our wishes or our duty to engage in public services, it may still be highly to our advantage to trace the steps and to mark the progress by which great men have arrived at eminence. Many of the very same qualities are requisite to make a good tradesman or skilful mechanic, which are needed to form a great statesman or general.

We shall probably find that such a man was early distinguished from the frivolous or dissolute around him by devotedness to his object; that he made it his study, his pleasure, — not merely engaging in it as a matter of course, or of necessity. We shall find that he was not discouraged by difficulties, but rather stimulated by them to more vigorous efforts; that he never consulted his own ease or gratification, when they stood in the way of his grand design; that he was characterized by a disregard to trifles of all sorts, and by a steady aim at the most important ends. Now as these, among other good qualities, insured to him success and distinction, so we may be assured that the same causes will produce the same effects, in whatever situations they are applied. Thus far a little apprentice-boy may learn of Peter the Great; and become, by and by, as distinguished in his trade as the Czar was in his empire.

When we read the lives of distinguished persons, we are generally struck with the lamentable mixture of mean qualities and bad actions which sullied the glory of their highest achievements. In the whole history of mankind there are but a very few exceptions to this remark. From which we may learn not to envy that eminence of rank or talent which so peculiarly exposes to temptation.

At the same time it should make us watchful of ourselves; since, if men thus eminently gifted, and possessed of such gigantic powers, had not wisdom sufficient to govern their passions, nor strength to resist
temptation, what need must there be for us to guard
against the danger ! For although it frequently appears
that clever men are wicked men, it by no means follows
that to be wicked one must needs be clever; on the
contrary, it is often seen that persons of the weakest
intellect sink into the lowest degrees of vice.

From the lives of distinguished bad men we may see
the small value, in themselves, of those shining qualities which dazzle mankind. What is genius without
virtue ? It is but a splendid curse ; proving still more
baneful to the individual himself than to those within
the sphere of his influence. But in tracing the career
of men distinguished alike by their talents and their
vices, it is especially profitable to observe the gradual
steps by which they arrived at the height or rather the
depth of their notoriety. There was a time when Nero
appeared amiable and humane. Let us not, therefore,
conclude that we shall never be guilty of a crime
because we now shrink from the thought of it; but
rather, if we find that we have not resolution to resist
the small temptations of the present moment, let us
remember that we are in the high road to vice,
although as yet but at its commencement. It is presumption and ignorance of ourselves, to imagine that
the power of resistance will increase with the strength
of temptation. By such self-deception some once
promising characters have become the tyrants and
scourges of society. From their example we should
learn, " when we think we stand, to take heed lest we
fall."

But if so much improvement may be derived from
the history of bad men, and of others who have eminently possessed " the wisdom of this world," how

much more profitable must it be to study the lives of those who became "wise unto salvation;" who were good and great in the truest sense of the words? Our libraries are richly furnished with such profitable records; and the young reader is amply supplied with animating accounts of those of his own age who had the courage to "come out and be separate" from a vain world. But are we not too apt to read the lives of eminent Christians with the same feeling of *distance* as those of heroes and philosophers?—as though the higher attainments of holiness were as much beyond our reach as the gifts of genius. This is a common but lamentable mistake, proceeding not from humility but indolence. Although perseverance and industry will in a great degree supply the want of great abilities, yet genius, it must be acknowledged, is so far a gift of nature that it cannot be acquired by our own endeavors; but this is not the case with regard to "the wisdom which is from above." Hence Christian biography is all *encouragement;* and it is only sinful sloth which tempts us to say, "I can never hope to make such attainments in religion as others." Here ambition is sanctified; and here to be contented with mediocrity is dangerous indeed. By what means does it appear that these "burning and shining lights" arrived at such eminence in their profession? Were they not such as are in the power of every reader, however humble in station, mean in intellect, or young in years? Is it not invariably by watchfulness and diligence, by self-denial, fervent prayer, and giving up the world,—in other words, by being deeply in earnest in religion,—that these "best gifts" are attained? Let us not then merely envy the attainments of those we read of, but with a holy ambition resolve to emulate their graces. There is no obstacle in the way but our own unwillingness. It is true, that, like every other good, this degree of growth in grace must be given from above;

but this surely is not a hindrance, but the highest possible advantage. " He giveth more grace" to those who desire more ; and they who ask "will assuredly receive." To young readers the encouragements and inducements are especially great ; because their course is but beginning, and it is yet for them to determine in what way to direct it. Now they may either become like stars of the first magnitude, or sink to the level of those common, careless, doubtful characters, who live in worldliness and die without comfort.

Closely connected with this subject is that department of religious reading which has proved very edifying to many, and with which our young readers are frequently presented ; we refer to obituaries. In reading of the *lives* of individuals, we observe various situations wherein they are placed, in which it is highly improbable we shall ever follow them. But in accounts of the *deaths* of our fellow-creatures, we are intimately interested ; since it is a scene through which we must certainly ourselves pass, — and to read such records without a deep, thoughtful impression of that fact is folly indeed. We too must die ; and as we know not how soon, it behooves us immediately to inquire what reason there is to suppose that we should enjoy the same tranquillity and hope on a dying pillow as we frequently read of. The agonizing doubts of a death-bed repentance call loudly to those yet in health to "remember their Creator before those evil days come ;" while the cheerful hope of those whose youthful and healthful days were devoted to Him, — whom sickness and death found " watching, "— should stimulate us to " be also ready." Especially, as the many early deaths that are continually recorded prove that we know not at what hour the angel of death may come : with some it is " at cock-crowing and in the morning."

THE WISE MAN.

FREDERIC and Philip, with their sisters Julia and Kate, were amusing themselves together one evening while their father and mother were engaged in conversation. The children paid no attention to what passed, till Philip (who was very lively and inquisitive) happened to hear his father say of some person he was speaking of, that he might be truly called *a wise man!* These last words, which were uttered emphatically, struck his attention.

"A wise man!" said he to his brother and sisters; "who is that, I wonder, that papa can be talking about?" "Nobody that we know, you may be sure," replied Kate.

"No, but papa knows him, and I should like to know him very much," said Philip; and he began to conjecture what kind of a person this wise man must be. He thought of the seven wise men of Greece; but he did not imagine there were any of that sort in England. As soon as there was a pause in the conversation, he asked his papa what this wise man's name was, and where he lived.

"He lives," replied his father, "not very far off; and his name is Johnson."

"Johnson! Oh, some relation to Dr. Johnson, no doubt," said Frederic.

"'That is more than I know," answered his father; "but if you are so curious to see a wise man, I will promise to take you all to call upon him to-morrow morning."

Philip and the rest thanked their papa for this promise; and very much pleased were they at the thought of it.

The next morning the children talked much of their expected visit; and wondered they did not hear their father give orders for the chaise.

"How many miles off is it, papa?" said Philip.

"Not half a mile," said his father.

PHILIP. Not half a mile! Well, now, I had no idea that there was what one could call *a wise man* living anywhere hereabouts.

FREDERIC. No more had I.

JULIA. I think I know where he lives. Don't you remember that old-fashioned looking house, just off the common, with tall narrow windows, and a high wall all around it, where they say a very old gentleman lives all alone? That is the place, I dare say.

PHILIP. I wonder whether he wears a long beard!

KATE. No, no; most likely nothing but a huge wig.

JULIA. A wig! no such thing! depend upon it he has his own white locks, waving about his temples.

PHILIP. We shall find him up to his elbows in old dusty books, I'll engage.

FREDERIC. Or perhaps with globes and glasses, and all sorts of apparatus.

PHILIP. He will not be very well pleased, I am afraid, to be interrupted in his studies by us.

JULIA. For my part, I shall take care not to speak one word while we are in the room.

KATE. And so shall I.

PHILIP. I hope he will not ask us any questions!

FREDERIC. Oh, as to that, you may depend upon it he will not notice one of us; perhaps not so much as know we are there.

KATE. I am afraid I shall laugh.

PHILIP. Laugh! if you do though, we shall get turned out, every one of us, depend upon it.

On these remarks their papa made no comment; he only smiled occasionally, and at length bade them make ready to accompany him on his visit to the wise man. When they set off, Julia was much surprised that he passed the turning leading to the common, and kept straight on towards the town. "*Now* I have no idea who in the world it can be," said she. When they entered the town, they looked at most of the principal houses as they passed, expecting to stop every instant. "*Doctor Somebody*," said Philip, endeavoring to read the name on a brass plate; "this is it, I dare say." But no; his father passed on, and soon turned down a narrow street, where the dwellings were of a humbler description; and knocked at the door of a mean-looking house. A plain, middle-aged man opened it, and courteously invited them to enter. "Papa has to call here first, for something," whispered the children to each other. He ushered them into a small parlor, where his wife was sitting at needle-work; while three girls, her daughters, were seated on a form before her, reading their lessons. The room was in perfect order; and the mother and her children were neatly dressed. The only decorations of the apartment were two or three maps; and a few portraits of some of the old divines, and other pious ministers, on the wall.

The young folks listened to the conversation which their father entered into with these persons; and they quickly perceived (for these children were well taught, and could discriminate) that they conversed sensibly; and that their father, although much their superior in education, regarded them with respect. After a few minutes thus spent, their papa told the master of the house that he would not detain him any longer from his employment; but that he had taken the liberty of bringing his children with him, in the hope that he would allow them to look on for a little time while he was at work. It would be, he said, both amusing and instructive to them, as they had never had an opportunity of seeing that operation before. To this request he most obligingly acceded; and, with a look of great good nature at the young folks, immediately conducted them to the uppermost room in the house, in which he carried on his business. It was a light, airy apartment; and there was a pleasant view of the adjacent country from its long low window. The children were much interested in watching the process, and in listening to the intelligent explanation he gave them of his trade, for he was a very ingenious mechanic, and he told them many things which they had never heard before.

When their curiosity was a little satisfied, they began to look around the room, where their attention was attracted to a few shelves, containing his small library. Upon examining the titles of the books, they found that several of them treated of subjects more or less connected with his own line of business. There were, however, a few of a more general nature, and such as the children were surprised to see in the possession of so plain a man. But the greater part of the collection were well-chosen books of divinity, with a Bible, which had the appearance of being well read. They now again listened to the stranger's discourse with their father; and were struck with the mild and pleasing expression of his countenance, when he was telling him how happily his hours passed in that solitary chamber.

" I often think, sir," said he, " that I cannot be sufficiently thankful that my calling is of a nature that allows me so much retirement and opportunity for thinking; so that while I am laboring for the meat that perishes, I am also able to seek after that which will endure to everlasting life. Indeed, sir," continued he, " I am a happy man. The cheerful hope of another life is surely enough to make a man unspeakably happy. In addition to this, God is pleased to give me

many comforts to render this life pleasant to me. I
have a wife like-minded with myself: and when my
working hours are over, I want no other recreation
than that of going down to her and our dear children,
whom it is our delight to train up, as far as we are
able, to wisdom and virtue. I have great pleasure in
reading to her and to them such books as we possess;
and thus we increase our little stock of knowledge, as
opportunity allows. But, sir, though I mention these
things, my happiness, I trust, does not depend upon
them; but is fixed upon that good hope which sweet-
ens every comfort, and softens every trial."

The father and his children were pleased with their
visit; which for some time after they took leave
formed the subject of their conversation; until Philip,
suddenly perceiving that they were on their return
home, exclaimed, "But are not we going to see the
wise man?"

"My dear," said his father, "we have but just left
him."

"What, was *that* the wise man?" said all the children at once.

FATHER. That was the person of whom you heard
me say last night, that he was a truly wise man.

PHILIP. But, papa — I thought —

FATHER. Well, what did you think?

PHILIP. Why although he appears very good, and
happy, and industrious, and all that, yet he certainly
is not at all the kind of person we expected to see.

FREDERIC. No, not at all.

FATHER. I cannot help that; and I still think that
what I said of him was perfectly correct. What kind
of a person did you expect to see?

PHILIP. Why, papa, we thought he would at least
be a scholar, you know, with his head stuffed full of
Latin and Greek; or a philosopher, or an author, or
something of that sort.

FATHER. You mean that you expected to see a learned man, or a clever man. But that was your own fault; I promised you no such thing. Are you not aware, children, that a man may be learned, or clever, or both, without being *wise;* and that a man may be *wise* who is neither the one nor the other?

FREDERIC. Yes, wise in some things.

FATHER. Wise in everything with which *he* has to do. Can you recollect, Frederic, that definition of wisdom we met with the other day?

FREDERIC. Something of this sort, was it not, — that " *wisdom consists in employing the best means for the attainment of the most important end* " ?

FATHER. Very well. Then I think we have unquestionably seen a wise man this morning. You heard from himself the grand object of this good man's pursuit; and this must by every one be allowed to be the most important of all objects. He aims at nothing less than eternal life; and to this end he appears to employ the best means, such as God himself prescribes. And this wisdom, which is from above, teaches him to conduct himself wisely in all the relations of life. He is wise as a tradesman, — being honest and industrious, and exerting his ingenuity in his calling, as a talent which God has given him; so that he is one of the most ingenious mechanics in the neighborhood. He is wise as a neighbor, — living in peace and charity with all around him. He is wise as the master of a family, — being contented with such things as he has; never attempting to vie with his superiors, nor aiming to be thought what he is not. He showed himself to be a wise man, by choosing for a partner a wise woman; that is, a pious and prudent woman; and he conducts himself wisely as a husband and a father, — guiding his house with discretion, and training his children to tread in his own steps. He eminently displays also one of the invariable characteristics of

true wisdom, by his modest and unassuming deportment. But above all, and as the cause of all, this man
is *wise*, in making it his chief concern to be a Christian ;
not merely by profession, but in earnest. His religion,
you see, is of the true sort. It not only gives him a
hope of being happy hereafter, but it makes him happy
now. It shines in his face, and reigns in his dwelling.
In that solitary room where many would think it a
punishment to pass an hour, he enjoys daily the high
honor and happiness of holding communion with his
Maker, while the noisy world below are disquieting
themselves in vain with every passing vanity. And in
his daily walk and conversation he has this testimony,
that he pleases God.

Now, children, have I not performed my promise ?
Tell me, if you have not seen, according to the strictest
sense of the word, A WISE MAN ?

THE CLEVER FOOL.

NOT very long after the father and his children had
paid their visit to the wise man, the effects of a gentleman lately deceased in that neighborhood were adver-
tised for sale by auction. As it was well known that
his house contained many curiosities, persons from
miles round flocked to attend the sale ; and amongst
the rest this gentleman and his children, for he was so
good a father that he suffered no opportunity to escape
that might afford instruction or rational amusement to
his family.

" Children," said he to them, as they were driving to
the place, " you remember that some time ago I took
you to see a wise man. You were surprised by that
visit ; perhaps you will be still more so when I tell you
that we are going this morning to the late residence of

a man who, according to all that appeared of his character, might with equal propriety have been called *a
clever fool.*"

PHILIP.   A clever fool !

JULIA.   It seems a contradiction.

FREDERIC.   Papa will explain it, I dare say.

KATE.   A clever fool, — how droll !

FATHER.   As this poor gentleman was a stranger to
you, and as our opinions can now do him neither good
nor harm, I do not scruple, with a view of its being
useful to ourselves, to relate to you what appeared
unfavorable in his character.   But let us, at the same
time,. indulge a charitable hope that we may, after all,
be mistaken in our judgment.   Indeed, I could wish
as much as possible to keep him, as an individual, out
of sight.   I only mean to explain to you that a person
living and acting, as it is commonly reported he did,
can claim no higher appellation than that of a *clever
fool.*

CHILDREN.   Well, papa, now tell us how it was.

FATHER.   Nay, stay till we arrive at his house and
have looked about us, and then you shall judge for
yourselves.

Upon their arrival at the destined spot, they were
charmed with the beauty of the situation and the
pleasant aspect of the residence.   The house and
grounds were rather compact and elegant than extensive or magnificent; but there was a symmetry and
beauty of design which at once pleased the eye, and
conveyed an idea of the good taste of the possessor.
And as the general view was striking, the detail, when
examined, excited still greater admiration.   Our party
at first amused themselves with walking through the
park and gardens, which exhibited at every turn some
ingenious contrivance for pleasure or utility.   The
gardens displayed a variety of the most beautiful flowers, in the greatest perfection.   The greenhouses were

of themselves thought worth going many miles to see, they contained so rare a collection of exotics and other curious plants, disposed in the most exact order ; while fruits, in and out of season, yielded their tempting fragrance in rich profusion. Stately swans adorned the river that wound through the park ; while shady al-coves, rosy bowers, classic temples, baths and fountains, at every turn surprised the admiring visitor. The recesses of a shady grove conducted to a cool and beautiful grotto, which was enriched with some of the most rare and curious specimens in mineralogy. Lastly, they visited a small botanical garden, which afforded them much instruction as well as amusement ; for the late possessor was a man of science, and took particular pains with this well-arranged collection.

The children were delighted ; and not less surprised when they were assured that of these various embellish-ments and contrivances he was himself the designer and inventor, and that it was his own taste and ingenuity that was displayed in every part.

Upon entering the mansion, the effect was not less striking. The apartments were disposed and furnished with great taste and elegance, and continually exhibited some novel invention for promoting ease or pleasure, or for avoiding inconvenience. But what were the most interesting were the valuable collections in the various departments of art and science with which this house was embellished. A capital collection of old pictures, by the best masters, occupied the long gallery. The library was extensive, and contained a well-ar-ranged assemblage of the works of the most cele-brated authors of every age and in every language.

They were next shown a cabinet, containing a valua-ble assortment of ancient coins and medals ; after which they visited the laboratory, for it appeared that the deceased possessed a thorough knowledge of chemistry, and had himself made some ingenious discoveries in

that interesting science. Another room was devoted to
mechanism, and exhibited models of many of the most
useful and ingenious machines of modern invention,
some of them displaying improvements of his own. Last
of all, ascending to the highest story, they reached the
observatory, which was furnished with its appropriate
apparatus, and contained the largest telescope these
children had ever seen. The gentleman, it was said,
frequently passed whole nights in this place; astronomy
was his favorite study. For all these things were not
collected by him (as is frequently the case in the houses
of the rich) as mere appendages to wealth. The curiosities of science, art, and literature, are commonly
enough to be seen in the possession of persons of trifling
and vulgar minds, wholly incapable of deriving any other
gratification from them than as articles of show, and
who value them merely as they do the other expensive
ornaments of their dwellings. But in this instance they
were possessed by a man of taste and science, who
derived genuine pleasure from the pursuits in which he
was engaged, and who was therefore so far happy, useful, and respectable. When the party descended to
the lower part of the house they found it filled with
company, and the great hall exhibited a scene of noise,
bustle, and confusion. The auctioneer was at that
moment expatiating on the value of an article before
him, which some were cautiously examining; others
were marking their catalogues, — each was intent on his
own interests, and nothing was less thought of than he
to whom all had so lately belonged.

"Let us leave this noisy place, papa," said Julia,
"it makes me melancholy."

They soon made their way through the crowd; and
leaving the mansion, their father led them through a
fine plantation to the outskirts of the park, where they
soon discovered a little ivy-clad steeple, embowered in
dark chestnut trees, surrounded by a few lowly graves,

and adorned with one or two stately monuments. "Here," said the father, pointing to one of these, "lie the remains of this accomplished person."

"Now then, papa," said Philip, "pray tell us — though I partly guess — why you called such a clever man a fool."

"Because," replied his father, "of his whole existence, which he knew would be endless, he apparently provided for no more than the exceedingly small proportion of sixty-eight years. It is true that to make these sixty-eight years pass pleasantly he spared no pains ; and we will allow that he so far succeeded as to enjoy, during that time, more rational pleasure than most men who live only for this world. But, granting this, is it not still the lowest degree of folly for a man to devote all the energies of his mind to securing the comfort and entertainment of so short a period, and to make no provision for an eternal existence? There he lies ! All that he ever appeared to care for he has lost forever ! Those curious collections which he made with so much pains and cost, — all those fruits of his patient and laborious studies, which we have been admiring, — will in a few hours be disposed of and dispersed ; the cheerful mansion will be empty and deserted, other inhabitants will occupy it ; in a few years his name will be no more remembered ! So that the only thing that was of any real consequence to him is that which, it is greatly to be feared, he totally neglected.

"But the extremity of his folly was this, — that this change which he has undergone, this loss of all that he valued, was what he was well aware must somewhere about this time befall him. He knew as well as all other men that he must die. He knew, too, that the great Creator, whose works he spent his life in investigating and admiring, had by an express revelation informed him, in common with others, of the only way of securing everlasting life and happiness. Of these things he could not be ignorant, nor did I ever understand that he professed to doubt them ; yet, strange to say, that divine volume stood unopened on his shelves. It is said this unhappy man rarely read the Bible ; that he who could spend whole nights in gazing on the heavens, bent not his knee to the Former of them all ; that while so plenteously partaking the bounties of His providence, he never (unless with the utmost formality) acknowledged his obligation, or appeared to feel his dependence. Even of late, when he knew he must be drawing towards the close of life, he appeared to engage with as much avidity as ever in his favorite pursuits. Though he loved conversation, and delighted to discourse on other subjects, yet he was never known to talk about the life to come, upon which he was so soon to enter. Thus he deliberately chose to enjoy these few poor years, and to neglect his concerns for immortality. Now if this clever man had purposely set fire to his beautiful house, and had calmly seen all his valuable collections consumed by the flames, everybody would have exclaimed, ' What a fool ! ' As it was, he was extolled and applauded by most men, although guilty of incomparably greater madness than this.

" Children, endeavor to conceive (though it is impossible you should fully comprehend it) the tremendous folly of neglecting a book which God has sent us to read ! It is only because it is so very common for men to disregard their Bibles, that we are not more struck with the strange absurdity of it. This gentleman was particularly admired for the universality of his talents ; and it was always spoken to his praise that, while so much engaged in scientific pursuits, he attended equally to the elegances and refinements of life ; he was as cheerful a companion, and as finished a gentleman, as he was a sound philosopher. But, alas, how very far, it is to be feared, he was from being *universally* sagacious ! How very partial and limited even was his cleverness ! He not only knew that in a few years he must die, but, in some ways, he deliberately prepared for the event. He made his will ; he gave particular directions as to what should take place after his decease ; he even caused this vault to be built, left directions for his funeral, and wrote an inscription for his monument. So that, you see, he left nothing undone but that one thing which, alone, was of real consequence to him. This poor clever fool had no forethought, made no provision for his soul !

"I have been told that the last thing that occupied his attention was an improved method of raising pine-apples. By a great deal of thought and ingenuity, he succeeded in raising them some weeks earlier, and of a finer sort, than any that were grown in the neighborhood. Yes, children, here was a man of nearly seventy, really interested about *pine-apples*, while the great business of his eternal welfare was still unattended to ! A party of friends was invited to dine with him, in order to partake of this rich dessert ; but on the eve of this intended entertainment it was said to him, ' This night thy soul shall be required of thee.' He was found the next morning dead in his bed ; and now, whose are those things that he possessed ? "

JULIA. Oh, papa !

FATHER. Now, children, let us leave this melancholy spot ; remembering that whether or not our fears of this individual are well founded, we are but too well assured that the world abounds with men and women who if not as clever are quite as foolish as we have supposed him to have been. Let it be *our* chief concern that we may not be of the number. But never, never, till that day when this sepulchre shall be torn open by the voice of the archangel, will any human mind be fully able to comprehend the dreadful difference between a *plain wise man*, and a *clever fool*.

POEMS.

TO. MADAME DE STAËL.

WRITTEN AFTER READING "CORINNE, OU L'ITALIE."

O WOMAN, greatly gifted! why
Wert thou not gifted from on high?
What had that noble genius done,
That knew all hearts — all things, but *one*,
Had that been known?   Oh, would it might
Be whispered, here she took her flight!
Where, where is that fine spirit hurled,
That seemed unmeet for either world?

While o'er thy magic page I bend,
I know thee, claim thee for my friend;
With thee a secret converse hold,
And see my inmost thoughts unfold.
Each notion crude, defined, expressed;
And certain, what I vaguely guessed.
And hast thou taught, with cruel skill,
The art to suffer better still;
Grief's finest secret to explore,
Though understood too well before?
Ah, well! I 'd thank thee if I might;
Although so wrong, thou art so right!
While I condemn, my heart replies,
And deeper feelings sympathize.

Thy view of life, that painful view, —
How false it is ! and yet how true !
" Life without love — a cheerless strife ;
Yet love so rarely given to life."
And why must truth and virtue, why,
This mighty claim of love deny?
What was this earth, so full, so fair ?
A cheerless desert, bleak, and bare —
God knew it was — till love was there.
Say, has the heart a glance at bliss —
One — till it glance or gaze at this?
Ah, no ! unblessed, unsoothed the lot,
Fair though it seem, that knows it not !
'T is true ! and to the truth replies
A thousand joyless hearts and eyes, —
Eyes beamless, hearts that do not break —
They cannot — but that always ache ;
And slowly wither, day by day,
Till life at last is dried away.

" Love, or Religion ; " yes, she knew
Life has no choice but 'twixt the two.
But when she sought *that* balm to find,
She guessed and groped, but still was blind.
Aloft she flew, yet failed to see
Aught but an earthly deity.
The humble Christian's holy love,
Oh, how it calmly soars above
These storms of passion ! Yes, too much
I 've felt her talent's magic touch.
Return, my soul, to that retreat
From sin and woe — thy Saviour's feet !
There learn an art she never knew,
The heart's own empire to subdue :
A large, but willing sacrifice ;
All to resign that He denies ;
To him in meek submission bend,

Own Him an all-sufficient friend ;
Here, and in holy worlds above,
My portion — and my only love !

September 23, 1822.

TO THE MOON.

WHAT is it that gives thee, mild Queen of the Night,
    That secret intelligent grace ?
Oh, why should I gaze with such tender delight
    On thy fair, but insensible face ?

What gentle enchantment possesses thy beam,
    Beyond the warm sunshine of day ?
Thy bosom is cold as the glittering stream,
    Where dances thy tremulous ray.

Canst thou the sad heart of its sorrow beguile,
    Or grief's fond indulgence suspend ?
Yet where is the mourner but welcomes thy smile,
    And loves thee almost as a friend ?

The tear that looks bright in thy beam as it flows
    Unmoved thou dost ever behold ;
The sorrow that loves in thy light to repose,
    To thee it has never been told.

And yet thou dost soothe me, and ever I find,
    While watching thy gentle retreat,
A moonlight composure steal over the mind,
    Poetical, pensive, and sweet.

I think of the years that forever are fled ;
    Of follies by others forgot ;

Of joys that are vanished, of hopes that are dead,
   Of friendships that were, and are not.

I think of the future — still gazing the while,
   As thou couldst those secrets reveal ;
But ne'er dost thou grant an encouraging smile,
   To answer the mournful appeal.

Those beams which so bright through my casement
      appear,
   To far distant scenes they extend ;
Illumine the dwellings of those that are dear,
   And sleep on the grave of my friend.

Then still I must love thee, mild Queen of the Night,
   Since feeling and fancy agree
To make thee a source of unfailing delight,
   A friend and a solace to me.

1811.

A STORY.

THERE once was a man who contrived a balloon,
To carry him whither? — why, up to the moon.
One fine starlight night he set sail for the sky,
And joyfully bid our poor planet good-by.
He mounted aloft with incredible speed,
And saw the green earth every moment recede.
" Farewell," he exclaimed, " to thy pride and conceit,
Oppression and injury, fraud and deceit ;
Thy flagrant abuses, thy luxury too,
And all thy gay pageants, — forever adieu.

Thy festivals, spectacles, learning and lore ;
My share in thy pleasures I gladly restore, —
Thy kings and thy nobles, lords, ladies, and squires,
And all the poor world in its dotage admires.
From its factions and parties and politics free,
The statesmen and heroes are nothing to me ;
Bonaparte in his cage, on Helena's wild shore,
And all his devices, to me are no more.
Farewell to thy valleys, in verdure arrayed ;
Farewell to thy merchandise, traffic and trade ;
Thy wide-swelling rivers that roll to the seas ;
Thy dark waving forests, that sigh to the breeze, —
From Britain to China, or Ganges' wide stream ;
All fades on my sight like a vanishing dream."

He spoke, and with pleasure soon darted his eyes on
The moon, just appearing above the horizon ;
And sitting upright with his hand in his pocket,
Shot up the dark sky into space, like a rocket.
But the swiftness with which his light vehicle sped
Brought on such a giddiness into his head,
That he lay a long time in his boat without knowing
How long he had been or which way he was going.
At length he aroused from his stupor, when, lo !
The beautiful planet was shining below !
Already so near was he come, as to see
Its mountains and valleys, as plain as could be.
With feelings no language could well represent,
He quickly prepared his machine for descent.
A fine open plain, much resembling, he said,
Some spots in old England, before him was spread,
Whose smoothness and verdure his presence invited ;
And there, all amazement, our traveller alighted.
What thrillings of rapture, what tears of delight,
Now melted this signally fortunate wight ;
And thus he expressed his astonishment soon :
" Dear me, what a wonder to be in the moon !"

'T was now early morning, the firmament clear ;
For there the sun rises, the same as down here.
He took out his pocket-book, therefore, and wrote
Whatever he saw that was worthy of note.
For instance, the soil appeared sandy and loose ;
The pasture much finer than we can produce.
He picked up a stone, which he wished he could hand
To some learned geologists down in our land.
A blue little weed next attracted our writer,
Not very unlike to our hare-bell, but brighter,
And looked, as he said, most decidedly *lunar*, —
He wished he had come on this enterprise sooner.
But still he was far more impatient to trace
What sort of inhabitants lived in the place.
Perhaps they were dragons, or horrible things,
Like fishes with feathers, or serpents with wings.
Thus deeply engaged in conjectural thought,
His eye by an object was suddenly caught ;
To which, on advancing, he found, you must know,
'T was just such a mile-stone as ours are below.
And he read, all amazed, in plain English this line,
" Twelve miles to old Sarum, to Andover nine."
In short, the whole wonder at once to explain,
The man had alighted on Salisbury Plain.

RECREATION.

WE took our work, and went, you see,
To take an early cup of tea.
We did so now and then, to pay
The friendly debt, — and so did they.
Not that our friendship burnt so bright
That all the world could see the light ;
'T was of the ordinary *genus*,

And little love was lost between us.
We loved, I think, about as true
As such near neighbors mostly do.

At first, we all were somewhat dry ;
Mamma felt cold, and so did I.
Indeed, that room, sit where you will,
Has draught enough to turn a mill.
" I hope you 're warm," says Mrs. G.
" Oh, quite so," says mamma, says she ;
" I 'll take my shawl off by and by."
" This room is always warm," says I.

At last the tea came up, and so
With that our tongues began to go.
Now in that house you 're sure of knowing
The smallest scrap of news that 's going.
We find it there the wisest way
To take some care of what we say.

Says she, " There 's dreadful doings still
In that affair about the will ;
For now the folks in Brewer's Street
Don't speak to James's, when they meet.
Poor Mrs. Sam sits all alone,
And frets herself to skin and bone.
For months she managed, she declares,
All the old gentleman's affairs ;
And always let him have his way,
And never left him night nor day ;
Waited and watched his every look,
And gave him every drop he took.
Dear Mrs. Sam, it was too bad !
He might have left her all he had."

" Pray, ma'am," says I, " has poor Miss A.
Been left as handsome as they say ? "

"My dear," says she, "'t is no such thing,
She 'd nothing but a mourning ring.
But is it not *uncommon* mean,
To wear that rusty bombazine !"
"She had," says I, "the very same,
Three years ago, for — what 's his name ? "
"The Duke of *Brunswick ;* very true,
And has not bought a thread of new,
I 'm positive," said Mrs. G.
So then we laughed, and drank our tea.

"So," says mamma, "I find it 's true
What Captain P. intends to do, —
To hire that house, or else to buy — "
"Close to the tan-yard, ma'am," says I.
"Upon my word it 's very strange,
I wish they may n't repent the change ! "
"My dear," says she, "'t is very well
You know, if they can bear the smell."

"Miss F.," says I, "is said to be
A sweet young woman, Mrs. G."
"Oh, excellent ! I hear," she cried ;
"Oh, truly so !" mamma replied.
"How old should you suppose her, pray ?
She 's older than she looks, they say."
"Really," says I, "she seems to me
Not more than twenty-two or three."
"Oh, then you 're wrong," says Mrs. G.
"Their upper servant told our Jane,
She 'll not see twenty-nine again."
"Indeed, so old ?   I wonder why
She does not marry, then," says I ;
"So many thousands to bestow,
And such a beauty, too, you know."
"A beauty !   Oh, my dear Miss B.,
You must be joking now," says she.

" Her figure 's rather pretty," —   " Ah !
That 's what I say," replied mamma.

" Miss F.," says I, " I 've understood,
Spends all her time in doing good.
The people say her coming down
Is quite a blessing to the town."
At that our hostess fetched a sigh,
And shook her head ; and so says I,
" It 's very kind of her, I 'm sure,
To be so generous to the poor."
" No doubt," says she, " 't is very true ;
Perhaps here may be reasons too, —
You know some people like to pass
For patrons with the lower class."

And here I break my story's thread,
Just to remark that what she said,
Although I took the other part,
Went like a cordial to my heart.

Some innuendoes more had passed,
Till out the scandal came at last.
" Come, then, I 'll tell you something more,"
Says she, — " Eliza, shut the door.
I would not trust a creature here,
For all the world, but you, my dear.
Perhaps it 's false, — I wish it may, —
But let it go no further, pray ! "
" Oh," says mamma, " you need not fear ;
We never mention what we hear."
" Indeed we shall not, Mrs. G.,"
Says I, again, impatiently :
And so we drew our chairs the nearer,
And, whispering, lest the child should hear her,
She told a tale, at least too long
To be repeated in a song ;

We panting every breath between,
With curiosity and spleen.
And how we did enjoy the sport,
And echo every faint report,
And answer every candid doubt,
And turn her motives inside out,
And each reputed virtue hide, —
Till we were fully satisfied !

Thus having brought it to a close,
In great good humor we arose.
Indeed, 't was more than time to go,
Our boy had been an hour below.
So, warmly pressing Mrs. G.
To fix a day to come to tea,
We muffled up in cloak and plaid,
And trotted home behind the lad.

THE CHURCH-YARD.

THE moon rises bright in the east,
  The stars with pure brilliancy shine ;
The songs of the woodland have ceased,
  And still is the low of the kine.
The men, from their work on the hill,
  Trudge homeward with pitchfork and flail ;
The buzz of the hamlet is still,
  And the bat flaps his wings in the gale.

And, see ! from those darkly green trees
  Of cypress, and holly, and yew,
That wave their black arms in the breeze,
  The old village church is in view.

18

The owl, from her ivied retreat,
  Screams hoarse to the winds of the night;
And the clock, with its solemn repeat,
  Has tolled the departure of light.

My child, let us wander alone,
  When half the wide world is in bed,
And read o'er the mouldering stone,
  That tells of the mouldering dead.
And let us remember it well,
  That we must as certainly die;
For us, too, may toll the sad bell,
  And in the cold earth we must lie.

You are not so healthy and gay,
  So young, so active and bright,
That death cannot snatch you away,
  Or some dreadful accident smite.
Here lie both the young and the old,
  Confined in the coffin so small,
And the earth closes over them cold,
  And the grave-worm devours them all.

In vain were the beauty and bloom
  That once o'er their bodies were spread;
Now still, in the desolate tomb,
  Each rests his inanimate head.
Their hands, once so active for play,
  Their lips, which so merrily sung,
Now senseless and motionless lay,
  And stiff is the chattering tongue.

Then seek not, my child, as the best,
  Those things which so shortly must fade;
Let piety dwell in thy breast,
  And all of thine actions pervade.

And then, when beneath the green sod
 This active young body shall lie,
Thy soul shall ascend to its God,
 To live with the blest in the sky.

SPRING.

Ah ! see how the ices are melting away !
 The rivers have burst from their chain ;
The woods and the hedges with verdure look gay
 And daisies enamel the plain.

The sun rises high, and shines warm o'er the dale,
 The orchards with blossoms are white ;
The voice of the woodlark is heard in the vale,
 And the cuckoo returns from her flight.

Young lambs sport and frisk on the side of the hill,
 The honey-bee wakes from his sleep ;
The turtle-dove opens her soft-cooing bill,
 And snowdrops and primroses peep.

All Nature looks active, delightful, and gay ;
 The creatures begin their employ ;
Ah ! let me not be less industrious than they, —
 An idle or indolent boy.

Now while in the spring of my vigor and bloom,
 In the paths of fair learning I 'll run ;
Nor let the best part of my being consume,
 With nothing of consequence done.

Thus while to my lessons with care I attend,
  And store up the knowledge I gain,
When the winter of age shall upon me descend,
  'T will cheer the dark season of pain.

SUMMER.

THE heats of summer come hastily on,
  The fruits are transparent and clear;
The buds and the blossoms of April are gone,
  And the deep-colored cherries appear.

The blue sky above us is bright and serene,
  No cloud on its bosom remains;
The woods and the fields and the hedges are green,
  And the haycock smells sweet from the plains.

Down far in the valley where bubbles the spring
  Which soft through the meadow-land glides,
The lads from the mountain the heavy sheep bring,
  And shear the warm coat from their sides.

Ah! let me lie down in some shady retreat,
  Beside the meandering stream;
For the sun darts abroad an unbearable heat,
  And burns with his over-head beam.

There all the day idle my limbs I 'll extend,
  Fanned soft to delicious repose;
While round me a thousand sweet odors ascend
  From ev'ry gay wood-flower that blows.

But, hark ! from the woodlands what sounds do I hear?
   The voices of pleasure so gay ;
The merry young haymakers cheerfully bear
   The heat of the hot summer's day.

While some with bright scythe, singing shrill to the tone,
   The tall grass and buttercups mow,
Some spread it with rakes, and by others 't is thrown
   Into sweet-smelling cocks in a row.

Then since joy and glee with activity join,
   This moment to labor I 'll rise ;
While the idle love best in the shade to recline,
   And waste precious time as it flies.

To waste precious time we can never recall,
   Is waste of the wickedest kind ;
An instant of life has more value than all
   The gold that in India they find.

Not diamonds, that brilliantly beam in the mine,
   For one moment's time should be given ;
For gems can but make us look gaudy and fine,
   But time can prepare us for heaven.

AUTUMN.

THE sun is far risen above the old trees,
   His beams on the silver dew play ;
The gossamer tenderly waves in the breeze,
   And the mists are fast rolling away.

Let us leave the warm bed and the pillow of down ;
  The morning fair bids us arise,
Little boy ; for the shadows of midnight are flown,
  And sunbeams peep into our eyes.

We 'll pass by the garden that leads to the gate, —
  But where is its gayety now?
The Michaelmas daisy blows lonely and late,
  And the yellow leaf whirls from the bough.

Last night the glad reapers their harvest-home sung,
  And stored the full garners with grain ;
Did you hear how the woods with their merry shouts
      rung,
  As they bore the last sheaf from the plain?

But, hark ! from the woodlands the sound of a gun !
  The wounded bird flutters and dies.
Ah ! surely 't is wicked, for nothing but fun,
  To shoot the poor thing as it flies.

The timid hare, too, in affright and dismay,
  Runs swift through the brushwood and grass ;
How she turns, how she winds ! and she tries every way,
  But the cruel dogs won't let her pass.

TO A LITTLE GIRL THAT HAS TOLD
A LIE.

AND has my darling told a lie?
Did she forget that God was by?
That God, who saw the thing she did,
From whom no action can be hid, —

Did she forget that God could see,
And hear, wherever she might be?

He made your eyes, and can discern
Whichever way you think to turn;
He made your ears, and he can hear
When you may think nobody's near.
In every place, by night or day,
He watches all you do and say.

You thought, because you were alone,
Your falsehood never could be known.
But liars always are found out,
Whatever ways they wind about;
And always be afraid, my dear,
To tell a lie — for God can hear!

I wish, my dear, you'd always try
To act as shall not need a lie.
And when you wish a thing to do
That has been once forbidden you,
Remember that, nor ever dare
To disobey — for God is there!

Why should you fear to tell me true?
Confess, and then I'll pardon you.
Tell me you're sorry, and will try
To act the better by and by,
And then, whate'er your crime has been,
It won't be half so great a sin.

But cheerful, innocent, and gay,
As passes by the smiling day,
You'll never have to turn aside
From any one your faults to hide;
Nor heave a sigh, nor have a fear,
That either God or I should hear.

MEDDLESOME MATTY.

Oh, how one ugly trick has spoiled
    The sweetest and the best !
Matilda, though a pleasant child,
    One ugly trick possessed,
Which, like a cloud before the skies,
Hid all her better qualities.

Sometimes she 'd lift the teapot lid,
    To peep at what was in it ;
Or tilt the kettle, if you did
    But turn your back a minute.
In vain you told her not to touch,
Her trick of meddling grew so much.

Her grandmamma went out one day,
    And by mistake she laid
Her spectacles and snuff-box gay
    Too near the little maid :
"Ah ! well," thought she, " I 'll try them on,
As soon as grandmamma is gone."

Forthwith she placed upon her nose
    The glasses, large and wide ;
And looking round, as I suppose,
    The snuff-box too she spied.
" Oh, what a pretty box is this !
I 'll open it," said little miss.

" I know that grandmamma would say,
    ' Don't meddle with it, dear ! '
But then, she 's far enough away,
    And no one else is near."

Besides, what can there be amiss
In opening such a box as this?"

So thumb and finger went to work
  To move the stubborn lid;
And presently a mighty jerk
  The mighty mischief did;
For all at once, ah! woful case,
The snuff came puffing in her face!

Poor eyes and nose, and mouth and chin,
  A dismal sight presented;
And as the snuff got further in
  Sincerely she repented.
In vain she ran about for ease,
She could do nothing else but sneeze!

She dashed the spectacles away,
  To wipe her tingling eyes;
And as in twenty bits they lay,
  Her grandmamma she spies.
"Hey-day! and what's the matter now?"
Cried grandmamma, with lifted brow.

Matilda, smarting with the pain,
  And tingling still, and sore,
Made many a promise to refrain
  From meddling evermore;
And 't is a fact, as I have heard,
She ever since has kept her word.

THE WORM.

No, little worm, you need not slip
Into your hole, with such a skip;
Drawing the gravel as you glide
On to your smooth and slimy side.
I'm not a crow, poor worm, not I,
Peeping about your holes to spy,
And fly away with you in air,
To give my young ones each a share.
No; and I'm not a rolling-stone,
Creaking along with hollow groan;
Nor am I of the naughty crew
Who don't care what poor worms go through,
But trample on them as they lay,
Rather than step the other way;
Or keep them dangling on a hook,
Choked in a dismal pond or brook,
Till some poor fish comes swimming past,
And finishes their pain at last.
For my part, I could never bear
Your tender flesh to hack and tear,
Forgetting that poor worms endure
As much as I should, to be sure,
If any giant should come and jump
On to my back, and kill me plump;
Or run my heart through with a scythe,
And think it fun to see me writhe!

Oh no, I'm only looking about
To see you wriggle in and out,
And drawing together your slimy rings,
Instead of feet, like other things.
So, little worm, don't slide and slip
Into your hole, with such a skip.

FIRE.

WHAT is it that shoots from the mountains so high,
  In many a beautiful spire?
What is it that blazes and curls to the sky?
  This beautiful something is Fire.

Loud noises are heard in the caverns to groan,
  Hot cinders fall thicker than snow;
Huge stones to a wonderful distance are thrown,
  For burning fire rages below.

When Winter blows bleak, and loud bellows the storm,
  And frostily twinkle the stars;
Then bright burns the fire in the chimney so warm,
  And the kettle sings shrill on the bars.

Then call the poor traveller, covered with snow,
  And warm him with charity kind;
Fire is not so warm as the feelings that glow
  In the friendly, benevolent mind.

By fire rugged metals are fitted for use, —
  Iron, copper, gold, silver, and tin;
Without its assistance we could not produce
  So much as a minikin pin.

Fire rages with fury wherever it comes,
  If only one spark should be dropped;
Whole houses, or cities, sometimes it consumes,
  Where its violence cannot be stopped.

And when the great morning of judgment shall rise,
  How wide will its blazes be curled!
With heat, fervent heat, it shall melt down the skies,
  And burn up this beautiful world.

AIR.

WHAT is it that winds about over the world,
  Spread thin like a covering fair?
Into each crack and crevice 't is artfully curled;
  This sly little fluid is Air.

In summer's still evening how peaceful it floats,
  When not a leaf moves on the spray,
And no sound is heard but the nightingale's notes,
  And merry gnats dancing away.

The village bells glide on its bosom serene,
  And steal in sweet cadence along;
The shepherd's soft pipe warbles over the green,
  And the cottage girls join in the song.

But when winter blows, then it bellows aloud,
  And roars in the northerly blast;
With fury drives on the snowy blue cloud,
  And cracks the tall, tapering mast.

The sea rages wildly, and mounts to the skies
  In billows and fringes of foam;
And the sailor in vain turns his pitiful eyes
  Towards his dear, peaceable home.

When fire lies and smothers, or gnaws thro' the beam,
  Air forces it fiercer to glow;
And engines in vain their cold torrents may stream,
  Unless the wind ceases to blow.

In the forest it tears up the sturdy old oak,
  That many a tempest had known;
The tall mountain's pine into splinters is broke,
  And over the precipice blown.

And yet, though it rages with fury so wild,
   On the solid earth, water, or fire,
Without its assistance the tenderest child
   Would struggle, and gasp, and expire.

Pure air, pressing into the curious clay,
   Gave life to these bodies at first;
And when in the bosom it ceases to play,
   We crumble again to our dust.

EARTH.

WHAT is it that 's covered so richly with green,
   And gives to the forest its birth?
A thousand plants bloom on its bosom serene;
   Whose bosom? — the bosom of Earth.

Hidden deep in its bowels the emerald shines,
   The ruby, and amethyst blue;
And silver and gold glitter bright in the mines
   Of Mexico rich, and Peru.

Large quarries of granite and marble are spread
   In its wonderful bosom like bones;
Chalks, gravel, and coals, salt, sulphur, and lead,
   And thousands of beautiful stones.

Beasts, savage and tame, of all colors and forms,
   Either stalk in its deserts, or creep;
White bears sit and growl to the northerly storms,
   And shaggy goats bound from the steep.

The oak and the snowdrop, the cedar and rose,
    Alike on its bosom are seen ;
The tall fir of Norway, surrounded with snows,
    And the mountain-ash scarlet and green.

Fine grass and rich mosses creep over its hills,
    A thousand flowers breathe in the gale ;
Tall water-seeds dip in its murmuring rills,
    And harvests wave bright in the vale.

And when this poor body is cold and decayed,
    And this warm throbbing heart is at rest,
My head upon thee, mother Earth, shall be laid,
    To find a long home in thy breast.

WATER.

WHAT is it that glitters so clear and serene,
    Or dances in billows so white?
Ships skimming along on its surface are seen, —
    'T is water that glitters so bright.

Sea-weeds wind about in its cavities wet,
    The pearl oyster quietly sleeps ;
A thousand fair shells, yellow, amber, and jet,
    And coral, glow red in its deeps.

Whales lash the white foam in their frolicsome wrath,
    While hoarsely the winter wind roars ;
And shoals of green mackerel stretch from the north,
    And wander along by our shores.

When tempests sweep over its bosom serene,
   Like mountains its billows arise ;
The ships now appear to be buried between, —
   And now, carried up to the skies.

It gushes out clear from the sides of the hill,
   And sparkles right down from the steep ;
Then waters the valley, and roars through the mill,
   And wanders in many a sweep.

The traveller that crosses the desert so wide,
   Hot, weary, and stifled with dust,
Longs often to stoop at some rivulet's side,
   To quench in its waters his thirst.

The stately white swan glides along on its breast,
   Nor ruffles its surface serene ;
And the duckling unfledged waddles out of its nest,
   To dabble in ditch-water green.

The clouds blown about in the chilly blue sky
   Vast cisterns of water contain ;
Like snowy white feathers in winter they fly,
   In summer stream gently in rain.

When sunbeams so bright on the falling drops shine,
   The rainbow enlivens the shower,
And glows in the heavens a beautiful sign,
   That water shall drown us no more.

MY MOTHER.

Who fed me from her gentle breast,
And hushed me in her arms to rest,
And on my cheek sweet kisses pressed?
> My Mother.

When sleep forsook my open eye,
Who was it sang sweet lullaby,
And rocked me that I should not cry?
> My Mother.

Who sat and watched my infant head,
When sleeping on my cradle bed,
And tears of sweet affection shed?
> My Mother.

When pain and sickness made me cry,
Who gazed upon my heavy eye,
And wept for fear that I should die?
> My Mother.

Who dressed my doll in clothes so gay,
And taught me pretty how to play,
And minded all I had to say?
> My Mother.

Who ran to help me when I fell,
And would some pretty story tell,
Or kiss the place to make it well?
> My Mother.

Who taught my infant lips to pray,
And love God's holy book and day,
And walk in wisdom's pleasant way?
> My Mother.

And can I ever cease to be
Affectionate and kind to thee,
Who wast so very kind to me?

My Mother.

Ah! no, the thought I cannot bear;
And if God please my life to spare,
I hope I shall reward thy care,

My Mother.

When thou art feeble, old, and gray,
My healthy arms shall be thy stay,
And I will soothe thy pains away,

My Mother.

And when I see thee hang thy head,
'T will be my turn to watch thy bed,
And tears of sweet affection shed,

My Mother.

For God, who lives above the skies,
Would look with vengeance in his eyes,
If I should ever dare despise

My Mother.

READING.

"AND so you do not like to spell,
Mary, my dear? Oh, very well;
'T is dull and troublesome, you say,
And you had rather be at play.

"Then bring me all your books again, —
Nay, Mary, why do you complain?

For as you do not choose to read,
You shall not have your books, indeed.

"So, as you wish to be a dunce,
Pray go and fetch me them at once ;
For as you will not learn to spell,
'T is vain to think of reading well.

"Now don't you think you'll blush to own,
When you become a woman grown,
Without one good excuse to plead,
That you have never learned to read?"

"O dear mamma," said Mary then,
"Do let me have my books again.
I never more will fret, indeed,
If you will let me learn to read."

———

IDLENESS.

SOME people complain they have nothing to do,
   And time passes slowly away ;
They saunter about with no object in view,
   And long for the end of the day.

In vain are their riches, or honors, or birth,
   They nothing can truly enjoy ;
They 're the wretchedest creatures that live on the earth,
   For want of some pleasing employ.

When people have no need to work for their bread,
   And indolent always have been,
It never so much as comes into their head
   That wasting their time is a sin.

But man was created for some useful employ,
　　From earth's first creation till now ;
And 't is good for his health, his comfort, and joy,
　　To live by the sweat of his brow.

And those who of riches are fully possessed
　　Are not for that reason exempt ; ⸚
If they give themselves up to an indolent rest,
　　They are objects of real contempt.

The pleasure that constant employments create,
　　By them cannot be understood ;
And though they may rank with the rich and the great,
　　They never can rank with the good.

THE PIN.

" DEAR me ! what signifies a pin,
　　Wedged in a rotten board ?
I 'm certain that I won't begin
　　At ten years old to hoard !
I never will be called a miser,
That, I 'm determined," said Eliza.

So onward tripped the little maid
　　And left the pin behind,
Which very snug and quiet laid,
　　To its hard fate resigned ;
Nor did she think (a careless chit)
'T was worth her while to stoop for it.

Next day a party was to ride
　　To see an air balloon ;·

And all the company beside
   Were dressed and ready soon ;
But she a woful case was in,
For want of just a single pin !

In vain her eager eye she brings
   To every darksome crack ;
There was not one ! and all her things
   Were dropping off her back.
She cut her pincushion in two,
But, no ! not one had slidden through.

At last, as hunting on the floor
   Over a crack she lay,
The carriage rattled to the door,
   Then rattled fast away ;
But poor Eliza was not in,
For want of just — a single pin.

There 's hardly anything so small,
   So trifling, or so mean,
That we may never want at all
   For service unforeseen.
And wilful waste, depend upon 't,
Is, almost always, woful want !

THE CHATTERBOX.

From morning till night it was Lucy's delight
   To chatter and talk without stopping ;
There was not a day but she rattled away,
   Like water forever a-dropping !

As soon as she rose, while she put on her clothes,
  'T was vain to endeavor to still her;
Nor once did she lack to continue her clack,
  Till again she lay down on her pillow.

You 'll think now, perhaps, that there would have been
    gaps,
  If she had not been wonderful clever;
That her sense was so great, and so witty her pate,
  That it would be forthcoming forever.

But that 's quite absurd, for have you not heard
  That much tongue and few brains are connected;
That they are supposed to think least who talk most,
  And their wisdom is always suspected?

While Lucy was young, if she 'd bridled her tongue
  With a little good sense and exertion,
Who knows but she might now have been our delight,
  Instead of our jest and aversion?

THE SNOWDROP.

I SAW a snowdrop on the bed,
  Green taper leaves among;
Whiter than driven snow, its head
  On the slim stalk was hung.

The wintry winds came sweeping o'er;
  A bitter tempest blew;
The snowdrop faded — never more
  To glitter with the dew.

I saw a smiling infant laid
   In its fond mother's arms ;
Around its rosy cheek there played
   A thousand dimpling charms.

A bitter pain was sent to take
   The smiling babe away ;
How did its little bosom shake,
   As in a fit it lay !

Its beating heart was quickly stopped,
   And in the earth so cold
I saw the little coffin dropped,
   And covered up with mould.

Dear little children, who may read
   This mournful story through,
Remember death may come with speed
   And bitter pains for you.

THE YELLOW LEAF.

I saw a leaf come tilting down
   From a bare, withered bough ;
The leaf was dead, the branch was brown,
   No fruit was left it now.

But much the rattling tempest blew
   The naked boughs among ;
And here and there came whirling through
   A leaf that loosely hung.

This leaf, they tell me, once was green,
　Washed by the showers soft ;
High on the topmost bough 't was seen,
　And flourished up aloft.

I saw an old man totter slow,
　Wrinkled, and weak, and gray ;
He 'd hardly strength enough to go
　Ever so short a way.

His ear was deaf, his eye was dim,
　He leaned on crutches high ;
But while I stayed to pity him,
　I saw him gasp and die.

This poor old man was once as gay
　As rosy health could be ;
Yes, and the youngest head must lay,
　Ere long, as low as he !

THE POPPY.

High on a bright and sunny bed
　A scarlet poppy grew ;
And up it held its staring head,
　And held it out to view.

Yet no attention did it win
　By all these efforts made,
And less offensive had it been
　In some retired shade.

For though within its scarlet breast
   No sweet perfume was found,
It seemed to think itself the best   •
   Of all the flowers around.

From this may I a hint obtain,
   And take great care indeed,
Lest I should grow as pert and vain
   As is this gaudy weed.

THE VIOLET.

Down in the green and shady bed
   A modest violet grew ;
Its stalk was bent, it hung its head
   As if to hide from view.

And yet it was a lovely flower,
   Its colors bright and fair ;
It might have graced a rosy bower,
   Instead of hiding there.

Yet there it was content to bloom,
   In modest tints arrayed ;
And there it spreads its sweet perfume
   Within the silent shade.

Then let me to the valley go,
   This pretty flower to see ;
That I may also learn to grow
   In sweet humility.

THE WAY TO BE HAPPY.

How pleasant it is at the end of the day
   No follies to have to repent;
But reflect on the past, and be able to say
   That my time has been properly spent!

When I 've done all my business with patience and care,
   And been good, and obliging, and kind;
I lie on my pillow, and sleep away there,
   With a happy and peaceable mind.

But instead of all this, if it must be confessed,
   That I careless and idle have been;
I lie down as usual to go to my rest,
   But feel discontented within.

Then as I don't like all the trouble I 've had,
   In future I 'll try to prevent it;
For I never am naughty without being sad,
   Or good without being contented.

THE CRUEL THORN.

A BIT of wool sticks here upon this thorn, —
   Ah, cruel thorn, to tear it from the sheep!
And yet, perhaps, with pain its fleece was worn,
   Its coat so thick, a hot and cumbrous heap.

The wool a little bird takes in his bill,
  And with it up to yonder tree he flies;
A nest he's building there with matchless skill,
  Compact and close, that cold and rain defies.

To line that nest, the wool so soft and warm
  Preserves the eggs which hold its tender young;
And when they're hatched, the wool will keep from
      harm
  The callow brood, until they're fledged and strong.

Thus birds find use for what the sheep can spare.
  In this, my child, a wholesome moral spy;
And when the poor shall crave, thy plenty share, —
  Let thy abundance thus their wants supply.

THE NOTORIOUS GLUTTON.

A DUCK, who had got such a habit of stuffing
That all the day long she was panting and puffing,
And by every creature who did her great crop see,
Was thought to be galloping fast for a dropsy, —

One day, after eating a plentiful dinner,
With full twice as much as there should have been in
      her,
While up to her eyes in the gutter a-roking,
Was greatly alarmed by the symptoms of choking.

Now there was an old fellow, much famed for dis-
      cerning, —
A drake, who had taken a liking for learning,

And, high in repute with his feathery friends,
Was called Dr. Drake : for this doctor she sends.

In a hole of the dunghill was Dr. Drake's shop,
Where he kept a few simples for curing the crop ;
Some gravel and pebbles, to help the digestion,
And certain famed plants of the doctor's selection.

So, taking a handful of comical things,
And brushing his topple and pluming his wings,
And putting his feathers in apple-pie order,
Set out, to prescribe for the lady's disorder.

" Dear sir," said the duck, with a delicate quack,
Just turning a little way round on her back,
And leaning her head on a stone in the yard,
" My case, Dr. Drake, is exceedingly hard.

" I feel so distended with wind, and oppressed,
So squeamish and faint, such a load at my chest ;
And day after day, I assure you it is hard,
To suffer with patience these pains in my gizzard."

" Give me leave," said the doctor, with medical look,
As her flabby cold paw in his fingers he took ;
" By the feel of your pulse — your complaint, I 've
        been thinking,
Is caused by your habit of eating and drinking."

" Oh no, sir, believe me," the lady replied
(Alarmed for her stomach as well as her pride),
" I am sure it arises from nothing I eat,
For I rather suspect I got wet in my feet.

" I 've only been roking a bit in the gutter,
Where the cook had been pouring some cold melted
        butter ;

And a slice of green cabbage, and scraps of cold
      meat,
Just a trifle or two, that I thought I could eat."

The doctor was just to his business proceeding, —
By gentle emetics, a blister, and bleeding, —
When all on a sudden she rolled on her side,
Gave a horrible quackle, a struggle, and died !

Her remains were interred in a neighboring swamp
By her friends, with a great deal of funeral pomp ;
But I 've heard this inscription her tombstone was put on,
" Here lies Mrs. Duck, the notorious glutton."
And all the young ducklings are brought by their
      friends,
To learn the disgrace in which gluttony ends.

THE CHILD'S MONITOR.

THE wind blows down the largest tree,
And yet the wind I cannot see.
Playmates far off, that have been kind,
My thought can bring before my mind ;
The past by it is present brought,
And yet I cannot see my thought.
The charming rose perfumes the air,
Yet I can see no perfumes there.
Blithe Robin's notes — how sweet, how clear !
From his small bill they reach my ear ;
And whilst upon the air they float,
I hear, yet cannot see a note.

When I would do what is forbid,
By something in my heart I 'm chid ;
When good I think, then quick and pat,
That something says, " My child, do that."
When I too near the stream would go,
So pleased to see the waters flow,
That something says, without a sound,
" Take care, dear child, you may be drowned."
And for the poor whene'er I grieve,
That something says, " A penny give."
Thus Spirits good and ill there be,
Although invisible to me ;
Whate'er I do, they see me still,
But oh, good Spirits, guide my will !

THE BUTTERFLY.

THE butterfly, an idle thing,
Nor honey makes, nor yet can sing,
   Like to the bee and bird ;
Nor does it, like the prudent ant,
Lay up the grain for time of want,
   A wise and cautious hoard.

My youth is but a summer's day.
Then, like the bee and ant, I 'll lay
   A store of learning by ;
And though from flower to flower I rove,
My stock of wisdom I 'll improve,
   Nor be a Butterfly.

THE SPIDER AND HIS WIFE.

In a little dark crack half a yard from the ground
    An honest old spider resided ;
So pleasant and snug and convenient 't was found,
That his friends came to see it from many miles round.
    It seemed for his pleasure provided.

Of the cares, and fatigues, and distresses of life
    This spider was thoroughly tired ;
So leaving those scenes of contention and strife,
His children all settled, he came with his wife,
    To live in this cranny retired.

He thought that the little his wife would consume
    'T would be easy for him to provide her ;
Forgetting he lived in a gentleman's room,
Where came every morning a maid and a broom, —
    Those pitiless foes to a spider.

For when — as sometimes it would chance to befall —
    Just when his neat web was completed,
Brush would come the great broom down the side of
      the wall,
And perhaps carry with it web, spider, and all, —
    He thought himself cruelly treated.

One day, when their cupboard was empty and dry,
    His wife (Mrs. Hairy-leg Spinner)
Said to him, " Dear, go to the cobweb and try
If you can't find the leg or the wing of a fly,
    As a bit of a relish for dinner."

Directly he went, his long search to resume
    (For nothing he ever denied her),

Alas ! little guessing his terrible doom, —
Just then came the gentleman into his room,
   And saw the unfortunate spider.

So while the poor fellow, in search of his pelf,
   In the cobwebs continued to linger,
The gentleman reached a long cane from the shelf
(For certain good reasons best known to himself,
   Preferring his stick to his finger),

Then presently poking him down to the floor,
   Not stopping at all to consider,
With one horrid crush the whole business was o'er ;
The poor little spider was heard of no more,
   To the lasting distress of his widow !

NEVER PLAY WITH FIRE.

My prayers I said, I went to bed,
   And soon I fell asleep :
But soon I woke, my sleep was broke,
   I through my curtains peep.

I heard a noise of men and boys,
   The watchman's rattle too ;
And " Fire ! " they cried — and then cried I,
   " Oh dear, what shall I do ? "

A shout so loud came from the crowd,
   Around, above, below ;
And in the street the neighbors meet,
   Who would the matter know.

Now down the stairs run threes and pairs
　　Enough to break their bones,
The firemen swear, the engines tear
　　And thunder o'er the stones.

The roof and wall, and stair and all,
　　And rafters tumble in ;
Red flames and blaze now all amaze,
　　And make a dreadful din !

And horrid screams, when bricks and beams
　　Came tumbling on their heads ;
And some are smashed, and some are crashed ;
　　Some leap on feather beds.

Some burn, some choke, with fire and smoke !
　　And, oh, what was the cause?
My heart 's dismayed, last night I played
　　With Tommy, lighting straws !

———

THE LARK.

FROM his humble grassy bed
　　See the warbling lark arise !
By his grateful wishes led
　　Through those regions of the skies.

Songs of thanks and praise he pours,
　　Harmonizing airy space,
Sings, and mounts, and higher soars,
　　Towards the throne of heavenly grace.

Small his gifts compared to mine ;
   Poor my thanks with him compared, —
I 've a soul almost divine ;
   Angels' blessings with me shared.

Wake, my soul ! to praise aspire,
   Reason, every sense, accord ;
Join in pure seraphic fire ;
   Love, and thank, and praise the Lord.

THE TRUANT BOYS.

The month was April, and the morning cool,
   When Hal and Ned,
To walk together to the neighboring school,
   Rose early from their bed.

When reached the school, Hal said, " Why con your task
   Demure and prim?
Ere we go in, let me one question ask :
   Ned, shall we go swim?"

Fearless of future punishment or blame,
   Away they hied
Through many verdant fields, until they came
   Unto the river side.

The broad stream narrowed in its onward course,
   And deep and still
It silent ran, and yet with rapid force
   To turn a neighboring mill.

20

Under the mill an arch gaped wide, and seemed
   The jaws of death !
Through this the smooth deceitful waters teemed
   On dreadful wheels beneath.

They swim the river wide, nor think nor care ;
   The waters flow,
And by the current strong they carried are
   Into the mill-stream now.

Through the swift waters, as young Ned was rolled,
   The gulf when near,
On a kind brier by chance he laid fast hold,
   And stopped his dread career.

But luckless Hal was by the mill-wheel torn,
   A warning sad !
And the untimely death all friends now mourn,
   Of this poor truant lad !

GEORGE AND THE CHIMNEY-SWEEPER.

His petticoats now George cast off,
   For he was four years old ;
His trousers were nankeen so fine,
   His buttons bright as gold.
" May I," said little George, " go out
   My pretty clothes to show ?
May I, papa ? may I, mamma ? "
   The answer was, " No, no !

" Go, run below, George, in the court,
  But go not in the street,
Lest naughty boys should play some trick,
  Or gypsies you should meet."
Yet, though forbade, George went unseen,
  The little boys to see,
And all admired him when he lisped,
  " Now who so fine as me?"

But while he strutted to and fro,
  So proud, as I 've heard tell,
A sweep-boy passed, whom to avoid
  He slipped and down he fell.
The sooty lad was kind and good,
  To Georgy boy he ran ;
He raised him up, and kissing said,
  " Hush, hush, my little man ! "

He rubbed and wiped his clothes with care,
  And hugging said, " Don't cry !
Go home, as quick as you can go !
  Sweet little boy, good-by."
Poor George looked down, and, lo ! his dress
  Was blacker than before ;
All over soot, and mud, and dirt,
  He reached his father's door.

He sobbed, and wept, and looked ashamed,
  His fault he did not hide ;
And since so sorry for his fault,
  Mamma she did not chide.
That night when he was gone to bed,
  He jumped up in his sleep,
And cried, and sobbed, and cried again,
  " I thought I saw the sweep ! "

SOPHIA'S FOOL'S-CAP.

SOPHIA was a little child,
Obliging, good, and very mild,
Yet, lest of dress she should be vain,
Mamma still dressed her well, but plain.
Her parents, sensible and kind,
Wished only to adorn her mind;
No other dress, when good, had she,
But useful, neat simplicity.

Though seldom, yet when she was rude,
Or ever in a naughty mood,
Her punishment was this disgrace, —
A large fine cap adorned with lace,
With feathers and with ribbons too;
The work was neat, the fashion new!
Yet, as a fool's-cap was its name,
She dreaded much to wear the same.

A lady, fashionably gay,
Did to mamma a visit pay.
Sophia stared, then whispering said,
" Why, dear mamma, look at her head!
To be so tall and wicked too,
The strangest thing I ever knew!
What naughty tricks, pray, has she done,
That they have put a fool's-cap on?"

WASHING AND DRESSING.

AH ! why will my dear little girl be so cross,
  And cry, and look sulky, and pout?
To lose her sweet smile is a terrible loss,
  I can't even kiss her without.

You say you don't like to be washed and be dressed,
  But would you be dirty and foul?
Come, drive that long sob from your dear little breast,
  And clear your sweet face from its scowl.

If the water is cold, and the comb hurts your head,
  And the soap has got into your eye,
Will the water grow warmer for all that you 've said?
  And what good will it do you to cry?

It is not to tease you, and hurt you, my sweet,
  But only for kindness and care
That I wash you, and dress you, and make you look
    neat,
  And comb out your tanglesome hair.

I don't mind the trouble, if you would not cry,
  But pay me for all with a kiss.
That's right, take the towel and wipe your wet eye,
  I thought you 'd be good after this.

THE PLUM CAKE.

" Oh, I 've got a plum cake, and a rare feast I 'll make ;
    I 'll eat, and I 'll stuff, and I 'll cram :
Morning, noontime, and night, it shall be my delight,—
    What a happy young fellow I am ! "

Thus said little George, and, beginning to gorge,
    With zeal to his cake he applied ;
While fingers and thumbs, for the sweetmeats and plums,
    Were hunting and digging beside.

But — woful to tell ! — a misfortune befell,
    Which ruined his capital fun ;
After eating his fill he was taken so ill
    That he trembled for what he had done.

As he grew worse and worse, the doctor and nurse
    To cure his disorder were sent ;
And rightly, you 'll think, he had physic to drink,
    Which made him his folly repent.

And while on his bed he rolled his hot head,
    Impatient with sickness and pain,
He could not but take this reproof from his cake,
    " Don't be such a glutton again."

ANOTHER PLUM CAKE.

" Oh, I 've got a plum cake, and a feast let us make !
   Come, school-fellows, come at my call !
I assure you 't is nice, and we 'll each have a slice,
   Here 's more than enough for us all."

Thus said little Jack, as he gave it a smack,
   And sharpened his knife for the job ;
While round him a troop formed a clamorous group,
   And hailed him the king of the mob.

With masterly strength he cut through it at length,
   And gave to each playmate a share.
Dick, William, and James, and many more names,
   Partook his benevolent care.

And when it was done, and they 'd finished their fun,
   To marbles or hoop they went back,
And each little boy felt it always a joy
   To do a good turn for good Jack.

In his task and his book his best pleasures he took ;
   And as he thus wisely began,
Since he 's been a man grown, he has constantly shown
   That a good boy will make a good man.

NURSERY RHYMES.

THE COW.

THANK you, pretty cow, that made
Pleasant milk to soak my bread,
Every day, and every night,
Warm, and fresh, and sweet, and white.

Do not chew the hemlock rank,
Growing on the weedy bank ;
But the yellow cowslips eat,
They perhaps will make it sweet.

Where the purple violet grows,
Where the bubbling water flows,
Where the grass is fresh and fine,
Pretty cow, go there and dine.

GOOD NIGHT.

LITTLE baby, lay your head
On your pretty cradle-bed ;
Shut your eye-peeps, now the day
And the light are gone away.

All the clothes are tucked in tight ;
Little baby dear, good night !

Yes, my darling, well I know
How the bitter wind doth blow ;
And the winter's snow and rain
Patter on the window-pane.
But they cannot come in here,
To my little baby dear ;

For the window shutteth fast,
Till the stormy night is past ;
Or the curtains we may spread
Round about her cradle-bed.
So till morning shineth bright,
Little baby dear, good night !

GETTING UP.

Now, my baby, ope your eye,
For the sun is in the sky,
And he 's peeping once again
Through the frosty window-pane.
Little baby, do not keep
Any longer fast asleep.

There now, sit in mother's lap,
That she may untie your cap ;
For the little strings have got   .
Twisted into such a knot.
Yes, you know you 've been at play
With the bobbin as you lay.

There it comes, now let us see
Where your petticoats can be.
Oh ! they 're in the window-seat,
Folded very smooth and neat.
When my baby older grows,
She shall double up her clothes.

Now one pretty little kiss,
For dressing you so nice as this.
But before we go down stairs,
Don't forget to say your prayers ;
For 't is God who loves to keep
Little babies while they sleep.

———

BABY AND MAMMA.

WHAT a little thing am I !
    Hardly higher than the table.
I can eat, and play, and cry,
    But to work I am not able.

Nothing in the world I know,
    But mamma will try and show me.
Sweet mamma, I love her so,
    She 's so very kind unto me.

And she sets me on her knee,
    Very often, for some kisses.
Oh ! how good I 'll try to be,
    For such a dear mamma as this is.

THE STAR.

Twinkle, twinkle, little star,
How I wonder what you are !
Up above the world so high,
Like a diamond in the sky.

When the blazing sun is gone,
When he nothing shines upon,
Then you show your little light, —
Twinkle, twinkle, all the night.

Then the traveller in the dark
Thanks you for your tiny spark.
He could not see which way to go,
If you did not twinkle so.

In the dark blue sky you keep,
And often through my curtains peep ;
For you never shut your eye
Till the sun is in the sky.

As your bright and tiny spark
Lights the traveller in the dark,
Though I know not what you are,
Twinkle, twinkle, little star.

THE FLOWER AND THE LADY, ABOUT GETTING UP.

PRETTY flower, tell me why
　　All your leaves do open wide,
Every morning, when on high
　　The noble sun begins to ride.

This is why, my lady fair,
　　If you would the reason know,
For betimes the pleasant air
　　Very cheerfully doth blow.

And the birds on every tree
　　Sing a merry, merry tune,
And the busy honey-bee
　　Comes to suck my sugar soon.

This is, then, the reason why
　　I my little leaves undo.
Little lady, wake and try
　　If I have not told you true.

———

THE BABY'S DANCE.

DANCE, little baby, dance up high !
Never mind, baby, mother is by ;
Crow and caper, caper and crow,
There, little baby, there you go !
Up to the ceiling, down to the ground,
Backwards and forwards, round and round ;
Then dance, little baby, and mother shall sing,
While the gay merry coral goes ding-a-ding, ding !

FOR A LITTLE GIRL THAT DID NOT LIKE TO BE WASHED.

WHAT ! cry when I wash you ! not love to be clean !
Then go and be dirty, not fit to be seen.
And till you leave off, and I see you have smiled,
I can't take the trouble to wash such a child.

Suppose I should leave you a figure like this,
Do you think you could ask dear papa for a kiss, —
Or to sit on his knee and learn pretty great A,
With fingers that have not been washed all the day?

Ay, look at your fingers, you see it is so.
Did you ever behold such a black little row?
And now you may look at yourself in the glass ;
There 's a face to belong to a good little lass !

Come, come then, I see you 're beginning to clear,
You won't be so foolish again, will you, dear?

―――――

QUESTIONS AND ANSWERS.

WHO showed the little ant the way
    Her narrow hole to bore,
And spend the pleasant summer day
    In laying up her store?

The sparrow builds her nice, warm nest
    Of wool, and hay, and moss.
Who told her how to weave it best,
    And lay the twigs across?

Who taught the busy bee to fly
  Among the sweetest flowers,
And lay his feast of honey by,
  To eat in winter hours?

'T was God who showed them all the way,
  And gave their little skill;
He teaches children, if they pray,
  To do His holy will.

THE FIELD DAISY.

I 'M a pretty little thing,
Always coming with the spring.
In the meadows green I 'm found,
Peeping just above the ground;
And my stalk is covered flat
With a white and yellow hat.

Little Mary, when you pass
Lightly o'er the tender grass,
Skip about, but do not tread
On my bright but lowly head;
For I always seem to say,
" Surly winter 's gone away."

THE MICHAELMAS DAISY.

I AM very pale and dim,
With my faint and bluish rim,
Standing on my narrow stalk,
By the littered gravel walk;

And the withered leaves aloft
Fall upon me very oft.

But I show' my lonely head
When the other flowers are dead,
And you 're even glad to spy
Such a homely thing as I ;
For I seem to smile and say,
" Summer is not quite away."

THE LITTLE CHILD.

I 'M a very little child,
   Only just have learned to speak ;
So I should be very mild,
   Very tractable and meek.

If my dear mamma were gone,
   Oh, I think that I should die,
When she left me all alone,
   Such a little thing as I.

Now what service can I do,
   To repay her for her care ?
For I cannot even sew,
   Nor make anything I wear.

Well, then, I will always try
   To be very good and mild ;
Never now be cross or cry,
   Like a fretful little child.

How unkind it is to fret,
   And my dear mamma to tease,
When my lesson I should get,
   Sitting still upon her knees !

Oh, how can I serve her so,
   Such a good mamma as this?
Round her neck my arms I 'll throw,
   And her gentle cheek I 'll kiss.

Then I 'll tell her that I will
   Try not any more to fret her,
And as I grow older still,
   Try to show I love her better.

THE SHEEP.

LAZY sheep, pray tell me why
In the pleasant fields you lie,
Eating grass or daisies white,
From the morning till the night?
Every thing can something do,
But what kind of use are you?

Nay, my little master, nay,
Do not serve me so, I pray.
Don't you see the wool that grows
On my back to make your clothes?
Cold, and very cold, you 'd be,
If you had not wool from me.

True, it seems a pleasant thing
To nip the daisies in the spring ;

But many chilly nights I pass
On the cold and dewy grass,
Or pick a scanty dinner where
All the common 's brown and bare.

Then the farmer comes at last,
When the merry spring is past,
And cuts my woolly coat away,
To warm you in the winter's day.
Little master, this is why
In the pleasant fields I lie.

A FINE THING.

WHO am I with noble face,
Shining in a clear blue place?
If to look at me you try,
I shall blind your little eye.

When my noble face I show,
Over yonder mountain blue,
All the clouds away do ride,
And the dusky night beside.

Then the clear wet dews I dry
With the look of my bright eye ;
And the little birds awake,
Many a merry tune to make.

Cowslips, then, and hare-bells blue,
And lily-cups their leaves undo ;
For they shut themselves up tight,
All the dark and foggy night.

21

Then the busy people go,
Some to plough, and some to sow ;
When I leave, their work is done, —
Guess if I am not the Sun.

A PRETTY THING.

WHO am I that shine so bright
With my pretty yellow light,
Peeping through your curtains gray?
Tell me, little girl, I pray.

When the sun is gone, I rise
In the very silent skies ;
And a cloud or two doth skim
Round about my silver rim.

All the little stars do seem
Hidden by my brighter beam ;
And among them I do ride,
Like a queen in all her pride.

Then the reaper goes along,
Singing forth a merry song,
While I light the shaking leaves
And the yellow harvest sheaves.

Little girl, consider well,
Who this simple tale doth tell ;
And I think you 'll guess it soon,
For I only am the Moon. ·

THE SNOWDROP.

Now the spring is coming on,
Now the snow and ice are gone,
Come, my little snowdrop root,
Will you not begin to shoot?

Ah! I see your pretty head
Peeping on the flower-bed,
Looking all so green and gay
On this fine and pleasant day.

For the mild south wind doth blow,
And hath melted all the snow,
And the sun shines out so warm,
You need not fear another storm.

So come up, you pretty thing,
Just to tell us it is spring,
Hanging down your modest head
On my pleasant flower-bed.

GOING TO BED.

THE moon is up, the sun is gone,
Now nothing here he shines upon;
The pretty birds are in their nest,
The cows are lying down to rest,
Or wait, beneath the farmer's shed,
To hear the merry milkmaid's tread.

The pleasant flowers that opened wide,
And smelt so sweet at morning-tide,
Fold up their leaves, as if to say,
" Good-by, we 'll come another day ;
And now, dear little lady, you
Must sleep, as we shall seem to do." .

Yes, — here 's my pretty bed, and I   ·
Will kiss mamma, and say " by, by ! "
So nice and warm, so smooth and white,
So comfortable all the night !
And when my little prayer is said,
How could I cry to go to bed?

———

TIME TO GET UP.

THE cock, who soundly sleeps at night,
Rises with the morning light ;
Very loud and shrill he crows ;
Then the sleeping ploughman knows
He must rise and hasten too,
All his morning work to do.

And the little lark does fly
To the middle of the sky.
You may hear his merry tune,
In the morning very soon ;
For he does not like to rest
Idly, in his downy nest.

While the cock is crowing shrill,
Leave my little bed I will,

And I 'll rise to hear the lark,
Now it is no longer dark.
'T would be a pity there to stay,
When 't is bright and pleasant day.

———

THE LITTLE FISH THAT WOULD NOT DO AS IT WAS BID.

" Dear mother," said a little fish,
  " Pray is not that a fly?
I 'm very hungry, and I wish
  You 'd let me go and try.''

" Sweet innocent," the mother cried,
  And started from her nook ;
" That horrid fly is put to hide
  The sharpness of the hook."

Now as I 've heard, this little trout
  Was young and foolish too,
And so he thought he 'd venture out,
  To see if it were true.

And round about the hook he played,
  With many a longing look,
And — " Dear me," to himself he said,
  " I 'm sure that 's not a hook.

" I can but give one little pluck, —
  Let 's see, and so I will."
So on he went, and, lo ! it stuck
  Quite through his little gill.

And as he faint and fainter grew,
  With hollow voice he cried,
" Dear mother, had I minded you,
  I need not now have died."

———

THE LITTLE NEGRO.

AH ! the poor little blackamoor, see, there he goes,
And the blood gushes out from his half-frozen toes,
And his legs are so thin you may almost see the
    bones,
As he goes shiver, shiver, all along upon the stones.

He was once a merry boy, — yes, a merry boy was he,
Playing outlandish plays by the tall palm-tree,
Or bathing in the river like a brisk water-rat,
And at night sleeping soundly on his little piece of
    mat.

But there came some wicked people, and they stole
    him far away,
And then good-by to palm-tree tall, and merry, merry
    play ;
For they took him from his house and home, and
    everybody dear,
And now, poor little negro boy, he 's come a-begging
    here.

Oh, fie upon those wicked men, who did this cruel
    thing !
I wish some mighty nobleman would go and tell the
    king.

For to steal him from his house and home must be a
    crying sin,
Though he was a little negro boy and had a sooty
    skin.

THE LITTLE LARK.

I HEAR a pretty bird, but hark !
  I cannot see it anywhere.
Oh ! it is a little lark,
  Singing in the morning air.
Little lark, do tell me why
You are singing in the sky ?

Other little birds at rest
  Have not yet begun to sing ;
Every one is in its nest,
  With its head behind its wing.
Little lark, then, tell me why
You 're so early in the sky ?

You look no bigger than a bee,
  In the middle of the blue ;
Up above the poplar tree,
  I can hardly look at you.
Little lark, do tell me why
You are mounted up so high ?

" 'T is to watch the silver star,
  Sinking slowly in the skies ;
And beyond the mountain far,
  To see the glorious sun arise.
Little lady, this is why
I am mounted up so high.

" 'T is to sing a merry song
To the pleasant morning light ;
Why stay in my nest so long,
When the sun is shining bright ?
Little lady, this is why
I sing so early in the sky.

" To the little birds below,
Here I sing a merry tune ;
And I let the ploughman know
He must come to labor soon.
Little lady, this is why
I am singing in the sky."

THE LITTLE ANTS.

A LITTLE black ant found a large grain of wheat,
Too heavy to lift or to roll ;
So he begged of a neighbor he happened to meet,
To help it down into his hole.

" I 've got my own work to see after," said he ;
" You must shift for yourself, if you please."
So he crawled off, as selfish and cross as could be,
And lay down to sleep at his ease.

Just then a black brother was passing the road,
And seeing his neighbor in want
Came up and assisted him in with his load ;
For he was a good-natured ant.

Let all who this story may happen to hear,
Endeavor to profit by it ;

For often it happens that children appear
  As cross as the ant, every bit.

And the good-natured ant, who assisted his brother,
  May teach those who choose to be taught,
That if little insects are kind to each other,
  Then children most certainly ought.

———

THE MEADOWS.

WE 'LL go to the meadows, where primroses grow,
  And buttercups, looking as yellow as gold ;
And daisies and cowslips, beginning to blow, —
  For it is a most beautiful sight to behold.

The little bee humming about them is seen ;
  The butterfly merrily dances along ;
The grasshopper chirps in the hedges so green,
  And the linnet is singing his liveliest song.

The birds and the insects are happy and gay,
  The beasts of the field they are glad and rejoice ;
And we will be thankful to God every day,
  And praise His great name in a loftier voice.

He made the green meadows, He planted the flowers,
  He sent his bright sun in the heavens to blaze ;
He created these wonderful bodies of ours,
  And as long as we live we will sing of His praise.

THE WASP AND THE BEE.

A Wasp met a Bee that was just buzzing by,
And he said, " My dear cousin, can you tell me why
You are loved so much better by people than I?'

" Why, my back is as bright and as yellow as gold,
And my shape is most elegant, too, to behold ;
Yet nobody likes me for that, I am told ! "

Says the Bee, " My dear cousin, it 's all very true ;
But indeed they would love me no better than you,
If I were but half as much mischief to do !

" You have a fine shape and a delicate wing,
And they own you are handsome ; but then there 's
    one thing
Which they cannot put up with, — and that is your
    sting.

" Now I put it at once to your own common-sense,
If you are not so ready at taking offence
As to sting them on even the slightest pretence ?

" Though my dress is so homely and plain, as you
    see,
And I have a small sting, they 're not angry with me,
Because I 'm a busy and good-natured Bee ! "

From this, pray, let ill-natured people beware ;
Because, I am sure, if they do not take care,
That they 'll never be loved, if they 're ever so fair.

THE END.

𝔉𝔞𝔪𝔬𝔲𝔰 𝔚𝔬𝔪𝔢𝔫 𝔖𝔢𝔯𝔦𝔢𝔰.

MARGARET FULLER

By JULIA WARD HOWE.

" A memoir of the woman who first in New England took a position of moral and intellectual leadership, by the woman who wrote the Battle Hymn of the Republic, is a literary event of no common or transient interest. The Famous Women Series will have no worthier subject and no more illustrious biographer. Nor will the reader be disappointed, — for the narrative is deeply interesting and full of inspiration." — *Woman's Journal.*

"Mrs. Julia Ward Howe's biography of *Margaret Fuller*, in the Famous Women Series of Messrs. Roberts Brothers, is a work which has been looked for with curiosity. It will not disappoint expectation. She has made a brilliant and an interesting book. Her study of Margaret Fuller's character is thoroughly sympathetic ; her relation of her life is done in a graphic and at times a fascinating manner. It is the case of one woman of strong individuality depicting the points which made another one of the most marked characters of her day. It is always agreeable to follow Mrs. Howe in this ; for while we see marks of her own mind constantly, there is no inartistic protrusion of her personality. The book is always readable, and the relation of the death-scene is thrillingly impressive.' — *Saturday Gazette.*

"Mrs. Julia Ward Howe has retold the story of Margaret Fuller's life and career in a very interesting manner. This remarkable woman was happy in having James Freeman Clarke, Ralph Waldo Emerson, and William Henry Channing, all of whom had been intimate with her and had felt the spell of her extraordinary personal influence, for her biographers. It is needless to say, of course, that nothing could be better than these reminiscences in their way." — *New York World.*

"The selection of Mrs. Howe as the writer of this biography was a happy thought on the part of the editor of the series ; for, aside from the natural appreciation she would have for Margaret Fuller, comes her knowledge of all the influences that had their effect on Margaret Fuller's life. She tells the story of Margaret Fuller's interesting life from all sources and from her own knowledge, not hesitating to use plenty of quotations when she felt that others, or even Margaret Fuller herself, had done the work better." — *Miss Gilder, in Philadelphia Press.*

Sold by all booksellers. Mailed, post-paid, on receipt of the price, by the publishers,

ROBERTS BROTHERS,

BOSTON, MASS.

Famous Women Series.

◆

MARIA EDGEWORTH.

By HELEN ZIMMERN.

◆

" This little volume shows good literary workmanship. It does not weary the reader with vague theories; nor does it give over much expression to the enthusiasm — not to say baseless encomium — for which too many female biographers have accustomed us to look. It is a simple and discriminative sketch of one of the most clever and lovable of the class at whom Carlyle sneered as ' scribbling women.' . . . Of Maria Edgeworth, the woman, one cannot easily say too much in praise. That home life, so loving, so wise, and so helpful, was beautiful to its end. Miss Zimmern has treated it with delicate appreciation. Her book is refined in conception and tasteful in execution, — all, in short, the cynic might say, that we expect a woman's book to be." — *New York Tribune.*

" It was high time that we should possess an adequate biography of this ornament and general benefactor of her time. And so we hail with uncommon pleasure the volume just published in the Roberts Brothers' series of Famous Women, of which it is the sixth. We have only words of praise for the manner in which Miss Zimmern has written her life of Maria Edgeworth. It exhibits sound judgment, critical analysis, and clear characterization. . . . The style of the volume is pure, limpid, and strong, as we might expect from a well-trained English writer." — *Margaret J. Preston, in the Home Journal.*

" We can heartily recommend this life of Maria Edgeworth, not only because it is singularly readable in itself, but because it makes familiar to readers of the present age a notable figure in English literary history, with whose lineaments we suspect most readers, especially of the present generation, are less familiar than they ought to be." — *Eclectic.*

" This biography contains several letters and papers by Miss Edgeworth that have not before been made public, notably some charming letters written during the latter part of her life to Dr. Holland and Mr. and Mrs. Ticknor. The author had access to a life of Miss Edgeworth written by her step-mother, as well as to a large collection of her private letters, and has therefore been able to bring forward many facts in her life which have not been noted by other writers. The book is written in a pleasant vein, and is altogether a delightful one to read." — *Utica Herald.*

◆

Sold by all booksellers. Mailed, post-paid, by the publishers,

RORERTS BROTHERS,

ROSTON, MASS.

FAMOUS WOMEN SERIES.

EMILY BRONTË.

By A. MARY F. ROBINSON.

One vol. 16mo. Cloth. Price, $1.00.

" Miss Robinson has written a fascinating biography. . . . Emily Brontë is interesting, not because she wrote 'Wuthering Heights,' but because of her brave, baffled, human life, so lonely, so full of pain, but with a great hope shining beyond all the darkness, and a passionate defiance in bearing more than the burdens that were laid upon her. The story of the three sisters is infinitely sad, but it is the ennobling sadness that belongs to large natures cramped and striving for freedom to heroic, almost desperate, work, with little or no result. The author of this intensely interesting, sympathetic, and eloquent biography, is a young lady and a poet, to whom a place is given in a recent anthology of living English poets, which is supposed to contain only the best poems of the best writers." — *Boston Daily Advertiser.*

"Miss Robinson had many excellent qualifications for the task she has performed in this little volume, among which may be named, an enthusiastic interest in her subject and a real sympathy with Emily Brontë's sad and heroic life. 'To represent her as she was,' says Miss Robinson, 'would be her noblest and most fitting monument.' . . . Emily Brontë here becomes well known to us and, in one sense, this should be praise enough for any biography." — *New York Times.*

"The biographer who finds such material before him as the lives and characters of the Brontë family need have no anxiety as to the interest of his work. Characters not only strong but so uniquely strong, genius so supreme, misfortunes so overwhelming, set in its scenery so forlornly picturesque, could not fail to attract all readers, if told even in the most prosaic language. When we add to this, that Miss Robinson has told their story *not* in prosaic language, but with a literary style exhibiting all the qualities essential to good biography, our readers will understand that this life of Emily Brontë is not only as interesting as a novel, but a great deal more interesting than most novels. As it presents most vividly a general picture of the family, there seems hardly a reason for giving it Emily's name alone, except perhaps for the masterly chapters on ' Wuthering Heights,' which the reader will find a grateful condensation of the best in that powerful but somewhat forbidding story. We know of no point in the Brontë history — their genius, their surroundings, their faults, their happiness, their misery, their love and friendships, their peculiarities, their power, their gentleness, their patience, their pride, — which Miss Robinson has not touched upon with conscientiousness and sympathy." — *The Critic.*

"' Emily Brontë ' is the second of the ' Famous Women Series,' which Roberts Brothers, Boston, propose to publish, and of which ' George Eliot ' was the initial volume. Not the least remarkable of a very remarkable family, the personage whose life is here written, possesses a peculiar interest to all who are at all familiar with the sad and singular history of herself and her sister Charlotte. That the author, Miss A. Mary F. Robinson, has done her work with minute fidelity to facts as well as affectionate devotion to the subject of her sketch, is plainly to be seen all through the book." — *Washington Post.*

Sold by all Booksellers, or mailed, post-paid, on receipt of price, by the Publishers,

ROBERTS BROTHERS, Boston.

FAMOUS WOMEN SERIES.

GEORGE SAND.

By BERTHA THOMAS.

One volume. 16mo. Cloth. Price, $1.00.

"Miss Thomas has accomplished a difficult task with as much good sense as good feeling. She presents the main facts of George Sand's life, extenuating nothing, and setting naught down in malice, but wisely leaving her readers to form their own conclusions. Everybody knows that it was not such a life as the women of England and America are accustomed to live, and as the worst of men are glad to have them live. . . . Whatever may be said against it, its result on George Sand was not what it would have been upon an English or American woman of genius." — *New York Mail and Express.*

"This is a volume of the 'Famous Women Series,' which was begun so well with George Eliot and Emily Brontë. The book is a review and critical analysis of George Sand's life and work, by no means a detailed biography. Amantine Lucile Aurore Dupin, the maiden, or Mme. Dudevant, the married woman, is forgotten in the renown of the pseudonym George Sand. "Altogether, George Sand, with all her excesses and defects, is a representative woman, one of the names of the nineteenth century. She was great among the greatest, the friend and compeer of the finest intellects, and Miss Thomas's essay will be a useful and agreeable introduction to a more extended study of her life and works." — *Knickerbocker.*

"The biography of this famous woman, by Miss Thomas, is the only one in existence. Those who have awaited it with pleasurable anticipation, but with some trepidation as to the treatment of the erratic side of her character, cannot fail to be pleased with the skill by which it is done. It is the best production on George Sand that has yet been published. The author modestly refers to it as a sketch, which it undoubtedly is, but a sketch that gives a just and discriminating analysis of George Sand's life, tastes, occupations, and of the motives and impulses which prompted her unconventional actions, that were misunderstood by a narrow public. The difficulties encountered by the writer in describing this remarkable character are shown in the first line of the opening chapter, which says, 'In naming George Sand we name something more exceptional than even a great genius.' That tells the whole story. Misconstruction, condemnation, and isolation are the penalties enforced upon the great leaders in the realm of advanced thought, by the bigoted people of their time. The thinkers soar beyond the common herd, whose soul-wings are not strong enough to fly aloft to clearer atmospheres, and consequently they censure or ridicule what they are powerless to reach. George Sand, even to a greater extent than her contemporary, George Eliot, was a victim to ignorant social prejudices, but even the conservative world was forced to recognize the matchless genius of these two extraordinary women, each widely different in her character and method of thought and writing. . . . She has told much that is good which has been untold, and just what will interest the reader, and no more, 'n the same easy, entertaining style that characterizes all of these unpretentious biographies." — *Hartford Times.*

Sold everywhere. Mailed, post-paid, on receipt of price, by the publishers,

ROBERTS BROTHERS, Boston.

FAMOUS WOMEN SERIES.

MARY LAMB.

By ANNE GILCHRIST.

One volume. 16mo. Cloth. Price, $1.00.

"The story of Mary Lamb has long been familiar to the readers of Elia, but never in its entirety as in the monograph which Mrs. Anne Gilchrist has just contributed to the Famous Women Series. Darkly hinted at by Talfourd in his Final Memorials of Charles Lamb, it became better known as the years went on and that imperfect work was followed by fuller and franker biographies, — became so well known, in fact, that no one could recall the memory of Lamb without recalling at the same time the memory of his sister." — *New York Mail and Express.*

"A biography of Mary Lamb must inevitably be also, almost more, a biography of Charles Lamb, so completely was the life of the sister encompassed by that of her brother; and it must be allowed that Mrs. Anne Gilchrist has performed a difficult biographical task with taste and ability. . . . The reader is at least likely to lay down the book with the feeling that if Mary Lamb is not famous she certainly deserves to be, and that a debt of gratitude is due Mrs. Gilchrist for this well-considered record of her life." —*Boston Courier.*

"Mary Lamb, who was the embodiment of everything that is tenderest in woman, combined with this a heroism which bore her on for a while through the terrors of insanity. Think of a highly intellectual woman struggling year after year with madness, triumphant over it for a season, and then at last succumbing to it. The saddest lines that ever were written are those descriptive of this brother and sister just before Mary, on some return of insanity, was to leave Charles Lamb. 'On one occasion Mr. Charles Lloyd met them slowly pacing together a little foot-path in Hoxton Fields, both weeping bitterly, and found, on joining them, that they were taking their solemn way to the accustomed asylum.' What pathos is there not here?" — *New York Times.*

"This life was worth writing, for all records of weakness conquered, of pain patiently borne, of success won from difficulty, of cheerfulness in sorrow and affliction, make the world better. Mrs. Gilchrist's biography is unaffected and simple. She has told the sweet and melancholy story with judicious sympathy, showing always the light shining through darkness." — *Philadelphia Press.*

Sold by all Booksellers. Mailed, post-paid, on receipt of the price, by the Publishers,

ROBERTS BROTHERS, BOSTON.

www.ingramcontent.com/pod-product-compliance
Lightning Source LLC
Chambersburg PA
CBHW030820110726
47900CB00006B/1677